An Invitation to Forever

Anna Tikvah

2nd Edition May 2013

An Invitation to Forever

Chapter One	Frigid, Black Water
Chapter Two	Voices in the Courtyard
Chapter Three	A New Job
Chapter Four	An Orange Piece of Paper
Chapter Five	Something to Think About
Chapter Six	A Ride with "Mr. Blue"
Chapter Seven	Sandra Asks Questions
Chapter Eight	The Promise
Chapter Nine	A Closed Door
Chapter Ten	Heavenly *Yogurt!*
Chapter Eleven	Another Promise
Chapter Twelve	An Evening in the Courtyard
Chapter Thirteen	The Purple Invitation
Chapter Fourteen	Confrontation
Chapter Fifteen	The Kingdom Feast
Chapter Sixteen	To Rise
Chapter Seventeen	Soar Like the *Seagulls?*
Chapter Eighteen	Dinner in the Courtyard
Chapter Nineteen	A Birthday at the Bryant's
Chapter Twenty	Two Invitations
Chapter Twenty-One	The Lunch Date
Chapter Twenty-Two	The New Man
Chapter Twenty-Three	An Invitation to Forever
Chapter Twenty-Four	A Wonderful Surprise
Chapter Twenty-Five	Apologies
Chapter Twenty-Six	Help With the Car and a New Idea
Chapter Twenty-Seven	The Wedding
Chapter Twenty-Eight	In the Moonlight
Chapter Twenty-Nine	James has Some Questions
Chapter Thirty	Lay Down Your Life
Chapter Thirty-One	Warm, Cleansing Water

"The things which are impossible with men are possible with God."

Luke 18:27

All Scriptural quotations in this book are from the New King James Version, unless otherwise stated. Copyright © 1979, 1980, 1982 by Thomas Nelson, Inc. Used by permission. All rights reserved. Italics are at the emphasis of the author.

Frigid, Black Water
Chapter One

It was dark. Everything seemed so cold and dark. Earlier in the day thick clouds had moved in and now it was a moonless night without stars. The black, murky water rolling towards the harbour front crashed noisily against the concrete barrier. Wrought-iron lamps lining the boardwalk shed an eerie glow into the approaching fog, but it was barely noticeable to the young woman slumped against the wooden railing.

I never wanted to teach grade eight in the first place! Sandra Carrington thought miserably, watching the restless, churning waves. *And yet that's been the only opportunity I've had for the past two weeks. Everything has gone wrong since I moved to Nova Scotia...and I still haven't seen my brother!*

With a heavy sigh, Sandra thought back on all the trouble Mitchell and Ty had instigated. *I can't control them; it's as simple as that,* she told herself. *They've taken over the class. I can hardly believe how many students I sent to the office this week! They've been throwing chalk brushes across the classroom, swearing out loud, openly cheating on tests, shooting spit-balls whenever my back was turned...it's been a nightmare!*

A multitude of 'if onlys' went through her head. After being summoned to speak to the principal at the end of the day, Sandra had a premonition she wouldn't be asked to supply-teach at *any* school in Stirling, Nova Scotia. "Sandra," Ms. Ferrier had said regretfully, looking up with steady, brown eyes, "I don't understand why you're having such trouble with this class. Their regular teacher says they're quite an easy group to work with." After a meaningful pause, she had added, "I wonder if you might want to consider a course on classroom management? I have a registration form here, if you're interested."

The suggestion had been pleasantly given but miserably received. Sandra knew she would no doubt benefit from such a course, but it wouldn't be offered until the summer and it would cost a fair deal. Having subsisted on only an irregular supply-teaching income since September, she was already struggling just to keep up with her rent and the repayment of university loans.

Watching an old, dimly-lit fishing boat chug in to dock, Sandra sighed again. It was early May. *There are only two months left of the school year,* she thought despairingly, *and four months of my lease. What if I'm not called in again? Ms. Ferrier thinks I'm a failure. If only I could have had a chance to teach the younger children! I've always done well with the early grades. But that hasn't happened once all year, and now she'll probably inform the board that I'm unable to manage a classroom. Who will give me a call now? Will I be evicted if I can't pay my rent?*

Turning to look into the distance, Sandra couldn't see the lights of Margaret's Manor. Usually from where she now stood on the boardwalk, she could see the lights clearly, beckoning softly, high above the subdivisions below. That was where she lived, in the *far* too expensive, fourth- floor apartment. Oh, it was lovely and new with an indoor pool, exercise room and quaint stone courtyard. Gorgeous country gardens encircled the patio and had been in full bloom when she'd first moved there in August. As advertised on the internet, it was close to the harbour and had fantastic views. Had she been given the full-time position she had been offered, it would have been the perfect place to live! But at the last minute, after she had signed the rental agreement, the teacher she was to relieve had decided to return.

They've let me down so badly! she thought. *They promised me a job. At the very least, couldn't they have given me a steady year of supply-teaching?*

A lively group of girls ambled past as Sandra straightened up to wipe the salty mist off her glasses. Sliding them back into place, she watched as they walked close together, laughing and talking loudly, sharing dinner from the cardboard-boxes they held in their hands.

The smell of french fries and battered fish wafted tantalizingly behind the girls. It smelled so good! But "take-outs" were a luxury Sandra could not afford, at least, not anymore. Unnoticed in the gloomy shadows, she slouched back against the railing. Only five foot-four, Sandra had never been an imposing figure, and now she was slimmer than ever - almost too thin. The short, dark hair that she kept carefully straightened was becoming unruly in the damp, moist air. Her pretty blue eyes were filling with tears.

It's not fair, she thought. *I struggled through university in a tiny, claustrophobic, basement apartment so that I could get a decent job, live in a nice place, eat out at restaurants when I felt like it, and enjoy life. But here I am, two years later - still struggling!*

Loneliness flooded over her. Last August, she had left everyone she knew in Ontario, and driven east to Stirling, Nova Scotia, hoping to be re-acquainted with her brother. They hadn't seen each other for eighteen years. Laurie hadn't even come to their mother's funeral last year! He'd been on a business trip to China. A fantastic flower arrangement had been sent with his name attached; but it didn't compensate for his failure to be there himself. Since moving out East, Sandra had often made plans with Laurie to get together but on every occasion, he had cancelled out. Laurie had cancelled again just last night. It was always the same – something more important came up. Laurie was always so busy! "Why don't you care about me?" she whispered forlornly across the bay. "I'm only here in Nova Scotia because of you!"

Sandra had never found an answer to that question and tonight she wondered if she ever would. For the most part, through all the hard knocks life had dealt her, Sandra had maintained a friendly, positive outlook, but there were times, such as now, when life seemed almost unbearably painful. There were times when hope seemed like a pathetic delusion. *Is there any point to life when it hurts this much?* she wondered. Looking down from the wooden railing, Sandra watched the waves roll in, one after another. The frigid, black water was so dark; the heavy mist was creeping closer. Now she could only see thirty yards or so into the distance.

I wonder how long it takes for hypothermia to set in? she mused.

Three young teens came rushing past. Two of them were racing on skateboards. The other who was on foot was trying to keep pace, holding tightly to the leash of a large brown Labrador. "I can't run this fast!" he panted loudly to his friends. "Rambo's trying to catch up to you."

Turning to watch, Sandra hoped no one would get hurt. Always instinctively a teacher, she considered telling them to be careful but decided they weren't likely to listen. When they reached the end of the boardwalk, one teen kick-flipped his skateboard, landing perfectly, while the other did a grind down the handrail.

Sandra breathed a sigh of relief when the skateboarders stopped to wait for their friend to catch up.

As the boys ventured off into the shroud of fog with the Labrador vying for the lead, Sandra turned back towards the water. Gloomy thoughts filled her mind. *If I swam out far enough,* she told herself, *no one would see me or rescue me. But what if...*she pondered fearfully, *what if I got out there and changed my mind?*

Even as she contemplated such a foolish end, Sandra knew she would never be so reckless. Still she wondered, *Would that be the end...the final end of everything? Or is there...something else?*

Out of the corner of her eye, Sandra noticed a scrawny cat slinking through the shadows. *Tiger!* she thought anxiously, recalling her own little tabby at home. *Who would look after Tiger? What if no one knew I was missing? What if Tiger had no one to feed him? I couldn't do that to Tiger!*

The cold, ocean spray was seeping through her coat. Morbid thoughts had chilled her to the bone. Beginning to shiver, Sandra couldn't stand still any longer. Moving despondently away from the railing, she headed home.

At least, Tiger would be happy to see her.

Voices in the Courtyard
Chapter Two

Approaching the stone archway that led into the Manor's courtyard, Sandra could hear a disagreement taking place behind the wall. Living in downtown Stirling, it was nothing out of the ordinary to overhear private conversations, laughter, and even arguments at any hour of day or night. For the most part, Sandra paid little attention to what she heard or saw. However, as she drew closer, the muffled, masculine voices in the courtyard became more intense.

I hope I can get past them safely, she thought. *I'm so cold!* The pathway through the courtyard was the quickest way to warmth and shelter. *I really don't want to walk all the way around to the front.*

"Just hear me out," one voice begged earnestly.

Sandra stopped, still hidden on the other side of the courtyard wall, uncertain as to what she should do.

With less emotion, the other voice replied quietly. Sandra could only hear a few snippets of the conversation, "I respect your... please respect mine... leave it at that."

"But this is important!" the earnest voice pleaded.

There was a short laugh and then she heard, "...don't agree...I'm *not interested!*"

"Please... a couple of passages..."

Passages? Sandra wondered. *Passages to what? Is this some kind of secret mission?*

After a pause, the calmer voice answered. A little louder now, his words drifted more easily over the wall. "People can twist things to prove anything they want. I don't pretend to know... but... God is in control. I'm at peace... stuff that's not nailed down perfectly. I know I'm good *if I'm with Jesus!"*

A heavy sigh was quite audible.

Sandra deliberated what she should do. *I really don't want to disturb this conversation,* she thought, *but it's so far to walk all the way around.* She ran her fingers nervously through her damp, wavy hair. *Sounds like it's just a religious argument, so I'm probably safe enough...*

"All right... how *you* want it," the earnest voice replied unhappily. "I will respect your feelings."

There was no response from the other.

"But please just remember this," the earnest voice implored loudly. "I've only pestered you so much about this, because you mean *so much to me.* You're my brother. *I love you,* man! I want you to be with us forever!"

The earnest voice captured Sandra's attention. *He's telling his brother he loves him when his brother won't even hear him out? He must really care...a lot!*

A sudden cool breeze and mounting curiosity compelled Sandra to choose the shortcut through the courtyard. Shivering as she walked forward into the archway, she gazed inquisitively towards the tall figures. Silhouetted against the misty glow of the carriage lights, they were totally oblivious to her. *Imagine if Laurie would bug me - even once, because he cares!* she thought enviously.

"If I mean anything to you at all," one of the tall figures replied curtly, "then please relay the message that I don't want to talk to any of you about this again, not Mom, not Dad, not even Andrew! I've had enough..."

The voice broke off in mid-sentence as the men suddenly became aware that they were no longer alone. Both looked startled and one man moved back politely out of Sandra's way. Trying not to stare or shiver as she passed by, Sandra took only a quick look. She readily determined that both men were over six feet tall. The one who stepped back was tall and lean, while the other had a heavier build. Such a brief glance at their shadowy faces, however, was not enough to distinguish any recognizable features.

Neither man spoke until she reached the Manor's back entrance. However, just as she was about to open the door, the earnest voice spoke again quietly. He spoke so quietly that Sandra could just barely hear his last few words. "Truth fears no questions. Truth sets you free."

The soft words puzzled Sandra. *Truth fears no questions? Truth about what?* She wished she could turn around to ask what he meant but knew it wouldn't be right to intrude. With a sigh she opened the glass door and walked into the Manor, leaving the perplexing conversation behind. *I doubt that I'll ever recognise them even if I do bump into them again,* she thought disappointedly. *It was too dark to see clearly.*

When she entered her fourth floor apartment, Sandra took off her damp coat, wrapped herself in a big fleece blanket and slumped down on the sofa. Taking a long leap a little tabby cat landed on her lap. She wrapped her arms around his warm, furry body and Tiger snuggled in. He had been her constant companion since university days.

"It's been a horrible day, Tiger," she told him, looking down into his yellow-green eyes, "and I'm not sure what the future holds. We might have to move back to Ontario. Maybe I'd have better luck getting a job back there. At least I know people who would help me."

Tiger didn't seem too worried. His loud purrs indicated that he would be happy wherever she was. His eyes shone with a deep devotion.

"I'm so glad I have you, Tiger," Sandra told him, patting his silky fur. "You're the best little friend!"

Warm, vibrating purrs were comforting, even on such a gloomy, bad day. Leaning back against the couch, Sandra's gaze shifted to a small picture frame that sat alone on the marble mantle above the gas fireplace. Tucked inside were the faces of two children and their smiling, young mother. All three had the same bright, blue eyes and dark, wavy hair. The older boy's arm was draped around his little sister's shoulders. It was her only picture of Laurie. Sandra had been almost ten when Laurie left home. Not having any recollection of her father and having lost her mother in a car crash last year, Laurie was now all the family she had left. From what she'd gathered, he had become a 'big-wig' at the Stirling Royal Bank, with plenty of money, a downtown mansion, a cottage *and* a yacht!

Turning resolutely away from the picture, Sandra flicked on her small TV and propped up her tired feet on the coffee table. A cop chase was playing out on the screen. Sirens were wailing and tires screeching as the getaway car manoeuvred around various obstacles in nearly impossible ways. After Tiger, the TV was Sandra's second-best friend – the TV and novels. Whenever it hurt to think, fantasy helped numb the pain.

However, the cop chase seemed to go on and on. As the occupants of each car tried to shoot each other again and again, Sandra couldn't determine which car held the good guys and which held the bad. It really wasn't her kind of show. She picked up the remote and flicked the channels.

Unable to find anything she wanted to watch, Sandra settled for a news update; in half an hour her favourite soap opera would be on. As the announcer rambled on about a freak snowstorm in Calgary, her mind drifted back to the disagreement she'd overheard in the courtyard.

Truth fears no questions, she pondered. *I suppose that's a fair statement. I guess if you know you are telling the truth about something, then you aren't afraid to be asked questions. And if you want the truth, you aren't afraid to be the one who asks the questions! But what* truth *was that man talking about?*

I wish I'd had a better look at their faces, she thought regretfully. *They must live in the Manor somewhere - at least one of them must. But how will I ever recognize them?*

Riding on a deep sigh, Tiger stirred and opened his big, round eyes solemnly. He stretched out his front paws to gently push against Sandra's chin. Smiling down sadly at her little cat, Sandra instinctively scratched behind his ears. Her thoughts, however, drifted far away. She could still see the black, murky water rolling ominously towards her. Life had certainly not been fair – at least, not for her!

A New Job
Chapter Three

Sandra woke the next morning with sunlight streaming though the curtains of her large bedroom windows. The pain and discouragement from the day before didn't seem so overwhelming. Hope for a better day was possible once again.

Having taught grade eight every day for the past two weeks, Sandra's apartment needed a thorough clean. She spent the morning tidying things up, all the while looking out the windows at the bright, beautiful day and promising herself an hour in the courtyard sunshine. At noon, she looked around at the spotless apartment with satisfaction. A clean house always made her feel so much better. Picking up a fork and a bowl of buttered brown rice, she took the elevator down to the foyer. There she retrieved the *Stirling Gazette* from her mail slot and headed outside.

Daffodils and tulips were in full bloom, nodding freely in the soft spring breeze. The pink striped tulips were so beautiful that Sandra stopped to have a closer look. *If I were an artist, I'd paint a picture full of them!* she thought with a smile.

Looking out towards the harbour, she noticed that the water was a sparkling, brilliant blue. *Things don't seem quite so bad today,* she thought, recalling the despair she'd felt the night before. *I hate it when everything crashes in like that. If I just had someone to share things with, I'm sure I would sort it out a lot better. Mom was always so good at listening and understanding, but now I feel like I have no one to talk to. I can't complain about things to my friends in Ontario, because they don't understand why I chose Nova Scotia in the first place. They'd just tell me to come on home.*

"I miss you, Mom," she whispered sadly. "I'd do anything to bring you back to me!"

Taking a seat at one of the fancy, white metal tables scattered throughout the courtyard, Sandra was glad that the metal was pleasantly warm. A month earlier she might have instantly frozen to the seat! It was hard to spread out the newspaper on the small, round tabletop, but she did her best. The *Stirling Gazette* was only a freebie paper that came every Saturday morning, but it was full of ads. Turning anxiously to the help-wanted section, Sandra whispered, "Oh, please let there be some primary teacher in a little, private school that needs the next two months off! Even a daycare position would be wonderful."

Resumes had already been sent out to all the places that Sandra could think of, several times, but there was always the possibility that they had been mislaid. On such a fresh spring morning Sandra was clinging to hope that this might be her lucky day.

However, as usual, it didn't appear that luck was on her side; nothing stood out. She quickly scanned the help-wanted section just to make sure her own ad was still there. Very succinct, in twenty-five words or less, it read: "Tutor Available. Get your child the professional help they need. All subjects. Any evening. $30 an hour." Below she had listed her phone number.

A tall, athletic man walked past her table on his way through the courtyard. She had dubbed him 'Mr. Blue' because of the reflective-blue sunglasses he usually wore. Today they were perched on top of his head. "Nice day!" he called out cheerily, with an admiring glance in her direction.

"Sure is," Sandra replied with an admiring glance of her own. Well-dressed and good-looking, Mr. Blue's attention was warmly received.

One of these days I'll get up the courage to ask his real name, Sandra told herself. Suddenly she noticed his height. Could Mr. Blue have been one of the men she had overheard in the courtyard? Was he the man who cared so much for his brother?

Watching him stroll through the arched entrance towards his red Mustang parked on the street, Sandra took careful note of his blond, wavy hair and black leather jacket. Even though she knew there was little chance she'd ever identify the two brothers, she could hardly stop herself from trying.

As the Mustang roared off down the street, Sandra idly pondered how she might inquire about the conversation she'd overheard. It was easy enough to imagine Mr. Blue asking if he could take a seat across from her at the table. Of course she would nod graciously with a welcoming smile. She could see herself inquiring after his name and offering hers. And then they would probably compare notes about how long they had each lived in the Manor and what they thought of the luxurious accommodation and the high rental fees. But when she tried to imagine herself probing after the conversation she'd overheard, she truly didn't know where to start. *I hope you don't mind me asking,* she joked silently to herself, *but you wouldn't, by any chance, have been outside in the courtyard last night, having ...well...um, having an argument with your brother?*

Right! she thought with a smile, shaking her head. *As if I could ask a complete stranger such a personal question!*

Turning back to the newspaper, Sandra saw an ad for a dish washer in the local restaurant down the street, but it was five days a week. Just in case she might still receive calls to supply-teach she didn't feel she could take on anything with inflexible hours. It was the same problem with the landscaping position - plus she didn't have the experience required - and a host of other ads. Then one request caught her eye: Housecleaner Required. Five hours per week. $15 an hour. Margaret's Manor.

"A housecleaner! Right here in the Manor!" she exclaimed to herself. "I could probably do that. Mom taught me well." The hours sounded flexible enough. Regardless of whether or not she might get further calls to supply-teach, she could certainly fit in *five hours* per week. The wage wasn't too bad and the location was excellent! Without any further hesitation, Sandra ran upstairs and placed a call. She was disappointed when only an answering machine responded.

"Sorry I am unable to answer your call right now," a friendly, firm voice replied, "but please leave a message and I'll get back to you as soon as possible. Have a great day!"

Hoping for the best, Sandra left a message of her own and hung up. Then, tossing the newspaper on her kitchen counter she went back to work on her favourite project – organizing a kindergarten curriculum. If ever Sandra found the job she wanted, she planned to be one hundred-percent prepared. All year long she had been taking out books from the library and researching the most exciting, educational activities she could find. From the supplies she had collected during her university years, three big cardboard boxes now sat in the spare bedroom with various games and special crafts neatly packaged in plastic Zip-lock bags. Today she planned to begin a large felt calendar and weather chart.

Turning on the TV, Sandra quickly skipped to her favourite cooking show. It was always on Saturday afternoons. With her ears open to Chef Jeff, who was explaining how to make fantastic frozen yogurt, Sandra kept her eyes on the felt, sketching in the shapes she needed to cut out.

Sandra was still hard at work that evening, sewing clear plastic pockets on the weather chart and listening to a sitcom when the phone rang.

"Hi," the caller said, "is this Sandra Carrington?"

"It is," she replied.

"I got your message," the friendly voice said. "If you'd like to meet me in the foyer at seven, we can talk about the housecleaning job."

Seven sounded fine to Sandra. She finished off one last plastic pocket, had a bowl of brown rice and tomatoes, and took a look in the mirror. Not pleased with her dishevelled reflection, she made things right.

Tiger's hair was all over the black yoga pants she was wearing, so she decided to change clothes. From a tidy drawer, Sandra chose her best jeans and the blue, cotton sweater her mother had given her on her twenty-fifth birthday. Setting her glasses back on, she looked in the mirror carefully and then laughed.

"Why am I dressing up?" she exclaimed to Tiger, who was purring contentedly on the bed. "If I'm hoping to be a housecleaner I might make a better impression with sweatpants and rubber gloves!"

Shortly after seven, Sandra stepped into the elevator and hit G for ground floor.

Now what did he say his name was? she asked herself. *Oh, I can't remember. Maybe he didn't tell me. I wonder how old he is? What's he like? I hope he's nice. His voice sounded pleasant enough.*

Only one man was standing in the marble foyer. From the apprehensive way he looked over at her, Sandra guessed he must be the one she was supposed to meet. When she met his glance and stepped towards him, he smiled and stretched out his hand.

"Sandra Carrington?" he asked uncertainly.

She nodded, stretching out her own hand. *Another tall man,* she observed, mentally adding him to the list of possible 'courtyard disputants'. With a lanky, slim build and a receding hairline, he wasn't nearly as good-looking as Mr. Blue, but he did have kind, brown eyes.

"Molly Maid, at your service," she said whimsically as they shook hands and then she regretted her words. *What a dumb thing to say!*

"I wasn't expecting someone so young," the tall man replied awkwardly.

He probably thinks I'm still in my teens, Sandra thought. It was a common occurrence. Not many guessed that she was almost twenty-eight. "You wanted someone with more experience?" she asked.

"Oh, no, it's not that," he mumbled uncomfortably. "It's just I expected some little old granny would want this job...you know," he chuckled, with a rather animated expression, "someone with a pink hair net and a great, big green apron!"

They both laughed.

"I knew I should have worn my rubber gloves!" she smiled.

He chuckled. "Well, good to meet you. I'm James and... well, um, I'm glad to hear you do this professionally."

"I... don't," Sandra said a little uneasily, hoping she wasn't off to another bad start. "I've never cleaned houses professionally before."

"So you aren't really Molly Maid?"

Sandra laughed. "No, I was just joking."

"Do we even have Molly Maid in Nova Scotia? Or is that..." he looked at Sandra inquisitively, "an Ontario-ism?"

"I think Molly Maid is everywhere," she said, "but I *am* from Ontario. I just moved here last August."

"Really! I'm from Ontario, as well," James said amiably. "Only it was a long time ago."

They compared notes about where they had grown up, discovered that neither of them were familiar with the other person's birthplace and the similarities ended there.

"Are you comfortable having a look around my place?" James inquired hesitantly. "It would probably be easier to show you where things are than try to tell you. But if you're not comfortable..."

Sandra looked up in surprise. She had only known James for five minutes but already she was fairly certain he was a trustworthy person; it shone from his eyes.

"I'd like to have a look," she said.

Apartment 226 wasn't a total disaster and it was the exact same layout as hers. Sandra noticed that the floor needed a wash and the dust had been collecting for a while, however, the dishes were all done and the kitchen was reasonably tidy. Glancing into the living room, she was immediately drawn to the enormous, flat-screen TV. *Lucky guy!* she thought.

"Yeah, it's messy all right," James said with an uncomfortable laugh. "This is going to be kind of embarrassing for me. I've always cleaned for myself, but…well, lately I just haven't been able to keep up with it. I started a new job a few months ago and right now I'm working eighty hours a week." He sighed, running his hand through his gray-speckled, dark hair. "I hope things will settle down soon," he added, somewhat doubtfully, "but for now when I come home I just need time to relax."

Sandra nodded. "It's actually tidier than I expected," she smiled, wondering if James always looked so flustered. "At Uni, some of my friends only did the dishes when they ran out of something clean to eat from."

"Really?" he laughed. "Not me. I like things tidy. Usually I do it myself," he reiterated. Then he seemed to absorb the information she'd given him.

"So you went to university?" he asked.

By the look on his face Sandra could tell he was perplexed why a university graduate would be offering to do housecleaning.

"I'm an elementary school teacher," she explained. "I came out last year thinking I had a job lined up but it fell through. So I've been supply-teaching ever since and there just hasn't been enough work. Your ad sounded like you might be flexible with hours and…," she paused to catch her breath, "well, if you don't

17

mind when I clean, then I can leave myself open to take any other work that comes my way."

"So, you're a teacher?" he clarified, looking at Sandra with that same flustered expression. There was a look of hesitation on his face and Sandra wondered if he was questioning her suitability. "Um, well, I don't mind when you clean," he said, "as long as it's during the day. I don't really want to come home to the sound of a vacuum cleaner running…"

With a laugh, Sandra realised James was thinking she might choose to clean after dinner. "No, no, of course not! I'll do it when you're at work," she assured him.

"Well then, let me show you what needs to be done," James said hesitantly, leading her through the various rooms. He explained he needed someone to do laundry, mopping, vacuuming, dusting, windows and clean the bathroom.

"This really is embarrassing," he explained again to Sandra with a sigh, after showing her the bathroom. "I've never had someone clean my house before and I don't think I'd want to clean someone else's…but… you're okay with this?"

"Of course," Sandra laughed, appreciating how he must feel. "I'm thankful for the work."

"I suppose I should ask for a reference or two…"

Sandra gave him Ms. Ferrier's number, hoping Ms. Ferrier would at least have confidence in her cleaning ability.

"Well then…if you have the time, I'd appreciate it if you could start with two days next week," James suggested. "I'm quite behind with it all. The shower, the fridge and the oven are in bad shape and the cupboards need some reorganization."

"As far as I know I have nothing else on," she assured him. "Should I start Monday?"

James handed her a key with a grin. "Sounds great! You have no idea how much I'll appreciate a clean house!"

"Do you want to do this on a trial basis?" Sandra inquired hesitantly, taking the key. She needed to know whether or not she could count on the work until her lease had expired.

"How about we give it a month?" James suggested. "We'll see how things go and talk it over in June."

Only a month? Sandra hid her disappointment. *I do hope he'll keep me on at least till August!* "Thank you," she smiled, placing the key in her pocket. "I'll start Monday then."

An Orange Piece of Paper
Chapter Four

It was with a strange feeling that Sandra entered apartment 226, Monday morning. She had never let herself freely into a stranger's apartment before. Besides that, she was wearing her old, gray shorts, a bleach-stained t-shirt and bright yellow gloves. Sandra had waited till nine-thirty and then run down the stairs and across the hall hoping no one would see her. *I hope he doesn't have to come home from work to get something,* she thought, heading to James' room to collect the laundry and strip the bed sheets. *I would be so embarrassed to be seen like this!*

However, once the laundry was going and she'd found her favourite station on the radio, Sandra began to relax. For a moment or two she stood and stared out the large, floor-to-ceiling windows. The view of the sparkling bay waters was almost the same as hers. Rays of sunshine were coming in through those windows, illuminating the dirty glass *and* every speck of dust! Housecleaning was not Sandra's favourite profession, but, aside from being a little squeamish about cleaning someone else's bathroom, she didn't mind the work. Growing up, she had taken on many of the household duties, as her mom, an obstetrics nurse and single parent, was far too busy.

I may not be Molly Maid, but I couldn't have had more stringent training, she thought with a smile, mopping sticky marks off the cream-coloured kitchen tiles, leaving them fresh and glossy. *Mom was a perfectionist! She knew too much about bugs and bacteria. But there is satisfaction in the work when it makes a difference like this!*

The hours flew by quickly and Sandra saved the living room for last, because it was the easiest. Taking the dust cloth, she began with the bookshelf. Four photo frames sat on the top shelf.

James must have done some travelling recently, she guessed, picking up one to dust off the frame. The pristine, white beach and turquoise water looked very inviting. *I wonder where that is?* She looked more closely at the other photos, marvelling at the monstrous, ornate cathedral in the largest frame and the snow-capped mountains in the other. Another photo in a glass frame sat in behind the first three. A tall, smiling man with dark curly hair stood behind a boy's hockey team. He looked similar to James, only not nearly so thin. *Is this another brother, or just a younger James?* she wondered.

After dusting each picture frame that sat on the shelf, Sandra turned her attention to the family photo that hung above. *Oh, this must have been taken at a wedding,* she decided. A stylish older couple were in the foreground, seated on a fancy bench, with three young men in gray suits clustered behind them. *The skinny one in the middle is certainly James,* she decided, *although he must have been still in his teens. What a mop of curls!* She glanced at the others. *Maybe those are his brothers standing beside him?...although they don't really look alike.* While James was tall, dark and slim, the other two were fair with heavier builds.

Tall – slim...! *Hmm,* she thought, remembering the courtyard contention, could *James be one of the brothers?* She laughed. *That would be quite a co-incidence if I'm cleaning his house!* She tried to imagine what James would sound like if he was pleading with his brother to listen. *He does have a nice voice,* she considered thoughtfully. But James didn't quite fit the mental picture she was developing of the earnest, caring brother, at least, he didn't fit as well as Mr. Blue. *I do hope it was Mr. Blue,* she thought. Then her more rational side took over. *There are so many people in this condominium. There could be fifty tall men!*

With a shake of her head, she straightened the books, wondering all the while, *Why am I letting this bother me? Does it really matter? So, two brothers had an argument...it's their business. Who am I to get involved?*

I want to know, she argued back, *because I want to know what they were talking about.*

How nosey is that!

But it sounded important. I want to know what it's about.

His brother won't give him the time of day.

His brother hasn't bothered to listen.

Maybe he won't listen because he knows his brother has nothing worthwhile to say.

But he sounded so sincere!

One of her favourite songs began playing on the radio and Sandra hurried over to turn it up louder. Returning to her cleaning, she sang along. As she lifted heavy reference books into place and tidied up the collection of CDs, Sandra envisioned herself in the words of the song; standing outside on the balcony in a long, flowing dress calling down to the man she loved...

The song lasted for the entire time it took to dust the lampshades, TV and the stereo. Still singing, her thoughts drifted idly from the family wedding photo sitting up on the book shelf, to her own brother Laurie and his girlfriend Michelle. Laurie had never married. Sandra had never been to a wedding but she often imagined what such a special day might be like.

I wish someone would promise to love me forever, she thought wistfully as her favourite song came to a haunting end; *someone kind and devoted. I'd love to wear a beautiful white dress and ride off to live happily ever after.* But that wasn't all she wanted! She also hoped that whomever she married had a sister or two and a mom and a dad. She longed to be part of a family! Throughout the years Sandra had often dreamed of the family she yearned for. She and her mom had been good friends but unfortunately the men in her life had been rather disappointing. Books and movies had been most instrumental in developing her family ideals. What she liked she held on to and what she didn't like, she cast away. It was easy enough to do in a make-believe world – a safe, self-pleasing, fully-controlled, make-believe world. Reality, however, hadn't seemed so kind.

Vacuuming the floor, Sandra pictured her brother standing in the open doors of a large stone mansion in downtown Stirling. "My dear sister," Laurie was saying with great compassion, "We're happy to welcome you into our home, at last! Michelle and I have been waiting to see you and we're sorry that we've had to cancel our invitations to you over and over again. It's just the way things go sometimes; work has been very demanding - we've really had no choice. Thank you for being so patient."

Sandra smiled as she imagined the lovely, warm feeling of Laurie's embrace and the caring concern in his eyes. *One day,* she thought, *it'll all work out and Laurie will care about me.*

Polishing the windows, the reverie continued. "I'm thankful you've moved out to Stirling," Laurie was saying sincerely. "I've often told Michelle about *my* sister, and now, look at you – you're all grown up!"

With Laurie's gentle, guiding hand on her shoulder, she imagined he would give her a tour of his grand home. "I want you to know, Sandra, that we're more than happy to have you stay here," he would assure her. "You're our guest. Michelle and I have been well-blessed financially and we're thankful to have the opportunity to share this with you."

Wiping the dust off James' windowsills, Sandra imagined Michelle joining in. She wasn't really sure what Michelle looked like but in her mind's eye Laurie's girlfriends were always blond and beautiful. "Let's show Sandra the room we've fixed up for her," Michelle beamed happily, taking Sandra's arm. "You're going to love it!"

The daydream didn't stop there. Often, in the past few years, Sandra's thoughts had wandered to this very moment in time. Having been an avid day-dreamer all her life, Sandra had imagined every inch of the four-thousand-square-foot mansion that Laurie apparently owned. Occasionally, she updated her vision with a new kitchen or decor if she saw something she liked on TV or in a magazine. Sometimes she even envisioned visiting Laurie at his cottage down by the ocean, especially in June and July when the weather was warm. Always, in both places she was welcomed, cared for and completely happy. The only trouble was… she had been waiting an awfully long time!

Wandering into the kitchen to wash off her cloth, Sandra heard the hourly news report. "…the fourth homicide in Stirling, this year. Police are investigating the situation…" Having heard the same news five times already, she was well aware that there had been another homicide last night, a boating accident and one armed robbery. Back in Ontario, General Motors was calling for major cutbacks and layoffs and another large company had just declared bankruptcy. On top of all of that there was rising panic about an influenza outbreak. It was all rather depressing. *I think I'll bring some music next time,* she thought, glancing over at the small CD player that sat on the kitchen counter. There was an elaborate stereo system next to the large TV but she was sure that would be off limits.

Walking back into the living room, Sandra heard a clip from a speech that the Israeli prime minister had given to the Jewish Congress in the United States. "We will never compromise on security," he said. "If there is no security there can be no peace…"

Peace? Security? Will they ever have either? Sandra mused. It seemed to her that the Palestinian-Jewish conflict was intractable. *Israel has taken over the Palestinians' land,* she thought to herself. *Until they give back what doesn't belong to them, how can they ever expect to have peace?*

James' computer desk was covered with dust. Plenty of lint lay in the keyboard. Sandra removed it patiently and organized the pencils and pens that lay scattered on the desktop. She tidied up a few handwritten notes and printed papers. *I don't know what's important and what isn't,* she thought, *so I'd better be very careful what I throw out.* However, the plastic bin underneath the desk was already overflowing. Picking it up, Sandra dumped the contents into the garbage bag that she was filling by the door. Most of the rubbish consisted of computer print-offs and discarded bills, but a fancy, lilac envelope fell out on top of everything else. Curiously, Sandra plucked it out from the pile. It was a beautiful invitation with a broken silver seal.

It's a wedding invitation! she marvelled, scanning the words. *What a pretty, pastel purple! And James has thrown it out.* The RSVP card and self-addressed envelope were still tucked inside. *I guess he's not planning to go,* she thought. *But why wouldn't he want to go to a wedding? I'd jump at the chance!* Her eyes glanced briefly over the names on the front, but they were completely unfamiliar. Then she had another thought. *Maybe the invitation fell into the garbage by mistake.*

Just to be on the safe side, Sandra returned the envelope with its contents to the empty plastic bin, setting the bin back in its place under the computer desk. *If it was thrown out by accident, then at least it's still in his house,* she thought. *Maybe he'll see it the next time he sits down at his desk.*

There was only one task left to finish. Sandra collected all the take-out boxes neatly stacked in the kitchen and the newspapers that had piled up on the coffee table to take down to the Manor's recycling bin. There were at least three-weeks worth of papers – *good papers!* Being content with freebies, Sandra didn't subscribe to *The Stirling Star* as James did. An article on "Early Learning Disorders" caught her eye and she decided she might as well take it home before throwing it out. She set the newspaper aside. Shuffling everything else into one big pile, she noticed a bright orange flyer still lying alone on the floor. *Is this important?* she wondered. It was an advertisement for an upcoming presentation to be held in the public library.

She read the title. "Israel – An Unwilling Witness that God's Word is Truth". Underneath in smaller print were the words, "Forget Nostradamus, or Astrology! Thousands of years ago God predicted, in great detail, the future of the Jewish people. In the last 100 years His Word has been miraculously fulfilled before our very eyes! And there's more to come! The future of the whole world is intertwined with these events. Come and hear why the Miracle of Israel will soon involve YOU!"

How on earth could anything going on in Israel involve me? Sandra considered. She shook her head dubiously and tossed the flyer onto the stack of papers. The phrase, 'God's Word is truth', stood out to her eyes once more. *What does Israel have to do with 'truth'? If the Bible was written thousands of years ago, how could there possibly be accurate predictions about today?* She stole another glance at the flyer. "God predicted, in great detail..." caught her attention. *Is that just hype?* she questioned, *or will this talk really give me evidence that God is real?*

The concept of 'God' wasn't completely foreign to Sandra. Her mom had believed in "a higher power" and some of her friends at school had been Christian. However, in Sandra's mind, God was an interesting consideration - yet an unproven possibility. Reading the words on the bright orange paper one more time, her curiosity increased. She wondered if James may have purposely singled the flyer out and left it on the floor. Perhaps he was planning to attend the presentation. *If I could be assured that something God said thousands of years ago has actually come true – in great detail,* she considered, *then that would be strong evidence that He is real. Maybe I should go to this.*

Just in case James had singled the flyer out to keep, she placed it on the computer desk with a little note:

> Hope the housecleaning meets with your approval. Let me know if there are any problems.
> I wasn't sure whether to throw this flyer out or not. It was by itself and I thought it might be important.
> Do you mind if I use your little CD player while I work? I'll do the fridge, stove and cupboards tomorrow.
>
> Sandra

Taking one last look at the lovely, clean rooms, Sandra left apartment 226 and darted up the stairs to her own place, hoping once again that no one would see her. Unfortunately, in the corridor, just as she was unlocking her door, Mr. Blue stepped out of the elevator. Their eyes met.

"Hey, how's it going?" he asked in his kind, charming way.

"Great!" she replied quickly with a radiant smile. "It's been a good day for housecleaning." Embarrassed to be seen in such shabby clothing, Sandra tried to scurry inside.

"Hey, you can do mine too, if you like!" he called out.

Sandra laughed and closed the door behind her.

"Okay, that does it!" she told Tiger, as he purred happily, curling around her bare legs. "From now on, I'll wear nice clothes *overtop* of these bleach-stained ones until I get where I'm going."

Tuesday morning Sandra made her way back to finish the housecleaning job with a *Top Hits* CD in hand. Outside the rain was pouring down in sheets and the skies were gray and heavy. With jeans and a sweatshirt overtop of her designated cleaning outfit, Sandra had a leisurely ride with three other people on the elevator – *unfortunately, no tall men* - and strolled casually across to door 226. Enthusiasm wasn't bubbling up in quite the same way as it had the day before. The weather had dampened her spirits even though she hadn't set a foot outside.

The first thing Sandra checked, once she had taken off her jeans and sweatshirt, was the computer desk. She hoped James had written a reply to her note, or left further instructions. Sure enough there was a small message.

> *Feel free to use the CD player or the stereo if you like. Instructions for the stereo are on top of the TV.*
>
> *You may take all the papers you like, but please only from previous weeks. I wasn't quite finished reading the latest one.*
>
> *House looks fantastic!*

Oops! she thought to herself. *I'd better go and get that newspaper before I forget.*

A few minutes later, the paper was back on James' coffee table and Sandra was heading to the bathtub to get a large bucket of hot water. The fridge and oven were Tuesday's assignment and she wasn't exactly looking forward to the task.

Since she had been generously offered the use of the stereo, Sandra found the instructions and turned it on. An I-pod was already docked into the system and Sandra decided it would be interesting to listen to James' music collection. Leaving it on 'random', the first piece was classical and the second was by U2.

Spraying the oven, Sandra left it to sit for a while and began to take everything out of the fridge. There wasn't really very much there, besides milk and margarine - just a couple mouldy containers of restaurant food and a few limp, wilted vegetables; all of which she tossed into the compost bin. When she opened the small freezer she discovered a sirloin roast and a bag of frozen raspberries. *Ah, just imagine how lovely that roast would smell in the oven,* she thought. *And if there were some crispy, spiced potato wedges, and lemon-buttered broccoli, it would be the most amazing meal!* As she scrubbed away at the sour milk spill that had hardened at the bottom of the fridge, Sandra imagined the bag of frozen raspberries in a flaky, golden-crusted pie, warm and runny, fresh from the oven, with a big scoop of vanilla ice cream on top. Having maintained a 'healthy' brown rice diet for the last month, in order to try an experimental 'detox' and save on her grocery bill, the raspberry pie was a tantalizing idea.

Suddenly a wonderful plan came to her. *I'll make James a pie!* she determined. *Surely he would love to come home to a warm, raspberry pie. That's got to be better than take-outs!* The dreary day that lay ahead of her, was suddenly full of colour. Sandra loved to cook! Having deprived herself of anything beyond the basics for quite some time, this seemed a splendid opportunity. It would be something special for her employer and she would enjoy it *vicariously!*

Now that there was something to look forward to, Sandra worked more energetically. When the oven and fridge were clean, she tried to find the ingredients to make the pie. There wasn't any Crisco shortening or butter in the fridge so she picked up the container of Becel margarine. *I guess I'll give it a try,* she thought. She looked in every cupboard for flour but could find none of that either. Thinking she might have a little bit left in her own cupboards, Sandra ran quickly back up the stairs to the fourth floor, avoiding the elevator once again in her bleached-stained shirt. She was very pleased to find she had over two cupfuls of flour.

The pastry didn't turn out exactly as she'd hoped. With only a little flour left to dust the countertop, and soft margarine instead of shortening, the pastry kept sticking to the counter and falling apart when she lifted it up. However, she managed to patch together a half-decent crust in a square, glass baking pan. She found enough sugar and cornstarch to mix with the raspberries and couldn't resist setting aside a few of the lovely, red berries to nibble on.

Now, I'd better make sure there's a cookie sheet underneath this, she thought with amusement as she turned the clean oven on, *or it might boil over and make a big mess. Mom used to get so mad when I did that!*

As she cleaned up the counters, Sandra opened the kitchen cupboard under the sink to dispose of the plastic bag from the raspberries. A bright, crumpled, orange wad of paper was sitting on top of the rest of the garbage.

The flyer, she mused, remembering the ad that she'd left on James' computer desk. *I guess he didn't want it.*

Had Sandra never seen the orange flyer again she may not have given it a second thought. She decided against plucking it out from the trash, knowing she would likely find others in the Manor's recycling bin. *I'll have to have another look at it,* she told herself. *The topic sounded interesting to me.*

Once the cupboards had been cleaned and reorganized and the pie was baked to a crispy, golden brown, Sandra pulled her good clothes back on. She hastily scribbled another note to James about the pie, and then reluctantly closed the door on the enticing aroma. Heading for the elevator, she pressed the down arrow. The recycling bin was on the basement floor.

Something to Think About
Chapter Five

As Sandra expected there were plenty of discarded, orange flyers. Just as she was picking one up, another man came by with a huge stack of papers in his arms. "Lose something?" he asked.

"Oh, no. I'm just taking one of these orange flyers," she told him, glancing briefly in his direction. He wasn't tall, so one glance sufficed.

"You can have mine," he grunted, dropping his newspapers into the bin. "I don't know why people waste money and trees on ads like that. Look how many there are!"

"I think I might like to hear this talk," she said cheerfully, glancing at the flyer she had retrieved. She smiled teasingly, "If I learn anything interesting, do you want to hear about it?"

"I can tell you right now, you'll be bored to tears!" the older man grinned. "Better to stay home and watch hockey. Big game this weekend!"

Sandra laughed pleasantly as she walked away. Even if she planned to stay home and watch TV on a Sunday night, a hockey game wouldn't be her first choice.

When Sunday evening finally came, Sandra drove her car - her mother's old car, carefully out of the narrow, enclosed, parking garage. Most of the tenants only used the garage when the weather was bad, since the parking spots were tightly crammed in. With the orange flyer spread out on her lap so that she could refer to the directions, she drove past a tall man climbing out of his truck. She observed him carefully. His hair was completely gray and he was fairly stout. *I don't think either brother was quite that large,* she told herself, *but that makes three tall men in the Manor!*

Thinking about her list of possibilities, Sandra clearly favoured Mr. Blue. *He seems so kind,* she thought, stopping for a red light. *I'd like to get to know him better somehow - someway.*

James was second on the list although Sandra doubted that he was religious. There was certainly nothing in his apartment to suggest otherwise. *And besides, he hasn't even called to thank me for the pie,* she thought dismally. *I made it five days ago! He can't be very thoughtful or caring. Hmm... maybe...he's the brother who wouldn't listen...but no, I think that brother was still religious...he just had his own beliefs.* Then a new, rather discouraging thought popped into her mind. *Perhaps the two brothers don't even live in the Manor. What if they were just out for a walk and ducked into the courtyard to get out of the wind?* Sandra sighed. *I may never figure this out. I'm certainly not a good detective.*

Picking up the orange flyer, Sandra had a quick look at the map. She crossed the Harbour Bridge. *Windsor Street,* she mused to herself, *that's what I need to find.*

Sandra's white Ford Escort was making an unusual noise as she drove along Windsor Street looking for the Northcliffe Centre. She'd never been to the west side of town before and wasn't familiar with any street names. Squealing noisily every time she accelerated, Sandra's car attracted lots of embarrassing attention. Some of her gauges began to bounce back and forth. "Oh please," she begged no one in particular, "please don't let there be something else wrong. I just paid for a new muffler last month. I can't afford another repair!"

At last she spotted the community center. A large sign sat on the lawn which said, "Israel – An Unwilling Witness that God's Word is Truth." It was the same message the orange flyer had advertised.

Parking the noisy car, Sandra walked nervously inside the blue clapboard building, wondering who she would meet and what would be said. She was greeted by a pleasant young woman.

"Hi," the young woman said, extending her hand with a warm, welcoming smile, "I'm Jessica Symons. I'm so glad you could join us tonight."

"I'm Sandra Carrington," Sandra said, shaking Jessica's hand and looking up at her. Jessica was nearly a head taller than Sandra and seemed much younger. Her straight, light brown hair was twisted up into a loose knot.

Unsure of what to say next, Sandra asked, "Does it matter where we sit?"

There were plenty of empty chairs in the large meeting room and Sandra felt silly asking the question but Jessica only smiled.

"You can sit beside me if you like," she suggested warmly, "There's plenty of room in my row."

Happy to have the company, Sandra followed Jessica up to the front row and sat down. A moment later, a tall, blond man joined them. Rugged in appearance, he looked as though he spent a great deal of time outdoors. .

"This is my fiancé - Peter," Jessica said, making introductions. "Peter, this is Sandra…Sandra…" With a look of dismay in her pretty blue eyes, Jessica looked over at her new friend.

"Carrington," Sandra reminded her with a laugh.

Peter and Sandra shook hands. Peter's hands were rough and worn. "Good to meet you, Sandra," he said sincerely. "I hope you enjoy the presentation tonight." Noticing that she didn't have a Bible, he added. "We have a stack of Bibles to give out, would you like one?"

"That would be wonderful," she replied, somewhat embarrassed. "I don't own a Bible."

When Peter returned with a new Bible for her, Sandra thanked him appreciatively.

Waiting for the talk to begin, Sandra flipped through the new book carefully. She had only a vague idea of what it was about, based on what she'd heard from friends at school and bygone Christmas pageants. Her mother had been an honest, good-living person, who believed there was a God but never talked much about Him.

Jessica and Peter explained how the Bible was organized into sixty-six different books and showed Sandra how to use the index to find a reference. A couple of times Peter scurried off to get Bibles for other people who had come in without one.

Having attended very few church services, Sandra wasn't sure what to expect; especially when they weren't even in a church. Two men were sitting up in front of a big screen that stood against the white wall and Sandra presumed they would be giving the presentation. One looked to be around fifty, with gray hair and a well-trimmed beard. The other she supposed was in his late twenties. For a moment or two she looked at him carefully. *He looks a little like Laurie,* she thought, *except he has a different nose. Maybe he's my cousin, or some distant relative I didn't know I had. Maybe he's my dad's nephew and knows my dad really well. Maybe...* When the man looked up and caught her eye, Sandra turned away embarrassed. *I've got to stop hoping that people are related to me!* she told herself. *Am I becoming obsessed?*

As advertised, at six o'clock, the older man stood up and introduced the subject for the evening.

"We're happy to see so many of you were able to make it out tonight," he began with a smile. "My name is Craig Symons and I'm a local High School teacher. Our speaker tonight, is Mr. Thomas Lovell - a keen Bible student. You may recognize him as the friendly, produce manager at the Atlantic Superstore just down the road."

"Lovell," Sandra considered. *The name doesn't sound familiar. He can't be related...*

"Mr. Lovell has been studying the Bible for the last ten years," Craig continued, "and will speak to you tonight on a subject that is dear to his heart *and* to the heart of many others. We have the privilege, my friends, to be able to look back on thousands of years of fulfilled Bible prophecy and see how incredibly accurate God's Word has been with *every* prediction in the past. This gives us total confidence that any remaining prophecies will likewise transpire exactly as God has said they will."

This is what I came to hear! Sandra thought, sitting up straight in her chair.

Before calling on the speaker, Craig began the evening with a prayer. Listening carefully, Sandra took mental notes on how the prayer was given. It was all new to her. She noticed with interest that everyone bowed their heads and closed their eyes until the last Amen.

When the prayer was over, Thomas stood up at the podium and looked out at the audience with a friendly smile. "Welcome everyone," he said. "I wish we had six hours to discuss this subject tonight! Maybe then, as Craig has said, I could truly do justice to the evidence of fulfilled Bible prophecy and the vast detail of what God has in store for this earth.[1] Bible prophecy touches on the history and future of many nations; however, tonight we are going to look specifically at the Jewish people."

There's that much fulfilled Bible prophecy? Sandra wondered. *Could he really talk for six hours about it?* She paid close attention as Thomas took them through Deuteronomy twenty-eight. Using a PowerPoint slide show he demonstrated pictorially how this chapter had accurately predicted the Jews' sad

---

[1] For more evidence see the Appendix.

and fearful history. Very clearly in the chapter, God had instructed them that if they followed His laws they would be blessed in every aspect of their lives and all nations would see that God was with them. However, if they refused to obey, as they often did, they would suffer disease, persecution, sieges, poverty, captivity, and many other terrible consequences.

They have certainly suffered a lot, Sandra mused as Thomas displayed one slide after another.

Thomas then took everyone to the words of Jesus at the end of Luke chapter nineteen. There Jesus lamented over the Jewish people's failure to accept him as their Messiah and prophesied that because of this, their land would be taken from them, their temple destroyed and they would be scattered into all the other nations.

"And so it happened in AD 70," Thomas stated. "After the Romans had driven the Jews from all the surrounding cities, they finally took Jerusalem and burned the temple to the ground. The Jewish people were taken captive, scattered into many nations and for almost two thousand years they were without a national presence in their land. It happened just as God said it would!"

So, God took the Jews out of their land because they wouldn't accept Jesus as their Messiah, Sandra considered. *But then, why did they get to come back?*

Taking everyone to the prophecies of Ezekiel chapters thirty-six to thirty-nine, Thomas explained that God prophesied, almost three thousand years before it came to pass, that He would have favour on Israel again *in the future*. In chapter thirty-seven, Thomas read the verses which said that God would bring His people back to their land. Sandra followed along. "Surely I will take the children of Israel *from among the nations*, wherever they have gone, and will gather them from every side and bring them into *their own land*; and I will make them *one nation* in the land, on the mountains of Israel...²"

"Very plainly in these chapters, God explains that it is not because His people deserve to return to their land that He will do this,³" Thomas explained. "God promises to bring His people back to His land because He wants all the nations to know that *He is God!* ⁴ By returning the Jews to their homeland, God is demonstrating *to us and to them* that He has power to fulfil His Word! It's a modern-day miracle!"

Sandra was surprised. *But if God wanted all the nations to know that he brought the Jews back to their land,* she considered, *why has no one ever told me this before? Did God's plan not have the effect that He wanted?*

Thomas showed the audience a ten-minute video collage of old, relevant news clips from the 1900's. Some of the clips were black and white and a little hard to see, but they were an authentic, graphic review of the events that transpired to resurrect a nation that had ceased to exist. There was a speech in the British parliament, where the Balfour Declaration was read, stating that the Jewish people had the right to return to their land. There was a clip of Jewish men and women dancing in a circle, singing the "HaTikvah," as they celebrated the legal establishment of their nation, even though they knew this would lead immediately to a declaration of war from the Arab countries nearby. There were several dramatic clips from the war of 1948 where the newly-formed Jewish nation miraculously defeated the much better equipped, far more numerous Arab armies.

A shiver went down Sandra's spine. *It does seem to be a miracle, but why hasn't more been made of this? I've never heard*

---

[2] Ezekiel 37:21-22
[3] Ezekiel 36:17-23;31-32; 39:23-29
[4] Ezekiel 36:35-36; 37:21-18; 39:25-27

anything about this on the news, or even from my Christian friends!

When Thomas directed their attention to the rest of Ezekiel chapter thirty-seven, Sandra was sceptical. The prophecy indicated that one king would be king over them all, and it sounded as though the new nation would believe in God and serve Him.[5]

Well that isn't true, Sandra pondered. *Israel doesn't have a king and I know they aren't all religious."*

"We are in the *middle* of the fulfillment of this prophecy," Thomas clarified as he spoke. "It began in 1917 with the Balfour declaration giving Jews the opportunity to return to Palestine. As we saw in the video, other lands had been suggested, including a tract of land in Uganda - but it was to their ancient homeland that the Jews returned! Since then, they have immigrated to their land from "many nations" just as God said they would. [6] In 1948 they became *a nation* – against great odds – as you saw from the news clips, with so many hostile, Arab countries declaring war on them at the very moment of their birth! How could such a tiny, unprepared, fledgling nation, unauthorized at that time to own *any weapons*, defeat such a massive, well-armed Arab assault... *unless...* some greater force was behind the events?"

True! Sandra nodded, thinking, *maybe it is a miracle. So then,* she considered, *if God has brought the Jews back to Israel, perhaps they have a right to the land. But why are the Jews so important to God?*

Sandra still wasn't completely convinced. *They don't have a king...*she thought. *They aren't all religious and in the chapter that Thomas read, God says all the nations would know that He has made this happen. This isn't common knowledge today. It certainly wouldn't be presented like that on the news.*

---

[5] Ezekiel 37:21-18
[6] Ezekiel 36:20-24; 38:8,12; 39:27-28

Thomas took everyone to the prophecy of Zechariah and skimmed through chapters twelve to fourteen, to show that God foretold the Jews would also *regain Jerusalem*. "It is over this city that another great battle will be fought," he said. "True to God's Word the Jews took control of Jerusalem as *their own* capital city in 1967. Slowly, bit by bit, prophecy has been fulfilled before our eyes, and more is yet to come."

"But they don't have a king," Sandra whispered to Jess. "They have a prime minister..."

Jessica smiled. "They will have a king – *a very important king!*"

"Look at what is *left* to happen from Ezekiel chapter thirty-seven," Thomas directed, pointing to a list displayed on the screen.

Sandra looked up. *Okay, so he's willing to admit that some of this hasn't come true yet.*

"God specifically says the Jews will exist on *the 'mountains of Israel'* which is the disputed West Bank,"[7] Thomas said, pointing to his list. "This is still a work in progress, while the world is calling for a 'freeze on settlements' and insisting that Israel agree to a 'two-state solution'.[8] God says that in the future the Jews will have *one king* – [9]not the democratically elected, ever-changing government we see in Israel today. God says His *tabernacle* will once again be built in their land. [10]Today, the Jews would love to have their own temple but to build one would incite the wrath of the world. God says that in this future time they will live *righteously* in His eyes as His people [11]– *forever!* Today, most of the Jews in the land are secular and uninterested in their Creator.

---

[7] Ezekiel 37:22
[8] A two-state solution refers to the plan to divide up the land of Israel, giving part to the Arabs and another to the Jews.
[9] Ezekiel 37:22-25; 34:23-24; Jer. 23:5; 30:9; Hosea 3:5; Luke 1:32; John 10:16
[10] Ezekiel 37:26; Isaiah 2:2-5; Micah 4:1-4
[11] Ezekiel 37:22-28; 36:16-36; Isaiah 60; 61

And finally, God says *all the nations of the world* will understand that what has happened in the land of Israel is a miracle *God has performed!*[12] Today, world opinion is on the side of the Palestinians, pressuring the Jews to give up more and more of the Promised Land."

"However," Thomas paused, looking confidently out at his audience, "having seen that God has begun to fulfil this prophecy, we hold on *in faith* to these details, believing that God will fulfill His Word completely."

Sandra looked the list over carefully. It was hard to believe that the six 'future' details Thomas had listed there would ever occur! *He needs faith all right,* she thought. *And even if it all comes true, I really don't see how the whole world will ever acknowledge that any of this is a miracle from God! Most people are like me – completely unaware of these prophecies."*

"Now, it's easy enough to see something in hindsight," Thomas went on to say, "but I'd like to show you a paragraph from a book that was written in the mid-1800's, well before the Jewish people had any hope of re-establishing their own nation. This author never claimed to have any *special* inspiration from God; he was simply a man who devoted himself to reading the Bible and searching for God's truth. This is what he said in the mid-1800's, based on the Bible prophecies he read in the Old Testament:

'There is, then, a partial and primary restoration of Jews....which is to serve as the nucleus, or basis, of future operations in the restoration of the rest of the tribes after he [Jesus] has appeared in the kingdom. The...colonization of Palestine will be on purely political principles; and the Jewish colonists will return in unbelief of the Messiahship of Jesus, and of the truth as it is in him. They will emigrate thither as agriculturists and traders, in the hope of ultimately establishing their commonwealth, but more

---

[12] Ezekiel 37:28; 36:23; 20:41-44

immediately of getting rich in silver and gold by commerce with India, and in cattle and goods by their industry at home under the efficient protection of the British power. And this their expectation will not be deceived; for, before Gog invades their country, it is described by the prophet, as "a land of unwalled villages, whose inhabitants are at rest, and dwell safely, all of them dwelling without walls, and having neither bars nor gates; and possessed of silver and gold, cattle and goods, dwelling in the midst of the land" (Ezekiel 38:11-13)[13]'"

It was a lengthy section and Sandra gave up trying to write it all down. She was quite impressed that someone had been able to foresee these events in such detail long before they had transpired – just from reading the Bible! *Maybe God is behind this,* she considered.

"Incredible, isn't it?!" Thomas said, looking out at his audience. "And this man wasn't the only one who understood the Jews would return to their land well before it occurred. Isaac Newton, the famous scientist and avid Bible student, wrote in an early eighteenth-century manuscript, under the title "Of ye… Day of Judgement & World to come" his strong belief that the Bible prophesied the Jews would return.[14] The historicist, H. Grattan Guiness, and theologian, George Stanley Faber also left behind writings in the nineteenth century that anticipated the Jews would come back to the land of Palestine.

"Now," Thomas said, "we've looked at prophecies concerning Israel; let's take a brief look at the world we live in. Let me read what *Jesus* said *our world* would be like right before his return. As I read, think about whether or not this describes the general state of affairs we see all around us."

---

[13] John Thomas, *Elpis Israel* (The Christadelphian, 1849, revised in 1973), pp. 441-442.
[14] www.isaac-newton.org/snobelen.pdf

Sandra followed along closely as Thomas read Luke chapter twenty-one, verses twenty-five to twenty-eight. "And there will be signs in the sun, in the moon, and in the stars; and on the earth distress of nations, with perplexity, the sea and the waves roaring; men's hearts failing them from fear and the expectation of those things which are coming on the earth, for the powers of heaven will be shaken. Then they will see the Son of Man coming in a cloud with power and great glory. Now when these things begin to happen, look up and lift up your heads, because your redemption draws near."

There is a lot of fear in society today, she mused.

"Think about the concerns we hear addressed in the news," Thomas prodded. "Violence, global warming, global recession, flu epidemics, nuclear capabilities of rogue nations like Iran, an aggressive Russia restocking arms and warships, intractable wars in Afghanistan and Iraq, the United States trillions of dollars in debt – where is this all headed? And why does God say that when we see this time of trouble, we should look up and lift up our heads?"

Sandra waited anxiously for the answer to that question.

Thomas didn't give the good news first, instead he warned every one of the hardships that were yet to come. "There will be a time of trouble on this earth," he said, "bringing distress to the nations and causing men's hearts to fail them for fear, perhaps even more than what we see today.[15] As we read in Zechariah fourteen and Ezekiel thirty-eight, Russia will develop an alliance with Germany, France, Ethiopia and Iran, invade the Middle East, [16]have success for a time, [17]but will eventually be overthrown *by the Lord Jesus Christ and his saints on the mountains of Israel!*

---

[15] Luke 21:25-36
[16] Ezekiel 38:1-12
[17] Daniel 11:40- 12:3

[18]This will usher in a time when the *Kingdom of God* will be set up on earth![19]

"So, we're looking for Jesus Christ to return!" [20]Thomas said with elation. "Jesus Christ will soon intervene and take control of the world. He will be *the King* in Jerusalem! [21]He will build *the temple* in God's land[22] and turn all the Jewish hearts to *worship God in truth.* [23]It will be at this time that the nations of the earth will finally understand that God has brought it all to pass. [24]So look up and lift up your heads because your redemption draws near!"[25]

Sandra nodded thoughtfully, mulling it over. Thomas had put the last few pieces of the prophecy together in a flash. *Jesus will be the king! How interesting,* she thought. *And he's coming back! Will we actually get to see him? If Thomas is right, this world is going to be a very different place! Will I get to see this happen?*

"So," Jessica said, turning to Sandra when it was all over, "how did you find the presentation this evening? Do you have any questions?"

"Lots!" she nodded, feeling rather overwhelmed. "I've never read the Bible before so it was all very new to me. But I was impressed. You really expect Jesus to return soon?"

Jessica nodded.

"Really soon? Like in our lifetime?" Sandra clarified.

"Any day now," Jess replied. "Maybe he'll come tonight; or maybe it will be twenty or thirty years from now. We can't be sure exactly but we know it will be soon. Thomas only touched on

---

[18] Ezekiel 38:18- 39:7; Zechariah 14:1-16;
[19] Daniel 2:36-44; 7:13-27; Zechariah 14:16-17; Ezekiel 39:21-29; Rev. 5:9-10
[20] Acts 1:11; 1 Thessalonians 4:16; 2 Thessalonians 1:7-10; Revelation 22:12
[21] Luke 1:31-33; Matthew 5:35; John 18:36-37
[22] Zechariah 6:12-13; Isaiah 11:1-5; Jeremiah 23:5-8; Revelation 21:24-27
[23] Zechariah 12-13
[24] Revelation 1:5-7: Matthew 24:30; Ezekiel 39:7,21-23
[25] Luke 21:28

some of the prophecies that relate to Jesus' return. There are many that show us there's not much left to happen before he comes."

Sandra shivered. *How exciting!* "I'd really like to know more about the Bible," she said. "Is there anything else I could come to?"

"Well, we have a women's Bible study class every Wednesday morning," Jessica suggested. "You're more than welcome to come to that."

"Do you go?" Sandra asked hopefully.

"Only if her boss gives her the time off," Peter responded, joining into the conversation with a playful tug at Jessica's hair.

Jessica laughed and patted Peter's leg. "I have *the best* boss in the world!" With a happy smile she said, "I know he'll give me the time off."

A small pang of jealousy skittered across Sandra's heart. It was obvious that Jessica worked for Peter and they were both very much in love. *Lucky girl!* she thought.

"Do you know where the Bloomfield Library is?" Jessica asked.

"Oh yes, I go there all the time."

"Well, if you'd like to come to our Bible study, it will be in the library, in the large, downstairs meeting room, Wednesday morning at ten."

"I'll make sure she's there," Peter promised Sandra with a wink. "God willing, that is."

"Thank you," Sandra smiled. She stole a curious glance in Peter's direction as he turned to talk to his fiancé. *There's something vaguely familiar about his kind brown eyes. Have I seen him before?*

A Ride with Mr. Blue
Chapter Six

Monday night Sandra mustered the courage to call Laurie and see if they could set up another date to get together. She waited till after nine to call, hoping he would be home, but Michelle answered instead.

"Oh, hello, Sandra," she said. "Sorry, but Laurie's in Vancouver for a few days. Can I help you?"

"I was just wondering if we could set up another time to get together," Sandra explained almost apologetically.

"We're just not having any luck, are we?" Michelle laughed kindly. "Let me check our appointment book." There was a pause while Michelle walked to another place in the house and began shuffling through pages. "Hmmm," she pondered, "where are we now? Early May? Maybe we could do something at the beginning of June…Oh, no, I forgot! We have a wedding to go to that weekend…its down in the Dominican - if you can believe it!"

Sandra listened patiently as Michelle rhymed off all the activities they had planned for every weekend in June.

"We really do want to get together with you, Sandra," Michelle assured her. "It's just such a busy time of year!"

It's been a busy time of year since last August, Sandra thought despondently.

"I really don't know what to say," Michelle conceded at last. "I'll have to talk to Laurie when he gets back. He tends to only think of one week at a time, but we do have holidays coming up in July. Perhaps we can work something out then…maybe even at the cottage."

"That would be nice," Sandra replied, trying not to sound disappointed that it was so far away and still uncertain. "So, you'll get back to me then?"

"I'll tell Laurie that you've called," Michelle assured her, "and I'll write a big note on the fridge to remind him to get back to you. Usually when I write things on the fridge he remembers," she laughed.

It's that hard to remember me? Sandra felt like crying. "Okay, I'll look forward to hearing from him. Thanks for your time."

Taking Tiger into her arms, Sandra curled up by the large picture windows and stared out dismally. Other than the twinkling lights of the city, it was a black, dark night. *I feel so alone,* she thought, caressing the warm, furry head that rubbed against her face. *What would I do without you Tiger?* Tears trickled down her cheeks and Tiger did his best to wipe them away with his rough little tongue. "After last night's talk though," she told her cat, "I think it's possible there may be a God. But...if there is, do you think He cares about *us?* Do you think it's worth trying to talk to Him?"

Having been without a dad for as long as she could remember, a loving, Heavenly Father was hard to imagine and yet the idea intrigued her. A former, Christian friend from high school had often referred to God in that way.

Tiger was looking up at her devotedly and purring with contentment.

"I don't know who else to ask for help," she told him miserably. "We're in trouble, Tiger! But if God really does exist and has this whole world in His control, like Thomas said He does, then I guess... I guess I might as well give it a try."

Looking up to the stars, Sandra timidly pleaded for God's help. "I can't pay my rent this month," she told Him mournfully. "I don't know how I'm ever going to make it through the summer. I might get evicted unless I find another job and then...where would I go? And my *only* brother, who could help me so easily, keeps forgetting that I even exist! Please, God, if you're there, please make him realize I'm a human being. Please help him to want to spend time with me. Please help me out."

The first thing Sandra did, Tuesday morning when she arrived at James' place was to look for a note on the computer desk. If he wasn't going to thank her for making the pie, she certainly wasn't going to make him anything else. But, sure enough there was a message.

> Sandra,
> It was very kind of you to make that beautiful pie! Unfortunately, I have to watch my cholesterol - had a heart bypass just over a year ago - and so I couldn't enjoy such a delicious looking treat. I stuck it in the freezer. Please feel free to take it home with you.
> James.
> P.S. I hate to tell you this, but I spilled juice in the fridge the other day. I hope you don't mind fixing that up. ☹

I get the raspberry pie! Sandra thought with delight. *I guess I should have told him it was made with Becel, not shortening...Oh well, this is my lucky day!* Before beginning work, Sandra took the pie out of the freezer so it could begin to defrost. *Mmmm, yummy!* she thought, imagining how good it would taste warmed up in the microwave. *Forget the detox today!*

Then again, she considered reluctantly, the frozen pie still in her arms, *maybe I should tell him it's safe. After all, I used up his whole bag of raspberries and a lot of his margarine.* With a sigh, she stuck the pie back in the freezer.

Opening the fridge door, she had a look at the mess. Juice had spilled everywhere. Sandra had to redo the cleaning she had done the week before and this time she didn't see anything that inspired culinary creativity. The roast was gone. Aside from a carton of milk, a new container of Becel margarine, two apples and a package of almonds, there wasn't much there. *I guess it'll be another take-out, tonight,* she thought, *but maybe he'll have a piece of pie to go with it.* She looked over at the pile of cardboard in the corner. *I wonder where he goes to get healthy restaurant meals?* There were a variety of boxes – Garden Trends, Eden Delights, Fresh and Fancy. Sandra didn't recognize any of the names, but then, she never ate out.

After everything was sparkling clean again she wrote a message to James.

> James,
> I think the pie will be safe for you. I made it with Becel, not shortening. Just so you know, cooking isn't work for me – it's fun. So if you'd ever like me to leave you a meal, just give me an idea of what you want to eat and leave me the ingredients to make it with.
> Sandra

Wednesday morning, as usual, Sandra began with an internet check on her computer to see if anyone had responded to her job applications. Tiger curled up in her lap, gently kneading his paws against her. As usual there were no requests. It seemed that there weren't any private schools hiring for the upcoming school year and there were no public school opportunities either – at least, not for her. Ever since the principal had suggested the course on class management, there hadn't been a single call to supply.

However, there were a couple of short emails from her university friends and to her great delight - there *was* even an email from her brother!

Hey Sandra,

Michelle and I have holidays in July. We'd like to invite you for a weekend at the cottage, July 4th – $6^{th.}$ We'll take the yacht out for a spin and show you around Cape Breton. Beautiful country up there! Hope that works for you.

Laurie

"Yes! A whole weekend! A ride on his yacht!" Sandra exclaimed ecstatically to Tiger. Until now, her brother had only ever suggested meeting for dinner at a local restaurant. "This is incredible! Laurie, I forgive you for everything," she said happily. She emailed back immediately:

Dear Laurie,

That would be amazing!! Of course I'll keep that weekend free! I am so looking forward to sailing on the yacht! Thanks for thinking of such a wonderful idea!

Your sister, Sandra

After a quick bowl of left-over brown rice and honey, Sandra straightened her hair and dressed for the ladies' Bible study class. She wasn't really sure what to wear, so she chose her best jeans and her favourite blue sweater. All the while, her mind was fixated on the yacht! It was a chance of a lifetime. Such an adventure would go a long way to make up for years of neglect!

Oh thank you, Laurie! she thought over again and again. *Thank you so much!*

Unfortunately, when Sandra tried to start up her car to head to the library, the squealing sound was even worse than before. She didn't know what to do. *If I take it to the auto shop,* she thought, *I'll be handed another bill I can't afford. Oh dear! Will this car make it to the library, or not?*

As she sat there in the parking garage, watching the erratic gauges on the dashboard, there was a knock at her window. Much to her surprise, Mr. Blue stood there in his black leather jacket and familiar reflective-blue sunglasses. Sandra quickly rolled the window down.

"Hey there," he said, with a charming smile. "It sounds like you've got car troubles. Would you like me to take a look?"

What a nice guy! she thought, nodding appreciatively. "That would be wonderful!"

"Just pop the hood," he directed, peering in underneath the instrument panel to see if he could point out the right latch.

Sandra didn't have any idea what was wrong with her car, but she did know how to pop the hood. She quickly pulled on the handle. There was a click and the tall, good-looking man with the wavy, blond hair pushed back his sunglasses and made his way around to the front. He lifted the hood. In a minute he was back at her window.

"It looks like your fan belt is going," he reported. "Are your gauges stable?"

Sandra shook her head. "They're going haywire."

Leaning in, with a pleasant, aftershave aroma, Mr. Blue had a look for himself. "I don't think your alternator is working properly," he reasoned. "Do you have far to go?"

"I'm just heading over to the library for a ten o'clock meeting."

He looked down at his watch briefly. "Why don't I give you a lift," he said. "If that belt goes, you won't be getting anywhere. You'd be better off to save your last run for a trip to the auto shop."

"I would be *very* grateful for a ride!" she told him. There wasn't time to catch a bus and *what an opportunity!* "Thanks!"

"No problems," he assured her.

Turning off the squealing engine, Sandra picked up her purse and the Bible that Peter had given her. *Time for a little detective work,* she thought. *Choice number one is giving me the perfect chance to ask a few questions.*

Once they were comfortably settled in the red Mustang – very comfortably settled that is - in soft, cushioned, black leather seats, Mr. Blue introduced himself. "Brett Lawson," he said, extending his hand.

"Sandra Carrington," she smiled, reaching out to shake hands. Brett's hand was big and tanned, and folded around hers in a comforting way. His real name suited him much better than "Mr. Blue."

"You live on the fourth floor, right?" Brett inquired, as he backed out of the crammed garage. "I think you're just down the hall from me?"

"Yes. I've been there since August," she said, looking at him carefully. Brett had a square jaw-line and very Roman nose. His eyes were such a pale, sapphire-blue! "What about you?"

"I've lived here for the last five years," he told her, as they approached a major intersection, "ever since the Manor first opened. I love it! My brother lives a few blocks away. We both wanted to be close to the harbour. The fishing is great."

A shiver ran down Sandra's spine. *He has a brother...only a few blocks away!*

There was a pause in the conversation as Sandra tried to think of how she could ask if Brett was religious. Thankfully, when the light turned green, he set her up perfectly. "So, what kind of a meeting are you going to at the library?"

"I'm going to a ladies' Bible study," she told him. "This is my first time."

"Good for you," he said approvingly. "I thought you might be going to something of that nature, with a Bible on your lap! I'm just getting back into it all, myself. I go to a Bible study on Thursday evenings. It's great. I learn a lot…although the Pastor we have now isn't nearly as good as the one I had, growing up."

He's religious! Sandra's palms became sweaty.

"So what do you do for a living?" Brett asked.

They were almost to the library, so Sandra gave him the quickest version ever, of her teaching woes, trying not to sound too dour about it.

"If you love teaching the early years," he reiterated when she was finished, "I suppose that means you like teaching children how to read?"

"I do!" she exclaimed. "It's so rewarding to see a child develop the ability to read. It's a precious key that opens so many doors for them. It's like helping a blind person learn to see."

Brett nodded. "Do you do any tutoring, one on one? Or would you be interested?"

"I'd love to tutor," she told him. "I've actually had an ad in the newspaper for the last few months offering my services."

"Well, maybe this is a lucky day for both of us," Brett smiled. "My brother was just saying last night that he needed someone to help his six-year-old son learn to read."

Sandra could hardly believe it! Brett went on to explain that his nephew, Matt, was in a private school, but both his parents worked and they didn't have time to help their son practise his reading at home.

"They feel kind of bad about it," Brett continued, pulling into the library parking lot, "but when they get home from work they just don't have the patience to sit there for half an hour while Matt stumbles over the easiest words." He paused as he stopped outside the front doors. "Do you mind if I tell my brother about you?"

Being desperate for work, Sandra was delighted. It seemed certain that Brett was the tall, compassionate man she'd been searching for! "Please do!" she said. "I'll give you my number." However, when she searched her purse for paper and a pen, she could only find the paper.

Brett found a pen in his glove compartment.

Sandra hastily scribbled down her name and number and handed it over.

"Great!" he said, accepting the piece of paper with a grin. "Hopefully this will work out. Thanks for being so willing. And by the way..." he said looking over admiringly, "you probably hear this a lot – but you have the most gorgeous blue eyes!"

"Oh, thank you," Sandra replied, somewhat taken aback by the unexpected compliment. She opened the door to get out, unsure of what to say next. It was only after Brett drove off that she remembered she should have thanked him for the ride. She waved and called out, "Thanks for the ride!" but he was so far down the road that she doubted he heard.

Sandra walked into the Ladies' Bible study dizzy with excitement. *It has to be him!* she thought. *Brett must be the man I overheard! He's compassionate; he's religious and he has a brother close by! This is so amazing! I hope I see him again...soon! Maybe I'll finally discover what that courtyard conversation was all about. And maybe... I'll find a friend...*

The ladies' Bible study was a welcoming group of about ten. They met in a large conference room around a big mahogany table. Jessica was there and had saved a chair for Sandra. The lady leading the class was introduced to Sandra as Jessica's mother, Beth Symons. Looking at her closely, Sandra didn't see much resemblance between the two; Beth's short hair was completely gray and her eyes were a dark coffee colour. *They're both tall though,* she noticed, *but then, compared to me, most people are tall!*

Beth introduced everyone to Sandra and told her that they were studying the book of Revelation, the last book of the Bible. After a prayer and a reading from Revelation chapter seven, Beth led the group discussion. While Sandra could tell that it was a great class for everyone else, with lots of participation, the subject matter was too deep for her. Beth was talking about twelve tribes with strange sounding names being sealed in their foreheads by angels. People from all nations and languages were standing in front of 'the Lamb' – which Beth said was Jesus! *How can a lamb be Jesus?* Sandra wondered. It was even stranger when one of the ladies mentioned 'the bride - the Lamb's wife'! *This is too much!* she thought. *Jesus – a lamb - is going to get married? I don't get it!*

Not only were the details and symbols of Revelation hard to comprehend but Sandra kept drifting off to visions of her own - sailing on a yacht with her rich, generous brother and riding in a red Mustang with a tall, compassionate man. As of that morning her future seemed quite bright and exciting all on its own! It was only near the end of the class when they read the last few verses of chapter seven, that Sandra gathered her thoughts and understood what they were reading. The verses spoke about a time when there would be no more hunger or thirst, or any scorching heat. "And God will wipe away every tear from their eyes," Jessica read.

"When?" Sandra questioned eagerly, thinking, *That's an intriguing promise. Imagine no hunger and no tears ever again!* "Is that what will happen when Jesus comes back?" she asked.

Beth nodded happily, and went on to explain that the chapter they were studying in Revelation was a glimpse into the future when Jesus will return and establish God's kingdom on the earth. She talked for a while about what that time period will be like, turning up other references which gave more detail. While Sandra was interested in what she heard, she was also confused. It was all so new.

She expressed her bewilderment to Jessica when everything was over.

"It *was* a bit deep," Jessica admitted. "Everyone in this class has been coming along for a few years. With a pause, Jessica thought carefully. "Look, if you like, I could go over the basics with you," she suggested. "We could start at the very beginning and work through things together."

"Just the two of us?"

"If that's what you'd like."

"That would be fantastic!" Sandra said with relief. "I really don't know a thing about the Bible. I'm not even sure if I believe in God."

Jessica nodded and reached for something in the back of her Bible. Producing a little pamphlet, she gave it to Sandra. "You can take this home with you," she said. "It will give you some reasons to believe the Bible is God's inspired Word."

Sandra took the pamphlet with interest.

"Would you be more comfortable coming over to my house for a discussion, or having me come over to yours?" Jessica asked.

Remembering the alternator problems she was having, Sandra wasn't sure when she'd be able to drive again. She certainly couldn't afford to fix it anytime soon. "If you don't mind coming to my place, I'd be very appreciative."

"Of course," Jessica said. "Would Thursday evenings be okay?"

It seemed that the long, lonely weeks might be a little less lonely. Sandra was hopeful she would get to tutor Matt, and now Thursday evenings would be with Jess.

"Sure. Can we start tomorrow night?"

"I'd love to," Jessica smiled. "And where do you live?"

When Sandra explained how to get to Margaret's Manor, Jessica gave a little laugh.

"Oh, I know the Manor," she said. "Peter's brother lives there."

Sandra Asks Questions
Chapter Seven

It was a fifteen-minute bus ride home from the library. When Sandra entered her apartment, there was a message on her answering machine.

"Hey there, Sandra. This is Brett Lawson. Hope you got home okay from your Bible study – and learned lots! I talked to my brother and he would love for Matt to have tutoring. He wants to know if you'll start tonight! Just give him a call," he said, listing out his brother's phone number. "And let me know if you want help getting your car to the auto shop. See ya around."

He is so nice! Sandra thought with a whimsical smile.

The first session with Matt began later that night. However, Sandra didn't get to meet Brett's brother. Instead, Matt's mom, Patti, brought him over, still wearing her high-heeled boots and smart gray suit. She looked very professional. A laptop computer was tucked under her arm.

Matt resembled his mother, with a dark, Mediterranean complexion and straight, black hair. His chocolate-brown eyes were filled with anxiety, so Sandra kneeled down to his level and told him about the great books she had for him to look at.

"I have some about sharks," she told him excitedly, "and I have a really good one about *Cars*! Have you seen the movie *Cars*?"

"That's his favourite!" Patti nodded.

There was just a hint of a smile on Matt's face, so Sandra continued talking about the other books she knew little boys loved. However, Matt clung tightly to his mother's skirt until Tiger came over. Then his face lit up.

"A kitty!" he exclaimed.

"He just loves animals!" his mom said.

Tiger curled up in Matt's arms and purred loudly. From then on, Matt seemed to relax. They all took a seat in Sandra's living room and Patti opened her laptop.

"Do you mind if I do a little work?" she asked. "I'm so behind today!"

"Go right ahead," Sandra assured her, picking up a reading handbook from the coffee table.

Believing in a balanced phonics approach to reading, Sandra began with a fun song to learn the alphabet, teaching Matt the sounds the letters make as well as their names. Matt was soon clapping along and trying to join in. He hardly noticed when Tiger decided to find a more peaceful place to sleep.

Teaching grade seven and eight had been a struggle for Sandra, as the difficult students had often taken advantage of her gentle spirit. However, younger children were usually won over by the warmth and friendliness she exuded.

"Let's read *Cars* together, Matt," Sandra said near the end of the lesson. "You can read one word on each page and I'll read the rest of the story."

"I only have to read *one word?*" Matt asked, looking very pleased with the idea.

It worked well. Matt wasn't overwhelmed by pages of words and the story stayed exciting. His mom looked up from her computer.

"I never thought of doing that," she said with surprise. "I always thought he had to read it all."

When they finished, Matt's mother paid her thirty dollars and asked if they could come over two nights a week, Wednesdays and Fridays. Sandra was more than happy to agree.

In anticipation of Jessica's visit, Thursday evening, Sandra read through the pamphlet she had been given. A strong case was made for the Bible being the inspired Word of God, based on the advanced health laws given long before modern scientific discoveries of germs and bacteria, and the benefits of proper sanitation. There was also much to be said about archaeological finds, consistent detail from Genesis to Revelation and a multitude of fulfilled Bible prophecies.[26] By the time Jessica arrived, Sandra was examining the Bible she had been given with a new respect.

When Sandra welcomed Jessica in, Tiger was right behind her. Jessica loved cats, so Tiger was again in luck. She scooped him up saying, "Oh, what a gorgeous kitty!"

"Would you like a cup of tea?" Sandra asked, trying to remember how to be a good hostess. She hadn't hosted anyone since coming to Stirling.

"That would be lovely," Jessica said. "For the middle of May, it's still fairly cool."

Sandra agreed, as she plugged in the kettle and opened the tea drawer. She was dismayed to discover that she didn't have a single bag of tea left! Maybe there would be some in a different cupboard. As Jessica caressed Tiger and remarked on his affectionate nature, Sandra anxiously opened bare cupboard after bare cupboard. There was simply no tea.

"I'm sorry, Jessica," she confessed at last, opening the fridge. "I'm right out of regular tea. Do you like lemon and honey?"

"That would be fine," Jessica smiled placidly. "In fact, a glass of cold water is all I drink at home. Just a glass of cold water would be lovely."

Noticing that she was out of honey as well, Sandra was thankful Jessica had suggested water. She filled two glasses with ice cubes and cold water from the fridge.

Jessica wandered into the living room area with Tiger still in her arms.

---

[26] See Appendix for these details

"Wow! You have a great view of the harbour!" Jessica said. "You must be on the same side as James."

Sandra walked into the living room slowly, trying not to spill the water. "James?" she reiterated slowly. *"James who?"*

Jessica nodded her thanks and took a seat on the couch. "James Bryant. He's my fiancé's brother. We've visited him here a couple of times."

Peter has a brother named James! Sandra thought. *This is interesting!* Carefully setting both glasses onto the coffee table in between them, Sandra sat down in a chair. "I clean house for a James," she said; "and he lives right here in the Manor."

"Which apartment?"

When Sandra relayed that it was apartment number 226, Jessica was very surprised. "Why, that's James' apartment - Peter's brother!" she exclaimed.

"Really?" Sandra questioned. "James is your fiancé's brother?"

"Yes," Jessica smiled. "He's tall and thin with dark hair…"

"And a flat-screen TV," Sandra added.

"That's right," Jessica nodded. "How long have you been cleaning house for him?"

"This was my second week."

"I thought you were a school teacher?"

Once again Sandra went through her story. Jessica was very sympathetic to her plight.

"That's unfortunate," she said. "This is an expensive place to live without a steady income. How have you found working for James?"

"So far, so good," Sandra smiled. "He seems like a nice guy."

"James *is* a nice guy," Jessica mused sadly, looking out the large windows. "We love him a lot!"

Sandra noticed the look on Jessica's face and was perplexed. *Why would Jessica be sad that Peter's brother is such a nice guy?* she wondered. Then she remembered finding the orange flyer crumpled up in the garbage. It was the flyer advertising the Bible lecture that Peter and Jessica had attended. *Hmm...*

"I came to the talk Sunday night because of an orange flyer that I found in James' apartment," Sandra relayed.

"You found that flyer in *James'* apartment?" Jessica questioned with a wry smile.

"Yes," Sandra nodded. "I found it on the floor. It looked rather interesting to me and because it was lying by itself on the floor, I thought perhaps he had singled it out. So I left it on his desk with a message, but James never wrote anything back. The next day I found it in the garbage."

Jessica nodded, looking at Tiger and stroking him softly.

"Is James religious, like you and Peter?" Sandra prodded.

"He does call himself a Christian," Jessica replied sadly, "but he and Peter have had their differences."

Okay... Sandra thought. *Here we go. Two brothers – both tall, one lives here and they've had some disagreements.* Having been almost completely sure that Brett was the man she'd overheard in the courtyard, she reluctantly reviewed the case.

"*Religious* differences?" she probed uneasily, hoping Jess would say no. She wanted to hold onto her theory that Brett was the man who cared.

Jessica sighed, leaning back against the couch, "It's a long story," she said. "You see, Peter went through a rough stretch when he didn't want anything to do with God. When he was in his teens his girlfriend died of cancer, right around the time when they had both become interested in religion and reading the Bible together...[27]"

---

[27] "In Search of Life" by Anna Tikvah

"Oh, that's so sad!" Sandra interrupted. "Did you know Peter back then?"

"I did," Jess said sadly. "I knew both Peter and Verity, but they were in their late teens and I was only eight."

"So Peter is a lot older than you?"

"Almost ten years," Jess nodded.

"Were you…friends with them?" Sandra asked tentatively. "I guess if you were only eight…"

"I loved *Verity,* back then," Jess smiled. "They both used to come over to my place to talk to my dad about the Bible. So I saw them often and I just adored Verity! She was so friendly… and very kind to me."

Sandra couldn't resist asking, "What about Peter?"

With a slight blush, Jess laughed. "Oh, I was rather shy around Peter. He was all grown up and well…I guess I had a little girl's crush on him. He would try to talk to me but I was much more comfortable with Verity."

"Were you upset when she died?"

"Devastated!"

"And then what happened?"

"Peter went away. He moved to Australia as soon as he finished high school and I didn't see him again until I was eighteen. He came back to be in his best friend's wedding…and that changed everything."

"He fell in love with you?"

"No," Jess smiled ruefully, shaking her head. "He hardly noticed me, at first. But, his brother James had a heart attack and Peter stayed to help him recover…and ended up living with my parents. That's how we got to know each other."

"Wow!" Sandra said, "That's quite a story."

"It has been," Jess agreed. "It's a story with a happy ending now," she mused. "For years, Peter was so bitter that God had let Verity die, that he wanted nothing to do with Him. But…

all through those years, he had a friend that never gave up on him – actually it was the fellow who gave the presentation that you came to."

"You mean Thomas?" Sandra clarified.

"That's right," Jessica nodded. "Thomas kept in contact with Peter all the time he was in Australia, trying to restore his faith in God and help him work through things. Finally when Peter came over to be in his wedding, Thomas was able to help Peter sort things through and…well, *forgive God*, I guess."[28]

"And that was just a couple of years ago?"

"That's right," Jess agreed. "It's been almost two years since Peter came back."

It was all very interesting to Sandra, and she wanted to ask many more questions, but she especially wanted to know why James and Peter were having their differences. After all, she had a mystery to solve! "So, what's happened between Peter and James?"

Jessica sighed deeply. "Well, you see, Peter is so thankful that Thomas never gave up on him, that he has tried really hard to help James. But now he thinks he might have overdone it. James has refused to even *talk* about the Bible with him and it's damaged their relationship."

It was all coming together. *Oh dear,* Sandra thought disappointedly. *If it was Peter and James that I overheard, then James must be the brother who wouldn't listen! How could that be? James seems so nice!*

Looking over at Jessica hesitantly, Sandra decided to tell her about the conversation she'd overheard. She was more anxious than ever to know the truth. Surely Jessica would know. "Can I tell you something?" she asked.

"Of course," Jessica replied.

---

[28] "Who Are You Looking For?" by Anna Tikvah

"A couple weeks ago," Sandra began soberly, "I overheard this argument between two brothers. I had gone for a walk in the evening and was on my way back to the Manor when I heard voices in the courtyard. The one brother was begging to show the other something from the Bible; something that he said was really important, and that he could show him with only a few passages. But his brother wouldn't listen and said he had his own beliefs and that he was good with God and Jesus and that's all that mattered. And, ever since then, I've been hoping to find out who those two men were and what it was that the one brother wanted to share."

Jessica stroked the sleeping cat sadly. "And you think it might have been Peter and James?" she pondered.

"I don't know. What do you think? All I could see in the darkness," Sandra clarified, "was that they were both tall. One was tall and thin and the other had a heavier build."

"It sounds like it could have been them," Jessica said. "Peter remarked just recently that without God's help he feels it's an *impossible* situation. He said that James has shut the doors on any future discussions."

I guess it wasn't Brett that I overheard, Sandra concluded disappointedly. *And Peter must have been the compassionate man who was trying to reach out to his brother, while James was the resister. Why? Why wouldn't James hear Peter out? He seems like a fairly nice guy. Why would he shut out his brother like that?* However, mixed with Sandra's dismay was the hope that if she had finally tracked down the voices she might now find the answers she was seeking.

"So, if it was them," Sandra surmised, "would you have any idea what Peter wanted to share with James?"

Jessica looked thoughtful for a moment or two. "I don't know for sure what it would be," she said. "There could be a number of things..."

That's okay, Sandra told herself. *At least now I know who to ask.*

"But," Jess began, sounding enthusiastic, "we were going to talk about the Bible tonight, so why don't I tell you what *I* would *love* to tell James, and if it's different than what Peter was going to tell him, we can discuss that another time!"

"That's a great idea!" Sandra agreed.

The Promise
Chapter Eight

Jessica began their little session with a prayer, asking God's blessing on their study. Sandra willingly bowed her head, listening carefully to the way Jess prayed. If she was going to start praying to God, she needed to know how it was done. Then Jessica opened her Bible and Sandra reached for hers.

"Well, this is what I would tell James," Jessica began with a smile. "I would tell him that in the Bible there are a number of promises that God made, way back in the Old Testament. Sometimes people overlook them because they think the Old Testament is no longer relevant, since Jesus Christ gave us the *New*. But, these Old Testament promises are the *foundation* of the Gospel message [29] and tie in beautifully with what is revealed later. They involve us! Jesus himself, referred to the Old Testament many times as the basis for his own message.[30]"

Sandra listened carefully. She wasn't really sure what either testament was about.

"So, let's start at the first book of the Bible, in Genesis chapter thirteen," Jessica suggested. "It would be really helpful to read right through the whole book of Genesis," she encouraged, "but tonight I want to start by showing you one of God's promises."

Sandra found Genesis thirteen easily enough and Jessica explained that the man to whom the promise had been given, was a faithful man named Abram, whose name was later changed to *Abraham*. Abram had responded to God's call to leave the large city, Ur of Mesopotamia, to go to the land of Canaan – which is the modern land of Israel. Abram's nephew, Lot, journeyed with

---
[29] Galatians 3:8
[30] Luke 24:25-27, 44-45; John 5:39,45-47; Luke 16:29-31

him. However, when the pastureland was unable to sustain all their livestock, Lot parted from Abram and chose a well-watered plain for himself.

"It was after they separated that God spoke to Abram," Jessica said, "and gave him this amazing promise!"

At Jessica's request, Sandra read verses fourteen to seventeen, which contained the promise.

"And the LORD said to Abram, after Lot had separated from him: "Lift your eyes now and look from the place where you are - northward, southward, eastward, and westward; for *all* the land which *you see* I give to you and your descendants *forever*. And I will make your descendants as the dust of the earth; so that if a man could number the dust of the earth, then your descendants also could be numbered. Arise, *walk in the land* through its length and its width, for I give it *to you.*""

"Do you see the things that God promised him?" Jessica asked.

Sandra studied the verses quietly. "Many descendants?"

"Yes, and what else?"

"Land?"

"Exactly," Jessica nodded. "He was told to *look* at the land all around him, which would have been the land of Israel and Palestine as we know it today. He was even told to *walk* in it, because God was going to give it to him. And do you see for how *long* God promised He would give it to him?"

It took Sandra a couple of glances before she noticed the word *'forever.'* She was thinking to herself that if God was real, and He had truly promised the land of Palestine to the Jewish people, then perhaps the Jewish people were justified in claiming it as theirs. After a momentary hesitation, she answered Jessica's question. "God promised to give him the land *forever,*" she said, "and to his descendants as well."

"That's right," Jess agreed. "And the interesting thing about this promise is that Abraham was *never* given this land during his life. The New Testament tells us that God didn't even give him 'enough to set his foot on.'[31] When his wife died he had to *buy* a plot of land to bury her; he had nothing he could call his own.[32] Why do you think that would be?"

Sandra thought hard. "Were there conditions to the promise? Conditions that Abram never met?"

"Good suggestion," Jess praised. She paused and then said with a smile, "Thankfully, in the New Testament, Hebrews chapter eleven explains it for us. Let's look at verses nine through eleven."

Sandra struggled to find Hebrews. Jessica gently reminded her about the index at the very beginning which listed the various books and the page numbers they could be found on. She showed her that every book was divided into chapters and every chapter into numbered verses. "It's just an easy way to find a quotation quickly in such a large book," she explained.

Once Hebrews eleven was found, Jessica read it through, emphasizing certain phrases, "By faith Abraham obeyed when he was called to go out to the place which he would *receive as an inheritance*. And he went out, not knowing where he was going. By faith he dwelt in *the land of promise* as in a foreign country, dwelling in tents with Isaac and Jacob, the heirs with him of the same promise; for he waited for the city which has foundations, whose builder and maker is God."

"What do we learn from those verses?" Jess asked.

Sandra read it through again silently. "Well," she attempted, "we learn that Abraham *lived* in the land God promised to him, and so did Isaac and Jacob and they were all given *the same* promise."

---

[31] Acts 7:5
[32] Genesis 23

"Exactly," Jess agreed. "And it says they were waiting for a city that God would make. But, does it say they received it?"

"No," Sandra shook her head. "Did they?"

"Let's read on in verse thirteen," Jessica smiled, her eyes twinkling. "The answer is in this chapter but you'll have to think about it."

Sandra continued, "These all died in faith, not having received the promises, but having seen them *afar off* were assured of them, embraced them and confessed that they were strangers and pilgrims on the earth. For those who say such things declare plainly that they seek a homeland. And truly if they had called to mind that country from which they had come out, they would have had opportunity to return. But now they desire a better, that is, *a heavenly country*. Therefore God is not ashamed to be called their God, for He has prepared a city for them."

"Okay, I get it," Sandra smiled, remembering various conversations she'd had with her friends in the past. "They'll get their promise when they get to heaven. Isn't that what Christians believe?"

Jessica looked puzzled. "What brings you to that conclusion?" she asked gently.

"Well, they saw it afar off," Sandra explained, "as in up in the sky, I guess. And it says they desire a 'heavenly country', and they were 'strangers *on the earth'."*

"Remember the promise we read about in Genesis thirteen," Jess kindly reminded her. "Why would God ask Abram to walk through *the land of Canaan, look at it* in all directions and *live in it,* if he wasn't actually going to receive that land?"

"True," Sandra mused. "Perhaps God is going to give him that exact land in heaven?"

"Is there another way of looking at it," Jessica prodded. "Does 'afar off' necessarily mean 'distance from the earth', or could it refer to something else*?"*

"Hmmm," Sandra mused. "It could mean far off in time, I guess."

"Yes, it could be that they understood the promise would be given sometime in the distant future, just as I might say my birthday is a long way away," Jess smiled. "And what about *'a heavenly country'*? Does that mean it has to be in heaven?"

"I don't know," Sandra replied candidly. "It sounds like it does to me."

"Well, when we talk about 'heavenly ice cream' do we mean that it was actually produced in heaven?"

Sandra giggled. "Of course not."

Jess smiled. "So why would anyone call it *'heavenly* ice cream'?"

"Because it's so good," Sandra reasoned; "it's as though God wrote the recipe!" *And I'd love a bowlful right now!* she thought with a smile.

Nodding, Jess agreed. "We use 'heavenly' and 'divine' quite often to describe things that are extraordinarily good. So, think of this - right now our earth is ruled by human beings. Generally speaking, it is a world dominated by mankind, where man's rules, intelligence, desires and aspirations are glorified and govern everything that happens here. Now imagine if God intervened and took control of this world and *'wrote the recipe,'*" she said to Sandra with a smile, "for everything that was going to happen here. If God's rules, intelligence, desires and aspirations governed *all* our activities on earth, wouldn't it then be *a 'heavenly'* country or *a divine* world – the sort of world that followers of God would love to inherit?"

"Okay, I see what you're getting at," Sandra agreed. "You're saying that Abraham and the others were looking forward to a time in the future when the land they had been promised would be governed by God, not man."

"Exactly," Jess smiled. "When God's will is done *'on earth'*, as Jesus taught us to pray, [33]we will be living in a divine world, or a 'heavenly country'."

"And is that really going to happen?"

"It's the foundation of the gospel message," [34] Jessica stated. "Have a look at the last few verses of this chapter in Hebrews." She paused for a moment waiting for Sandra to find the verse, and then she said, "After telling us about so many of the faithful people in the Bible throughout chapter eleven, the writer ends with: 'And all these, having obtained a good testimony through faith, *did not receive the promise*, God having provided something better for us, *that they should not be made perfect apart from us.'*[35]

"And so, when Jesus was here on the earth," Jess went on to say, "not only did he tell people about his death and resurrection – which is absolutely central to our salvation – but he also preached *'the kingdom of God.'*[36] He talked about himself as the king,[37] about his disciples sitting on twelve thrones judging the twelve tribes of Israel.[38] He talked about Jerusalem being the city of the great king[39] and Abraham, Isaac and Jacob sitting down in the kingdom[40] – *alive again!"*

"So, what is left to happen before this kingdom comes?" Sandra wanted to know.

Jessica looked over thoughtfully. "Remember the talk you went to last Sunday night?" she reminded Sandra. "Thomas spoke about how there is going to be a time of trouble coming upon this earth. Russia and the other countries will soon invade the Middle

---

[33] Matthew 6:10
[34] Galatians 3:8; Matthew 4:23; 9:35; Mark 1:14; Luke 8:1
[35] Hebrews 11:39-40
[36] Luke 4:42-43
[37] John 18:37
[38] Matthew 19:28
[39] Matthew 5:34-35
[40] Luke 13:28

East. We can already see that Russia is building up her military and aligning herself with the countries that Ezekiel thirty-eight said she would. Initially, this alliance will have some success. But at some point, whether it is days, months or years away, Jesus Christ will return to rescue Israel from total destruction and set up his throne in Jerusalem.[41] This will be the beginning of God's intervention and the Kingdom of God on earth!"

"And Abraham will have a part of this?" Sandra clarified.

"He will," Jess replied, "because remember, God promised him he would inherit the land *forever.* We'll want to talk about the resurrection later, and how Abraham and many others will be brought back to life. However, there's just one more passage I'd like to show you tonight, that I would *love* to share with James. It ties everything together and makes this all so exciting!"

Sandra smiled. Jessica's enthusiasm was contagious. "What is it?"

"Galatians chapter three," Jessica answered, as she flipped over a few pages of her Bible. "It's in the New Testament, close to the four gospels."

Using the page numbers from the index, Sandra eventually found the tiny book of Galatians. When Sandra turned to chapter three, Jessica suggested they read the last three verses.

Sandra read, "'For as many of you as were baptized into Christ have put on Christ. There is neither Jew nor Greek, there is neither slave nor free, there is neither male nor female; for you are all one in Christ Jesus. And if you are Christ's, *then you are Abraham's seed, and heirs according to the promise.*'"

"That's interesting!" Sandra said, reading it carefully through again, "so if we belong to Christ, *we* will also inherit the promise made to *Abraham*?"

---

[41] Ezekiel 38-39; Zechariah 14

"Yes! Isn't that exciting?" Jess smiled. "If you read the whole chapter through, you will see that God considers faithful believers to be Abraham's *true* descendants. [42]Jesus Christ himself, as it says in verse sixteen, is the *ultimate descendant* of Abraham to whom all the promises relate. The land, the blessings and so many other details that we can investigate later, *are his* – and his to share with those that are *in him*."

Jessica waited for Sandra to think it all over; then she asked, "How does it say we *put on Christ?*"

Glancing at the verses again, Sandra soon had the answer. "By being baptised."

"Right," Jess agreed. "And that's why Peter and I would love to share this passage with James. He thinks he's on good terms with Jesus already, just because he's a Christian and leads a decent life. He doesn't understand there are conditions to having a part in this wonderful promise."

Sandra nodded slowly. It was all so new.

"Next Thursday, I'd like to show you the promises God made to David – who was another descendant of Abraham and forefather of the Lord Jesus Christ," [43] Jessica suggested, glancing down at her watch to see that it was getting late. "David's promises relate to this future kingdom as well," she added.

"Okay!" Sandra smiled. "That would be great."

---

[42] Galatians 3:9
[43] Matthew 1:1

A Closed Door
Chapter Nine

The phone rang at seven-thirty the next morning. Still half asleep, Sandra reached over to pick it up, hoping that it might be a call to supply-teach. "Oh, please," she thought, "please let it be for the primary grades!"

Instead, the caller was Jess and she had a different type of work to offer.

"Hi, Sandra," she said. "I hope I didn't wake you up, but Peter told me last night that we would be potting containers today and it's a *mammoth* job! He asked me if I had any friends that might help us out and I thought of you. Do you think you could spare the day?"

With a laugh, Sandra agreed readily and then she remembered the state of her car.

"Jess, where will we be working? My car has broken down and I haven't had a chance to get it fixed. Can I get there by bus?"

"Believe it or not," Jess replied merrily, "we're starting along the harbour front. If you meet us at eight, just where the boardwalk begins, we can take you to all the other places and drive you home."

As soon as she'd hung up the phone, Sandra jumped out of bed and spun around happily. *Yes!* she thought. *A whole day of work – and working outside with friends! How wonderful!*

The weatherman had been calling for a warm, summer day in the low-twenties, with plenty of sunshine. Sandra dressed accordingly.

It was a delightful walk out to the harbour. So many trees were in blossom, birds were singing cheerily and all along the docks, fishermen were coming and going. Sandra soaked up the warm rays of the sun with a great deal of happiness.

As she approached the boardwalk, she could see Peter and Jess filling the large, wooden barrels that were stationed all along the railing. Peter's pickup was loaded with topsoil. Nearby, with its side door open was a van filled with trays of flowers – beautiful, vibrant flowers!

Jessica introduced Sandra to the other workers. "This is Derrick," she said, motioning towards a scruffy-looking young man with straggly, blond curls and bright orange sunglasses.

Derrick extended his hand cheerfully. "Glad for some extra help today!" he said, shaking Sandra's hand. "Pete says we've got to get these all done before dinner!" With a shake of his head, he looked sceptically towards the two vehicles overflowing with soil and plants, as though he didn't believe it was possible.

"And this is my brother, Allan," Jessica said, giving a lanky young teen a pat on the back. "He has the day off school today, so he's able to help out. Allan, this is Sandra."

Sandra and Allan shook hands and then Peter explained what they were going to be doing that morning and assigned jobs to each worker. It was a lot of work planting all the wooden barrels along the harbour front. Sandra had never considered how many there were, or the great variety of flowers that went into them. Peter and Derrick drove the pickup next to each tub and shovelled in the fresh soil, while Jess and Sandra arranged the spikes, flowers and vines. There were even Martha Washington geraniums! *Mom's favourite!* Sandra thought, watching Allan bring over the plastic tray of flowers.

Lunch was not a leisurely picnic overlooking the harbour, as Sandra had hoped, but only a quick snack in the vehicles as they headed out to the next place. There she and Jess had the job of raking up the winter debris around the Country Inn while the three guys went back to the nurseries to pick up more soil and plants. When they returned, everyone resumed their position in the potting routine. Sandra soon felt she had never spent a busier morning, but she was loving every minute.

"It's not always like this," Jess explained, as Sandra popped tiny plugs of lobelia out of the plastic trays and handed them to her. "Right now, since the threat of frost is hopefully over, all Peter's customers want their hanging baskets and containers done - *this week!* Usually, we would at least have a proper lunch break."

By six o'clock that evening, the last plant had been potted and everyone was exhausted. Peter and Jessica drove Sandra home.

"So, I hear you've been housecleaning for my brother," Peter remarked as he merged onto the highway.

"I just started two weeks ago," Sandra replied.

"What do you think of him?" he probed.

"He seems nice enough, but I only met him once briefly when I went to see about the job."

"Sandra thinks she may have overheard you and James talking one night," Jess added.

Peter glanced back at Sandra in the rear view mirror. "Really? When?"

Sandra explained that she had been out for an evening walk a couple weeks earlier and had overheard two brothers in the Manor courtyard. When she described the conversation they had been having, Peter gave a dismal laugh.

"Yeah, that was us all right!" he said. "We haven't talked since." He ran his hand through his straight, blond hair wearily. "And now James doesn't want anything to do with me."

"I could tell that you cared for him a lot!" Sandra remarked quietly.

"You could?" Peter looked up at her in the rear view mirror. "I wish James could see that."

Sandra wanted to ask what it was that Peter was trying to share with his brother, but she wasn't sure she should pry. However, after a moment's silence, Peter spoke freely.

"You're probably wondering why I was so intense that night," he mused thoughtfully.

With a smile, Sandra nodded.

"Well, you see," he began, "a couple of years ago, James had a major heart attack and I thought he wasn't going to make it. I was always very close to James; we were only a couple years apart in age and both of us have been bachelors for ages." Smiling at Jess and reaching over to take her hand, he added, "But not for much longer!"

"Just five weeks!" Jess cheered, bringing Peter's hand up to her cheek.

"I wish it was tomorrow!" he said, beaming into her eyes.

Before the car swerved completely off the road, Peter quickly brought it back in line.

"Anyway, James is older than I am," he continued with a sheepish grin, "and he knows the struggles I once had with religion…and accepting God's will. So I don't think he looks at me as any reliable sort of guide. And unfortunately, while he was travelling the world last year he didn't appreciate all the emails I kept sending him."

Ah, Sandra thought, remembering the pictures she dusted, *so James did do some travelling recently!*

"It probably wasn't just the frequent emails that bothered him," Jess clarified with a smile, "but your attempts to share your faith in those emails."

"That's true," Peter agreed. "And looking back, I realize I was far too pushy, but… it was only because I care so much about him. I love my brothers! I want James to share in this amazing hope that God has offered the world. I want him to be there with us – *to live forever!* I couldn't bear to go to his funeral and feel I

77

didn't try hard enough. But…he's shut the door. He won't let me in."

Sandra was quiet, thinking things through. She remembered Peter's quiet words in the courtyard, "Truth fears no questions." *Why has James closed the door?* she wondered. *Is he afraid of truth? Is he afraid of what he will find, or what he doesn't have? Or has Peter been so pushy that he's just turned James off from listening?*

Peter looked up into the rear view mirror. "Sorry, Sandra," he said. "You probably didn't want to know all that. Sorry for the rant."

"Don't be sorry," she assured him. "Now I understand a little better."

Mulling over the conversation, Sandra found it hard to imagine Peter as someone who had struggled to accept God's will, or to 'forgive God', as Jessica had relayed the day before. Bitterness seemed so far removed from his cheerful, trusting demeanour. *But he says he used to struggle with it,* she mused, watching Peter exit the highway towards the downtown district. Regardless of who was right and who was wrong on the religious side of it all, Sandra was impressed by Peter's strong feelings. *If only I had a brother who cared like this,* she thought. *Even a friend would be nice!*

Jess and Peter were talking quietly in the front seat. She heard Jess say, "Has he got back to you yet?"

"No," Peter sighed, shaking his head. "He still hasn't let me know one way or the other. My guess is that he doesn't want to come – especially not now."

I wonder how James feels about Peter? Sandra thought. *Is he completely indifferent to such loving concern? Did he ever care the same way for Peter? Peter said they used to be close. What's happened between them?*

Heavenly *Yogurt!*
Chapter Ten

When Sandra opened the door to James' apartment the next Tuesday morning, she stepped in with an air of intrigue! So much had happened in the week since she'd last been there. She now knew James was the man who had turned his back on his brother's urgent appeal. She now felt a strong empathy with Peter and Jessica with whom she had spent a whole day, but she was also *very* curious to hear James' side of the story.

There was another note sitting on the computer desk, along with two white envelopes and a large cookbook. She read the note first.

> Sandra,
>
> That pie was fantastic! If you're serious about making meals, I'll be very appreciative! No doubt about that! Everything in this HeartSmart cookbook should be safe for me to eat.
>
> I've left you two envelopes. The one with your name on it is what I owe you for cleaning. The money in the other envelope is so you can buy whatever supplies you need to make a meal. Will two extra hours cover the time you need to get supplies and cook? Let me know what you think. I don't have much experience in that regard.

James

P.S. If you have the time, I need a couple white shirts ironed.

P.P.S. Not sure what went through the wash last time, but there are some strange spots on my t-shirts – I left them on the washing machine.

P.P.P.S. I should be home at 6:00 tonight – just so you can plan the dinner – if you're happy to plan one. ☺

Oops, Sandra thought, wondering about the spots on the t-shirts, *I probably forgot to check his pockets. I'm always forgetting to do that. You'd think I'd have learned after ruining mom's gold watch!*

However, the note also brought a smile to her face. *I like the way he asks for things,* she thought. *And imagine that – I get paid to cook and there's money to buy whatever supplies I need! This will be fun!*

Sandra sprayed the spots on the t-shirts and carefully checked all the pockets for the next wash. Sure enough, in a pair of navy shorts there was a package of gum and two lifesavers. Then she checked James' black, hooded sweatshirt. There was something bulky inside the front pocket. It was his Blackberry! *Whew!* she thought, laying the digital device carefully on the computer desk. *If he hadn't written that note, I may never have checked. That would have been even worse than mom's gold watch!*

After she had tackled the bathroom and had the worst job out of the way, Sandra turned on the stereo and sat down at the kitchen table to quickly pick out a few recipes. *Sesame-crusted salmon on greens, served with basmati rice,* she decided, looking at the picture, *and maybe a big salad.* She looked at the desserts but she already had frozen yogurt on her mind. Ever since she had learned how to make it from listening to Chef Jeff, she had been longing to give it a try! *Surely that will be healthy enough and the perfect thing for a summer evening. Yum!*

Suddenly, lively music sounded in the apartment and it didn't harmonise at all with the Brandon Heath song on the stereo. Perplexed, Sandra rose from the chair and searched for the source. She laughed when she realized it was coming from the Blackberry she'd rescued! *I wonder if that's James calling looking for his phone?* she thought. *Maybe I'd better answer it.*

It was James!

"Ah… I am *so-o-o* relieved you answered this call!" James sighed.

"Did you think your Blackberry might be spinning around in soapy suds?" she giggled.

"Sandra, thank you so much for taking it out of my pocket!" he exclaimed earnestly. "I only just realized I'd left it there…"

"It's a good thing you wrote me that note," she replied.

He chuckled. "I was hoping you wouldn't take offence."

They talked a minute more and then James said he had to run and that he could make do without his Blackberry for the day. Sandra set it back down on the desk with a smile.

The grocery store was just a block away, so it didn't take long to run over and get the supplies. Sandra searched through the cupboards looking for the right cooking equipment; there wasn't much. James' kitchen had a few appliances stored away, including a crock-pot that was still in the box, with a "Love Mom" tag. However, he didn't have a blender, so Sandra ran back to her apartment to get her own. By the time she had made the meal and cleaned up all the dishes, she estimated that altogether it had added another three hours to the day – but they were three very fun hours! She finished cleaning the rest of the house and then tried a small helping of the frozen yogurt.

"Blueberry coconut!" she whispered with delight. "It's absolutely delicious – hmm, maybe even *'heavenly'!"*

However, Sandra felt guilty helping herself to James' food. *Would he mind?* she wondered. *After all, if I don't sample it, I won't know whether I've got it right!* But she still felt uncomfortable. *I guess I better say something,* she thought.

Before she left, she wrote another message for James.

> James,
>
> I sprayed the t-shirts and put them through another wash, but the spots didn't come out – sorry about that. I'll try to remember to always check your pockets.
>
> I hope you like the meal. I sampled the frozen yogurt just to make sure it was okay ☺ Cooking was fun. Thanks for leaving the money. The receipt and change are in the envelope. Two extra hours would be great. If I'm going to make a trip to the grocery store every week, feel free to leave me a list for anything else you might need.
>
> I could only find one white shirt, so I ironed a blue one as well.
>
> Sandra

Another Promise

Chapter Eleven

Thursday evening Jessica came over again. Her eyes sparkled merrily. "Do you want to see my ring?" she asked, as Sandra welcomed her in.

"Oh! I'd love to! When did you get it?"

"On the weekend," Jessica smiled, turning her hand back and forth so the diamond would catch the light. It was a curvy, solid gold ring with a lustrous diamond. Sandra tried not to feel too envious. "We've been engaged since March," Jess explained happily, "but it's taken a while to pick out our rings."

Sandra smiled and picked up the teapot. She had restocked the tea bags that morning in anticipation of her guest and just recently prepared the tea. "Would you like a cup of tea? It's already made."

"I'd love one."

"Do you take milk or sugar?"

"A little of both, please," Jessica replied.

When Sandra opened her nearly empty fridge to take out the milk, Jessica noticed all the bare shelves and was quiet for a moment. "Do you always eat out?" she asked.

"The grocery store is just down the road," Sandra explained evasively, "so I only buy what I need when I need it." As she spoke the words, Sandra wished she had the courage to admit how tight things were, but she didn't.

"Yes, I guess that makes sense," Jess replied. "My mom shops only once a week, so when she brings the groceries home the fridge is stuffed-full for a while. I guess I'm used to seeing it that way."

"So, you had *a special weekend,"* Sandra prodded, quickly changing the subject. She passed Jessica a cup of tea and they both headed to the sitting area.

"I had an amazing weekend!" Jess began, her face shining as she sat down on the couch. Tiger came out from Sandra's bedroom and leapt up beside her. "Peter has been looking at this little house in the country," Jess said as she stroked Tiger's back, "and on Saturday morning he took me to see it. It's just so perfect!" she smiled. "It's a sage-green clapboard, with the prettiest little carved, white shutters and big evergreen trees all around. All the floors are hardwood – newly-finished hardwood - and there are three nicely-decorated bedrooms, a fully-finished basement and a *brand new* kitchen! The people who are selling it have fixed it up beautifully. Oh, and it even has a hot tub!" Jessica exclaimed. "We met the neighbours and they're an older couple and just so sweet! So, we put an offer in on it and I just heard today that it's been accepted. *I am so happy!"*

"That's very exciting!" Sandra agreed. "I love those painted clapboard houses. And when did Peter give you the ring?"

Jessica twisted the ring on her finger with a smile. "Peter is such a romantic! He packed us a picnic lunch – a *really nice* picnic lunch! After we made the offer on the house, we drove out to his parent's place and took a walk along the shore. They live right down by the ocean, near Peggy's Cove."

Sandra nodded knowingly. She had visited Peggy's Cove before; it was only about twenty minutes away.

"And then," Jessica continued, as Tiger stretched out on the cushions, resting his head against her side, "sitting on the rocks, watching gigantic, foaming waves crash in, Peter asked me all over again if I'd marry him. And when I said yes, he gave me this ring."

"That's so lovely," Sandra smiled, as wispy daydreams swirled into her mind. How she would love to be walking barefoot on a beautiful, sandy beach, with foaming waves lapping against her ankles, hand in hand with a tall, good-looking man with wavy blond hair...! Sandra brought herself back to reality. "And you're getting married in July?"

"That's right, July fifth at Peter's parent's place."

"And who is going to be in your wedding?" Sandra asked, wishing with all her heart that she might be invited to attend. *I'd love to see a wedding!* she thought.

"I have five bridesmaids and Peter has four groomsmen," Jess relayed, explaining that Thomas, the man who had given the talk on Israel, was to be Peter's best man, and Thomas' wife, Purity, would be her matron of honour.

"And I'm having my sister and Purity's sister, plus a good friend from Jamaica and one from college," Jess added. "Peter has asked my brother Allan, a friend from Australia and *both* his brothers to be groomsmen, but...," Jessica sighed and looked out the window sadly, "James has said he can't come."

"He can't come to *his brother's wedding?!*" Sandra asked with astonishment.

"Apparently he has a very important convention to go to that weekend," Jessica explained. "If he had told us about the convention before we sent out the invitations, we would have changed our date, but he only sent an email last night. He's known our wedding date for two months."

Why wouldn't James go to his brother's wedding? Sandra wondered; *especially if he's been asked to be in it. How inconsiderate! Convention or no convention.*

"Peter must feel rather hurt," she said to Jess.

"It's been hard on Peter," Jessica agreed. "He blames himself. But, anyway," she said with a laugh, "I guess if we're going to have a class tonight we should get on with it."

Taking out her Bible, Sandra wanted to clarify just one more thing. "So you're going to have five bridesmaids and Peter will only have four groomsmen? Won't that look rather unbalanced?"

"We'll make it work," Jessica shrugged.

"There's no one else that Peter can ask?"

"He doesn't want to ask anyone else," Jessica smiled sadly. "He keeps hoping James might change his mind."

As Jessica opened her Bible, Sandra couldn't stop thinking about the sad situation. *Peter must feel like I do, when Laurie lets me down,* she thought. *I can't believe James would let work get in the way of being in his brother's wedding! Has he no compassion?*

Jessica began their evening session with a prayer. Sandra struggled to focus her thoughts.

"So, we talked about the promises to Abraham last week," Jessica began. "Do you remember what they were and why they are significant to us?"

Sandra thought back on the promises Jess had told her about. "God promised Abraham the land of Israel, for himself and his descendants," she recalled. "You said that Jesus was the most important descendant of Abraham, so he will also inherit that land, along with anyone who is baptised into him."

"Good memory!" Jessica praised. "Yes, so last week we talked about *the land* of the kingdom – the royal state - or the King's domain!"

Sandra nodded absentmindedly; disappointment with James was still clouding her thoughts.

"Okay," Jess said, "I want to show you another promise tonight and this one involves *the king* who will *reign forever!* Have a look at Second Samuel chapter seven."

With some help from the index Sandra found the chapter to which Jessica was referring.

"Have you ever heard the story of David and Goliath?" Jessica asked.

Sandra shook her head. "I've heard the names but I don't know what the story is about."

"You'll love reading about David!" Jess promised enthusiastically. "There are so many chapters about David it's like reading a novel. David was just a shepherd boy to begin with, but he had a tremendous faith in God. As a teenager, David fought Goliath, a giant over nine feet tall! He had faith that God would help him win, even though he only had a sling and five stones, because the giant had blasphemed God. God did help and David won! [44] God made *David* a promise in those early years, that one day *he* would be *the King* of Israel.[45] But before that promise came true, David spent many years running for his life."

"Running for his life?" Sandra repeated. "Why?"

"Because there was already a king – King Saul, who had been told that due to his disobedience, God would give His kingdom to another man.[46] King Saul began to suspect that God had chosen David to be the next king and so he spent years trying to kill him. [47]However," Jessica went on, "after Saul had died and David was finally established as the next king, God made a promise to David that he would have a very special son. This son would build a house for God's name. He would sit on David's throne and God would establish His kingdom on earth *forever!*"

Jessica and Sandra read through the promise in Second Samuel seven, verses twelve to sixteen.

"'When your days are fulfilled and you rest with your fathers, I will set up your seed after you, who will come from your body, and I will establish his kingdom. He shall build a house for My name, and I will establish the throne of his kingdom *forever*... I will be his Father, and he shall be My son ...your house and your

---

[44] 1 Samuel 17
[45] 1 Samuel 16
[46] 1 Samuel 15:22-23
[47] 1 Samuel 18-31

kingdom shall be established forever *before you.* Your throne shall be established *forever.*'"

"And did this happen?" Sandra asked.

"It did," Jessica replied, "to a certain degree. You see, many prophecies in the Bible have an immediate, partial fulfillment but will have a much greater, complete fulfillment in the future. When Israel became a nation they were God's Kingdom on earth at that time.[48] David had a son, Solomon, who ruled on his throne, just as the prophecy said, and built a temple for God's name. It was the pinnacle of Israel's history. [49] They had peace on all sides and fantastic wealth pouring in from all the nations around them, [50]but it was *just a foretaste* of what is yet to come." With a pause, Jess asked, "Based on those verses we just read, why could Solomon's kingdom not be *the complete* fulfillment?"

Sandra looked over the verses carefully. Since she didn't know the details of the story she wasn't sure she would be able to give an answer. At last she made an attempt, "I guess because Solomon's kingdom didn't last *forever?"*

"Is it still there today?" Jess prodded.

"No, obviously not."

"You're right. So, those verses couldn't be *just* referring to Solomon then," Jessica said. "And there are two other details that help us understand this promise was never intended to apply only to Solomon."

"Like what?"

"See in verse sixteen," Jess pointed out, "God says '… your house and your kingdom shall be established forever *before you.'* God is promising that David will be there when this promise is fulfilled. It will be established *before his eyes!"*

---

[48] Exodus 19:5-6; Psalm 114:1,2; 1 Chronicles 29:11 – The kingdom was "lost" when Judah was taken captive by Babylon (Ezekiel 21:2,19,25-27)
[49] 1 Kings 5-10
[50] 1 Kings 10

"Oh," Sandra pondered.

"And..." Jessica's eyes twinkled, "this same promise is repeated to someone else, much later in the Bible. That someone was Mary, the mother of Jesus! Have a look in Luke chapter one, verse thirty to thirty-three."

Sandra found the Luke passage and read it out loud. It was a promise to Mary by the angel Gabriel, "'And behold, you will conceive in your womb and bring forth a Son, and shall call His name JESUS. He will be great, and will be called *the Son* of the Highest; and the Lord God will give Him *the throne of His father David.* And He will *reign over the house of Jacob forever,* and of His kingdom there will be no end.'"

They compared the two promises for a minute.

"Hmm, they both speak about David's throne ..." Sandra considered.

"Yes," Jess agreed. "And they both speak about God *giving, or establishing* the kingdom. What other significant word do you see appearing in both?"

"They both speak about *'forever,'*" Sandra said excitedly. She was making the connection.

"That's right!" Jess agreed. "All these promises that we've been looking at, are primarily about a *very significant* future event! Abraham and his descendants have been promised the land *forever,* David was promised his throne will be established *forever,* and Mary is told that Jesus will reign *forever!*"

Sandra was impressed. She looked at the Luke passage again more carefully. "When it says that Jesus will reign over 'the *house of Jacob,*'" she pondered, "what does that mean?"

"Jacob was Abraham's grandson," Jessica explained. "He had twelve sons of his own, which became the twelve tribes of

Israel. [51]The *'house of Jacob'* is another way of saying *'the nation of Israel'*."

Looking confused, Sandra asked, "But if Jesus is going to reign over *the whole* earth, why does this promise only mention Israel?"

Jess looked thoughtful. "That's a great question, Sandra," she smiled. "It's like this: Jesus said that Jerusalem 'is the city of the great King'.[52] As we read tonight, David's throne was in Jerusalem, and that's the throne promised to our Lord Jesus Christ.[53] Jerusalem will be the capital city, the place where Jesus will establish his kingdom. From there, as we read in Daniel chapter two, Jesus' influence and power will gradually extend across the whole earth."[54]

"Gradually?" Sandra questioned.

"It will take time," Jessica replied. "Jesus will first establish himself in Israel and then call on the whole world to submit."[55]

"And of course, everyone *will* submit to him?"

Jess smiled. "*Eventually* the world will recognize Jesus for who he is…" she paused, "but it won't be instantaneous. Many people have an unbalanced view of who Jesus is and don't understand what the Bible says he will do in the future. There are prophecies that indicate the nations will gather together in an attempt to oust him from power before he is recognized as the true Messiah."[56]

Sandra was looking at Jessica with alarm.

"Anyway, that's another topic we could look at some time," Jess said.

---

[51] Genesis 32:28; 1 Kings 18:31
[52] Matthew 5:35
[53] See also Isaiah 9:6-7
[54] Daniel 2:31-45
[55] Isaiah 2:1-4; 60:12; Zechariah 14
[56] Psalm 2; Revelation 17:12-14

"I'd like to," Sandra nodded, realizing it might be a lengthy discussion. "However, I have another question about the Jews," she said. "If God has promised the land of Palestine to Abraham's descendants, what will happen to the Palestinian people? Doesn't God care about them?"

"God cares about everyone," Jess assured her. "Oddly enough, the Jews and the Arabs are both descended from Abraham. Ishmael was Abraham's eldest son and became one of the fathers of the Arab people, [57]but Isaac was the son of the promise and the father of the Jewish people. God promised to bless both sons,[58] but the special promise that involved the land was given to Isaac and his son Jacob."[59]

"Why?"

"Well, we learn from Galatians four, verse twenty-two to the end that Isaac was the son that God chose based on spiritual reasons." Jess told her. "A lot of jealousy and anger has been stirred up over the years towards the Jews because of this, but in reality, if we all just submit to God's choice, *everyone* can be saved through Abraham's descendant - the Lord Jesus Christ! God's promise is a Jewish hope – just as Jesus is a Jewish Messiah, but through faith and obedience the whole world can be blessed, as we read in Galatians chapter three.[60]"

"Will God give the Jews the promise, regardless of whether they have faith or not?" Sandra queried.

"Yes and no," Jessica replied. "If we were to read through Ezekiel thirty-seven, we would see that God has brought the Jewish people back to their land, even though they aren't faithful to Him. He is fulfilling the promise He made to their fathers – it's not based on the faith of the Jewish people in the land today.

---

[57] Genesis 16; 25:1-9
[58] Genesis 17:15-21
[59] Genesis 17:15-21; 28:1-4;13-15
[60] Galatians 3:26-29

However, as we read in Galatians chapter three, to inherit the land 'forever' as an immortal in the future, both Jews and Gentiles must be baptised and faithfully follow Jesus' commands.[61]"

"Okay. And what about the Arabs?"

"God has given the land that we call Palestine to the Jewish people,[62] but He has also made *land* promises to Abraham's other descendants - the Arab people,"[63] Jessica smiled. "God has promised that those of Egypt and Syria who accept Jesus as God's chosen King will live peacefully and happily in the Kingdom age."[64]

"So if God has brought the Jews back to their land, will they have a special position when Jesus is the King in Jerusalem?"

"Unfortunately, many of the Jews who live in Israel today will be wiped out in the Russian invasion," Jessica replied sadly. "In the Zechariah prophecies that refer to the coming invasion of Israel, we learn that two-thirds of the Jewish people will be cut off.[65] However, Ezekiel indicates that those who survive and accept Jesus Christ will help with the work in the new temple."[66]

Sandra felt overwhelmed. The more questions she asked, the more awestruck she became. There seemed to be so much detail concerning the future Kingdom age! "I suppose we could talk all night," she smiled at Jess, "but I know you have to work in the morning. What will we discuss next week?"

"Perhaps we should discuss the resurrection," Jess suggested. "We've talked about the faithful people who have died and are still waiting to receive the promises God made to them. To live forever, they need to be brought back to life."

---

[61] Galatians 3:26-29; John 14:15,21-23
[62] Genesis 15:18; Deuteronomy 11:24; Joshua 1:4
[63] Genesis 16:11-12; Deuteronomy 2:5,9,19
[64] Isaiah 19:23-25
[65] Zechariah 13:8-9 & 14:1-2
[66] Ezekiel 44:10-31

"Sounds great!" Sandra agreed, thinking that death was no longer the ultimate unknown. The 'something more' that she'd often wondered about was turning out to be something much grander than anything she had ever imagined!

An Evening in the Courtyard
Chapter Twelve

The month of May went by very quickly for Sandra, without one single call to supply-teach. Somehow she managed to get enough money together for her rental payment but not her university loans. She had no choice but to pay the interest charge, hoping next month would be better.

Matthew was coming over twice a week now with his mother. Once he had even stayed for the hour on his own, while his mother ran some errands. The little, dark-haired boy loved to play spelling games and to look at the readers that Sandra borrowed from the library. Occasionally he had even tested out some of the special activities she kept stored away in the big cardboard boxes.

She had a good laugh one evening near the end of May, when Matthew said, "I wish I could come to your house *every day*. I love doing the stuff in your treasure boxes!"

Thinking about Matt, Sandra realised she had not yet met Brett's brother, the father of the boy. It seemed like a long while since she had last seen Brett.

Sunday evening, the last day of the month, was particularly warm. Sandra took her meal of buttered brown rice, carrots and celery sticks and went down to the courtyard to eat. One of these days she was going to give up the brown rice detox diet but for now it was saving a lot of money on groceries. Underneath one arm was her Bible. As she had promised herself several times that week, she intended to read right through Genesis. *Tonight I am finally going to read chapter one!* she thought.

Sandra took a seat at her favorite table; it was the closest to the gardens. Fat, white peony buds were almost ready to bloom and some of the blue irises were already showing. *It will be June tomorrow,* she thought pleasantly. June meant sunshine and warmth and beautiful walks along the harbour. Then suddenly she remembered, *My one month contract with James is up next week. I hope that he wants me to keep cleaning. I don't think I've messed up too badly on anything other than the t-shirts.* However, from all that she had heard about James, she worried that he might be somewhat unpredictable.

"Hey, Sandra, how's it going?" a familiar voice rang out.

Sandra looked up to see Brett Lawson hand in hand with a lovely brunette. *Oh no!* she thought to herself, as a huge wave of disappointment engulfed her. *How come the nice guys always belong to someone else?*

"Hi," she said quietly.

"How's your car?" he asked with a puzzled expression. In the setting sun, his blond wavy hair was edged with gold. "It looks like it hasn't moved for a couple of weeks. Do you need someone to drive it to the shop for you? I'd be happy to help."

"Thanks, but I haven't really needed a car," Sandra explained lamely. "I've been working right here in the Manor, so I haven't had far to go."

Brett didn't look convinced. His girlfriend looked over at Sandra with a friendly smile. "Well let me know if you need any help. By the way, I've heard that Matt really enjoys his time with you. His parents say his reading has improved dramatically!"

"Oh, thanks," Sandra said with a wan smile, "and thanks for offering to help with the car."

"Anytime," Brett assured her, as he and his girlfriend waved goodbye and strolled off.

Sighing deeply, very deeply, Sandra opened the Bible she had brought out and picked up a carrot stick. *Lucky girl!* she mused, watching the couple stroll across the courtyard to the street and get into Brett's shiny red Mustang. *She gets the good-looking guy and the sweetest car!*

Watching them speed away, Sandra picked glumly at her food. *Another daydream evaporates,* she despaired. *Why did I get my hopes up?* However, there was not much she could do about it. Brett obviously belonged to someone else. Opening her Bible, Sandra tried to concentrate on the words before her but it was difficult. She sat staring blankly at the page.

I wonder if I should pray before I read? she considered finally, *Jessica always prays before we have a class.* Having heard a number of prayers in the past few weeks, Sandra had more of an idea about what she should say. "Heavenly Father," she whispered forlornly, reminding herself to start with the positives. "Thank you for this food I'm eating and this book I've been given. Thank you for the little bit of work I've found and please send more. Thank you for letting me find out who the two brothers were and I pray that somehow I might be able to help both of them. I'm hurting all over right now but I really want to know what you've promised us for the future and how to have a part in the kingdom that Jessica has told me so much about. Please be with me, In Jesus' Name, Amen.

Sandra had half-heartedly read through about twenty verses when another tenant came walking into the courtyard. *This is a busy place,* she thought. *It's rather distracting out here.* Glancing up curiously, she was surprised to see James. *I haven't seen him since that very first day,* she thought. *That was almost a month ago.*

James caught her eye and a slow look of recognition came over him. "Sandra?" he asked hesitantly.

"Hi, James," she said, forcing a smile.

"Hey, how are you?" he said cheerily, sliding into the seat across from her. "I hardly recognized you," he apologized. "It's been a while...and well, we only talked briefly last time."

"That's okay," Sandra said, thinking, *you haven't been looking at my photos every Tuesday, as I have yours.*

"Have you been out for a walk?" she asked.

In denim shorts and a loose-fitting, red t-shirt, James certainly hadn't been at work.

"Yes, I was," he admitted. "It's such a nice evening."

Looking down at what she was eating, James looked perplexed. "Rice and carrots sticks?" he remarked. "Aren't you the girl who makes gourmet meals and frozen yogurt?"

A blush crept over Sandra's face. She didn't think James would be open to the virtues of a brown rice diet, or the financial savings. "It's fun to cook for other people," she replied, smiling sadly. "I can't be bothered cooking for myself."

James didn't look convinced. He said, "I'm not sure if my notes have conveyed my full gratitude, but please know that I really look forward to Tuesday nights. Coming home to a sparkling, clean home and the most amazing, delicious smells coming from my kitchen is the highlight of my week!"

So, I guess he's not about to fire me, Sandra mused, appreciative of the compliments. "I'm thankful for the work," she smiled.

"Then it's good for both of us," James nodded. Glancing down at the book she held in her hands, he asked, "You're reading the Bible? Are you a Christian?"

"I'm not really anything," Sandra confessed. "This is actually the first day I've tried to read on my own." She pointed to the page. "See, I'm only in Genesis chapter one."

"What made you decide to begin reading the Bible?" he probed.

The orange flyer you threw out, she thought impishly. *But no, I don't think I'll mention anything about Peter and Jessica just yet. As soon as I do, James might shut the door on me.*

"I have a friend I've been talking to about religion," Sandra relayed instead. "We've only had a couple of discussions and I've been amazed by the promises God has made in this book."

"Such as?" James queried.

Looking up into James' hazel-brown eyes, Sandra liked the sincere, caring expression she saw there. *I don't understand what's going on between Peter and his brother,* she thought, *but I'm going to share what Jess has told me and see how he reacts.*

"Have you heard about the promises God made to Abraham and David?"

"I'm not exactly sure," James admitted. "What are they?"

James listened politely as Sandra described the promises and the way they relate to believers today. There was no way she could explain everything exactly as Jessica had, but starting with Abraham, she tried her best. However, when Sandra tried to explain that David had been promised a son who would sit on his throne forever, build a temple and bring the kingdom of God to earth in the future, James disagreed.

"I don't know about that, Sandra," he said with a shake of his head. "I'm fairly certain that Solomon was the complete fulfillment of that promise on earth. Can I look at your Bible for a sec?"

"Sure," Sandra said, passing it to him.

For almost five minutes James searched diligently for a passage he wanted to find. Sandra watched as he flipped page after page, running his finger down the side as he skimmed through the words. Finally, he found what he was looking for.

"Listen to this," he said. "This is what Solomon said after he had finished building the temple for God: 'Blessed be the LORD, who has given rest to His people Israel, according to *all that He promised.* There *has not failed one word of all His good promise,* which He promised through His servant Moses.'"[67]

"You see," he said. "Solomon completely fulfilled God's promise to David on this earth."

For a moment, Sandra was puzzled. *But Jess explained it all so clearly,* she thought. Eventually, she remembered the angel's words to Mary, the mother of Jesus. "Then what did the angel mean in Luke chapter one?" she asked. "He repeated this promise to Mary."

James looked up the promise, turning the Bible sideways so that they both could see. Perusing verse thirty to thirty-five thoughtfully for a moment, James shook his head. "Jesus reigns over spiritual Israel now," he insisted, "in the Church. His kingdom is here already. Besides, believers are going to be raptured from this earth and it's going to be burned up. Our hope is in heaven."

"Where does it say that?"

"Somewhere in the Epistles of Peter," James replied, flipping to the end of her Bible. He scanned a few pages before finding the passage he wanted. "Here it is," he said, "in Second Peter three, verse ten, it says, 'But the day of the Lord will come as a thief; in the which the heavens shall pass away with a great noise, and the elements shall be dissolved with fervent heat, and the earth and the works that are therein shall be burned up.'"

Sandra was confused, but she didn't feel she knew enough to debate the matter and she certainly didn't want to argue with James. She would have to ask Jessica about it. However, she still hadn't shown James the passage Jessica had especially wanted him to see. "Can I show you one more exciting verse?" she asked.

With a smile, James shrugged. "Of course."

---

[67] 1 Kings 8:56

Galatians chapter three captured James' attention more than any of the others. He read the verses over a number of times. "That's interesting," he said. "So if we belong to Christ, then we have a part *in Abraham's promises.* I've never really thought much about the Old Testament promises. I just assumed they were for the Jewish people."

"And if we want to belong to Christ," Sandra reiterated, remembering the most important point that Jessica longed to share, "then we need to be baptised."

"We need to be baptised?"

Sandra pointed to verse twenty-seven. "Isn't that what it says?"

"I'm not sure," James said hesitantly, skimming through the verses once more. "On the surface it seems to be saying that...but my Pastor says that we just have to believe in Jesus and ask him to come into our heart. If Jesus is in our heart then we're good with God."

"Really?" Sandra said, wondering if there was another way to see it all.

"Do you mind if I just have a look at something," James said.

"Okay."

James took the Bible again and shuffled to the very end. After flipping back and forth between a few pages, he put his finger on a verse thoughtfully. "It is interesting what you're saying about the promises," he admitted. "I've been reading through Revelation on my own, lately, and there's *plenty* that I don't understand, but I remember reading this verse and wondering how it fit."

Moving the Bible sideways again, so that Sandra could see the passage, James pointed to it and said, "Right here the believers are in heaven talking to Jesus and it says, 'And they sang a new song, saying: "You are worthy to take the scroll, and to open its seals; for You were slain, and have redeemed us to God by Your blood out of every tribe and tongue and people and nation, and have made *us kings and priests* to our God; *and we shall reign on the earth.*[68]"

"I thought it was a little strange that it didn't say 'reign *over* the earth'," James explained. "But if what you're saying is right," he reasoned, "then maybe the believers will come down from heaven, at some point, to reign with Jesus *on* a new earth – in this Kingdom that you're talking about."

"They'll come *down* from heaven?" Sandra questioned. "But…" Sandra almost said Jessica's name, but she caught herself just in time. "So, we go to heaven after we die and *then* we come back to earth?"

"Maybe," James replied with a smile. "We definitely go to heaven…the coming back to an earth is a new thought for me."

Sandra was curious. *This is interesting!* she thought. From what she remembered of the rare religious discussions she had had in the past with her Christian friends, heaven had been a place they believed they would go. *Perhaps Jessica is mistaken. Maybe James is right after all!* "Does it say somewhere in the Bible that we go to heaven?" she inquired.

James looked at her thoughtfully for a moment. Then he flipped through some pages until he came to the Gospel accounts. "Here you have it quite clearly," he said, turning the Bible around for her. "When Jesus was dying on the cross, two other men were crucified beside him. One of them, a thief, confessed his sins and begged that Jesus would remember him when he came into his kingdom. Jesus said, 'Verily I say unto thee, Today shalt thou be with me in paradise.[69]'"

---

[68] Revelation 5:9-10
[69] Luke 23:42-43

Sandra silently read the passage a couple of times. "So Jesus and the thief both went to heaven when they died?" she clarified.

"Sounds like it to me. Doesn't it to you?"

"Yes, it does," she replied, wondering what Jessica would say.

With a friendly smile, James stood up. "Anyway, thanks for the conversation," he said. "I'd never paid much attention to those promises before. I'll have to talk to my Pastor about them. You sure know a lot for someone who is only starting to read the Bible!"

A little shiver ran down Sandra's spine. *James is thanking me for this conversation,* she thought. *This is what Jessica and Peter wanted to show him! But what if he finds out that I have been talking to them? Will he feel that I set him up for this? Should I have levelled with him from the very start?*

Sandra suddenly hoped that James wasn't going to ask who her friends were, or whether he could join them the next time they got together. She was most relieved when he changed the subject.

"So you're happy with everything?" he inquired, having moved only a few steps away from the table. "The cleaning job is working out for you? You're still okay with it all?"

"It's been fun," Sandra smiled. "Oh…and sorry for taking your newspaper before you had finished reading it."

James chuckled. "That's okay. Thanks for returning it. And sorry for making a mess of the fridge after you'd just cleaned it. I hated to leave you with that twice in a row!"

There were other apologies to make. James explained where the other white shirts had been hiding. Sandra apologized for the permanent spots on his t-shirts.

Suddenly, James looked down at his watch. "Oops, got to go," he said, pulling his Blackberry out of his belt clip and beginning to text. "My mom invited me for dinner and I was supposed to be there fifteen minutes ago!"

Lucky guy, Sandra mused, watching James head to the outdoor parking lot; *his mom invites him over for dinner. He has all his family close by.* She turned back to her Bible with very mixed emotions. They'd had such an interesting discussion. James had been so open and easy to talk with, not antagonistic at all! He'd given her some good points to ponder and Sandra could hardly wait to tell Jessica about it the next time they got together. *But...but why do I feel uneasy?* she wondered. *I feel like I wasn't totally honest with James. Will he find out who I've been talking to? Will he be upset?*

The Purple Invitation
Chapter Thirteen

There was more landscaping work for Sandra on Monday morning with Peter and Jessica. She was so thankful. She needed all the work she could get. She hoped she would be able to pay all her June bills.

It was another sunny, warm morning and Sandra met the others on the harbour front boardwalk at eight. All the petunias and geraniums they had planted now had to be "dead-headed". In other words - the dead blooms needed to be removed. Peter and Jessica looked after that job, while Sandra and Derrick were asked to water everything. Derrick drove the pickup from barrel to barrel, while Sandra gave all the flowers a good soaking from the large containers of water in the back. All morning, she was dying to tell Peter and Jess about the conversation she'd had with James the night before, but eventually, as the hours rolled by, she decided against telling them anything just yet. *I don't think James would want them to know about it,* she thought. *I'd better keep it to myself for now.*

The last place they worked at was a large country estate; which was the weekend home of a wealthy family. Since there was no one around to be disturbed, Peter left the van hatchback up so that everyone could hear the music he had playing. Derrick and Peter seemed to know most of the songs well and sang along as they trimmed the hedges.

"I hope you like Peter's music," Jess said to Sandra, as they worked side by side in the rose garden. "It's not really my kind of music, but every now and again there's a good song."

"What's your kind?" Sandra asked.

"I love classical music and hymns," Jess smiled, ripping dandelions out of the rose bushes. "But most people think I'm kind of strange and old-fashioned."

Sandra felt she would prefer Peter's music over Jessica's, but she didn't say so. Giving the last rose a good soaking around the roots, she was about to go on to the next garden, when Jessica held up her hand.

"Oh, you've got to listen to this song!" she said, pointing towards the van. Soft strains of a new song were just beginning. "It's one of Peter's favourites."

Sandra listened as she walked over to water the bed of hot pink impatiens. The song began quietly as a prayer – a prayer that God would help in an impossible situation. Peter joined in from where he stood pruning the hedge. "Lord, it is to you I pray. You open eyes. Please help my friend to see your way…" Peter's voice harmonized beautifully and captured Sandra's attention. The short song came to an end far too soon.

"That's how Peter feels about James," Jessica explained, joining Sandra to weed the bed of impatiens. "He says that James can build all the walls he likes and close every door tight, but he can't stop Peter from praying."

"He really loves his brother," Sandra mused. "I would think that most people would just give up!"

"Peter loves James," Jess agreed. "But he knows he's tried too hard and now…now he just has to leave it in God's hands *and* accept His will. Sometimes God's will is very different from ours," Jess added, more to herself than to Sandra. "But we trust that He knows best."

"It is a beautiful song," Sandra remarked sincerely.

"It is," Jessica agreed.

Sandra pondered Jessica's words as she carried the hose from garden to garden, bringing much needed moisture to the parched soil. 'Sometimes God's will is very different from ours,'

Jessica had said. *I've never really thought about that before,* Sandra thought. *What if it isn't God's will that I'm reacquainted with my brother?* She shuddered. *I couldn't handle that,* she decided. *Laurie and I **have** to be reunited! I have to have a family again! I can't go on alone like this forever!*

It was on the way home from work that Peter remembered an order he had to make. "Hey, Jess," he said, "did we ever phone Seaside nurseries back?"

"I did," she smiled. "They say they will have eight ornamental evergreens for us, Friday morning."

"I *love* having a secretary!" Peter laughed, taking her hand. "Especially one who remembers everything I forget."

Sandra clutched the door handle beside her, as Peter leaned over to give Jessica a kiss. It was rather awkward being the third party in the backseat sometimes, especially when the driver was so easily distracted by his front seat passenger that he forgot to keep his eyes on the road! Peter swerved back into his lane just in time to miss the gravel truck coming the other way. Sandra consoled herself that it was only a ten minute ride.

"Ooops! Sorry Sandra." Peter chuckled, glancing back in the rear view mirror.

"Any time you'd like me to be the chauffeur, just say!" Sandra chided teasingly.

"Now, there's an idea!" Peter remarked.

Jess laughed and turned around to face Sandra. "Speaking of the landscaping order, I just remembered that I was going to tell you about the 'Kingdom Feast' we're having this Friday evening. We hope to use the little, ornamental evergreens as decorations at the feast."

Passing back a pretty, violet-purple card with silver lettering, Jessica said, "Here's an invitation."

"It's beautiful!" Sandra exclaimed. "It looks like a wedding invitation."

"It's meant to," Jess smiled. "We've been giving these out to friends and neighbours, and I'm sure you'll want to come. When I was in Jamaica we had an evening like this and it was so inspirational!"

"It's a *real* feast?" Sandra enquired hopefully as she read the invitation over.

"Yes, we'll have a big table set out with all kinds of *scrumptious* food, and we'll read some of the Bible passages about God's kingdom. The kids will do a few songs and a little play and each of us will talk about something that we're looking forward to when Jesus Christ returns."

"That sounds great!" Sandra said. "Where will it be?"

"At our hall," Jessica stated. "Would you like a ride?"

"I'd love one!"

A moment or two later, Peter sighed. "I sure wish we could invite James to something like this. I know he'd enjoy the evening so much...but..."

A tingle of excitement ran down Sandra's spine. How she longed to tell both of them about her recent conversation with James! *One day I will,* she told herself, *but not yet.* An idea sprang into her mind.

"Why don't I leave some invitations in the foyer of the Manor?" Sandra suggested. "Then if James sees them he can pick one up, and if he doesn't, other people may be interested in coming."

Jessica looked up at Peter and Peter nodded his head. "Yeah, that would be good," he smiled.

A kingdom feast! Sandra mused to herself. *What an interesting idea.* Then she pondered what James had told her. *The kingdom is now,* she recalled. *Jesus is already ruling over the Christian church on earth...*

"I was talking to a friend, a few days ago," she spoke up, "and I'm somewhat confused. He said that Solomon completely fulfilled the promises to David. He even showed me a passage where Solomon said, not one thing that God has promised has failed. He said that Jesus was reigning over the Church from heaven and that it was a 'spiritual Israel' or something like that. How do we know for sure that Jesus will actually come back to *this earth?*"

"I used to think the same way as your friend," Peter replied, looking back briefly at Sandra. "But then I started reading the multitude of prophecies in the Old Testament dealing with God's restoration of the land and the kingdom to Israel. There were so many details - right down to the very rivers, and the seas, and the exact territories which match up with the place names that are still in use today.[70] I came to see that these promises must be about *this* earth that we know. They can't all be spiritualized away.

"Do we have a Bible here in the car?" he asked Jess, keeping his eyes on the road.

"I have one in my purse," she offered.

"See if you can find that passage in Jeremiah where God says He will never break His covenant with David."

Jessica skimmed through a number of pages before she said. "Here it is. I think you're thinking of Jeremiah thirty-three."

"Could you please read those verses to Sandra for me?" Peter requested. "I think they'll be helpful."

Glancing over them quickly, Jess explained the context to her friend. "Jeremiah was a prophet right around the time when the nation of Israel was about to lose everything that Solomon had worked so hard to build. The beautiful temple was to be destroyed and the walls of Jerusalem broken down. Most of the Jewish people and their king would be taken away…and they have never had another Jewish king reigning since. But at this tragic time, Jeremiah was given this beautiful promise that one day, *which is*

---

[70] Psalm 48; 72; Ezekiel 36-39; Isaiah 2:2-4; 60-62; Zechariah 14; Micah 4:1-4

still in the future, God would restore Israel's fortunes. Here's what he records in chapter thirty-three:

Sandra listened closely as Jessica read a lengthy section: "'Behold, the days are coming,' says the LORD, 'that I will perform that good thing which I have promised to the house of Israel…In those days…I will cause to grow up *to David a branch of righteousness*; He shall execute judgment and righteousness *in the earth.* In those days Judah will be saved, and *Jerusalem will dwell safely*…Thus says the LORD: *'If* you can break My covenant with the day and My covenant with the night, so that there will not be day and night in their season, *then* My covenant may also be broken with David My servant, so that he shall not have *a son to reign on his throne…'"*

"See," Peter explained, "that chapter is saying that as long as there is day and night, God will keep His promise to David, that one day a son will reign on his throne again. This promise was made to Jeremiah, long after Solomon had passed away, therefore the son promised to David here, could not have been Solomon.*"*

"So when Solomon said all the promise had come to pass, what did he mean?"

Peter asked Sandra to read the passage she was referring to, carefully. Jessica helped her find it in First Kings chapter eight, verse fifty-six, and Sandra read it out loud. "'Blessed be the LORD, who has given rest to His people Israel, according to *all that He promised.* There *has not failed one word of all His good promise,* which He promised through His servant Moses.'"

When she was finished, Peter asked, "Did you notice that when Solomon says all the promises have come to pass, he refers specifically to the promises made to *Moses?*"[71]

Sandra skimmed through the passage again. Peter was right.

---

[71] 1 Kings 8:56; Deuteronomy 12:1-14; 17:14-20

"Solomon is referring to the promise that temple worship would be established in the place God would choose – Jerusalem. Solomon isn't talking about the promises made to *David – the forever promises."*

Peter reminded Sandra about the very first talk she had come to, when Thomas had read from Ezekiel thirty-seven. There God plainly stated that He would "take the children of Israel *from among the nations,* wherever they have gone, and will *gather them* from every side and bring them into their own land; and I will make them *one nation in the land,* on the mountains of Israel; and *one king shall be king over them all."*

"You see, it's all tied together," Peter explained. "The return of the Jews to their own land in 1948, and the restoring of their nation is just the beginning of these latter-day prophecies. They will conclude with Jesus Christ returning to the earth and establishing his Kingdom in Jerusalem. The prophecy is being fulfilled right now in a *very literal way* with real Jewish people returning to the real Promised Land, and actually calling themselves the 'nation of Israel.' Since it has begun to be fulfilled in a literal way, we have every reason to believe it will continue to unfold in the same literal way."

It all seemed quite clear to Sandra and suddenly it occurred to her, as they turned onto her street, that even though she and James had had such an open discussion, she still didn't know exactly what message *Peter* had planned to share with his brother. Had Jessica guessed correctly or not? Had Peter wanted to talk to James about the promises? Feeling much more familiar with both Peter and Jess, Sandra felt free to ask, "Whatever was it that you wanted to tell James that night in the courtyard?"

Peter laughed sadly, as he pulled into the Manor parking lot. "There's *so much* that I'd love to share with him!" he said with a heavy sigh. "Unfortunately, when James and I first began talking about religion, I was reading some Christian End-Times novels and was really interested in discovering what the Antichrist was all about. So, naturally, I shared what excited me, but, unfortunately, it had the opposite effect on James. For whatever reason, I think I came off sounding totally negative about his beliefs and rather harsh. If I had the chance to do it all again, I'd start where you and Jess have started – with God's incredible promises to the world. That was what Jesus preached – *the kingdom of God* – and that's what I wish I could tell James about…now."

Jessica turned around to wink at Sandra. They shared a smile. Jess had guessed right.

Walking into the Manor that evening, Sandra held twenty purple invitations in her hands. *They are so much like wedding invitations*, she marvelled, looking at them with pleasure. *Why did Peter and Jessica choose to make them that way? What does a wedding have to do with Jesus coming back to the earth?* Unable to answer those questions for herself, she began to wonder, *Are Peter and Jessica's own wedding invitations as beautiful as these?* Suddenly she remembered the wedding invitation she had found in James' trash bin, the very first week she had cleaned house for him. At the time the names had meant nothing to her and she could hardly recall any of the details. She hadn't seen it since. *I wonder if that was the invitation to Peter and Jessica's wedding?* she thought in dismay. *James, did you throw out your own brother's wedding invitation?!*

Tuesday, throughout the day, as Sandra cleaned James' house and ironed his shirts, she thought about the upcoming Kingdom Feast and how much Peter wanted his brother to come. *I'd like James to be there as well,* she thought. *Imagine how happy Peter and Jessica would be if he showed up! Perhaps after everything I shared with him Saturday night in the courtyard, he might welcome this invitation. Maybe I should just invite him myself. He hasn't been antagonistic to me.*

But what if it changes things? she argued internally, hanging the white shirts carefully on hangers. *If I give him one of these invitations James will know who I've been talking to and he may never want to talk to me about the Bible again. I might even lose this job!*

But what if he comes? Maybe he'll enjoy the evening and become as excited as I am about the Kingdom! Maybe everything will be all right again between James and Peter and he'll want to come to the wedding...

No, I'm not sure it's a good idea...I'd better just stay out of it!

It took Sandra longer than usual that day to finish the work, as she picked up a long list of groceries for James, and had to tackle a pile of dirty dishes left in the sink. It was unlike James to leave so many dirty dishes. She assumed he must have worked late the previous few nights.

As she dusted the living room, Sandra saved the computer desk for last. Many papers lay scattered on the table top and Sandra tried to arrange them neatly in one pile. A logo at the top of one letter caught her eye. It was a simple silhouette of a man and a boy skating together with hockey sticks in their hands. Underneath were the words, "Big Brother Hockey Program."

Without a second thought, Sandra picked up the letter. *Is James involved in this?* She wondered. *Is he a Big Brother?*

Skimming quickly over the words she read, "It's been four years since you won the "Big Brother of the Year" award. It was a most deserving award. Everyone greatly appreciated your hard work and loving commitment to all the children in our hockey program during the fifteen years you coached. We appreciate your ongoing support financially and fully understand your need to withdraw from coaching after your recent heart attack. However, we are writing in hope that you may consider returning to the program now that your situation has stabilized. As always we have many children…"

Sandra suddenly realized she was reading James' private mail and put the letter back down. "Oops!" she said, *But wow! That's really special. I had no idea James would do something like that. He must have a compassionate side!* Then she remembered the photo that sat behind all the others on the top shelf. Walking over she lifted it up and took another look. The man with the big grin, standing in behind the hockey team had to be James. He was a lot heavier; he had more hair, but the eyes were unmistakably James' – those kind, trustworthy, brown eyes.

It was past five-o'clock when Sandra finished all the housework. Marinated, barbequed chicken and veggie strips awaited James in the crock-pot. They smelled so delicious that Sandra was very tempted to sample one. *He doesn't know how many I made*, she considered. *He'd never know if I ate just one.*

No. It would be stealing, she argued with herself. *I didn't buy the food. It doesn't belong to me. I'd probably feel terrible if I ate one!*

Just before leaving the apartment, Sandra poured brown rice and water into the rice cooker and turned it on. She took the bubbling apple crisp from the oven and left it to cool on the stovetop. *Mmm, James, enjoy!* she thought.

Pulling a navy t-shirt and denim shorts over her cleaning 'uniform', Sandra picked up the pile of invitations that she had brought with her. Looking over at the newspaper that sat unfolded in the living room, she made a spontaneous, last minute decision to stick one of the invitations inside. After numerous debates during the day whether she should do so or not, on a whim it seemed to be the right decision. *Oh, it can't hurt,* she thought, tucking it in inconspicuously. *I'm sure James will just think it came with the rest of the advertisements. And this way he won't miss the chance to learn more about the kingdom on earth. I sure hope he comes!*

Everyone will be so happy to see him! Before she could second-guess the decision again, Sandra scurried out the door and locked it behind her.

Down in the foyer, Sandra looked around for a good place to put a few more invitations. It was illegal to stuff any into the mail slots, but she tacked one up on the corkboard. The violet purple stood out quite distinctly; the silver lettering shone softly. *I guess that's all I can do,* she thought, *unless I leave some on the floor.* Then she saw the coffee table in the foyer sitting room. *Maybe I could put some there!*

"Hi, Sandra," a cheerful voice called out from behind her. "Can't wait to get home and smell what's cooking!"

Sandra turned around in total surprise. A tall man in a black suit with a bright red tie was smiling warmly at her. He held a laptop in one hand and keys in the other.

What! James is never home this early! she thought in a panic.

"I hope you like it," she smiled nervously, as James glanced at the pile of purple invitations she still held in her arms. Suddenly it all seemed like a bad mistake. *Oh, I wish I hadn't left one in his newspaper!* she moaned inwardly. *I hope he doesn't make the connection!*

"See you around," he called out with a slightly puzzled expression, as the elevator door opened and Sandra didn't follow him towards it.

Sandra waved politely but as soon as James was gone she quickly ran over to snatch off the invitation she'd pinned to the notice board. Regardless of who might miss out on the feast, she didn't want James to make any connections he hadn't already.

Heading back to her apartment she wondered if she had over-reacted in gathering up all the invitations. *Chicken!* she told herself, running up the stairs.

No, I'm not a chicken, she argued back. *I just want to keep the doors open between us.*

But now no one in the Manor has the opportunity to go to the feast.

If James finds out I've been talking with Peter and Jess, he's going to be very upset!

Maybe he will and maybe he won't, she thought. *If we talk it through, I'm sure he'll understand why I didn't tell him initially.*

Brett Lawson was walking out of the elevator with his girlfriend when Sandra burst through the stairway door.

"How's it goin?" he called out to her. "Found any more kids to tutor?"

"Not yet," Sandra replied merrily. "But you're welcome to send more my way."

Brett laughed and the pretty brunette took his arm. They stood still, waiting for Sandra to catch up to them. "What are all the purple cards for?" Brett asked.

Happy to be asked, especially by Mr. Blue, Sandra had no anxieties about giving an invitation to him. She pulled one from her stack and held it out. "There's going to be a Kingdom Feast this Friday evening," she smiled, filling them in on all the exciting details. "You're both welcome to come."

"Just might do that," Brett replied, as his girlfriend nodded her head politely.

It was at that moment that Sandra noticed the diamond ring on Brett's girlfriend's finger. The diamond was huge! *So they're engaged,* she thought dismally. *She's not just his dinner date.*

"Catch ya later." Brett smiled, as he and the brunette turned towards his apartment.

"Oh my," Sandra said to Tiger, as she burst into her apartment and closed the door behind her. "I can't believe I ran into both Brett *and James tonight!* And Brett's engaged! I guess I won't be dreaming about him anymore!" she sighed, laying the invitations down on the kitchen counter and picking up her little cat. "But *what on earth* was James doing home at five-thirty?!" she murmured. In a daze, she walked over to check the messages on her answering machine. There weren't any. "Why, I might have been still cleaning his house!"

After filling up Tiger's water bowl, Sandra filled the rice cooker with her dinner rations. *Let's see, tonight I'll have parmesan rice,* she decided, *and hopefully I can salvage a few more green beans. They sure don't last long when I buy them from the discount table!*

The purple invitations stood out very visibly on her white counter. *I don't think James saw them,* she thought, opening the fridge. *But all the same, I wish I hadn't left one in his newspaper. I hope I don't get an angry phone call tonight!*

Confrontation

Chapter Fourteen

There was a bold knock on Sandra's door later that evening, as she sat quietly making a reading chart for Matt and watching the end of the news. Tiger jumped down from her lap and ran to hide. Sandra looked up in surprise. *No one has ever knocked on my door before,* she thought. *I wonder who it could be?* Putting down her work, Sandra walked slowly over. The knock sounded loudly again.

It was James who was standing at her door when she opened it and he had a purple invitation in his hand. Her heart missed a beat and her mouth went dry. Searching his tense face quickly, Sandra could see that this wasn't a friendly visit. Instead of his usual kind, gentle glow, James looked quite perturbed.

I have a feeling I'm about to see the other side of James, Sandra thought anxiously.

"Do you know anything about this?" he asked bluntly, holding up the invitation.

"I do," she admitted.

"Where did you get it from?" With a searching glance, James' eyes came to rest on the eighteen purple cards sitting boldly on the kitchen counter.

"Your brother and his fiancée."

"How did you *ever* meet *them?!*"

Sandra laughed nervously. "Because of you," she smiled. She felt strangely confident.

"What? How?!"

"Do you remember that orange flyer, a few weeks back?" she asked hesitantly.

With a frown, James shook his head.

"I left it on your desk and...and... you threw it in the garbage," she explained awkwardly. "But it looked interesting to me, so I decided to go to the talk it was advertising. That's where I met Peter and ..."

"I see," James nodded angrily. "I get it! So they're the friends you've been talking to. And I guess that discussion that you and I had about the Bible was based on stuff *they've* told you about!"

Sandra flinched as she nodded uncomfortably. *How can James be so antagonistic towards his family?* she wondered. *Peter and Jess are so nice!*

"Did *they* ask you to put one of these in my newspaper?" James probed, nodding his head towards the bright purple stack.

James' voice was getting louder. Sandra stepped back and motioned for him to come in. Reluctantly, he moved forward and she closed the door behind him.

"No, that was my idea," she said.

Looking rather sceptical, James asked, "How much do you know about my relationship with my brother?"

Sandra wasn't sure what to say, so she only shrugged with an anxious smile.

Uncomfortably, James eyes shifted from hers to the living room and back. And then they shifted again with surprise as though he had noticed something on the floor.

What's he looking at? Sandra wondered. From her vantage point she couldn't see anything unusual.

But when James turned his gaze back to Sandra, fiery sparks were dancing in his eyes. "I'm sick and tired of having this forced on me, everywhere I turn," he explained firmly. "I can't believe Peter would get *you* involved!"

Okay, he sees this as a big set up, Sandra told herself, *and on the surface it could look that way, but I know that it isn't. Peter would never pressure me to do that!*

Shaking her head, she tried to speak but James continued. "Listen, Sandra, I don't want to hear *anything* about what my brother believes. I don't want *any* of his flyers in my house and if you're going to work for me, then you need to respect that *decision*."

"I'm sorry, James," she said sincerely. "I shouldn't have given you that invitation. It was a mistake. It was my idea not Peter's. I know that things aren't great between you and Peter, but I just hoped that maybe you'd want to come. It sounds so exciting..."

"And what about when you and I talked in the courtyard?" he continued angrily. "Why didn't you tell me who you'd been talking to? You *must have known* I'd be upset!"

Sandra sighed sadly, certain that they would never have another open discussion. "I'm really sorry, James," she said sincerely. "I knew that you didn't want to listen to your brother, but I wanted to see if the problem was just between the two of you..."

"What do you mean I don't want to listen to my brother?!" James asked defensively. "Is that what *he* told you?"

So this is the angry James, Sandra thought, surprised that she didn't feel more intimidated. Looking down at the floor, she carefully considered how to respond. *I may as well tell him everything,* she thought, *it's the only way he might believe me.*

With a deep breath she spoke earnestly, "Over a month ago, I heard both of you talking, outside. I was coming back from a walk and you and Peter were in the courtyard talking loudly; I couldn't help but overhear. I didn't know who it was then, but I do now. Peter was trying to tell you something and you wouldn't let him. He was pleading with you to listen and you didn't seem to care..."

"*Didn't care?!*" James argued. Sparks were still igniting in his hazel-brown eyes; the kind, trustworthy look seemed to have completely vanished. "If Peter *cared about me* he would have respected our differences of opinion *ages ago* and stopped *hammering* this down my throat!"

"But what if it is truly a matter of life and death?" Sandra reasoned boldly, coming to the defense of her new-found friends. "Don't you appreciate...how much Peter cares? He's only tried so hard because he loves you. He told me he couldn't bear to be at your funeral and think he hadn't done everything that he could to help..."

James was shaking his head angrily. "Who says he's going to be at *my* funeral? Maybe I'll be at his!"

Sandra suddenly realized that she was setting James off by the things she was saying. *Slow down and think through your words carefully*, she told herself. *Don't make the situation worse!* But on the other hand, she wanted to make sure James understood the truth of the matter. Taking a deep breath, she added slowly, "Please don't think that either Peter or Jess have told me to do anything. They haven't. And they don't know about our conversation the other day in the courtyard. Everything I said to you, I said because it makes so much sense to me. For the same reason, it was my idea to post the invitations and leave one for you. I'm planning to go and *I* hoped *you* would too."

James considered this new information thoughtfully. With a heavy sigh, he turned to leave. "Sorry. I shouldn't have reacted so strongly. I jumped to some conclusions," he admitted. "Just please remember," he begged, "I don't want *anything* to do with Peter, right now! It's a raw, sore situation."

It sure is! Sandra thought. *I guess I should have known he felt this strongly. There were plenty of clues. But...how can James hate someone who cares about him so much?*

As James opened the door, Sandra murmured softly, "My brother could hardly *care less* what happens to me. All my life I've longed to have a brother like yours!"

Standing still, James looked at Sandra with surprise. He glanced over to the picture on the mantle and then quickly all around the bare-looking rooms, especially that one spot on the floor which she couldn't see from her vantage point. Sandra watched him quietly, bewildered, realizing that as much as she didn't like confrontation, she had finally had the opportunity to hear James' side of the story.

I actually do feel a little sorry for him, she decided, *even though I doubt we'll ever be friends now. He's angry and frustrated because he doesn't understand where Peter's coming from. He sees his brother's persistence as ruthless attacks on his beliefs, rather than anxious, loving concern.*

Without another word, James left, closing the door quietly behind him.

Feeling a little shaky, Sandra rubbed her face with her hands. *Oh my,* she thought. *That was intense. What a dumb mistake on my part! He'll never speak freely to me again! If we were on a friendship track, we've both been flung off. But… at least he didn't fire me as his housekeeper – not yet.* She sighed deeply and then remembered how James kept glancing at the floor. *Whatever was he looking at?* she wondered.

Walking over to the place where James had stood, she looked in the same direction but all she could see was the back of the couch, a floor mat and a few specks of dust. There was nothing to attract attention. With a shrug of her shoulders, she sighed, shook her head and headed back to watch TV and finish her work.

The Kingdom Feast
Chapter Fifteen

It was still light outside when Peter and Derrick drove Sandra to the little white hall on the outskirts of town. Jessica had been there most of the day getting everything organized. Sandra still had not told anyone about her confrontation with James, but it was very much on her mind.

"So why was the invitation to this Kingdom Feast – so much like a wedding invitation?" Sandra inquired.

"Because that's how God has described the uniting of Jesus and his faithful believers when he returns[72]," Peter told her. "A marriage is when two people agree to become one – one in mind and purpose for the rest of their lives. Jesus prayed that [73] the believers might be one with he and his Father. "

"Jesus is going to marry the believers?"

"In a symbolic way," Peter replied. "The believers are spoken of in Revelation nineteen as a bride. When Jesus returns and raises the dead to immortality, it seems that he will first hold a feast called, "the marriage supper of the Lamb"[74] before he and the saints set out to call the world to worship their new King. [75]

Sandra nodded politely, but she wasn't completely sure what it all meant.

The hall where Peter and Jess and all the others in their congregation met was surrounded by lovely gardens, large spruce trees and mature oaks. One prominent, red maple stood in front and a small lake sparkled brightly in the distance.

---

[72] Matthew 22:3-12; 25:10; 2 Corinthians 11:2; Ephesians 5:23-32
[73] John 17:20-24
[74] Revelation 19:6-9
[75] Zechariah 14 (especially vs. 5); Revelation 19

"So, your church is out in the country," Sandra remarked, more to herself than anyone else.

"It is," Peter nodded. "The kids love being out here. There's lots of room to run around."

"It's so peaceful," Sandra smiled, taking a deep breath as she stepped out of the van.

Derrick opened the heavy front door of the hall and held it back for the others to walk through.

Inside, only candles and tiny white lights wrapped around ornamental trees lit up the darkened, main room. Planters brimming over with flowers gave the appearance of an outdoor, garden setting. Soft, instrumental music filled the hall. Lengthwise down the room were several tables arranged in a row, lined with crisp, white tablecloths and laden with a variety of food. In between tall ivory candles, were huge fruit trays, on which lay carved watermelon bowls overflowing with pineapple, kiwi, strawberries and cantaloupe. Ornate, glass platters were laden with stacks of rolled chicken, salami and roast beef. Fancy, flowered china dishes on elevated wooden stands held many types of cheese and crackers, decorated with sprigs of parsley and red radish curls. There were veggie trays, mini quiches, soft bread rolls, dainty flaky pastries and bottles of sparkling grape juice. Sandra could hardly take her eyes off the food. *I'm in paradise tonight!* she thought to herself with a smile.

Brett didn't arrive and neither did James, but with Derrick and his girlfriend on one side and Jessica and Peter on the other, Sandra felt only a momentary regret. This was going to be a special evening!

Jessica's father, Craig Symons, rose to begin the proceedings. "We're so happy that all of you are able to share this special evening with us," he said. "The Bible says that, 'Where there is no vision, the people perish.'[76] So, tonight we hope to enrich our vision of the promised kingdom. Throughout the ages, believers have become 'citizens' of this kingdom in anticipation of the day when our Lord Jesus Christ returns to be the King of the world. [77]

Gesturing towards the table, Craig added, "Before us we have a wonderful feast prepared by many loving hands. This is to give us a little taste of what it will be like to live in a land that God has blessed, when corn will grow on the tops of the mountains and streams will flow in the desert.[78] But first we'll thank our Heavenly Father for the many blessings we enjoy today."

The prayer touched Sandra's heart as she marvelled at how many blessings there were to be truly thankful for. Perhaps life wasn't so hard after all!

Craig waited until everyone had filled their plates and then he explained that while they ate, Mark Benito would read some of the kingdom prophecies from the Old Testament, in conjunction with a slide show of beautiful pictures from around the world.

As Sandra munched on a sweet slice of pineapple, she quickly discovered why Mark had been chosen to read. Mark had a booming voice and put such expression into the words he read that no one could possibly be lulled to sleep, or fail to appreciate the significance of each sentence. As the beautiful music continued to play softly in the background, Mark began with Psalm seventy-two, "Give the king Your judgments, O God, and Your righteousness to the king's son... He will bring justice to the poor of the people; He will save the children of the needy..." Pictures flashed steadily onto the screen of a king in royal robes, high, snow-capped mountains and little children with happy, shy smiles and bowls of white porridge.

---

[76] Proverbs 29:18 (KJV)
[77] Matt. 4:17; 11:11-12; Luke 19:11-27; Col. 1:12-13: Heb. 11:8-16
[78] Psalm 72:16

"Those are the Kenyan orphans we sponsor," Jessica whispered. "They now have food to eat every day. They get to go to school and they're learning to read the Bible."

The poverty in the background struck Sandra forcibly. The children looked happy enough in hand-me-down clothes with their bowls of maize, but the dilapidated shack in the background didn't look very inviting. *I complain about eating brown rice every day,* she thought, *but I live in a palace compared to that rickety mud hut.*

Mark read, "In His days the righteous shall flourish, and abundance of peace, until the moon is no more. He shall have dominion also from sea to sea, and from the river to the ends of the earth." Beautiful pictures of rain showers, a full moon in a dark sky and a satellite view of the oceans played across the screen.

Sandra listened, wide-eyed as Mark read that *all the kings of the earth* would bow down before this King who would be set over the world. They would bring gifts of gold, prayers and praise, and "men shall be blessed in Him; all nations shall call Him blessed."

Why, that's just what Jess was telling me about, she marvelled. *Through Jesus - Abraham's promised heir - all nations will be blessed!*

"Reading from Isaiah chapter two," Mark continued dramatically, as the pictures on the screen focused on an enormous temple with huge arched entrances, tall trees and a flowing river. "'Now it shall come to pass *in the latter days* that the mountain of the LORD'S house shall be established on the top of the mountains, and shall be exalted above the hills; and *all nations* shall flow to it. Many people shall come and say, 'Come, and let us go up to the mountain of the LORD, *to the house of the God of Jacob*; He will *teach us His ways,* and *we shall walk in His paths.*' For out of Zion shall go forth the law, and the word of the LORD *from Jerusalem.*'"

This seemed new to Sandra. She leaned over to Jessica, whispering, "There will be a temple in Jerusalem?"

"Yes," Jessica whispered back, her eyes sparkling with anticipation. "Remember we talked about God's promise that David's descendant would build Him a house for His Name. Jesus will build this temple.[79] This is where he will rule from - his throne - or his headquarters, so to speak. The temple will be big enough for people all over the world to visit, and worship, and learn."

Mark read from Isaiah eleven, which foretold that Jesus would descend from the stem of Jesse – who was King David's father, and that he will judge the world with righteousness. "'In those days,'" Mark read, "'the wolf will dwell with the lamb, the cow and the bear will feed together, lions will eat straw like the ox, and the earth will be filled with the knowledge of God as the waters cover the earth.'"

Sandra was astounded to hear that even the relationships between the animals will be altered when Jesus rules the world. She loved the wildlife pictures that came up on the screen. *Imagine that, Tiger,* she thought to herself with amusement, thinking of her own little cat, *perhaps you will be friends with the squirrels!*

Isaiah thirty-five added new colour to the vision that was steadily emerging in Sandra's mind. Mark read of a time when the desert would blossom as a rose. The eyes of the blind would be opened, the ears of the deaf unstopped. "Then the lame shall leap like a deer, and the tongue of the dumb sing. For waters shall burst forth in the wilderness, and streams in the desert."

"Would you like a drink?" Derrick whispered, holding up a bottle of sparkling-red grape juice. He had just poured himself and Laura a glass.

Sandra realized she had become so awe-struck by the presentation that most of her food was still sitting untouched on

---

[79] Ezekiel 40-48 (master plans); Zechariah 6:12-13; 14:16-20; Isaiah 11:1-5; Jeremiah 23:5-8; Isaiah 2:2-5; Luke 1:30-33

her plate. "Oh yes, thank you," she nodded with an appreciative smile.

Derrick filled her glass and Sandra took a sip. "It's lovely!" she whispered. Derrick smiled.

Looking down at her plate, Sandra picked up a little quiche that looked very appetizing. It was delicious!

Mark read from Isaiah chapters sixty, and sixty-two. His pleading voice cried out, "I have set watchmen on your walls, O Jerusalem; they shall never hold their peace day or night. You who make mention of the LORD, do not keep silent, and give Him no rest till He establishes and till He makes Jerusalem a praise in the earth."

Jerusalem must be a very special place to God, Sandra considered; *if we are to keep begging God about it.* Then she remembered, *Of course, it will be the capital city in the future! The city of the great King!*

When Mark began Zechariah chapter fourteen, the pictures changed briefly from serene, stunning scenery, to destruction and war. "'For I will gather all the nations to battle against Jerusalem;'" he read in an alarming way, "'The city shall be taken, the houses rifled, and the women ravished. Half of the city shall go into captivity, but the remnant of the people shall not be cut off from the city. Then *the LORD will go forth and fight* against those nations, as He fights in the day of battle. And in that day *His feet will stand on the Mount of Olives,* which faces Jerusalem on the east. And the Mount of Olives *shall be split in two,* from east to west, making a very large valley; half of the mountain shall move toward the north and half of it toward the south... *Thus the LORD my God will come, and all the saints with You.*'"

Sandra shivered.

"This is what has to happen before God's Kingdom will be established," Jessica whispered to her. "Many nations of the world will come against Jerusalem in the near future. God has promised that He will intervene to save Jerusalem, sending Jesus and the saints to defend His holy city."[80]

The gloom didn't last long. The tone of the chapter soon changed with the words, "And the LORD shall be King over all the earth. In that day it shall be -"The LORD is one," and His name one... and no longer shall there be utter destruction, but Jerusalem shall be safely inhabited... And it shall come to pass that everyone who is left of all the nations which came against Jerusalem shall go up from year to year to worship the King, the LORD of hosts, and to keep the Feast of Tabernacles."

After the PowerPoint presentation had concluded and Mark sat down to enjoy the good food himself, the children put on a presentation of their own.

A lanky young teen that Sandra knew well from the gardening crew, took his place at the podium and announced that they were going to present "The Marriage Supper." It was based, he said, on the parable Jesus told in Matthew and Luke.[81]

"Allan's narrating!" Sandra whispered to Jessica with surprise.

"Yes," Jessica replied quietly. "And Peter's nephews and nieces are the main actors."

What a shame James is missing the show, Sandra thought. *These are his nephews and nieces too.*

As Allan narrated the story, one of Andrew's twin boys, dressed in a king's costume stood stirring a large pot. "The kingdom of heaven is like the story of a certain king who arranged a marriage for his son," Allan said in a lively way. "He sent out his servants to call those who were invited to the wedding; but they were not willing to come!"

Right beside the king, the other twin in fancy clothes was pacing back and forth. A home-made, golden crown sat crookedly

---
[80] See Zechariah 12; Joel 2 & 3
[81] Matthew 22:2- 14; Luke 14:16-24

on his short blond hair. Two teen girls, in long gowns, stood at attention waiting for orders.

The king spoke, "Servants, the supper is ready. Tell those that we have invited to the marriage that it is now time to come."

Both girls curtsied and ran out of the room. In a minute they were back, looking very nervous. "Oh King," they said, "we're very sorry, but... no one ...wants to come."

"What?" the king roared, his dark eyes flashing, "They've been invited to *a feast*!" At this point the king's beard began to fall off his face and he hastily tried to stick it back on. "Why on earth would they not want to come?" he said angrily, holding his beard on with one hand.

"Well," said the younger, dark-haired girl in a very sweet voice, "George said he's just bought some land and he has to check it out. You know, he has to make sure there's a good well on it and stuff like that..."

"And Fred just bought some oxen," the older girl explained, "and he has to test them. He wants to make sure they're strong enough to pull his plow..."

"And what about Bob?!" the king asked with dismay. His beard began to fall again and a hand reached out from behind the stage curtain to give him two pieces of tape.

"Oh, well you see," the older girl replied, looking uneasily towards the king as he fixed his beard, "well, Bob says he just got married....so he can't come."

"What lousy excuses! Bob could have brought his wife!" the king roared, shaking his head. This time the beard stayed firmly in place. "All of those things could be done at some other time, but the wedding is *today!*" Motioning to the servants the king commanded, "Since those we've invited have proved themselves unworthy, go out to the highways and invite the poor and the lame and the blind..."

The little play continued to a grand finale when the whole group joined together to sing a song. The chorus was a catchy little ditty that echoed for the rest of the evening in Sandra's head:

"I cannot come to the wedding, don't trouble me now,
I have married a wife, I have bought me a cow,
I have fields and commitments that cost a pretty sum,
Pray have me excused, I cannot come!"

Everyone clapped for the actors as they exited the stage.

The king ripped his troublesome beard off on his way out, grinning at his audience. It made people laugh.

As everyone continued to eat the good food, there were a few beautiful songs sung by various individuals. Jessica and Peter's song was Sandra's favourite. Jess played the piano and sang along with Peter and they harmonised so well together. It was a soft melody about a bride and a groom, which Sandra thought would be very fitting for a wedding ceremony.

When they returned to the table she quietly asked Jess, "Are you going to sing that at your wedding too?"

Jess smiled and whispered back, "We have an even better one to sing. But you'll have to wait till the wedding!"

Am I invited? Sandra wondered, unsure that she should ask. She didn't want to put Jessica on the spot. *Maybe she is intending to invite me,* she hoped.

Craig stood up. "Before dessert is served," he began, "we will ask Mark to read us a few passages from the New Testament. Of course, we are only scraping the surface tonight. There are many, many passages that tell us what God's kingdom will be like, but tonight we don't have time to include them all. It's so important that we take the time to make this vision our own; to make it real and vibrant and alive that we might desire it above all the temptations and trials that come our way in this life. As Paul writes in Second Corinthians chapter four, "Therefore we do not lose heart. Even though our outward man is perishing, yet the inward man is being renewed day by day. For our light affliction, which is but for a moment, is working for us *a far more* exceeding and *eternal* weight of glory, while we do not look at the things which are seen, but at the things which are not seen. For the things which are seen are temporary, but the things which are not seen *are eternal."*

It's kind of like creating a daydream, Sandra considered. *Rather than just allowing random thoughts to fill my mind, I could choose to think about all this instead!*

The last few readings were sections taken from First Corinthians fifteen and Revelation twenty-one to twenty-two. Sandra loved the descriptive language, which Mark emphasized so well, as she imagined the glorious scene in her mind. "And he showed me a *pure* river of water *of life, clear as crystal,* proceeding from the throne of God and of the Lamb. In the middle of its street, and on either side of the river, was *the tree of life,* which bore *twelve fruits,* each tree yielding its fruit *every month.* The *leaves* of the tree were for the *healing of the nations.* And there shall be *no more* curse, but the throne of God and of the Lamb shall be in it, and His servants shall serve Him. They shall *see His face,* and His name shall be on their foreheads… And the Spirit and the bride say, *"Come!"* And let him who hears say, *"Come!"* And let him *who thirsts come.* Whoever *desires,* let him take the water of life *freely."*

It's an invitation, she thought. *God is inviting us all to come! He's almost pleading with us to come. And now that I know what it's all about, of course it's where I want to be!*

The lovely, haunting music began to play again after Mark finished reading and Jessica left to help serve dessert. Craig stood up once more to say that the last session of the evening would be a chance for everyone to share what they most looked forward to in the coming kingdom.

Jessica and the young actors, still in their costumes, helped to serve dessert, tea and coffee. Each tray they brought around held a lavish selection of cheesecakes, chocolate truffles, caramel slices and for the health-conscious - Banana Flambé over frozen vanilla yogurt. One of Andrew's identical twin boys, who both looked much more like Peter than Andrew, served Sandra's table. There were still red marks on his cheeks where the tape had been stuck.

"Hey, Zach," Peter called out to him, "That was good acting tonight! You've got quite a roar! If I had been one of your servants I'd have been shaking in my boots!"

Zach laughed. "I just wish my beard didn't keep falling off."

"You covered well, man!" Peter said, giving him a friendly pat on the back. "So what do you recommend on that tray?"

"My mom made the truffles," he grinned, "and they're *so* good!"

"You've tried them?" Peter asked.

"Sure did! I tried three!"

"And they were all good? Every single one?"

Zach nodded his head vigorously.

"I'll take your word for it then," Peter said, quite seriously, reaching for a truffle. "I know you're the dessert connoisseur!"

The young boy proudly moved on to Sandra.

With all the delicious fruit trays, Sandra hadn't realized that dessert was still to come. She was so full! But such opportunities didn't come along very often, so after a little more input from Zach, she finally chose the caramel slice.

"Hey," Peter said, amused by her indecision, "If you'd like to share that with me, I'll share the chocolate truffle with you."

"It's a deal!" Sandra smiled. "And you can take the bigger halves. I've already eaten too much."

"Bigger halves!" Peter chuckled, looking over with a friendly grin. "Who taught you fractions?"

Sandra laughed, insisting more accurately that Peter take two-thirds of each.

Setting aside her small portions of dessert for later, Sandra sat back in her chair and listened eagerly as everyone began to share their most cherished hope for the future to come. All the faces around the dark table were softly lit by the golden, flickering candlelight. Soft mellow music created a very relaxed atmosphere conducive to sharing. An older woman was first in the circle to tell of her greatest longing. With snow-white hair and a pale, wrinkled face, her blue eyes still sparkled earnestly as she expressed her desire to finally see the Lord Jesus face to face. "I want to hear his voice with my own ears, see his eyes with my own eyes and experience Jesus as my friend, my brother and King!" she exclaimed. "I long to thank him, personally, for laying down his life in such an agonizing way, so that we can all have forgiveness for our sins!"

This is reason enough, Sandra felt. Many heads nodded in agreement and a few 'amens' were heard around the circle. To see Jesus and experience friendship with someone so loving, self-sacrificing, and so much like his Father in all righteousness, could only be the ultimate desire of everyone in the room!

The list of cherished hopes didn't stop there however; one man was excited to help build the enormous, elaborate temple in Jerusalem, well-described in Ezekiel forty to forty-eight. Others longed to be free of a physical ailment they struggled with daily. Craig Symons expressed his desire to travel the world, teaching willing, open minds about the new King. Derrick and Laura, who were both experiencing estrangement from their families due to their religious convictions, hoped that their loved ones would witness Christ's return and have a change of heart before it was too late.

"I just hope we've shared enough with them," Derrick added, "so they will recognize Jesus Christ for who he truly is, and not be misled by the popular Christian view of it all."

Sandra was rather nervous to say anything, as this was still very new to her. However, she remembered the little orphans in the slide show and said she would love to see the day when *all* the children of the world had enough to eat, comfortable homes and good health to enjoy.

Jessica and Peter had been quietly conferring together and Sandra was curious to hear what they had to say. When it was Jessica's turn, she took a deep breath and spoke softly. The candlelight gleamed against her smooth skin and sparkled in her eyes. "Peter and I are both looking forward to the resurrection," she said. "There will be so many people who will be reunited with their loved ones. We both want to see Verity again and throw our arms around her and tell her how much she's been missed. I can't wait to see the look on her face when she sees Peter and knows that her greatest wish…," Jess suddenly choked up and she covered her mouth with her hand momentarily. She spoke again with great emotion. "Her greatest wish…was answered…" Jess could barely finish her thought.

Sandra felt tears come into her eyes, although she knew so little about the situation to which her friend was referring. Peter put his arm around Jessica's shoulders and drew her close. "And I long to apologize to Verity," he expressed, "for being such a fool when she was dying. I'll be so happy to tell her that her friendship eventually led me to accept Christ. It took a long time," he smiled, "but by God's mercy I'm here. And I'm sure there are many other people who will gratefully tell their loved ones what their lives accomplished and their sacrifices won," he continued. "The disciple Stephen who was stoned to death, as Saul of Tarsus stood by consenting to the murder will see Saul alive again as the beloved Apostle Paul. Isaiah, who was killed by King Manasseh, will learn that his words may have contributed to the king's eventual conversion in prison. Even someone like William Tyndale, who gave his life to translate the Bible into English, will rise to find out that his dying prayer was answered; God did open the King of England's eyes and now almost everyone in the world can read the Bible freely in their own language! So many people who died with a sense of failure will be able to rejoice when they're told the end of their story!"

There were nods of agreement all around the table.

"Well, what I long for," the older man beside Peter said next, "is the complete change of nature. I'm looking forward to serving God with a completely pure heart, without any self-deceit creeping in or fleshly motives taking over. I long to serve God *faithfully*, every day, forever!"

"I can say Amen to that," Sandra heard Peter say. Others agreed.

Just before the evening concluded, there was a special five-minute presentation. It was intended to sound like a message from God. Pre-recorded, a deep voice, with an Australian accent, spoke over stirring music telling everyone how much He loved them and desired them to be in His Kingdom. The voice assured everyone that they would have plenty to do to subdue the earth and restore it to a paradise condition. It encouraged the listeners to press on, to believe His promises and patiently wait for His Son to return. It ended with the words, "…do not seek what you should eat or what you should drink, nor have an anxious mind. For all these things the nations of the world seek after, and your Father knows that you need these things. But seek the kingdom of God, and His righteousness, and all these things shall be added to you. Do not fear, little flock, for it is your Father's *good pleasure* to give you the kingdom."[82]

---

[82] Luke 12:29-32; 1 Timothy 2:3-4; 1 Thessalonians 5:9-11; 2 Peter 3:9

That's so comforting, Sandra thought. *God really wants us to be there!* She was amazed that the passage also seemed to promise that God would care for her temporal needs now if she would only seek His kingdom and His righteousness first. *Is that true?* she wondered. *Will He really find a way to provide for me?*

Once the feast was over and Sandra had helped the others clean up, she wandered over to a table advertising free literature. She was especially drawn to a pamphlet that was all about the kingdom of God. As she quickly skimmed through it, she saw that it had almost everything that she and Jessica had discussed. Thinking it would be very handy for review, Sandra put it and a few others into her purse.

Later that evening, as Peter and Jessica were driving her home, Sandra willed herself to ask a question that she hoped wouldn't cause offense. "I'm just wondering," she said, "and I hope you don't mind me asking…but won't it be rather awkward for both of you in the Kingdom when Verity is alive again? I know you both love her, but won't she be jealous that you're… you're married to each other?"

Jessica looked back with a smile. "That's something we didn't really discuss tonight;" she said, "relationships in the Kingdom. How does that verse go, Peter?"

"You'd know better than I would," he replied, squeezing her hand.

Opening up her Bible, Jessica found the verse she was looking for. "This is what Jesus said in Luke twenty," she told Sandra. "'The sons of this age marry and are given in marriage. But those who are counted worthy to attain that age, and the resurrection from the dead, neither marry nor are given in marriage; nor can they die anymore, for they are equal to the angels and are sons of God, being sons of the resurrection.'"[83]

---

[83] Luke 20:34-36

"So, there won't be *marriage* in the Kingdom?" Sandra reiterated.

"There won't," Peter agreed. "We will all be the best of friends together. And because we'll be immortal, there won't be any more envy, or self-pity, or misunderstandings, or feeling left out. All of us will be perfectly happy and fully content to work together in whatever way God asks of us."

"So, you, Jessica and Verity will be great friends together, without any awkwardness?" Sandra clarified.

"Exactly," Peter nodded. "And our great friendships won't be just with the people we know *now,* but with all those who have lived *before us,* and those who come *after."*

"Imagine, being friends with King David," Jessica said to Sandra excitedly, "or getting to know the Rachel and Leah you've been reading about in Genesis."

Wow! There really is so much to think about! Sandra marvelled.

That night, as she lay in bed trying to go to sleep, a new, very exciting dream was developing. No longer did it involve a tour of a massive, downtown stone mansion and a promise of help with the rent. This new dream was full of the people who had been at the feast, all with their great longings for the future, fulfilled. In it was a temple much grander than anything Laurie would ever own, filled with smiling people who were warm and welcoming, much like those she was getting to know. Rivers and trees, gorgeous gardens, an abundance of food, happy, well-fed children, friendly animals on *a vegetarian menu,* overflowed the new vision she was developing, like never before. And above all, she imagined Jesus, a king, a righteous, incorruptible king who will never die, or neglect, or desert anyone – a King who will live *forever!*

This is something to believe in! she marvelled. *It's not just a fantasy. My foolish imaginations are always letting me down.*

But Jessica says that God's promises are for real. God won't let us down.[84]

But how does heaven fit into all this, she wondered. *I don't remember anyone mentioning anything about heaven tonight. Will it be just as exciting? Or is everyone up in heaven just kind of waiting to get back to the earth for the kingdom to begin? I should have asked Jess about it tonight but I forgot.*

Other questions began to pour into her mind. *What will we be like when we're immortal? Will we have bodies like we do now? Will we enjoy food like we did tonight? Will we need to eat? Will we look the same? Will we get to travel anywhere we want to go? Will we remember everything we did before we were immortal?*

I cannot come to the wedding, don't trouble me now... ran through her head for the umpteenth time. *No way! That won't be me,* she thought sleepily. *I've been invited. I want to be there!*

---

[84] Numbers 23:19; Titus 1:2; Hebrews 6:17-19

To Rise
Chapter Sixteen

Sandra met Brett later that week, when he brought Matt over for his lesson. Wearing only his black Nike bathing shorts, Brett had a white towel slung over one shoulder. *He's so good-looking!* Sandra thought. *And those abs!* she marvelled, noticing the well-defined muscles that rippled across his chest. *He must work out to have a body like that.*

"We were just having a swim in the pool," Brett told her. "Matt's parents aren't home yet, but they plan to pick him up when you're finished."

Matt was quite comfortable with Sandra now and wandered into her apartment in search of Tiger.

"Sorry I didn't make it to your Kingdom Feast," Brett apologized earnestly, leaning against her doorway. "I was planning to come, but at the last minute a client called me up and needed to meet right away. Was it fun?"

"It was beautiful!" Sandra smiled. "I had no idea there were so many verses about the future Kingdom of God on this earth. And the food was incredible!"

Brett looked sorry to have missed out. "Well, see you around," he said, reluctantly turning to leave.

There was something in Brett's parting glance that caused Sandra's heart to race. Maybe it was the long searching look; or the way his eyes travelled from her head to toe and back up. Whatever it was, it was more than just a caring look between friends; it was intense…it made her feel…*wanted.*

Don't do that to me, she thought breathlessly, closing the door to her apartment. *You belong to someone else. Don't make me feel that you're in love with me.* But was he? Was it possible she was attracting Brett's attention somehow? Or was Brett just another charmer - intent on capturing as many hearts as he could? Sandra had had enough of 'charmers' from earlier days. Looking around for Matt, knowing he was probably checking out her 'box of treasures', she tried to thrust the look from her mind.

Matt had chosen a 'memory challenge' game from her box and was excited to play it. Half the cards were pictures, while on the other half were the matching words. Sandra was happy to test it out with him.

Neither Matt's mother nor father came to pick him up later that evening. Instead a pretty brunette with a familiar face, stood at the door when Sandra answered the knock.

"Hi," the young lady said with a lovely smile. "I'm Natalie, Brett's fiancé. Matt's parents still aren't home from work and Brett's on the phone with a client, so he sent me to get Matt."

"Nice to meet you," Sandra said, a little surprised. She reached out to shake hands with Natalie. "We've kind of met in passing," she laughed, "but it's nice to know your name...I'm Sandra Carrington by the way."

"I know," Natalie smiled. "Matt thinks the world of you. He talks about Ms. Carrington all the time."

"Look Natalie," Matt exclaimed, holding up the memory challenge. "We played this game and I won...at least, I won *one* of the games," he clarified.

"You sure did," Sandra agreed. "You almost won *both!* You're very good at remembering where everything is!"

"Can we go to the park?" Matt begged, handing the game to Sandra.

"The park might be a good idea," Natalie nodded. "We'll have to ask your Uncle Brett, when he gets off the phone."

"Thanks so much, Sandra," Natalie said, as she took Matt's hand.

Waving goodbye, Sandra slowly closed the door behind her. *I'm glad Brett sent Natalie,* she thought. *I needed to meet her today, especially after that look! She's so sweet...*

Sandra sighed. The look was something she wanted to hold onto; it was exciting; it was satisfying but, *it isn't right,* she told herself. Then a new thought struck her. *Was I looking at him that way? Did my feelings show through my eyes?* Seeing Brett in his bathing suit had been rather distracting. With embarrassment, she suddenly realized how unguarded she had been, *I never knew how much can be said just through looks! I'd better be careful. I don't want to cause confusion or hurt anyone. I wouldn't want someone to do that to me.*

It wasn't often that Sandra dwelt on the past; she felt she had enough heartache in the present. But standing there in front of the mirror, everything darkened as she drifted back five years. "It's over? So soon?" she could hear herself saying.

"I'm sorry, Sandra. Look, we've had a great time together..."

"But..."

"I'm sorry. I've met someone else and I just need some space..."

"But you said..."

"Sandra, there's no use staying together. I'd just be pretending..."

"Gavin, you said this would be *forever!* It hasn't even been a year!"

A chill went down her spine and she turned quickly away. *I know that heartbreak all too well. I never want to bring it on someone else!*

Thursday night when Jessica came over she brought a basket of muffins and a box full of supplies. "My mom was cleaning out her cupboards this week," she said in a matter-of-fact sort of way. "If you can use any of this stuff you're welcome to it."

"Oh, thank you," Sandra said, accepting the box gratefully. "I'm sure it will all come in handy!" She took a brief look. There were boxes of crackers, cereal and tins of food. It was a very welcome sight! *A week off brown rice!*

"Then my mom will be happy it's not clogging up her cupboards," Jess said with a sad smile. "And I made muffins today and thought you might like to try some. It's a new recipe."

She probably thought I needed this after seeing my bare fridge last week, Sandra reflected. *But she's making me feel as though I'm doing her a favour by taking it all!*

"Can I get you a glass of juice?" Sandra asked as Jessica wandered into the living room. A furry bundle stretched out on the couch looked up invitingly towards Jess. "Or do you prefer tea? I can actually offer you both tonight!"

"Juice would be nice, please," Jessica replied quietly, picking Tiger up and sitting down in the same spot she always did. "It's such a warm evening."

When Sandra brought over the drinks, she noticed that Jessica lacked her usual sparkle. It was quite hot in the apartment, so Sandra turned the air conditioning on.

"Thank you," Jessica said, taking a sip of her juice right away. "We might as well start with a prayer."

Sandra took her seat and bowed her head. Jess prayed.

It was a rather flat prayer - very unusual for Jess. Sandra wondered if something was wrong. "So, we've talked about some of God's promises," Jessica began soberly, before Sandra could ask any questions, "and we've discovered that Abraham and King David recognized their promises would be fulfilled in the future. [85] They also realized their promises related ultimately to a future descendant of theirs who would also be the Son of God. [86] When this future descendant – who we know as Jesus – receives his

---

[85] Hebrews 11:8-19, 32-40
[86] Matthew 1:1; Luke 1:30-35

promise – so will they and everyone who has a part. [87] Now where are Abraham and King David today?"

Sandra looked up hesitantly. "Are they dead, or in heaven? I'm not sure." she confessed.

Jessica looked up thoughtfully. "Well, if you're not quite sure, let's look at Acts chapter two."

Using the index, Sandra soon found Acts chapter two. Jessica directed her to verses twenty-nine to thirty-four, and Sandra read, "Men and brethren, let me speak freely to you of the patriarch David, that he is both dead and buried, and his tomb is with us to this day."

"So, David's dead," Sandra mused. "But is he in heaven?"

"What does it say in verse thirty-four," Jess asked.

"'For David did not ascend into the heavens…,'" Sandra read. "Hmm, I guess not," she said.

"And David was a man 'after God's own heart',"[88] Jessica explained. "If David didn't receive his reward in heaven, then this must not be the reward promised to the faithful. It also says in John three, verse thirteen, 'And no man hath ascended up to heaven…,' except Jesus."

The discussion Sandra had had with James in the courtyard was still causing confusion. "But what about the thief on the cross?" she asked. "Didn't he go to heaven *with* Jesus when he died?"

With a thoughtful look, Jessica said, "That's a really good question. We can look at that passage, if you like." Jessica knew exactly where it was, and told Sandra to turn up Luke twenty-three, verse forty-three.

"You see," Jess explained, as Sandra turned to Luke, "in the original Greek there weren't any punctuation marks like we have in the English; therefore, translators have to decide where to

---

[87] Galatians 3:14-19; Luke 13:23-29
[88] Acts 13:22

put the commas and periods. As such, the verse can convey different meanings depending on where you put the punctuation. However, if you were to take out all the commas, how might you read that verse?"

Sandra looked at the verse. Silently she read the thief's request as well as Jesus' answer without taking any punctuation breaks. "'Then he said to Jesus, 'Lord remember me when you come into your kingdom.' And Jesus said to him, 'Assuredly I say to you today you will be with me in Paradise.'"

Pondering Jessica's question, Sandra replied, "Well Jesus could be saying, 'I say to you, Today you will be with me in Paradise.' Or I suppose he could be saying, 'I say to you today, you will be with me in Paradise.'"

"That's good," Jess agreed. "And one way to determine how Jesus intended his words to be understood, would be to find out where Jesus went himself, the day that he died. Did he ascend to heaven that very day to be with his Father? Or did he simply die and wait unconsciously in the grave for three days until his resurrection?"

"That would be very helpful to know," Sandra nodded.

"There are two passages to help us," Jess replied. "One tells us what Jesus said to Mary immediately after his resurrection."

Turning up John twenty, verse seventeen, as Jess suggested, Sandra was surprised to see that Jesus had said to Mary, "Do not cling to Me, for I have *not yet ascended to My Father;* but go to My brethren and say to them, 'I am ascending to My Father and your Father, and to My God and your God.'"

"Okay," Sandra mused. "I guess if Jesus is saying that he hadn't yet ascended to God, then he must not have gone to heaven on the day that he died."

"Right. He didn't go to heaven until forty days after his resurrection," [89]Jess agreed. "The other passage I want to show you is actually in the same chapter we were looking at in Acts, which spoke about David."

Jessica suggested that they read Acts chapter two, from verse twenty-two to thirty-two. It was a longer section which quoted the prophecy David had penned in the Psalms concerning Jesus' death and resurrection. The Psalms, Jess told Sandra, had been written a thousand years before Jesus was even born. The last two verses clarified the point she was making: "he [David], foreseeing this, spoke concerning the resurrection of the Christ, that *His soul was not left in Hades,* nor did His flesh see corruption. This Jesus God has raised up, of which we are all witnesses."

"So where was Jesus Christ, during the three days after his crucifixion?" Jessica continued.

"Well, it says 'His soul was not left in Hades', so I suppose that means he must have been in Hades for only a short time," Sandra replied dubiously. "Where exactly is Hades?"

"Hades is one of the Greek words for 'hell'," Jess replied. "It is also translated in the King James Version as 'the grave'. You can find that out if you look it up in a reference book called a concordance, which gives the various meanings of all the original words used in the Bible. This passage in Acts indicates Jesus lay in the grave for three days until God resurrected him. So, would he have been with the thief in heaven the very day that they died?"

"I suppose not, if he was in the grave," Sandra replied. "But then what did Jesus mean?"

"What did the thief ask for?" Jess prompted gently.

Sandra read the passage again. "Then he said to Jesus, 'Lord remember me when you come into your kingdom.' And

---

[89] Acts 1:1-11

Jesus said to him, 'Assuredly I say to you today you will be with me in Paradise.'"

She noticed the words the thief had used. The thief hadn't asked to go to heaven!

"Ah..." Sandra murmured with a smile to herself. "The thief asked to be in the Kingdom, which still hasn't come!"

Jessica nodded.

"So, why did Jesus reply that he would be with him in Paradise?" Sandra inquired. "What does 'Paradise' mean?"

"If you looked up 'paradise' in a concordance," Jess explained, "you would find it means 'an Eden, a place of future happiness.'"

Sandra nodded. She thought back on all the beautiful slides she had seen at the Kingdom Feast, and all the flowery language of the prophecies they had read. 'Eden' would be a fitting description of the coming Kingdom of God. *Yes, I'd call that Paradise,* she thought.

"So, there are many faithful people who have been promised this wonderful future inheritance," Jessica reminded her, "including the repentant thief on the cross. But all these people are lying dead and unconscious in a grave just like Jesus did for three days. What must God do to give them the promises?"

"I guess they have to be resurrected just like Jesus," Sandra considered.

"That's right," Jessica agreed. "There was a section we read from First Corinthians fifteen at the Kingdom Feast that we should look at in more detail. This chapter is often read at funerals because it deals specifically with the resurrection."

Reading through the chapter together, Jessica stopped to explain various verses along the way. "The Apostle Paul, who wrote Corinthians, is making a case for the importance of the resurrection in this chapter," she stated. "There seems to have been a group of people at that time who didn't believe it would happen.

So Paul says that if there's no resurrection, then Jesus didn't rise, and 'if Christ is not risen, your faith is futile; you are still in your sins! Then also those who have fallen asleep in Christ *have perished*. If in this life only we have hope in Christ, we are of all men the most pitiable.'"

"Do you see why he says the resurrection is vital?"

Sandra looked carefully. "Because if Jesus didn't rise, then those who have died have perished?"

"That's right," Jessica smiled. "All the faithful of old have been waiting in their graves for the day when Jesus will return to the earth and call their name. If Jesus never rose from the dead, and if there is no resurrection, then the promises that have been given by God will never be fulfilled."

Reading the passage to herself again, Sandra saw further implications. "And if there's no resurrection," she pondered out loud, "it says that those who have fallen asleep in Christ have *perished.*"

"Therefore, they can't be in heaven waiting for the resurrection," Jess agreed; "the resurrection is their only hope for life again."

When Sandra nodded, Jessica said, "Please read on."

Sandra read, "'But now Christ is risen from the dead, and has become *the firstfruits* of those who have fallen asleep. For since by man came death, by man also came the resurrection of the dead. For as in Adam all die, even so *in Christ all shall be made alive*. But each one in his own order: Christ the firstfruits, *afterward those who are Christ's at His coming.*"

"What is meant by the 'firstfruits,'" Sandra asked.

Jessica explained that in the Old Testament the Jewish people had to give the first of the crops they gathered to God. "Jesus is the 'firstfruits' of the resurrection," she explained, "because he was the first human being to rise from the dead and *be* made immortal. It says in Colossians," she added, "that he is 'the firstborn from the dead.'"[90]

"And when will everyone else rise?" Sandra asked.

"Have a look further down in this chapter," Jess suggested. "Look at verse fifty-one."

Sandra read, "Behold, I tell you a mystery: We shall not all sleep, but we shall all be changed-- in a moment, in the twinkling of an eye, *at the last trumpet.* For the trumpet will sound, and the dead will be raised incorruptible, and we shall be changed. For this corruptible must put on incorruption, and *this mortal must put on immortality.*"

"We'll be raised at the last trumpet?" she clarified. "When is the last trumpet?"

Jessica took her to First Thessalonians four, which read, "But I do not want you to be ignorant, brethren, concerning those who have fallen asleep, lest you sorrow as others who have no hope. For if we believe that Jesus died and rose again, even so God will bring with Him those who sleep in Jesus. For this we say to you by the word of the Lord, that we who are alive and remain until the coming of the Lord will by no means precede those who are asleep. *For the Lord Himself will descend from heaven with a shout, with the voice of an archangel, and with the trumpet of God. And the dead in Christ will rise first.*"[91]

"That's beautiful," Sandra said sadly, thinking of her mother. *Mom wasn't 'in Christ'. She didn't ever read the Bible. What a comfort it would be to me if I knew Mom had this hope!*

"It must be very comforting to know that the people you love will one day be brought back to life," she said to Jessica. "Will we be just as we are now? Will we have the same memories; the same physical appearance, or will we be different?"

---

[90] Colossians 1:18; Acts 26:23
[91] See also John 6:39,40,44

"Well, since Jesus was the first to rise from the dead in this way," Jessica reasoned, "then we can learn what we'll be like, by examining what he is like as an immortal being. But that would take some time to consider. Why don't we save that for our next class?"

It wasn't until Jess closed up her Bible, that Sandra noticed the gloom return to her face.

"Is something wrong?" Sandra asked compassionately. "You don't seem to be quite yourself tonight."

Jessica looked up unhappily. "Oh," she said, "it's nothing really. It's just that Peter found out today that the money he thought would be coming to him - isn't coming anymore. Thankfully we had a conditional offer on the house, or we'd be in deep trouble now."

"Oh no!" Sandra cried. "You can't buy the little green house?"

Jess shook her head sadly.

I don't want to pry," Sandra said tentatively, "but if you don't mind me asking, what happened?"

With a big sigh, Jess explained. "Peter lived in Australia for ten years after Verity died, and he built up a highly successful landscaping company. He had lots of heavy equipment - backhoes, a couple dump trucks, bulldozers, and all the stuff you need to do a complete landscaping overhaul. Well, when he decided to stay over here in Canada, he asked his employees to buy him out, so that they could have their own company and he could set up a new one here. They paid him a small portion last year, but the majority of the money was supposed to come through last week. Unfortunately, they reneged on their part of the deal, saying that without Peter, the business isn't what it used to be. They say they're barely making enough profit to survive."

"Why doesn't he just sell off his assets and close it down?" Sandra asked.

"I guess he could," Jessica admitted, "but Peter already feels bad that he's let his friends down by not returning. He doesn't want to see them all out of work in this recession. They stuck by him faithfully in the early years when he was building up the company. He figures that with God's blessing, he can slowly build up another company here; it will just take time." With a pause, Jess mumbled sadly, "but of course that means we can't afford a house…"

"So, what will you do?" Sandra inquired.

"We talked about postponing *everything*… but then we decided we'll be content to live in his parent's RV for the rest of the summer and find some place to rent in the fall. If necessary, we can always stay with my parents."

"That doesn't seem fair!" Sandra exclaimed. "You and Peter care so much about other people. I don't understand why James, and these friends in Australia don't show the same care for you. That must…really hurt!" *Even more than Laurie's lack of consideration hurts me!* Sandra considered. "How do you deal with it?" she asked.

Jessica looked up at Sandra. "Let's go for a walk," she suggested, rising from the couch and finishing off her glass of juice. "It would be helpful to talk about it and I'd love to stretch my legs."

Soar Like the *Seagulls*?
Chapter Seventeen

It was a warm June evening, as Sandra and Jessica strolled out to the harbour front. The sun was just beginning to set. Soft, gilded clouds lined the deep blue sky. There were many people out walking on such a beautiful evening. A flock of noisy seagulls caught Sandra's eye as they swooped down to circle a small red fishing boat that was coming in to the harbour.

"I used to really struggle with hurts like this," Jessica admitted, looking over at Sandra as they walked along. "There was a time in my life, not so long ago actually, when I thought that if I showed God's love to the world, then all my relationships would be wonderful and everyone would want to know more about the hope God has offered."

Sandra nodded empathically, as she dodged around a group of runners. Such cause and effect sounded entirely plausible.

"The trouble was that such idealism didn't work so well in college," Jess said ruefully, shielding her eyes to watch the gulls soar back into the air. "I gave my all to my friends there, bent over backwards to do more than my share of the work, tried to be kind and forgiving and tell them about the coming Kingdom of God, and they *ditched me*...badly!

"What did they do?!"

"Well," Jess began with a sigh, "it all began after I spoke out against practising homosexuality. We were having an open discussion during a Christian Bible study group session. I assumed that since we all were interested in reading the Bible together, we would all equally respect the message.[92] However, it didn't quite work out that way. Everyone in the group turned against me and

---

[92] 1 Corinthians 6:9-10; 1 Timothy 1:10; Romans 1:26-32

thought that I was a bigot, even though I assured them that I believe God can 'save the sinner', just as He can save all of us from any sin that we confess and forsake. A month later my closest friends took me out to celebrate the completion of our final project – *or so I thought* – and then slipped some sort of drug into my drink. I was throwing up and hallucinating and not one of them cared. I was left to find my own way home across the city."

"How terrible!" Sandra exclaimed.

"It was devastating to me," Jess admitted, "and I took a long, long time to sort it all out in my mind. I thought that God's love would change the world for good. I thought that if I did my part faithfully, everyone would be won over to His cause – but now I've come to realize that Jesus warned us *it wouldn't be that way at all."*

"Seriously?!" Sandra asked. This seemed disconcerting.

"Jesus was the perfect manifestation of God's love," Jess said, as they approached the end of the boardwalk. A spent geranium flower protruded from the last of the twenty wooden barrels that they had planted in the spring. Jess reached over and plucked it off absent-mindedly. "Jesus healed the sick," she said, "he raised people from the dead, spoke words of life and truth, he was always providing for others and forgiving sins…and how did the world react to him?"

"They…they crucified him," Sandra said thoughtfully. She had never considered the immense betrayal involved in the crucifixion.

"Yes, and he was personally betrayed by one of his *closest friends,"* Jess added; "through a kiss!"[93]

Having reached the end of the wooden walkway, the girls automatically turned around to head back the same way they had come. Jessica looked over at Sandra. "And while Jesus was being

---

[93] Luke 22:47-48

mocked, tortured and put to death on that stake, what was he providing for the world?"

Sandra shook her head uncertainly.

"Forgiveness," Jess answered, walking closer to Sandra to avoid a nasty-looking dog straining against his muzzle.

"Don't worry. He can't bite," the owner assured her.

"Thanks," Jess smiled uncertainly, stopping for a moment to let the dog and his master pass by.

"The Bible says that Jesus died for us," she continued, as they started walking again, "while we were yet sinners; for the ungodly and for his enemies.[94] And Jesus says that, 'If the world hate you, you know that it hated me before it hated you.'"[95]

"How does this help?" Sandra asked anxiously, looking over at the gulls. A few of them had eaten their fill of fish and were gliding in towards shore. "It sounds very depressing..."

"It helps in this way," Jessica explained confidently. "If you make the effort in your life to show love to others, *expecting to receive the same back* – you will eventually be devastated when others fail to respond, or even worse - respond with scorn or hostility! *But*, if you change your expectations, and determine to be a loving person because Jesus was, and because you want to be *his* friend[96], regardless of the reactions of others, then you can... soar like...like those seagulls," Jess said, pointing in their direction. "You can soar above every hurt and misunderstanding, over all the lack of care and concern. You can trust that Jesus empathizes completely and one day he will recognize you as an 'overcomer' – just as he himself overcame."[97]

It was a whole new way of thinking and Sandra couldn't comprehend it all at once. They walked in silence for a while as

---

[94] Romans 5
[95] John 15:18-21
[96] John 15:12-21; 1 John 3:11-24; 1 Peter 2:19-24
[97] Revelation 3:21; 2 Corinthians 4:16-18; 1Peter 4:13-16

she tried to apply it to her own situation. *I'm not sure it fits,* she thought, *Laurie's lack of concern for me has nothing to do with religion or anything good I've done for him. How can I overcome the hurt that I feel?* Finally, she decided to pour out her problem to Jess.

"What you're saying makes a lot of sense," Sandra began. "I asked you how you overcome such hurt, because there's a lot of hurt in my life. I'm just not sure it's quite the same situation."

Jessica looked over kindly. She broke off another brown, withered geranium flower as they continued past the barrels. "What hurts you, Sandra?" she asked gently.

"It's my brother," Sandra explained. "He left home when I was ten and he was sixteen. I haven't seen him since. All these years he's never made any effort to get in touch with me; not even for *our mother's funeral!* Sure he sent an enormous bouquet of flowers and paid for all the expense, but *he* didn't come. He had to be in China for some business transaction…something more important! I've always been the one tracking him down, sending emails, making phone calls, and only rarely hearing back. I came out here hoping that we'd finally meet up but so far every date we've set up, he's cancelled. He just doesn't care, I guess, although I keep hoping he will. But he's *all the family I have now,"* she said, brushing away the tears that were welling up in her eyes, "so I keep trying…"

"Then you're doing the right thing," Jessica assured her. "Keep trying. Be the one who cares and don't expect anything in return."

"Really? Don't expect anything back?! But that's so hard to do. It's especially hard because I need his help!" Sandra stopped herself. She didn't want to let Jessica know how tough things were.

Jess looked over inquisitively. "It is hard, at first," she agreed, "but it gets easier. Just do whatever you do, because it's the right thing to do and you want to please God."

Putting her arm around Sandra's shoulders, Jessica spoke earnestly, "Remember this, God is *the only one* who will *never* let you down. He never breaks *His* promises and He can help in far greater ways than any human being ever can! God knows what's good for us and He's working for our eternal salvation." [98]

Sandra mulled things over quietly as they made their way to the other end of the boardwalk. The gulls continued their noisy show, skimming across the water, fighting over a little fish that one of them had managed to scoop up and then soaring back into the sky to fly high over all the fishing boats that bobbed up and down on the water.

What a beautiful world! Sandra thought quietly, looking out over the harbour. The colours of the sunset were deepening in intensity and a lovely cool breeze was drifting off the ocean. *I'm so happy to live here. I'm so happy I've met Jess!*

"I understand what you're saying," Sandra said at last. "I see how you can handle the bad things that happen to you and not become bitter. It's like you've found a way to look past everything to a wonderful vision in which none of these hurts and injustices matter. You've been...set free."

They had returned to the Manor entrance and it was time for Jess to go. She held out her arms to Sandra and they embraced.

"Be strong," Jess said, patting Sandra's back. "Our trials today are all part of God's plan to develop our faith and His characteristics in us. So forgive and forget and follow the example that Jesus gave to us.[99]"

---

[98] 2 Corinthians 4:16-18; Romans 8:17-18,28
[99] Luke 9:23-25

Dinner in the Courtyard
Chapter Eighteen

Another lonely weekend came. Sandra was feeling rather down again on Saturday. She still felt sad for Peter and Jessica's loss and quite anxious about how she would ever pay her rent that month. She was disappointed in James, still confused by Brett's glance and wondering if she would ever find someone who really cared. With plenty of time to spare, she finished reading a novel, replied to a chatty email from one of her friends in Ontario, did a little tidying and watched two movies. The last movie made her feel ten times worse than before. It was a beautiful love story with a handsome young prince who was wonderfully charming *and remarkably devoted!* When it was over, she felt even more wretchedly alone!

Why do I do this to myself? she thought. *It feels so good while I'm watching, but afterwards my own life seems so incredibly deprived! I want some handsome prince to hold me close like that and promise that he'll love me forever...and mean it.* She grabbed the DVD out of the player and snapped it back into its case. *Where will I ever find him? If only it could be Brett – but he's not mine – and he's probably just another charmer. I want someone who's kind, and loyal, and passionately believes in forever- forever with me!* Sandra tossed the case on the floor in disgust. Then she bent over, picked up both movies and placed them on her kitchen counter. She would take them back to the library Monday morning.

Am I just feeding myself foolish expectations with all this 'candy-floss'? she wondered, wandering back into her living room. *Will such fantasy make me want something I can never have?* A new thought suddenly occurred to her. *Maybe I'm looking for the wrong things. Maybe I overlook the kind of men who would actually be faithful, and loyal, and kind. I've made such huge mistakes in the past…I don't want to go through that again.*

Sandra was too distraught to work on her kindergarten project. It was getting late in the evening and she didn't feel like getting into anything big. More than anything she just wanted a friend - someone to talk to. *Oh, well, I guess I might as well go to bed,* she thought, *although I'll be awake for hours thinking about that movie! Maybe I'll read the magazine I found in the recycling bin.*

Her glance fell on the Bible that Peter and Jess had given her. *No! Forget all this trashy stuff!* she told herself. *I'm going to read through Genesis tonight, if it kills me!*

Lying in bed, with her head propped up on the pillows and Tiger curled up by her side, Sandra read past midnight. She read right through Genesis – the whole book! *That really wasn't so hard,* she thought to herself, rolling over to turn off the light. *In fact, it was surprisingly interesting. I loved the story of Joseph. He certainly had to forgive and forget! If only there were more brothers like him.* With a smile she decided, *I think I'll start Exodus tomorrow.*

Sunday morning she tried calling Jessica to see if Peter needed any help the next day, but there was no answer. *Oh right,* she recalled, *Jessica's at church. I should ask if I can come with her next Sunday. I'd like to find out what they do there. It's got to be better than staying home alone.*

After reading several chapters in Exodus, and being amazed by all the plagues God had brought upon Egypt for their refusal to let the Israelites leave, Sandra took a long walk down by the harbour. On the way home she picked up another bag of brown rice and a few discounted veggies. Instead of feeling depressed that this was all she could afford, she reminded herself, *This is probably a lot more than what many children in Third-World countries have for dinner!*

Tuesday morning Sandra was back at James' apartment to clean. After his angry remarks at her door, she wondered if there might be note saying he'd found another housekeeper. How would she ever pay her rent if he did? It was due in a week and she wasn't even close to having enough money saved.

There was no message on the computer desk but the envelopes of money and the handwritten grocery list confirmed that James expected things to continue, at least for now.

An extra special recipe caught Sandra's eye that morning and when she had finished most of the housework for the day, she made clam chowder, with a leek and potato soup base. She left a tray of biscuits on top of the oven, covered with a cloth and instructions on how long to bake them. Since black cherries were on sale at the grocery store that week, she made frozen cherry yogurt with a peach swirl! Mmmm, did it smell good! After pouring it into a plastic container and setting it into the freezer, Sandra licked out the blender. She didn't feel guilty about doing that; it would just go to waste otherwise. *Yum! Hope you like it, James,* she thought. *Maybe you'll forgive me for inviting you to the Kingdom Feast. I sure hope so!*

As Sandra polished the big windows and gazed across the calm, shining blue water, she found herself thinking again about her brother. It had been a couple of weeks since Laurie had promised to take her sailing on his yacht. Even after Jessica's inspiring words and the new vision she was creating, Sandra found it difficult to cast her old daydreams aside. *I hope Laurie doesn't let me down again,* she thought wearily. *Surely after all the cancelled dinners and get-togethers, this time our plans will be a priority! I can't wait to sail in his yacht...*

Vacuuming the living room, Sandra idly drifted off to imagine a warm welcome at the cottage; the beaming smile on Laurie's face; the friendly glow on Michelle's. "Ready for this big adventure, Sis?" Laurie was asking. "Michelle and I are so happy to have you come along."

"I brought some Gravol, just in case you get sea sick," Michelle said with genuine concern. "It's supposed to be a calm, beautiful day, but you just never know for sure."

"Thanks so much for thinking of me," she could hear herself saying. "I've never sailed before, but I'm really looking forward to it."

As she put the vacuum away, and started collecting the old newspapers, she could see herself being escorted to the yacht, her kind brother extending his hand to help her on. "Steady now," he was saying, holding her arm, "Just a little jump and...*there you go*. What do you think? Is this good enough for my sister?"

"It's beautiful!" she was saying, looking out over the sparkling blue water. "This is a dream come true!"

"And it's only just begun," Laurie chuckled kindly.

Sandra stacked all the papers by the door and picked up the duster.

"Just you wait and see what we're going to have for dinner!" Michelle chimed in pleasantly. "We have a famous New York chef aboard! I hope you like sirloin steak? Laurie thought you would."

"Oh yes," Sandra imagined herself responding. "It's my favourite!"

"I know!" Laurie laughed. "We always used to order steak for our birthdays."

"You remembered?" Sandra smiled; her heart aglow with wonder. She reached high to remove all the cobwebs in the corners of James' living room.

"Of course!" Laurie smiled, giving her a hug. "That's why I ordered it for our first meal together. This is a long overdue celebration!"

As Sandra walked over to dust the computer desk, she could almost feel the ocean breeze, soft and balmy against her face. Even though she'd never sailed before, from the movies that she'd watched and books that she'd read, she could well imagine the gentle, rhythmic motion of the waves, hear the seagulls cry and smell that delicious sirloin steak searing on the barbeque!

Hmm, she thought, making a slight change to her dream as she picked up a cloth to polish the computer monitor, *maybe we'll have a small luncheon first, with hot biscuits, imported wine and a vast array of cheese. Ah! That's nice!* With the wind ruffling her hair and billowing through the ruffled, white skirt that she wished she owned, she sat with the others around a food-laden table, munching happily on a biscuit as they set out to sea.

"And how are you doing financially?" she heard Laurie inquire. "It can't be easy on a part-time salary."

"Well no, it's been rather tight," she admitted.

"Really?" Laurie asked, with such genuine compassion in his deep blue eyes. "Look Sandra, if you ever need to come and stay with us for a few years, you know we'd be delighted to have you…"

Stacking all James' pens and pencils into one neat pile, Sandra savoured the beautiful feelings of acceptance, devotion and concern. As always, it lifted her spirits… only… she wished one day *it would be real!*

There was still the bookshelf to dust. Sandra glanced at the family photo she had become so familiar with, as she polished the glass. "You won't even go to your own brother's wedding," she remarked despairingly to the lanky, teenage James. "You don't know how lucky you are! You have a mom and a dad and two brothers. And you *even* have nephews and nieces and… soon you'll have *two* sisters-in-law!"

It was evening when Sandra returned to her own apartment. Reaching into the box of supplies Jessica had given her she took out a tin of tuna. "I think we'll skip the brown rice tonight," she said to Tiger. "I've detoxed long enough. Maybe we can have a tuna and Kraft dinner casserole for a splurge. Would you like to share that with me?"

Tiger purred happily. Sandra ran out to the grocery store and was back in twenty minutes with a package of Kraft dinner. Turning on a pot of water to boil, she opened the box and pulled out the package of cheese. Then the phone rang.

"Hey, Sandra," a friendly voice said nervously, "I'm just wondering…there's so much chowder… I can't possibly eat it all myself. Do you want to join me for dinner in the courtyard? Or… have you already eaten?"

"No, I haven't eaten. I was just making dinner," she said, somewhat taken aback.

"More rice?"

"No…um… *tuna casserole,*" she smiled slowly. "But… I'd be happy to join you…*right now?*"

"Just give me ten minutes to cook these biscuits," James said cheerfully. "That's right, isn't it? I've got the oven on. I just have to stick them in…." There was a clatter and then an "oops!"

"Did they all fall on the floor?" Sandra giggled nervously.

There was a pause and shuffling noise before James answered. "Ah, well…" he began sheepishly, "umm, yes. I guess I shouldn't have tried to do this with one hand. But this floor's so nice and clean, they'll be okay. Five-second rule – right?"

Sandra laughed. "Do you want some help carrying everything down?"

"Sure," James replied.

The biscuits were rather misshapen but beautifully golden brown. Sandra felt quite awkward meeting James again, after the argument they'd had, but she could instantly tell that he was trying to make things right. James was more courteous than ever, pulling out one of the metal chairs for her to sit down in and taking it upon himself to serve out the meal. When everything was laid in order, he looked over solemnly.

"I want to apologize for the other night," he began earnestly. "I've been feeling badly ever since. I shouldn't have been so upset. I hope I didn't scare you... like...*I scared your cat.*"

Sandra giggled. "You scared my cat?"

James laughed nervously. "It was under your couch the whole time, shivering with fear and staring at me with these *big* saucer eyes! It's a good thing you didn't have a dog, or he might have taken my leg off – and it would have served me right!"

The thought of Tiger staring fearfully at James from under the couch was inexplicably funny to Sandra. She laughed until the tears rolled out of her eyes. James joined in and the laughter became contagious between them. It was several minutes before they could stop.

Finally they settled down to enjoy the chowder. The tension had been released.

"Do you know how good this is?" James remarked sincerely. "Man, I wish I had someone cooking for me *every* night!" A look of embarrassment crossed James' face and he quickly added, "Ah, that's the life of a bachelor – pros and cons to everything."

"What are the pros?" Sandra asked impulsively. *Oops, that might be a rather personal question!* she chided herself.

James was still flushed. "Umm," he pondered evasively, looking down at his spoonful of chowder. "I'm sure there are some, but I can't really think of any at the moment." Then he looked up candidly and shrugged. "It's not like I've chosen to be on my own," he explained. "It's just that nothing's ever worked out."

There was an uncomfortable silence as they both sipped the chowder and munched on the biscuits. Then James asked, "What about you? Are you on your own?"

Sandra laughed, glowing pink herself. "I am," she admitted. "I've had a few relationships that have come and gone but I've always been rather occupied with helping my mom, getting through school, making ends meet and... *finding my brother.*"

"Does your brother live out here?" James asked, passing Sandra another biscuit. She could tell they were both relieved to change the subject.

"Yes."

"What's his name?"

"Laurie. Laurie Carrington."

"Do you have much to do with him?"

"No," she admitted. "So far, every time we've planned to get together he has had to cancel for one reason or another. He and Michelle work pretty hard," she explained. "But just recently he invited me to spend the first weekend in July with them. We're going to sail around Cape Breton on his yacht. I'm dying to see him again! It's been eighteen years."

"Eighteen years?" James replied with astonishment.

Sandra nodded. "When I lived in Ontario it was even more difficult to get together."

James swallowed hard. "Does he look like you?"

Sandra shrugged, sipping another spoonful of the chowder. *It's tasty,* she thought. *And it's so good to eat something other than rice!* "I don't really know what he looks like now," she confessed. "When he left, his hair was dark and curly and he had the bluest eyes. He was on all the sports teams and girls were always phoning to talk to him."

"Was he good to you?" James inquired, serving himself another bowl of chowder. Noticing that Sandra's bowl was close to empty, he asked politely, "Would you like a refill?"

Nodding eagerly, Sandra held out her bowl. James filled it.

"Thanks," she said, setting her bowl back down on the table. "He was never *bad* to me," she recalled. "But I was so much younger that we didn't have a lot to do with each other. I can remember he sometimes would read me books on the weekends. And I know he tried to teach me how to catch a ball, but I wasn't all that coordinated..."

James was listening and asking questions in such a concerned way, that Sandra soon spilled out her whole life story. She told him what it was like to grow up without a father, not really understanding why he had left, or why he didn't keep in touch, and how she had learned to clean house for her mom, since her mother worked full time. "And then my mom died just before I finished university," Sandra relayed. "She was killed in a car accident."

"Sandra, that's all so tragic!" James exclaimed. "It's so ...sad! I can't imagine not having a family," he said sympathetically. "I'd feel so... *alone.*"

Sandra didn't respond for a moment. There was sincere compassion in James' hazel-brown eyes. His voice sounded so earnest...and caring... *But would you really miss your family?* she wondered. *Are you really close to them? Every single member – or just your mom?*

"Tiger keeps me company," she smiled, realizing she had portrayed a rather dismal life story. She tried to lighten things up with an impish remark, "So whatever you do," she teased, "be *very* nice to my little pussy cat!"

James laughed. "Believe me, if your cat ever looks at me like that again, I won't be able to keep a straight face!"

Sandra giggled. She enjoyed James' animated way of expressing himself.

"Ready for the frozen yogurt?" he asked with a grin, his brown eyes sparkling. "I'll just have to get it out of my freezer."

"I'd love some!" Sandra replied.

"I'll be back in a sec, then," he said, getting up from his chair.

It was only a few minutes before James returned with the container, spoons and a couple of bowls.

"I'm amazed you're so slim," he remarked as he scooped out the pink, swirled, creamy dessert. "You ate as much as I did tonight."

It wasn't entirely true. Sandra had had just as many biscuits, but not a *third* bowl of chowder. She didn't respond and James handed her a bowl of the frozen cherry yogurt without further prodding.

"Anyway, I hope you understand," he said, scooping out a generous helping for himself, "that I fully regret blowing up at you last week. My family is fairly intense," he smiled, "not everyone can put up with us, or understand where we're coming from. I wrongfully assumed that Peter had put you up to give me that invitation...and...I have to admit... I was shocked to think you may have fallen for his *crazy ideas."*

"Crazy?" Sandra clarified with surprise, holding a pink spoonful up to her lips. "Are they only *his* ideas?"

"No... I guess not," James admitted uncomfortably. "But Peter was the first one to bring them into my family."

"And how does the rest of your family feel about it?"

Finishing off a big spoonful of the creamy dessert, James sighed. It was a deep, heartfelt sigh. "Sandra...," he tried to explain, "my older brother, Andrew, used to be the pastor of the biggest church in town. Everyone really respected him. He was an awesome pastor; the perfect guy for the job. I was a member of that same congregation ever since we both moved out here in our teens. We were at that church for over twelve years! When my parents came out to Nova Scotia, a year and a half ago, they became members too. It was great! We did a lot of good in this community.

"Then Peter came along," James said, digging fervently into the frozen yogurt as a bitter tone came into his voice. "He convinced my brother Andrew that he was wrong in a few areas of doctrine – and the next thing I knew *my brother Andrew had resigned!* He gave up his vocation, his house, his reputation and now, he and his wife and their *five* kids are living with my parents! He's had to go back to college at thirty-five, to try and become *an English teacher.* He's lost everything he's worked for in the last decade. It's *totally* ruined his life!"

"And what do your parents think of it?" Sandra asked.

"Oh, they're messed up too," James said regretfully. "Everyone in that house is trying to sort things out. It's mass confusion! None of them have actually joined Peter's church yet – but they go there all the time! I hope they'll see it for what it is and change their minds! I wish everything could be the way it used to be."

Looking thoughtful, Sandra tried to merge James' view of the situation with Peter and Jessica's. She could understand now, why James felt badly about it all, but was it truly *confusion* that Peter had brought to his family, or just...*change?*

"I understand how you feel," she said kindly, scooping up the last, pink spoonful in her bowl. "It must be hard to see your family go through such turmoil. But I haven't yet found anything to be confusing in what Jessica's told me. Maybe that's simply because it's *all new...* to me," she admitted candidly. "I don't have strong opinions on what is right or wrong."

"You can be easily misled," James warned.

"I can," Sandra admitted, and then a sudden thought came to her. She smiled invitingly. "But not if I have someone to talk it over with."

"Well it won't be me," James said firmly, shaking his head. "I can be as easily led astray as you. I'm not qualified to discuss religious matters."

Is that what you're afraid of? Sandra wondered, remembering Peter's remarks to his brother in the courtyard. *Are you afraid you'll be led away from truth or are you afraid to try and find it?* "But... you're *sure* that Peter's wrong?" she questioned.

"I really don't want to talk about Peter," James said flatly, shaking his head again.

"Did you hear he and Jess lost the house?" Sandra asked, not using Peter's name, but suddenly thinking James might want to know about the situation.

"What? I thought the offer had been accepted!"

"It was conditional on financing," she told him, "and his partners in Australia who were supposed to buy out his company, defaulted on the agreement. They're saying his company isn't worth as much anymore since he's not there to manage it. Therefore they can't afford to give him any more money."

"But they have all his heavy equipment!" James replied. "I hope he's not going to let them get away with that."

"I don't think he sees it that way," Sandra told him calmly. "He and Jessica say that they'd rather keep a good relationship with them all, than push to get their money out."

"See, my brother is crazy!" James sighed ruefully, shaking his head. "I really should have a word with him."

He stood up and collected the empty dessert bowls. "That was amazing, Sandra!" he smiled. "That cherry yogurt scores a ten! And listen, I don't think it's fair for you to do all that work and then have to make dinner again for yourself. From now on, whatever you make – you take half with you." He paused and then added, "Perhaps we can even have dinner together again…once in a while - if that works for you."

"Thanks," Sandra said, dumbfounded. 'That's a very kind offer." She hesitated for a moment and then clarified meekly, "I guess that means I still have a job?"

James looked at her with a measure of perplexity. *"Of course* you do! Why would you think otherwise?"

Sandra's blue eyes sparkled brightly. "I just needed to know for sure."

With an amused smile, James shook his head as if to say he would never understand women. Then piling everything on the tray, they walked into the Manor together. James pressed the up arrow at the elevator.

He can be so nice, Sandra mused, after they said goodbye at the second floor. The elevator continued to climb to the fourth. *I'm not afraid of his intensity; it's what I admire in Peter. But Peter is intense in a caring way. James seems to be intense in an antagonistic way... at least towards Peter! I understand now, why he feels Peter has messed things up, but does he really think Peter has done this to ruin their lives?*

As Sandra walked into her apartment and shut the door behind her, she pondered the situation. *Either James knows something about Peter that I don't, or he's lost sight of his brother's true motivation.*

A Birthday at the Bryant's
Chapter Nineteen

On Wednesday Sandra worked with Peter and Jessica. She was thankful they had called. Her rental fees were due in just a little over a week and so far she was still seven hundred dollars short. *Hopefully Peter will pay me today's wage on Friday,* she thought, *as he's done before. But will I get enough work this week to make another six hundred dollars?*

Sandra remembered to pray during the few quiet moments she had for lunch. "Dear God," she whispered, "I'm so thankful for the people you've brought into my life – especially Peter and Jessica. I'm so thankful for all the promises you've made and how you've invited me to become involved with your plans for the future. But please help me find a way to pay my rent. You promised to provide for those who seek Your kingdom and Your righteousness, and I'm in desperate need of Your help! And please, if it's possible, help me to meet up with my brother again…as soon as possible! Please don't let him cancel this time. In Jesus' name. Amen."

Peter's regular crew spent the remainder of the day mowing lawns and trimming grass around the gardens. Sandra's job was to do the watering. Since there hadn't been any rain for two weeks, the ground was parched and dry.

When they dropped Sandra off at the Manor around dinner time, Jessica said, "Hey Sandra, its Peter's birthday tomorrow and his mom is making a special meal. Would you like to work with us again tomorrow and join us for the party? I know it's our Bible study evening, but…"

A special meal, another day of work, a chance to meet James' family and see if they are as confused as he says they are?!

There was no hesitation on Sandra's part. "I'd love to!" she exclaimed.

Puffy white clouds began moving in the next morning and the forecast called for heavy rain later on in the evening. Every member of the gardening crew was very hopeful it would rain. All the gardens needed a good soaking. Sandra and Jess spent a few hours dead-heading endless peony plants and cutting back tall, wilted iris blooms. Then the entire crew drove out to Peter's parent's house for the afternoon to get the gardens ready for the wedding. The wedding was only three weeks away!

Sandra marvelled at the Bryant's family home. It was a large, purple-trimmed log house, surrounded by tall pines swaying in the strong breeze. In an elevated position on a low cliff, their home overlooked the vast, white-capped ocean. The view was amazing! The house looked warm and inviting. No one was there when they arrived so Peter and Derrick left their music on in the van, with the back hatch up, much to Sandra's delight. She quite enjoyed their music.

"All right, Jess," Peter said, surveying the grounds, "how about you and Derrick take charge of the rock gardens. Allan and I will figure out where to put the marquee and level the ground. And Sandra, maybe you could work on the stone pathway?"

Everyone grabbed the tools they needed and headed off to their locations while Peter took a moment to show Sandra what he wanted her to do.

"It's really overgrown," he said, lifting up one of the flat slate rocks. He pointed to the long, tubular grass roots that lay matted underneath. "This is a tough job," he apologized, as Sandra's eyes followed the length of the stone pathway all the way down to the sandy beach. "We need all these roots pulled out under every slab and the whole path needs to be edged. But if you get started on the roots, Allan and I will come and help in a few hours."

Sandra was quite happy to have an important job that she felt she could do. The work was somewhat hard and tedious, but the setting was stunning. As she worked steadily from stone to stone, she often looked up to enjoy the view. Billowing, white clouds were still moving in from the ocean, but there hadn't yet been a drop of rain. Huge waves thundered noisily against the enormous rocks along the beach and sometimes she could even feel the salty spray. The restless, slate-blue ocean filled the horizon as far as she could see. Seagulls squawked and glided on the fast-moving wind currents, soaring up and down all along the shore.

Soar like the seagulls, Sandra mused happily to herself, as she tugged away at the grass roots. *I love God's creation! It's too precise and majestic to have ever just happened by chance. I'm happy to be living in it. And I love working in all these gorgeous places!*

She looked up for a moment to see Jessica and Derrick arranging pots of plants in various places, discussing where each would look best. The wind knocked one pot over, rolling it along the ground and Derrick ran to get it. Sandra knew that Peter had great confidence in Jessica's sense of colour and always gave those decisions to her. Derrick, with his ripped jeans and unshaven appearance, was the powerhouse in many of the operations, always ready to do the heaviest jobs and carry out Peter's exact instructions carefully. Allan was young and inexperienced, and usually not a part of the crew during the school week, but when he worked he did his part well. As Sandra continued to move stones and pull roots, she watched Peter patiently explaining to the young teen where the tent was to sit and pointing out the uneven places that needed to be filled. A load of cedar shaving sat nearby, covered tightly with a tarp. Peter planned to spread those shavings over the grounds within the marquee. Peter was a good manager. There was no doubt that everyone highly respected his decisions. Working from place to place with them, Sandra had been very impressed by some of the gardens Peter had designed. It seemed to her that he had a knack for transforming the flattest piece of ground into a naturalised work of art.

Is Peter unique in his family? Sandra wondered. *Or are all three brothers just as special in their own way? He cares about James so much. Does James deserve that kind of affection? Does James care for anyone else in that same way?*

After many wheelbarrows of soil had been dug, transported, dumped and levelled into place, Peter and Allan joined Sandra on the pathway. Peter began to edge the grass on either side while Allan helped Sandra pull roots. Soft strains of music floated across the lawn, when the wind wasn't blowing it in the opposite direction, and Sandra suddenly recognized a song. It was the song that Jessica had told her about; the song she would always think of as, "Peter's Prayer". Hearing Peter join in the chorus, Sandra looked up to see the sad, distant look on his face.

"Do you like that song?" Peter asked, catching her eye.

"I do," Sandra admitted. "And Jessica told me that you think of James when you hear it."

"Yeah, I do," Peter nodded regretfully, stomping carefully with one foot on the edge-trimmer. "You know, I once was blind," he admitted. "It took me over ten years to accept that maybe I didn't have it all figured out like I thought I did, and that maybe the things my friends were telling me were worth investigation. So, I completely understand how James feels. I felt the same way. All I can do is pray that God will work in James' life like He did for me. Only God can open the eyes of the blind."

"I feel for you…both," Sandra said, unsure of what to say.

Peter sighed. "You know, Sandra," he said thoughtfully, "in all honesty, I think everyone needs to experience an impossible situation in their life. It's the only way we learn to have faith."

Sandra nodded but she didn't respond. *He's thankful for this pain!* she marvelled. *Will I ever learn to think like Peter and Jess? They're on such a different level than I am."*

Picking up the little tufts of grass, Peter threw them into the wheelbarrow. "There are a lot of good songs on that CD," he said. "I have an extra copy if you want it."

"That would be wonderful!" Sandra smiled.

Around four o'clock, Andrew's children jumped off the school bus and came running over to greet their uncle and wish him a Happy Birthday. Peter gratefully accepted hugs and kisses from his teenage nieces and lanky, twin nephews. He picked up the youngest child to spin her around. She shrieked with delight. The next time Sandra looked up she saw that the twins were carting off the wheelbarrow of grass to the compost bin, the youngest girl was collecting the plastic pots that were scattered all over the lawn and the teenagers were watering the plants that Jessica had put into the ground. *They'll all probably be part of the landscaping crew in a few years!* she thought with a smile.

Ten minutes later, Andrew, Peter's brother arrived home from university and then his wife and parents drove in together. Of course they all greeted Peter right away with hearty birthday congratulations.

Before going inside, Andrew and his wife strolled over to where Sandra was working. They introduced themselves cordially and Sandra took off her gloves to shake hands, glad to make their acquaintance. Andrew was very much like the picture she'd often viewed in James' apartment, only somewhat greyer and a lot stockier. His wife, Lisa, was a pleasant-looking woman, as round as her husband, with short, brown hair and happy, blue eyes.

After trading pleasantries, Andrew said, "So I hear you're working for both my brothers - a gardener for Peter and a housekeeper for James!" With a twinkle in his eye he asked, "Which one is easier to work for?"

"Andrew!" Lisa laughed. "Don't ask her a question like that!" Smiling at Sandra, she said, "Just be glad you don't work for Andrew. He never stops!"

But Andrew wasn't done teasing. "Come on," he prodded merrily, "my guess is that you come home from gardening exhausted, but James' place must be so clean it's hard to find enough to do!"

Sandra laughed. "I love working for both," she smiled. "James also pays me to cook – and I love cooking. Peter's work is all outside in beautiful gardens, so, I'm perfectly content."

Andrew laughed.

"You must be very good at what you do to meet James' high standards!" Lisa replied.

Sandra smiled at the compliment. "He's been good to me," she said sincerely.

"He's been good to us too," Andrew nodded. "If it wasn't for James, I wouldn't be back at university."

"James has been *very* generous!" Andrew's wife agreed earnestly, taking her husband's arm. She smiled up at him, "All the Bryants have hearts of gold!"

Andrew laughed and gave Lisa a kiss on the cheek. "Well, we'd better help get the birthday dinner ready," he said, turning to leave. "Great job on the pathway!" he encouraged Sandra.

As Sandra went back to weeding the pathway, she couldn't stop thinking about what Andrew and Lisa had just said. *James has helped them out?* she pondered. *It must have been a generous contribution if it has made the difference between Andrew returning to university or not. How surprising! James seemed so disappointed that Andrew resigned and needed to go back to school...and yet he's supporting him...*

Maybe James does care about his brothers after all, she considered. *Maybe he does have a heart of gold. Maybe I've misunderstood...*

When it was time to wash up and go in for dinner, Sandra gazed eagerly around the thick, wooden walls of the log home. The hallway entrance opened up on one side to a cozy living room area with the tallest stone fireplace Sandra had ever seen. Plenty of ocean-view windows flooded the house with light. An open pine staircase led to the lofts above. On the other side of the hallway, a large, multi-coloured Tiffany lamp hung above a long oak table in the kitchen. *This is a lovely home,* Sandra thought to herself. *It feels so warm and inviting! James – you're so lucky!*

Jessica showed her to the bathroom, where Sandra could clean up and change for the party. In the small cedar-lined room, there was a spicy-wooden aroma. Looking up, Sandra noticed a pretty painting of a white peony. She leaned closer to read the verse that was inscribed below the petals. It said, "For our light affliction, which is but for a moment, is working for us a far more exceeding and eternal weight of glory.[100]"

As Sandra scrubbed all the dirt from her hands and arms, she thought about the verse on the wall. It reminded her of the conversation she'd had with Jessica walking along the boardwalk. *That's how Jess soars above all her worries,* Sandra considered. *She's focused on what is to come, not the here and now. I need that perspective.*

Changing out of her work clothes, Sandra pulled on the dress she had brought with her - a soft, comfortable denim dress. Taking out a straightener from her bag, she fixed her fly-away hair.

When Sandra entered the kitchen, Jessica introduced her to Mr. and Mrs. Bryant and all the children. James' parents were getting on in years, but still able to get around without much difficulty. Sadie and Sue were in their early teens and the oldest of Andrew and Lisa's five. Jake and Zach, the twins, had just turned ten. With their brown eyes, blond crew-cuts and mischievous

---

[100] 2 Corinthians 4:16-18

smiles, they both looked like miniature Peters. Sandra was sure she would never be able to tell them apart. Little Esther was the youngest, very sweet, slightly plump and with sparkling eyes like her mom.

Under a brightly coloured Tiffany lamp, Sandra took a place at the long oak table with all the others. Looking around, she marvelled that thirteen people could fit so comfortably together. Then she noticed one place-setting in front of an empty chair. *Is it for James?* she wondered. There was no talk of waiting for him. Gazing sadly at the empty chair, Sandra noticed that Mrs. Bryant, who was sitting beside her, was looking in the same direction.

Mrs. Bryant's white hair framed a rather lined, but still attractive face. Mr. Bryant was tall and stocky with short gray hair and eyes that twinkled with amusement. *Who does James favour?* Sandra wondered, studying his parents carefully as they chatted with their family. *He doesn't really look like either,* she decided. Discreetly, she observed Mrs. Bryant again. *Maybe he has his mother's kind, brown eyes,* she decided. *Both James and Peter have those eyes - and perhaps James has her slender build as well.*

Regardless of the empty bowl and chair, there was a festive mood that evening with a clear focus on Peter and Jess. After Andrew gave thanks to God for the meal, Sandra watched everything with James' words echoing in the back of her mind. However, if there was confusion or regret due to Andrew's career change and Peter's crazy ideas, Sandra didn't see the evidence. The love and the bantering that went on between them all brought warmth to her heart. *Oh James,* she thought sadly, *how can you miss out on all this? If only you had come. I wish you were here!*

Clam chowder was one of the many wonderful items on the menu, and Sandra was pleased to discover it was a family favourite. Sadly, she noticed that the big crock-pot which was full of a rich cream soup was next to a tiny one, which was never served at all. *I bet that little crock-pot has a Heart-Smart recipe in it,* she thought, *made just for James.*

The birthday cake was brought in, once the plates had been cleared away. Thirty flaming candles bordered the outside and a lonesome male figurine stood in the middle. "It's the last birthday you'll have as a bachelor," Peter's mom teased merrily, setting the cake down in front of him.

Jessica draped herself around Peter's shoulders, as he leaned forward to blow out the candles. "Save one for me," she begged.

After a quick blow, Peter left *five* burning brightly.

"Five!" Jess exclaimed teasingly, with her cheek against his. "Are there that many special flames in your life?"

Laughing, Peter blew again carefully and this time *all* appeared to be extinguished. But after a flicker one little flame recovered. "There you go!" he told her, looking up with devotion. "One flame I'll *never,* ever blow out!"

Jessica kissed Peter on the cheek and he kissed her in return.

"Hey now," Andrew called out with feigned disapproval. "None of that till the wedding! Kids cover your eyes!"

"Dad!" Andrew' eldest daughter retorted with a laugh. "It's not like we haven't seen anyone kiss before!"

As Peter cut the cake and Jess served it out, a tall, lean figure sauntered quietly into the kitchen.

"Uncle James!" a happy voice rang out.

"Anything left for one overworked and underfed man?"

"You came!" Mrs. Bryant exclaimed happily as Jake left the table and hurled himself towards his uncle. Zach came running over as well, to give him a hug. "I thought you had to work till nine!"

"I got off early," James replied, returning his nephew's embraces. "Hey guys," he laughed. "Look what I have!"

The two nephews stood back in eager anticipation as James searched in his pockets. At last he produced a neon-coloured hockey puck.

"Ah, cool!" Zach said. "Can we play tonight?"

"It might be kind of late tonight," James replied reluctantly. "But I'm coming over this weekend and we can have a shoot-out."

"Yeah!" they both cheered.

"Okay, sit up now guys," Andrew called out. "Let Uncle James have something to eat."

Embracing his mom, James turned to find his place at the table. Suddenly he noticed Sandra. A look of astonishment came over his face.

"Jess invited me," Sandra tried to mouth across the room, pointing to Jessica at the same time.

James nodded to show he understood but he still looked surprised.

"Hi, James," Peter spoke up quietly, as his brother took his seat near the twins. "I was hoping we'd see you today."

"Gardens look good," James mumbled, avoiding Peter's eyes.

I can't believe how glad I am to see him, Sandra thought, as James unfolded the cloth napkin that had been beside his plate. *I feel like I want to run over and give him a big hug just like his nephews did. How silly! Why am I feeling like this?*

She considered the matter, as she watched James' mother scoop chowder from the mini crock-pot and set it down beside him. "Just for you, dear," Mrs. Bryant said with a smile.

Am I falling...? she asked herself incredulously. *No, I don't think so. James is a good guy to have as a friend, but I don't think I'm attracted to him...not in that way. But I do like looking after him and I care about him...a lot!*

Sandra noticed that James took a moment to pray before delving into the chowder. *Hmm, that's interesting,* she thought. *He didn't give thanks to God when we ate dinner together.*

Everyone began asking James how he was doing, whether he still liked his new job and where he had found the glow-in-the-dark hockey puck! Only Peter sat back silently, listening intently, but not asking any questions.

"Hey, look at the sunset!" Sadie called out. Everyone turned to look out the large glass windows that framed the ocean. The gray clouds that had been rolling in all day were streaked with soft pink highlights and pale purple shadows. Looking out the other windows toward the west, Sandra could see that the whole sky was ablaze with colour! Andrew grabbed his camera and he and Lisa ran out with their children.

"Come on, Peter," Jess said. "Let's have a quick look."

Sandra felt a little awkward remaining behind with only James and his parents but she wasn't finished her cake.

"So, is the convention still on?" Mr. Bryant asked his son, after the others had left.

"Dad, of course it is," James replied curtly.

"And are they still putting pressure on you to go?" his mother asked.

James looked up uncomfortably. "Mom, I *want* to go to this convention," he said. "It isn't a holiday. We'll be meeting with lots of representatives that we do business with. If I don't go I'll be completely out of the loop."

"We just find it hard to believe you'd miss your brother's wedding," Mr. Bryant explained gently, as his wife rose from the table to clear the dessert dishes.

James said nothing in reply and Sandra could feel the tension rising. Feeling uncomfortable, she took the last mouthful of cake and stood up to help.

As Sandra helped load the dishwasher, the silence in the kitchen was almost unbearable. She was so thankful when Peter and Jess came back in.

"Wow! They'll get some good pictures from that sky," Peter exclaimed, as he sat back down in his chair. "I've never seen it so red!"

"Let's order a sunset like that for our wedding," Jessica said with a laugh, picking up a basket of bread and setting it down closer to James.

"If only we could," Peter replied.

James savoured his second bowl of chowder and another slice of bread, as Jessica helped Mrs. Bryant and Sandra load the dishwasher.

"The gardens do look fantastic, Pete," Mr. Bryant said. "You and your crew sure can turn an overgrown jungle into a posh resort."

Peter laughed quietly. "Glad you're happy with it, Dad."

"So when are we setting up the marquee?"

"I'll be picking it up the day before we get married."

"So, in about two weeks from now," his father replied.

From there the conversation seemed to wane. For a few minutes no one spoke. There was just the clatter of dishes going into the dishwasher, the shuffling of feet walking back and forth and James' spoon clinking against his bowl. *Please someone speak*, Sandra thought, but she couldn't think of anything to say. What had been such a happy, fun-filled place only a few minutes before, was now heavy with uneasiness. Looking over at James, Sandra caught his eye. He pointed down at the bowl and mouthed the words, "Almost as good as yours."

Sandra smiled. James' compliments were healing-balm to her lonely heart.

The strained silence in the family continued. It made Sandra sad to think that James' presence had changed the merry mood. *He needs a friend,* she thought. *It must be hard for him to come here when he's the odd man out.*

At last Peter spoke up. "Say, James," he began awkwardly, "how's the chowder? Mom said she made you the healthy version."

James didn't look at his brother but he did reply, "It's great! I'm getting used to the healthy version of everything! Sandra's been leaving me a meal once a week and I tell you, it's like going to the best restaurant in town!"

"Really?" Mrs. Bryant said, looking over with surprise at Sandra, who blushed bright red. "That's awfully nice of you, dear," she remarked.

Peter's question eased some of the tension. James had a question for him. With his eyes focused on the bowl of chowder in front of him, he asked, "I hear that you've lost your house – the one you had an offer on."

Peter nodded with a puzzled look of surprise.

He wonders how James knows about this, Sandra thought to herself. *I hope it was all right for me to tell.*

"You're not going to just let those guys off the hook that easily, are you? How do you know they aren't just making things sound worse than they are?" Without waiting for an answer, James pressed his case. "They have all your heavy machinery, an established clientele base, and Jono took over your house and your sports car for next to nothing! Regardless of whether or not they're making money, they need to compensate you for all you've put into it. You've done enough for them already."

"They're my friends," Peter tried to explain, hesitantly. "They have paid me a considerable amount over the last year and I..."

"But Pete, you're getting married," James persisted. "Look, I know a really good lawyer that I deal with all the time. If

I ask him, he'll work things out for you in a fair way for both sides."

"I really appreciate your concern," Peter told him earnestly. "But Jess and I have talked this through and we're content to rent something, until the business grows here..."

With his arms folded and a studious look on his face, James pondered his brother's words. "I just hope they're not taking advantage of you," he said kindly.

Peter was quiet for a moment or two, resting his chin on his hands. Jessica had slowly made her way back into the chair beside him. She slipped her arm through his.

"It's like this...James," Peter explained quietly, looking straight at his brother. "I've preached Christ to them - forgiveness and love. I want them to find the hope that I have and realize that money and possessions don't even begin to compare with eternal life in God's Kingdom. I've got *to live* what I preach."

James looked over at Jessica. "And you're okay with that?" he asked.

"Yes," she replied gently. "I think Peter is doing the right thing. We'll be okay."

With a perturbed look on his face, James sat back in his chair. Sandra's heart went out to him. She wished there was some way she could give him a little friendly support. James seemed so alone in the midst of his family. *It's a difficult issue,* she thought, *and I'm not sure who's right and who's wrong. But I know that James only spoke up because...he cares; he cares about Peter and Jess. He does care about his family. I'm so proud he came tonight and that he actually tried to offer some assistance. Everyone needs to be thankful for that!*

However, silence hovered over the table. There wasn't any immediate appreciation for James' gallant attempt to reach out.

Empathy overwhelmed Sandra's heart. She wished she could catch James' eye and give him a smile but he wasn't looking over. Somehow she had to let him know how she felt. Seeing that he had finished eating, she decided to walk over and collect his dishes. Reaching from behind to take his bowl with one hand, she gently squeezed his shoulder with the other. When James looked up, she smiled down kindly. James held her gaze for a second. Then Sandra noticed that James' mother was looking over. Quietly, she left his side and brought the dishes to the sink.

Andrew and his troops came rushing in. "We've got the most amazing pictures!" Esther shouted. "Have a look, Nana!"

From that moment on until all the dishes were cleaned and put away, everyone had a turn viewing the gorgeous pictures on the camera. The western sky had been ablaze with colour.

"We're going to put them on Facebook," Sadie, the oldest girl declared. "Maybe we'll even enter them into that contest..."

"We'll win for sure," little Esther chipped in.

Peter stood up. "Well, mom that was a truly magnificent dinner! Makes reaching a new decade not quite so painful. But, I'd better take Jess and Sandra home. They've worked hard the last two days."

"I'll take Sandra home," James offered quickly, rising from his chair. "We're both at the Manor."

Sandra noticed an amused glance pass between Mr. and Mrs. Bryant. *Don't get too excited,* she felt like saying. *I don't think this is anything more than friends.* James walked over to hug his parents and give his mom and dad a kiss goodbye. His nephews crowded around.

"We'll look after the puck for you, Uncle James," Zach assured him. "Don't forget about Saturday!"

"I'll meet you in the park at ten," James promised.

"Can we go fishing afterwards?" Jake begged.

"Guys, guys!" Andrew laughed. "One thing at a time. Uncle James took you fishing last weekend – remember?"

"Keep practising your shots," James encouraged the boys. "I want to get a work-out in that net!"

Esther came skipping over to hug both James and Sandra, while Sadie and Sue approached in a more dignified manner, but there were hugs all around.

"Thanks Mom. That was a delicious meal," James stated appreciatively, opening the door for Sandra.

"Just one minute, Sandra," Jessica said, as though she had just remembered something really important. Running quickly over to where her purse lay by the door, Jessica reached in and took out a fancy, lilac-coloured envelope. She handed it to Sandra, "I hope you can come," she said, smiling brightly.

What could this be? Sandra thought to herself absentmindedly as she took the envelope. *Another invitation?* Thanking everyone for the meal, she followed James out the door.

Two Invitations
Chapter Twenty

James seemed unusually quiet as he opened the passenger door of his black Pontiac and helped Sandra get in. The brilliant sunset colours had disappeared and tiny stars glittered now in between dark masses of cloud. It still had not rained. Sandra was sad to be leaving. Other than a few tense moments the Bryant's home had been such a warm, colourful, happy place – filled with family and love. *You're so lucky, James!* she thought, glancing over quickly. *Now I know how much they all care about you.* She smiled, remembering the special bowl of chowder and two excited nephews. *And...I know you love them too. You may be in the middle of a family disagreement, but at least you're supporting each other. I wish I had a family like yours!*

The Pontiac Grand Prix wasn't nearly as flashy as Brett's red, convertible Mustang and it was older, but both were far superior to Sandra's white Ford! She watched as James slid in and turned the key in the ignition. His strong, lean hands guided the car smoothly as they drove down the long, winding lane.

Once they were on the highway, Sandra curiously picked up the envelope Jessica had given her.

"May I turn on the reading light for a sec?" she asked.

James reached up and turned it on for her.

She thanked him. With the little overhead light shining down, Sandra noticed the silver seal on the back of the envelope. She realized Jessica had given her *a wedding invitation!*

"Oh my goodness!" she exclaimed in delight. "I'm invited to *the wedding!* I've never been to a wedding before in my life."

James didn't say a word. He kept on driving. Sandra pulled out the invitation and looked closely at the date on the pale purple card - July 5th. And then, it suddenly occurred to her that it was the *very weekend* she had been invited to Laurie's cottage.

"No-o!" she moaned in dismay. "Oh, no! I'm supposed to go to Laurie's cottage that weekend!" She paused to consider the options. "Oh, I can't miss visiting Laurie," she remarked regretfully, "not for anything! We've had to cancel so many times and I've waited years and years!" She sighed heavily. "He's promised to take me sailing on his yacht."

"Sounds like fun!" James smiled. "How ironic that we both have conflicts that weekend."

For quite some time they rode silently along the country roads. After a few more deep sighs, Sandra regretfully dismissed the wedding option. There was nothing more important than time with her brother. As the minutes ticked by, she began to wonder why James seemed so quiet. She tried to think of something to jumpstart the conversation. She thought about Jessica's answer to James' points about the thief on the cross. *But James doesn't want to have any more religious discussions with me,* she told herself. Searching for something to say, compassion welled up in her heart when she thought back on all that had happened that evening. They were just entering the outskirts of Stirling when she decided to speak up. "I felt for you tonight," she said gently. "I know you wanted to help Peter. I thought it was very nice of you to try."

"Thanks," James said flatly with a shrug. "But he won't listen to me."

"I'm sure he appreciated your concern. I know *I* would have."

James didn't reply but his hands clenched the steering wheel tightly.

"You have such a beautiful family," Sandra said earnestly. "I guess any family is going to have some disagreements...Even though there was tension, I could feel the love you all have for each other. Your nephews think you're the greatest!"

A smile crept over James' face. "They're good kids," he said. "We've had some fun times together." He paused with a sigh. "Peter and I used to be good friends too," he confided. "We used to see eye to eye on most things. But ever since he came back from Australia, it's like he's from another planet. I just don't understand him and he just doesn't understand me."

So, even James says they used to be good friends, Sandra surmised. *He does care; he's just bewildered and confused and he doesn't understand what now motivates all the others.*

"Do you want to understand him?" she asked gently.

James didn't reply or even glance in her direction. Finally, just before they reached the Manor, he asked, "Is your brother's full name *Laurence* Carrington?"

"Yes," she said, looking up with interest.

"Does he work for the Stirling Royal Bank?"

She nodded. "He's high up in management."

"I think I met him last week," James said quietly. "He and I are negotiating a business contract."

"*Seriously?* You met my brother?!" Sandra replied in astonishment. "What's he like? What does he look like? Is he nice?"

Having parked the car in the outdoor parking lot, James opened the door to get out. Sandra followed suit.

"He's an interesting man," James replied noncommittally, waiting for Sandra to catch up to him. "From what I've heard he's your typical workaholic…and…well known as a shrewd businessman."

"What does he look like?"

"Well, he's quite gray and a little overweight. He has the same eyes as you…" Mumbling, James added, "They're quite striking eyes!"

Sandra missed the indirect compliment; she was mentally attempting to update the *outdated* vision of her brother. The attempt failed. Was Laurie really fat and gray? "Is he nice?"

"I don't know him well enough to say yet," James answered, as they walked through the courtyard. "But I have to meet with him again next Wednesday for lunch and I thought..." he paused for a moment before finishing, "well, I was wondering if *you* might like to come along?"

Sandra froze in mid-step, completely astonished.

"Sorry," James said, reaching out to steady her. "Are you...okay?"

"I'd love to see him..." Sandra mused hesitantly, her mind racing. "But won't I be out of place at a business luncheon?"

"I don't see why you would," James told her. "Sometimes other guys bring their secretaries along. It might be a good opportunity for you to see him again...just in case your July plans don't work out."

"Can I think about it?" Sandra begged.

"Of course you can," James replied with a shrug. "Just leave me a note on Tuesday."

The Lunch Date

Chapter Twenty-One

After four lonely, quiet days, Sandra was still unable to make up her mind about the luncheon. The weather had been cold and rainy and she'd spent a lot of time inside. Her upcoming rental payment weighed heavily on her mind. With all the rain there hadn't even been any landscaping to do. She had done plenty of reading, enjoying Exodus and then the Gospel of Matthew. Tutoring Matt had been her only real social interaction. He was sounding out words with more accuracy and gaining confidence. He loved playing the reading games that Sandra made up for him.

"I've been telling his teacher about you," his mother had told her as they were leaving one night. "I've told them they should hire you as a Reading Specialist."

"Thanks," Sandra smiled. "I hope they do."

"Really?" Matt's mother clarified. "You'd be willing to work in a private school? It doesn't have the same benefits."

Sandra had a fairly good rapport with Matt's mom after several weeks of tutoring. "Patti," she said, "I'm a teacher and I've been gardening and housecleaning for the last two months just to get by. I would love a job in *any* primary school."

"I'll let them know," Patti said. "There's a teacher who may be going on maternity leave."

After Sandra finished cleaning and cooking for James on Tuesday, she left him a little message.

> James,
> I'm sorry I couldn't get the pen stain out of your blue shirt. I've taken it home with me to try one more time.

> It seems really strange to take home half your meal, but I am very grateful! Thank you so much!
>
> Please give me a call tonight about my brother if you get a chance. I'm still not sure.
>
> Sandra

With her stomach in knots over the decision she had to make and all the worry about the rent, Sandra didn't enjoy the grilled salmon steak as much as she'd hoped. James had paid her, Peter had paid her, Matt's mom had paid, but she was still short the necessary funds. Getting up from the table, feeling quite nauseous, she put her slice of the berry flan in the fridge for later.

Tiger's digestive system was not in the least affected. He was more than happy to sample the tiny piece of salmon she gave him.

James called around seven to talk things over.

"So what are you most worried about?" he asked. "What's the worst that could happen?"

"He could think I was out of place in coming," Sandra expressed anxiously, "or think that I was being too pushy. Or he could be too busy to even talk to me."

"He could," James agreed calmly. "Or he could be very happy to finally have the chance to meet you. And if he has to cancel the cottage plans, for some strange, last-minute reason, at least you'll have already met him and it won't be so hard to keep waiting."

Sandra tried to consider both possibilities but it was all new to her. James' plan didn't follow any of the familiar reunions she had often imagined. "I don't know what to do," she admitted anxiously. "What would you do if you were me?"

With a laugh, James didn't hesitate. "I'd come along for sure," he said. "I'd want to meet this guy as soon as possible and see what he's all about."

"Okay," she said, faltering just a little. "I guess I'll come. Where should I meet you?"

James explained which bus she should take and how to get to his office. "You just have to walk one block north from the bus stop and you'll see Drayton's Engineering Firm on the corner. You can't miss it. There is a black sign with gold lettering and it's *big!*"

That night, Sandra lay awake for hours. Over and over she envisioned what it might be like to meet Laurie at a business luncheon. It wasn't that she intended to dream it all up in her mind; quite the contrary! In frustration she was trying to distract herself by other thoughts, so that she could get to sleep. She tried to remember all she'd learned about the coming Kingdom and concentrate on the wonderful new vision she'd begun to develop…but James had told her that her brother's hair was gray. It was hard to recreate her handsome, dark-haired brother with an older look. And now, instead of being welcomed as the guest of honour into a grand, stone mansion, she would have to share Laurie's lavish attention with his more important dinner guest - James. *I don't know about this,* she worried. *I have a feeling Laurie will be too busy to even notice me.*

Overshadowing the long-lost-brother dilemma was the looming panic Sandra felt over not being able to pay her rent. *It's due tomorrow,* she thought, *and I'm still four hundred dollars short. I don't want to be evicted! I have no place to go! Who would let me sign another contract without a steady job?* She was desperate for a knight in shining armour. It suddenly occurred to her, as she tossed and turned, that perhaps this luncheon date might be God's answer to her prayer. *Maybe Laurie will inquire about my financial situation tomorrow,* she thought. *After all he is a* banker. *Finances are his specialty; lending money is his business. Four hundred dollars is nothing to him.*

Earnestly she took the matter to God in prayer, pleading that all would go well and that she would say and do the right things. "And please," she begged, "please make my brother care about me."

Sandra took a long time the next morning getting ready for the luncheon. She still wasn't feeling well. Changing outfits three times, she decided at last on the fanciest dress that she had. She'd worn it at her university graduation ceremony. It was a closefitting, blue rayon, with a modest scoop neckline and flouncy skirt. With the gold chain necklace that her mother had given her years ago, Sandra thought she might pass for an accountant's secretary. She added some makeup, straightened a few of her top layers of hair once again, and picked up her purse. Then she stopped. Sometimes it was very difficult remembering to pray for God's help, but she knew she needed it today!

It was easy enough to find James' work. The big, black sign was visible in the distance as soon as she stepped off the bus. Entering through the heavy glass doors, Sandra walked nervously across the grand marble floor of a black and gold lobby. She made her way over to a massive, uniquely-carved, front desk.

"Hi, I'm Sandra Carrington," she explained quietly to the receptionist. "I'm here to meet James Bryant."

"I'll let him know that you are here," the receptionist smiled. She buzzed the office and a minute later James came walking in.

"You made it," he smiled admiringly. "I was worried you might chicken out."

I still might, Sandra thought, trying to smile back at him. *Oh, I hope this is a good idea.*

James drove over to the Mandarin, an all-you-can-eat Chinese restaurant, chattering casually about the deal he had to discuss with her brother. Sandra nodded politely but nothing registered; she was too overwhelmed with anxiety. *Will Laurie recognize me? Will he think I'm out of place? Will he care? Will he help me out financially?*

Before they entered the restaurant, James stopped Sandra with a hand on her shoulder. "Relax," he said with a bewildered smile. "Just relax and enjoy yourself."

It was easier said than done. They waited for Sandra's brother for at least twenty minutes. Sandra couldn't concentrate on anything James said, but was thankful that he kept talking.

Finally, a stout, middle-aged man in an olive green suit came around the corner. "James Bryant!" he said warmly, stretching out his hand, "Good to see you again."

"Laurence Carrington! Good to see you." James stood up and strode forward to shake his hand, while a rather astonished Sandra rose to her feet.

"I brought someone along to meet you," James said. "Can you guess who it is?"

Laurie glanced briefly over. "Your secretary... perhaps...?"

Sandra stared blankly at the gray-haired man. *He doesn't look at all like I thought he would. He looks so...old and rather...dull.*

"Does Sandra Carrington ring any bells for you?" James asked.

Laurie looked up from the papers he had pulled from his briefcase. His deep blue eyes rested on Sandra with a dumbfounded expression. "Well, I'll be..." he remarked, "if it isn't Sandra!" Keeping the papers in hand, he strode forward politely with his hand outstretched. "Good to meet you finally," he said, shaking her hand. "We've been having some troubles getting together, haven't we?"

"Yes, we have," Sandra agreed, forcing a laugh.

"So, shall we all go through the buffet?" Laurie asked, placing his papers on the table and picking up his plate. "Unfortunately, I only have an hour to spare."

James and Sandra followed suit. Disappointment was taking the place of anxiety as Sandra looked at the great variety of hot Chinese food. Hunger had fled long ago but she knew she had to put something on her plate. *I can't believe it,* she thought, *he didn't even hug me. He hardly seemed excited to see me. He hasn't even asked me any questions. Is this truly the brother I've dreamed about for years?*

Laurie and James were already talking business before they returned to the table.

However, as they were sitting down, James noticed Sandra only had three sweet and sour chicken balls on her plate. "Is that all you're eating?" he asked.

"I'm not very hungry," she apologized.

"Sandra, this is an *all-you-can-eat* restaurant," he smiled with a puzzled expression. "I know you can do better than that!"

She shook her head sadly.

"So, my files show that March thirteenth was the last instalment." Laurie said, his eyes on the screen of his laptop, "Does that correspond with yours?"

James gave Laurie his full attention. Sandra picked away at the three sweet and sour chicken balls that looked profoundly small on such an enormous white plate. She understood nothing about the conversation. On his laptop, James was making rapid calculations and taking notes on a pad of paper, while Laurie talked about the possible financial packages the bank was willing to offer. Sandra stole glances at her brother and tried to memorize his aged, well-rounded appearance. It was vastly different than the strong, athletic, handsome man she'd envisioned for so long.

Both men went back to the buffet for seconds, but James didn't touch the food on the clean plate that he brought back.

Continuing to talk until the waitress came by, James motioned her over. "Could I have this put in a take-home box?" he requested.

The waitress looked from his plate to Sandra's and nodded.

Now there's a way to get supper out of lunch, Sandra thought to herself in surprise. Such an action didn't seem characteristic of James.

"So, we'll have to talk again at the convention," Laurie said to James, as they were wrapping up. "We should be able to finalize the deal by then."

James nodded quietly, looking over at Sandra with uneasy regret.

Then Laurie turned to his sister. "Sandra, I know we've asked you to visit us at the cottage that first weekend in July, but some important business has come up. James and I have to attend a key convention. We really don't have a choice in the matter. However, we don't need to cancel our weekend plans completely. I'll only be away on Saturday and Michelle will be quite happy to look after you until I get back."

Sandra's heart sank. There would be no trip to Cape Breton on the yacht. It was another broken promise and one that she'd been looking forward to so much! *'Michelle will be quite happy to look after you,'* Sandra repeated to herself. *Not enjoy your company, or even 'spend time with you'…just 'look after you'! As if I was some nagging, little kid that he can't get rid of.*

Nodding dismally, Sandra told herself to be thankful that at least Laurie wasn't going to cancel the whole weekend. "Okay," she managed to say, sounding almost indifferent in an attempt to hide her feelings. "Maybe it will work out better some other time."

The waitress brought James his box of food, the bill and the credit card machine. James paid and Laurie stood up to leave.

Looking over at James, Laurie asked, "So, *is* Sandra your secretary…or your girlfriend…?"

Turning pink, Sandra didn't dare look at James but she quickly answered the question herself. "Actually, I clean house for James."

Laurie looked perplexed. "Last I heard you were going to university...Did that not pan out?"

"Oh, yes," she added, thinking that she may now have an opportunity to present her plight. "I'm a teacher. But ever since moving out here, I've only been able to get supply-teaching work. Housecleaning helps pay the rent."

Laurie nodded disinterestedly. Sandra's last hope that he might care to inquire about her financial well-being evaporated, along with everything else.

"Well, James," Laurie said, tidying up the papers he had spread out on the table. "If you can get back to me by the end of the week with that presentation, I'll take it to my superiors and we'll see what we can do."

James stood up to shake hands with Laurie and then Laurie turned to Sandra, "See you in July," he said, waving. "And good luck with the housecleaning. Sorry to duck out so quickly, but I have another meeting I should already be at."

'Good luck with the housecleaning,' was the final stab. *That's all he remembers,* she thought. *He didn't say 'I hope you find a teaching job soon.'* Tears welled up in her eyes as Laurie walked off.

James was smiling as he held the restaurant door open but when he noticed the look on Sandra's face, his smile quickly vanished away. He said nothing until they were both seated in the car.

"Why are you upset?" he inquired. "I thought that went fairly well."

"How could you think that went well?!" she replied with anguish.

"You finally got to meet each other."

"We haven't seen each other for eighteen years and he treated me like…like a…stranger!" Sandra blurted out, her face contorting with pain.

"But you are like strangers...since..."

"We are *not* strangers!" Sandra exclaimed indignantly. "He's my brother! But, he just doesn't care about me…*at all,*" she wailed, rummaging desperately in her purse for a tissue. "He breaks every promise he makes, and now he thinks I'm only *a housekeeper!*"

James handed her a tissue box he had from the back seat. "You didn't have to tell him you were housecleaning…"

"What else was I supposed to say?" Sandra sobbed, as she helped herself to several tissues.

"Well, I was going to tell him that we're friends."

Wiping tears away with the tissue, Sandra realized that James' response would have been much better than hers. "I wish I hadn't gone," she moaned.

"What did you expect the guy to do?" James asked kindly, even though he was obviously perplexed. "You haven't seen each other for eighteen years."

"I don't know," she admitted with a sob. "I just expected he would be happier to see me; that's all."

James shook his head and started the car.

Angry feelings began to rise out of the hurt. The seeming lack of understanding on James' part didn't help matters. "I would have thought that he might have spent more than five minutes talking to me," she explained miserably as they drove away. "I would have thought he'd have wanted to talk to me about the last eighteen years. And you'd think when I told him I had to clean houses in order to get by he might have cared enough to ask a few more details. He didn't even ask if I needed any help," she sobbed, so distraught that she no longer cared to hide her desperate situation. "There he is rolling in riches, with a mansion, a cottage and a yacht – and I can't even pay my *rent!* Don't families help each other out when times get tough? I came out here because of him," she cried, wiping away hot tears with one tissue after another, "and *I can't find a decent job!* I'm going to have to go back to Ontario!"

Sandra missed the look of concern on James' face. Her hand was over her face; her face was turned towards the passenger window and the flood of tears made it impossible to see anyway.

"I understand why you were disappointed," he said softly. "But maybe your expectations were just a little too high."

It wasn't the message that Sandra wanted to hear. *"Too high?"* she questioned between sobs, thinking that James had no compassion whatsoever. "Is it expecting too much for my brother to care about me? To want to spend time with me?" Shaking her head in despair, Sandra bemoaned her decision again. "I shouldn't have gone," she complained, as tears streamed down her face faster than she could wipe them away. "I should have just waited to meet them at the cottage – although now he'll only be there for half the time! Oh, why did I come?!"

There was no answer from James.

Minutes dragged by as Sandra sat crying, looking blindly out the window. A pile of used tissues piled up on her lap. James reached under his seat and pulled out a small plastic bag. Handing it to her, Sandra mechanically tidied up as she continued to mop her face. Suddenly she realized the tall, cream-coloured, rectangular building in the distance was the Manor. "Are you driving me home?" she sobbed with surprise.

"I didn't think you'd want to get on a bus right now."

"But won't you be late getting back to work?" she asked, wiping her nose with one tissue and then her eyes with another.

"If I'm late, I'll just have to work longer tonight," James replied curtly. "It's not a problem."

"Thank you," she said meekly. Overwhelmed by remorse, Sandra barely noticed the change in James' expression and tone of voice.

When the Pontiac rolled up in front of the Manor, James put his hand on Sandra's arm to stop her from getting out. His face was drawn and flushed but Sandra wasn't looking. "I just want to say this, Sandra," he stated evenly, "last week when I met your brother he told me he was thinking about coming to the July convention. I had a feeling he was going to let you down again. That's why I invited you today. I'm sorry that it didn't turn out the way you wanted it to. I only tried to help. I'm really sorry if I made things worse."

Placing the box of Chinese food on her lap, he added firmly. "Take this and have it when you're hungry."

Looking up at James blankly, Sandra's vision was still blurred. She didn't understand why he was apologizing or even fully comprehend what he'd just told her. In such an emotional state she hardly realised he'd handed her the box of food. "It's not your fault," she said uncertainly, reaching over to open the car door. "Don't worry about it," she sobbed. "And thanks... so much...for bringing me home and ... everything."

Taking the stairway so that she wouldn't have to meet anyone, Sandra ran up to her apartment, shoved the food in the fridge and flung herself across her bed. She sobbed so hard she started to cough. The daydreams she'd cherished for so long had dissolved in such a very disappointing way. "He breaks all his promises!" she wailed to the walls. "How can I ever trust him again? How can I trust anyone? I hate men. I hate Laurie so much! I never want to see him again. Never!" Even as she said the words she knew she was over-reacting, but it sure felt good to say it! With frustration and bitterness overflowing in her heart Sandra buried her face in her pillow and wept.

Tiger, sensing her need and wanting to do all he could to comfort his mistress, curled up contentedly in the small of her back.

The New Man
Chapter Twenty-Two

The next morning, Thursday morning, Sandra made her way to the landlord's office. Her rent was due and she simply wasn't going to have enough money. It didn't seem as though the missing four hundred dollars would miraculously appear. She saw no other choice than to beg for an extension. Sandra pleaded her case to the lady at the front desk. Since she had never missed a payment before, the receptionist readily agreed to give her another week.

"If you like, there are two apartments you could clean," the receptionist offered. "They were vacated just this week and we're short on cleaning staff. And I'm sure I could find more work for you, if you need it."

Even though the wage was much less than what James had been paying her, Sandra thanked her tearfully. She wished she had asked about such options earlier.

There was plenty to think over and sort out as she spent the day cleaning. Her high hopes had been dashed by Laurie so abruptly and in such a callous way that it would take time to forgive and forget. She had to figure out what was worth holding on to and what needed to be tossed away. As she vacuumed a living room floor, very much like her own and James', she poured out her confusion to God. "I thought You listen to prayers," she cried. "I prayed that You would make my brother care and he doesn't care at all. I thought you'd help me with my rent and I'm hundreds of dollars short. I don't understand how You work. I don't know if I can trust *anyone* anymore!"

Cleaning the big windows of the living room, Sandra looked out across the bright blue bay. The sparkling water contrasted sharply with her gloomy state. *I wish it was dark and*

201

stormy, she thought, recalling the frigid, black water of May. *My brother doesn't care about me at all! Life is always going to hurt like this. What is the point?* Yet, as the day wore on and she expended her grief, Sandra began to realise that intertwined with all her deep disappointment over Laurie, there was a strange secure feeling she didn't fully understand. As much as she told herself life wasn't worth living, she wasn't convinced that was true anymore. While she cleaned her second greasy kitchen sink for the day and mopped more cream-coloured tiles, she tried to sort through her feelings. *It's almost as though I've fallen off a tall, steep mountain cliff,* she thought, *and I should be dashed at the bottom, but I feel as though I've landed on some sort of ... an invisible safety net...or something. I'm dazed and very upset but I have no bruises or broken bones. There's something in my life,* she mused; *something that has never been there before. What is it?*

With a great deal of soul-searching she realized what it was. It was the hope for the future that Jess had been telling her about. There was something more now – something beyond the fanciful hopes and daydreams that had once been all she had.

When Jessica arrived for the class that evening, she brought a casserole. "My mom made too much for dinner tonight, so she told me to bring some to you."

Still very emotional, Sandra almost started crying again. This was *kindness* – kindness to her! She felt hot tears coming into her eyes as she gratefully accepted the casserole and took a quick peek under the foil. It was a rich looking lasagne! "Mmm, this looks so delicious!" she said, her voice wavering a little. "Please let your mom know that I'm so thankful!"

"Have you had a good week?" Jessica asked in a concerned way, as Sandra slid the lasagne into the fridge, right where the Chinese food had been. The Chinese food had tasted much better for dinner than it had for the previous day's lunch. She was thankful James had given it to her.

"Everything was fine..." Sandra began sadly as she tried to prepare two cups of tea. Tears were streaming down her face, once again, as she handed a cup of tea to Jessica.

Jess was all sympathy. "What happened?!"

The story spilled out in a tearful fashion as Sandra told Jessica about finally meeting her brother at the restaurant and the cruel disappointment that had followed.

Coming over to sit beside her, Jessica draped her arm warmly around Sandra's shoulders.

Sandra repeated her story of how she'd hoped for the last eighteen years that one day she'd meet up with her brother again. She described again how she had moved all the way from Ontario to Nova Scotia, believing that if she lived closer to Laurie she would get to see him more often. She told her about the yacht trip she had looked forward to with all her heart and listed off all the previous dates that had been set up and cancelled. She even admitted how tough it had been trying to exist in an upscale condominium on a supply teacher's wage and the particular financial crisis she was in that week.

"Laurie's my *only* brother," she sobbed, as the tears continued, "I just want him to care about me, accept me and be the family that I don't have."

Jessica held her close. "It must be really hard," she empathized, patting Sandra's back gently. "I can't imagine how lonely you must feel. But you do have friends who care! We'll help you."

Sandra returned her embrace. "Thank you," was all she could manage to say.

Jessica spoke very gently. "Sandra," she said, "tell me all you've done to try and gain your brother's attention."

"Everything I can think of," she replied in anguish. "For years and years I've tried calling him, emailing him, sending him birthday cards and he hardly ever responds. He just doesn't care!"

"It is heartbreaking," Jessica agreed. "I would be crushed if my brothers were like that to me. But do you really think he doesn't care about you, or is he just an insensitive person who is far too busy?"

"I don't know," Sandra sighed. "Is there a difference? I'd like to believe that he does care...deep down..."

"Well, I want you to remember something," Jessica said kindly, squeezing Sandra's hand. "Whether he does or not, there is someone who cares about you far more than your brother ever could."

Sandra looked up through her tears. *Who?* She wondered. *Is Jessica talking about herself?*

"Remember, He cares so much," Jessica smiled, "that He gave the Son He loved dearly as a sacrifice – for you – for all of us."[101] And His Son cares so much that he willingly gave up *his own life* so that we could all be saved." [102]

Sandra nodded dismally, trying to rein in her emotions. *It's too abstract,* she thought. *How do I know God really cares about* **me?**

"Just think," Jess encouraged. "You've done so much *hoping* your brother will want to have a relationship with you and so far he's always let you down. It has really hurt you and I can fully understand why. But imagine," she said kindly, "if you had offered to give up *your life* for Laurie and he *still* had no interest in seeing you or talking to you."

Okay, so things could be worse, Sandra sighed inwardly.

"It must be really hard to accept Laurie's disinterest," Jessica empathized tenderly, holding Sandra's arm, "especially when he's the only family you have." She paused and then said, "But I think it might help if instead of longing for Laurie's help and protection, you turn your hopes to the One who *has promised*

---

[101] John 3:14-17; Luke 20:9-16; Romans 5:7-8; 1 John 4:9-11
[102] John 10:14-18; 15:12-13; Ephesians 5:2,25

to be there for you. God will never let us down if we turn to Him. He's told us He won't. [103] The world deserves to be totally abandoned for how they have treated God, but in His patience He continues to give us the rain and sunshine, and grants complete forgiveness when anyone turns to Him." [104]

"True," Sandra nodded, "that *is* amazing love. But I prayed that God would help my brother care about me – and it didn't ...work. It didn't make any difference."

Looking thoughtful for a moment, Jessica pondered the matter. "Sometimes God answers our prayers in a different way than we expect," she said. "Sometimes He says 'yes', sometimes He says 'no' and sometimes He says 'wait'. [105]You might not see an answer now, but you may understand later on when you look back."

Sandra considered this possibility. "Really?" she said dismally. "It's hard to believe I'll *ever* understand!"

Jess had opened her Bible and was turning something up. "Have a look at this," she suggested, finding Luke chapter six and pointing out verse thirty-two to Sandra. "I'm showing you this," she explained, "because I think there's another way to look at your situation that will set you free and help you to rise above it. Remember the sea gulls?"

Trying to smile, Sandra pulled herself together and dried her eyes. She read, "'But if you love those who love you, what credit is that to you? For even sinners love those who love them. And if you do good to those who do good to you, what credit is that to you? For even sinners do the same. And if you lend to those from whom you hope to receive back, what credit is that to you? For even sinners lend to sinners to receive as much back. But love

---

[103] Psalm 37:23-24; 34:19-20; Hebrews 10:23, 35-39; 1 Chronicles 28:9; 1 Corinthians 10:13; 15:57-58; 1 Thessalonians 5:23-24
[104] Matthew 5:44-48; Deuteronomy 4:29-31; Isaiah 55:6-7
[105] Philippians 4:6-7; John 15:5-7; 1 John 5 :14-15; Psalm 34 :15-20; 66 :18; 130 :5

your enemies, do good, and lend, hoping for nothing in return; and your reward will be great, and you will be sons of the Most High. For He is kind to the unthankful and the evil.'"

Pondering the verses quietly, Sandra remembered the talk she'd had with Jess along the harbour front. "You're telling me," she clarified, "that I shouldn't be hoping for *anything* from my brother?"

"God wants you to trust *in Him* for your needs," Jessica replied. "He will never leave you or forsake you; He's promised[106]. But other human beings will *often* let us down. [107] God wants *us* to look to Him and be *like Him*. So, keep showing love to your brother but *don't expect anything in return* – because that's what God does for us. One day God will judge the world for their lack of response, but until then His desire is that all might come to Him and be saved."[108]

It was a radical change of thinking for Sandra and now that her long-held daydreams had vaporised, she was better able to understand Jessica's words. As she considered the message carefully, she became aware that everything she wanted from Laurie involved her own well-being. She had never really considered what she could do for Laurie, as it had seemed to her that he already had far more than he needed. But, sitting close to Jess, it began to be crystal clear. ... *set you free,* she remembered Peter telling James. *Maybe the truth will set me free from myself!* It was a shocking realization! *My life has been all about me - my needs, my wants; that's been my focus. God's promised to look after me if I serve Him and He wants me to look after others. Laurie never promised me anything – I was foolish to expect so much from him! God's promised everything! And Jessica says I can rely on God!* When she began to turn her thinking around and

---

[106] Hebrews 13:5; Deuteronomy 31:6-8; Psalm 37:25; 139:1-18
[107] Psalm 118:8-9; 146:3-9
[108] 2 Peter 3:9; 1 Tim. 2:3-4; Luke 12:32; Ezekiel 18:23

contemplate what she might do for Laurie rather than what she hoped he would do for her – the pain in her heart subsided dramatically.

"I think our class tonight might lift your spirits," Jessica smiled, squeezing Sandra's hand. "Remember, we were going to talk about immortality."

Sandra looked up. "Immortality," she repeated. "Yes, that will be interesting! I've been thinking a lot about it. One of my biggest questions is what will our bodies be like when we're made immortal? Will we look like we do now or be like…well…a ghost?"

Jessica smiled. "We know that we will be made like Jesus," she answered, "as it says in Philippians three, '…we also eagerly wait for the Saviour, the Lord Jesus Christ, who will transform our lowly body that it may be conformed to His glorious body… '[109] So…why don't we consider what Jesus was like after he had risen from the grave? But first, let's pray."

Beginning with "Dear Heavenly Father," Jessica prayed that God would be with them in their study of His Word, to give them wisdom and open their hearts to the message. But she also prayed for Sandra. "Please Lord," she begged, "strengthen Sandra's spirit and help heal her heart. Please help her to find work and overcome her financial stresses. Most of all, help her to see Your mercies and know that you are a faithful God to all who put their trust in You."

It was the first time anyone had ever prayed for Sandra and she was moved by her friend's kind words. Tears of thankfulness welled up in her eyes. Jessica gave her a big hug.

When they began their investigation on immortality, Jessica began with the last chapter of Luke. She pointed out verse thirty-nine, where Jesus had told his disciples, "Behold my hands

---

[109] See also 1 John 3:2; 1 Corinthians 15:49; 2 Peter 1:4

and my feet, that it is I myself: handle me, and see; for a spirit hath not flesh and bones, as ye see me have."

"Flesh and bones," Sandra considered thoughtfully. "So we will still have physical, tangible bodies?"

"Yes we will, but our bodies will be somewhat different than they are now," Jess added. "The Bible refers to *mortal human beings* as 'flesh *and blood.*'[110] In the Old Testament 'blood' represented 'life'[111] – the lifeblood of our mortality. As *an immortal* we will no longer have blood pumping through our veins, God will give life to our bodies through His Spirit!"[112]

Jessica turned back to First Corinthians fifteen and showed Sandra the last section of the chapter. It described the change that will take place at the resurrection. "And as we have borne the image of the man of dust, *we shall also bear the image of the heavenly Man."*

"The *'heavenly Man'* is Jesus," Jess explained.

They read the rest of the passage. "Now this I say, brethren, that *flesh and blood* cannot inherit the kingdom of God; nor does corruption inherit incorruption. Behold, I tell you a mystery: We shall not all sleep, but we shall all be changed-- in a moment, in the twinkling of an eye, at the last trumpet. For the trumpet will sound, and the dead will be raised incorruptible, and we shall be changed. For this corruptible must put on incorruption, and this mortal *must put on* immortality."

"So, God is going to transform our mortal bodies into immortal ones?" Sandra clarified.

"That's right," Jess agreed. "Instead of having bodies that corrupt and decay, we will have bodies that never grow old."

"Will we look just like we look now?" Sandra inquired.

---

[110] Matthew 16:17; Hebrews 2:14
[111] Deuteronomy 12:23
[112] Romans 8:11

"We're not told exactly," Jessica replied. "Jesus wasn't immediately recognized by some of his followers right after he rose from the dead, but when they did recognize him, no one said that he had changed drastically in appearance; in fact, he still had the nail holes in his hands. So, I would assume that we will be recognizable, but in a healthy, youthful form."

"And will we remember what we did in this life?"

"Jesus certainly remembered all his loved ones and his past experiences; his memory was fully intact."

"And if someone touches us," Sandra clarified, "will they feel something solid? They won't poke their hand right through us?"

Jess giggled. "We'll have a solid form," she assured Sandra. "As we read in Luke twenty-four, Jesus said, 'Handle me and see, for a spirit does not have flesh and bones as you see I have.' Jesus could be touched. He invited his disciples to feel the holes in his hands, and he could also eat and drink. But, in a miraculous way, he could also walk through walls, appear and disappear."

"Cool," Sandra said with a smile. "I'd like that."

"We can also learn about immortality from the angels," Jess said. "They were already immortal beings right at the beginning of Genesis."

Together, she and Sandra looked at the passage in Luke twenty, verse thirty-four to thirty-six, which spoke of believers being made, 'equal to the angels and are sons of God, being sons of the resurrection'. "Therefore," Jessica deduced, "the immortal nature which angels possess is that which believers hope to share." They discussed the important role angels had in the creation of the world[113] and Jess shared her ideas on how wonderful it would be to be involved in such a vast creative project. She also showed

---

[113] Genesis 1:26-27 (Hebrew 'Elohim' is used which is a plural form of 'El' (God) and occasionally refers to angels – Job 38:4-7; Psalm 8:5 and Heb. 2:7-8)

Sandra a number of passages where angels were mistaken for men, and other places where angels were so terrifyingly glorious that people fell to the ground in fear. Just like the immortal Jesus, angels can eat and drink, vanish and reappear, perhaps fly through the air and read people's minds. They are constantly at work, protecting the faithful, manipulating circumstances on earth to bring about God's will and even influencing human governments today.[114]

"Well, I'm sure I'll never get bored living forever," Sandra smiled. "It sounds like there will be plenty of interesting things to do!"

"Yes," Jessica agreed enthusiastically, "and God has promised to wipe away *all tears from our eyes,* so there will be *no more* death, or sorrow, or crying, or pain.[115] Therefore, we will *never* feel unhappy as an immortal being."

"Never unhappy…" Sandra mused.

"You know," Jess added, "the promises that God made are so wonderful, they helped Jesus endure the torture of the cross!"

"Really?"

Jess showed her the passage in Hebrews chapter twelve, which says, "Looking unto Jesus the author and finisher of our faith; who for *the joy that was set before him* endured the cross, despising the shame, and is set down at the right hand of the throne of God."

"God wants us to make this *our* vision," she encouraged gently, patting Sandra's arm, "so that we can be sustained by these promises regardless of *what* is happening to us now."

---

[114] Men: Hebrews 13:2; Genesis 18 & 19; Judges 13/ Fearful: Numbers 22:31; Luke 1:11,12; Matthew 28:3,4/ Eat and Drink: Genesis 18 & 19; Luke 24:42-43 / Vanish: Numbers 22:31; Judges 13:20-21: Luke 24:31,36/ Fly: Daniel 9:21; Acts 1:9/ Read Minds: Genesis 18:10-15; John 20:24-27/ Protectors: Psalm 34:7; Hebrews 1:14/ God's Will: Exodus 14:24-25; 2 Samuel 24:16; Psalm 103:20/ Influencing: Daniel 10:12-13; 4:17
[115] Revelation 21:4; 7:14-17

Lying in bed that night, with Tiger curled up in a fluffy ball beside her pillow, Sandra thought about everything she and Jess had discussed. *I know what is in my life now that was never there before,* she thought happily. *I have a hope for the future! I have something real to dream about,* she thought, s*omething better than all the 'candyfloss' I held on to so tightly before. God won't let me down – He's not like my brother!* With a wistful smile, she imagined how wonderful it will be to know we will *always* go on living and never again experience heartbreak, sorrow, pain, tiredness, hunger, *or rejection!* In her mind she replayed the beautiful pictures she'd seen at the Kingdom feast. She was just walking up the steps of the magnificent temple in Jerusalem, when the phone rang.

Sandra glanced over at her radio clock. *Eleven o'clock!* She thought. *This is rather late for someone to call. For a brief second she hoped James might be calling to ask how she was.*

It was Jessica.

"Sandra, I'm so sorry to call this late!" Jess apologized anxiously. "I was just talking to Peter and he really hopes you can work for us tomorrow, and Saturday *and* Monday. We still have to get his parents' place ready for the wedding, plus maintain all our regular customers. Would that be possible?"

"I'd love to help!" Sandra said without any hesitation. Mentally she quickly calculated whether another three days of work at ten dollars an hour, would add up enough to cover her overdue rent. *It will,* she thought. *If I tutor Matt on Monday night, and James pays me on Tuesday, as he always has, I'll have more than enough.*

"Great!" Jess exclaimed. "Then we'll pick you up at seven in the morning. Have a good night!"

"Good night and thank you so much!" Sandra said.

I must thank God for this, Sandra thought as she hung up the phone. *After all the complaining I did this morning, I must apologize and thank Him for providing a way.*

Bowing her head, she did just that.

An Invitation to Forever
Chapter Twenty-Three

It was a much happier Sandra who went gardening Friday morning. Having an extension on her rent payment and now enough work to cover that payment, she was no longer full of anxiety. There was plenty to do with the gardening crew and feeling emotionally drained from the past few days, Sandra was thankful to be with friends.

"If you're not tired of hanging around us," Peter said with a grin, as she got out of the car Saturday evening, "you're more than welcome to come with us to the Sunday service tomorrow."

"I'd love to come," Sandra agreed readily. "I've been meaning to ask if I could. But," she hesitated with a smile, "are you sure you aren't tired of me tagging along?"

They both assured her that they weren't and then Jess added, "We'll pick you up around nine, God willing, and there's a luncheon afterwards, if you can stay."

A luncheon! Fantastic! Sandra thought. "Sounds great," she replied.

There were two messages on her answering machine when she got home that evening. Sandra found herself strangely hoping once again that one of the calls might be from James. But no, neither was from James. The first message was from a friend in Ontario just calling to have a friendly chat. The second was a complete surprise!

"Hi Sandra," a pleasant voice said. "This is Marnie Teeter calling from Star Academy Private School. I've witnessed the dramatic improvement in Matthew's reading ability this year, due to the extra help you've given him. We have an opening this September for a grade one teacher and are wondering if you'd be interested in this position. I'd be happy to set up an interview for you later this week, if you like. Please give me a call. I'll be in tonight after six."

After jotting down the phone number that Marnie gave at the end of the message, Sandra sat down and cried tears of happiness. The opportunity she'd waited for all year long had finally come! *Oh, I hope I get this job!* she sobbed. *It will make all the difference in the world!*

As soon as she could compose herself Sandra called Marnie back and set up an interview for Thursday morning. Then she called her friend in Ontario and chatted for a while about simple 'candy-floss' matters and some of her new exciting news.

Sunday morning, when Sandra drove up with Peter and Jessica to the little white chapel near the lake, she noticed the large signboard in front. "The Christadelphians" stood out in bold, blue letters and Sandra wasn't sure how to pronounce such a name. She asked Jess what it meant.

"You've heard of 'Philadelphia'?" Jess asked.

"Yes, that's a city in America."

"That's right, and it's the city of 'brotherly love'," Jess explained. "'Phila' is Greek for 'love' and 'delphia' is Greek for 'brothers'. So, 'Christadelphian' is simply the Greek words 'Christos'- Christ, and 'delphia' which means 'brethren in Christ'."

"So, you call yourselves 'brethren in Christ'?" Sandra reiterated.

"Yes," Jess nodded pleasantly, "on the basis that Jesus said, 'whoever does the will of my Father in heaven is my brother and sister and mother.'"[116]

Peter noticed the look of confusion on Sandra's face. "The beauty of it all," he clarified, "is that Jesus is calling us to have a

---

[116] Matthew 12:50; Hebrews 2:10-12

very close relationship with him. He speaks of believers as his friends, his family and his bride.[117] He laid down his life for us because of love!

Sandra was still pondering the matter as Jessica's father stood up to give the exhortation that Sunday morning. With short gray hair and a closely-trimmed beard, Craig was wearing a navy suit and bright blue tie.

Smiling out at the audience, Craig Symons began, "You won't be too surprised by the theme I've chosen this morning. For the last two months, an upcoming wedding has often been on my mind. And when it's not on *my* mind, it's *always* on my wife's mind, so that brings it back to my attention!"

There were plenty of smiles all around and Peter, who was sitting in the same row as Sandra, put his arm affectionately around Jess.

"Now, there's a wedding that's been very much on God's mind," Craig continued earnestly, "for at least *two thousand years*. Imagine planning a wedding for that long!" he said, directing his smile towards his wife. "But the wedding that God is planning is *somewhat* different in a couple of ways. Firstly, many, *many* people are invited and those who come willingly, preparing as God has asked them to, will all be the bride.[118]

How unique, Sandra considered, as the little ditty the children sang at the Kingdom Feast rushed into her mind. Lately, any time the word 'wedding' was mentioned, that tune seemed to spring instantly to her mind. "I cannot come to the wedding, don't trouble me now. I have married a wife, I have bought me a cow…"

"Secondly," Craig went on to say. "It's a *royal* wedding. The bridegroom is about to receive his kingdom. He's going to be King of the World! He's given us a royal invitation. It's an

---

[117] John 15:12-17; Matthew 12:47-50; Ephesians 5:22-32
[118] Matthew 22:1-14; ; Revelation 19:6-9

invitation to *forever!*[119] We've been invited to a marriage with "Jesus Christ, the faithful witness, the firstborn from the dead, and the ruler over the kings of the earth. To Him who loved us and washed us from our sins in His own blood..." [120]

Why would anyone turn that down? Sandra mused. *What a tremendously, incredible invitation!*

Now we know that, if it's the Lord's will," Craig continued, "Peter and Jessica plan to be married next weekend and that date is coming up very quickly for all of us. We're quite sure when it's going to happen and that makes it easier to prepare. But with God's royal wedding," he paused, "we don't know for sure *when* the groom will arrive. He's given us signs by which we know it must be very close and asked us to be in a constant state of readiness, but it could be *tomorrow* and it might also be another ten or fifteen years away."

Turning up Matthew chapter twenty-five, Craig read the parable of the ten virgins who had been invited to meet the bridegroom. Five of the virgins had brought their lamps and extra oil, in case it ran out. The other five, the foolish ones, had brought lamps but no additional supplies to keep their lamps refuelled. The bridegroom took much longer to arrive than any of them had expected and they all slumbered and slept. It wasn't until midnight that the call went out and when they arose, their lamps were in dire need of attention. The foolish virgins pleaded with the wise to share their extra oil but," as Craig explained, "oil represents our own personal effort to apply God's Word in our lives, and that isn't something we can share. So, instead of going to the wedding, the foolish virgins tried to run to the store to buy oil. When they returned, the door was shut and the bridegroom was no longer willing to welcome them in. '"Watch therefore,"' Craig read, '"for

---

[119] Daniel 7: 13,14,18; Revelation 5:10; 20:6
[120] Revelation 1:5-6

you know neither the day nor the hour in which the Son of Man is coming.'"

Craig talked about the challenges in patiently waiting for Christ to return. He read from Second Peter three, emphasizing, "'scoffers will come in the last days, walking according to their own lusts, and saying, *'Where is the promise of His coming?* For since the fathers fell asleep, all things continue as they were from the beginning of creation...But, beloved, *do not forget this one thing,* that with the Lord one day is as a thousand years, and a thousand years as one day. The Lord is *not slack* concerning His promise, as some count slackness, but is *longsuffering* toward us, *not willing that any should perish* but that all should come to repentance. But the day of the Lord will come *as a thief in the night,* in which the heavens will pass away with a great noise, and the elements will melt with fervent heat; both the earth and the works that are in it will be burned up. *Therefore,* since all these things will be dissolved, what manner of persons ought you to be in holy conduct and godliness, looking for and hastening the coming of the day of God...? Nevertheless we, *according to His promise,* look for new heavens and a new earth in which *righteousness dwells.'"*

With a puzzled frown, Sandra turned to Jess and whispered. "But, if the earth is to be all burned up, how then can the promises be fulfilled?"

"It's a *new* earth in the sense that it will be a *cleansed* earth," Jessica softly whispered back. "There will be earthquakes and fires to destroy the works of men, but remember it is *this earth* that God promised to Abraham and told him to *look at, walk on* and *live in* as a stranger."[121]

Sandra listened carefully as Craig spoke about the state of the virgins when the bridegroom came, indicating that those who

---

[121] Genesis 13:14-17; Acts 7:5; Hebrews 11:8-10, 13-16; 39-40; Galatians 3:27-29

'slumbered' were those whose hearts were overcome by the cares of this life, and so Christ's return came upon them unexpectedly.[122] Those who 'slept' were the dead.[123] "You can see that Christ's return came at a time when the cares of this world were choking everyone," he pointed out. *"All* the virgins were having trouble staying awake."

"Now, looking more closely at this oil that we *must* have in order to light our lamps and follow our bridegroom into the wedding," Craig continued, "let's consider the following passages from Scripture."

Sandra listened eagerly. It seemed to her that this was the most important question. *Yes, what is this oil that the wise virgins have?*

It took a number of passages to establish the answer. Taking everyone to Psalm one hundred and nineteen, Craig read, "'*Your word* is a lamp to my feet and a light to my path...The entrance of Your words *gives light*; it gives *understanding* to the simple.'

"God's Word in the Bible, is a lamp to guide our way," Craig continued. "However, Jesus has asked *us* to shine *our* lights into this dark world,[124] so what is it that makes *us* shine? Is it not the influence of God's Word in our lives; the hearing and *then the doing*; the *faith* that is developed in us by what we've read? This morning I would like to suggest to you that 'faith' - based on a right understanding of God's Word - is what the five foolish virgins lacked. Faith is *personally* developed within your heart by reading God's Word;[125] it is not something that can be given away. It's *an individual response* that takes reading, prayer and an awareness of God's Hand in our lives. We need to have this faith

---

[122] Luke 21:34-36
[123] 1 Thessalonians 4:13-16
[124] Matthew 5:14-16
[125] Romans 10:17

before Christ's return. We can't be trying to sort things out when the angels call. Let's all awake from our slumber, which this world so easily induces us into and ensure we're staying close to the Word of God and practicing it in our lives daily. When the angels come to call us away to the wedding, we need to respond immediately with faith to believe."

Shuffling some papers in front of him, Craig looked up at his audience. "I'd just like to read you an interesting quotation that ties in with all this," he said. "It's from a book written well over a hundred years ago when Russia was nothing like the world power that it is today. This book was written by John Thomas, an author who was a dedicated Bible student. With all that has been in the news in the last year in regards to Russia's reawakening, it is a timely reminder."

Looking down at his notes, Craig read from the old book, "'The future movements of Russia are notable signs of the times, because they are predicted in the Scriptures of truth. The Russian Autocracy in its plenitude, and on the verge of its dissolution, is the Image of Nebuchadnezzar standing upon the mountains of Israel, ready to be smitten by the Stone. When Russia makes its grand move for the building up of its Image-empire, then let the reader know that the end of all things, as at present constituted, is at hand. The long-expected, but stealthy advent of the King of Israel will be on the eve of becoming a fact; and salvation will be to those who not only looked for it, but have *trimmed their lamps* by believing the gospel of the kingdom unto the obedience of faith, and the perfection thereof in 'fruits meet for repentance'.'"[126]

Craig then directed everyone's attention to the memorial table with the bread and wine, speaking specifically for a few minutes of the great sacrifice Jesus willingly made in order that we

---

[126] John Thomas, *Elpis Israel* (The Christadelphian, 1849, revised 1973), preface page xx.

– his bride - might join him forever. He ended with the words of Revelation nineteen. "Let us be glad and rejoice and give Him glory, for *the marriage* of the Lamb has come, and His wife *has made herself ready.* And to her it was granted to be arrayed in fine linen, clean and bright, for the fine linen is the righteous acts of the saints. Then he said to me, "Write: 'Blessed are those who are *called to the marriage supper of the Lamb!'"*

The marriage supper! Sandra thought, remembering the children's play. It was starting to all come together. *I've been invited to God's royal wedding. I've been invited to be part of the bride of the king! I'm not going to let the silly things of this life keep me from going to the wedding. I want to be there!*

There was an abundance of delicious looking casseroles and leafy green salads at the pot-luck luncheon after the service. Sandra filled her plate eagerly. When they sat down at one of the tables, Peter and Jessica introduced her to everyone nearby. Some she recognized from the Kingdom Feast. The gardening crew was also present. Derrick and his wife Laura were at the table. Allan was with the rest of the Symon family and all of the Bryants were there, except... James.

"So, I hear you got the job!" Craig was saying to Andrew as they sat down at the table next to Sandra and Jess.

"Yes. They called just last week," Andrew confirmed. "I have two grade nine classes, first semester, and a senior level class."

"I'm so pleased!" Craig said, patting Andrew on the back. "The English department is just down the hall from Math. I'm sure we'll be seeing each other every day once school starts."

"It's going to be weird having my dad for a teacher," Sadie chimed in. She was Andrew's oldest daughter. "I can't imagine calling him *Mr. Bryant!"*

"I'll be calling on you for all the tough questions," Andrew teased. "And if you don't get them right, you'll have *double* the homework."

Sadie giggled with a mischievous look. "Students can ask tough questions too!"

Everyone laughed and Andrew grinned sheepishly.

"I think she's got you there," Craig smiled.

After they'd finished dessert, Jessica suggested to Sandra that they go outside for a bit and have a look around. The hall was out of town on a small grassy lot with a lake just behind it. "Peter wants to find out if anyone owns this lake," Jess told her, as they strolled towards it, meandering through all the children who were playing a noisy game of tag. "He wants to see if he can bring in a load of sand, so we can use it for our Sunday school picnics. Right now it has a very slimy bottom – not much fun to swim in!"

Looking around, Sandra didn't see any other houses nearby. "Maybe no one owns the lake," she said.

A little boy threw a tennis ball at Jess. Seeing the ball coming, Jess caught it and lobbed it back with a smile.

"I don't know how you would feel about this, Sandra," Jessica said, when they had reached the water, "but my parents are quite happy to have you stay with them, if you'd like. It would sure save you a ton of money."

Sandra was awestruck. "Really?" she clarified; then she remembered a previous conversation. "But you and Peter might need a room if you can't find any place to rent."

Jessica smiled. "We'll be fine, I'm sure. And even if we're not, there will soon be two extra rooms in my parent's house. Peter used to board in our basement. There would be plenty of room for all of us, if necessary."

The offer was most welcome and it also brought to Sandra's mind an issue that was beginning to trouble her. Having read quite a few books of the Bible by now, she was beginning to appreciate that if she wanted to please God, her sense of morality would need revising. *Jess and Peter will only need one room after the wedding; right now they need two…*

"Jess," she said tentatively, "I don't know how to ask this…but I guess…is it okay to sleep together before you get married?"

"No," Jessica replied quietly. "God speaks very clearly about that in the Bible. Having a sexual relationship outside of marriage is called 'fornication'. And God says that if we give ourselves over to an immoral lifestyle we won't be in His Kingdom."[127]

"Really? God says it that strongly?"

Jess reached into her handbag and took out a small Bible. "Remember that God has asked us to seek His Kingdom *and His righteousness.*[128] That means that He asks us to *love* His laws of morality and take them into our hearts as our own. Let me read a passage to you," she said. Turning up First Corinthians chapter six, Jessica read verses nine to ten. "'Do you not know that the unrighteous will not inherit the kingdom of God? Do not be deceived. Neither fornicators, nor idolaters, nor adulterers, nor homosexuals, nor sodomites, nor thieves, nor covetous, nor drunkards, nor revilers, nor extortioners will inherit the kingdom of God.'"

"But it seems like almost everyone sleeps together before they get married!"

"That doesn't make it right," Jess replied. She turned up another passage. "In Colossians three, we're told that if we want to be with Christ in his glory when he returns, then we need to "'put to death your members which are on the earth: fornication, uncleanness, passion, evil desire, and covetousness, which is idolatry. Because of these things the wrath of God is coming upon

---

[127] 1 Corinthians 6:9: Ephesians 5:5; Hebrews 13:4
[128] Matthew 6:33; 7:21; John 14:15,21,23

the sons of disobedience, in which you yourselves once walked when you lived in them.'"[129]

"What if someone lived like that before they knew better?"

"There is forgiveness," Jess assured her earnestly. "If we stop doing things that are wrong and ask God to forgive us, He's promised that He'll have mercy on us.[130] God says that when we're baptised into Christ, all our past sins are washed away.[131] God will help us overcome our sinful desires, if we call upon Him for help."[132]

Sandra was relieved to hear that.

Turning to walk back to the hall, Jessica asked, "So would you be interested in staying with my parents?"

"That's a very generous offer! I don't know what to say."

"Just say 'yes'," Jess laughed; then she relayed some exciting news. "I don't think Peter and I will need to move back to my parents' house anyway, because last night we found out that one of our customers is going away for a year and he's wants us to live at his place and maintain it. It's a great place and we'll be very happy there, I'm sure."

"Jess, that's perfect!" Sandra laughed with astonishment. "Well, in that case, I'd love to board with your parents. My lease with the Manor lasts until the end of August, but after that I'd be so happy to get out."

When her parents strolled out of the hall, Jessica brought Sandra over to discuss the particulars of the boarding arrangement. Sandra was elated. The savings would be enormous and being part of a family again was…well…an unexpected answer to prayer!

---

[129] Colossians 3:2-7
[130] Ezekiel 18:21-23; Galatians 5:13-25
[131] 1 Corinthians 6:9-11; Romans 6:4-13
[132] Matt. 26:41; Heb. 12:1-17; Col. 1:21-23; Jude 1:24; Tit. 2:14

Then Sandra thought of something. "The only thing is," she said tentatively, "I have a little cat. Can I bring him along?"

"He's a *nice* cat," Jess added.

"That's fine," Jessica's mom assured her. "We haven't had a pet for quite some time. We'll enjoy a *nice,* little cat."

A Wonderful Surprise
Chapter Twenty-Four

Sandra made an important decision Tuesday morning as she was eating a bowlful of brown rice for breakfast. While she and Jessica were weeding gardens together the day before, Jess had inquired if Sandra had decided whether or not she was coming to her wedding. Sandra had assured her friend how thankful she was to have been invited and how much she would love to come, but she had explained the situation with her brother. Now as she sat at her lonely kitchen table she considered her options carefully.

Jessica and I have become really good friends, she thought. *She and Peter have done so much for me. Laurie's not even going to be at the cottage on Saturday...and it's a three-hour drive away. Knowing him, he may never get there anyway! And without a car that works, I can't get to the cottage independently; I'll have to depend on Michelle for a ride. Why would I miss a wedding that I really want to go to, for something so uncertain? The more I get to know Peter and Jess, the more special they've become. This is such an important event in their life. This is such an important event to me.* With only a momentary regret, Sandra made a decision that she never would have entertained a few weeks earlier. *I think I'll cancel the cottage plans and hope Laurie and I can get together some other time.*

Emailing her brother, Sandra explained her decision in the nicest possible way and then, picking up the phone, she called the Symons. Jessica and Peter had already left for work, but Beth answered.

"I'd really love to come to the wedding," Sandra told her happily. "I'm sorry I put off accepting the invitation until now, but I had other plans – plans which I've *just decided* aren't nearly as important! If there's still room *please* count me in."

"There's still room," Beth assured her, "and I know Jess will be so happy to have you there."

It was an easy phone call and Sandra was glad she'd made it. She left her apartment and headed down the elevator to apartment 226.

I should be able to finally pay my rent today, Sandra thought happily, as she opened James' door. She looked over at the desk and saw the two envelopes of money sitting in the usual place. *I'm so glad I can always count on James,* she thought.

There was only a small note on the computer desk along with the shopping list. Sandra picked it up and read.

Sandra,
I won't be home till 9:00 tonight.
James

That's all he has to say? she wondered sadly. All week long she had half-expected James might call, or send her flowers, knowing how upset she had been about her brother. *Oh well,* she thought, *he's probably been working a lot this week and just hasn't thought about me.*

Taking the money out of the wages James had left for her, she added the final twenty dollars to the wad of bills she had for the landlord. Then she went out, locking the door behind her. Heading down to the first floor, she made her way to the office. She wanted to get the overdue rent payment looked after as quickly as possible.

"Thank you so much for the extension," she said to the receptionist, handing her the money, "I finally have enough. It was a tough month!"

The receptionist looked up surprised. "Your rent has already been paid, Sandra."

"What?!" Sandra could hardly believe her ears. "But, I didn't have enough money until now. There...there must be a mistake. Are you sure it was mine? How was it paid?"

"An envelope was express-mailed to the Manor last Friday with a money order," the receptionist replied. "The note just said to apply it to your rent. There was no name or return address. We just assumed it was from you – or that you at least knew about it! Anyway – be assured – we have your money."

"Seriously?!" Sandra started to tremble. Happy implications swirled around inside her mind. *Then I only have two more months... to pay my lease,* she mused. *And now that I can clean other apartments and work for Jess and Peter - I can make it! I should be able to make it!*

Turning around in total astonishment, Sandra could hardly think straight. Not only was her rent paid but now she had one thousand, five hundred dollars to use as needed. *I can get my car fixed,* she thought. *I can buy groceries! I can pay my school loan... and maybe even get a new dress for the wedding!* She wandered back to James' apartment in a complete daze.

As she collected James' sheets and clothes, Sandra felt a deep peace and true happiness. *Jess was right,* she smiled. *I need to trust that God will provide for me...and He has! Somehow, my rent was paid. It's incredible! Starting tonight,* she promised herself, *I'm going to change! I'm going to read the Bible every day and get that oil Craig talked about, into my lamp. I'm going to change my life completely.*

Sandra began the laundry, faithfully checking all of James' pockets. She found nothing except some loose change. Once she had the washing machine going, she left the money on his dresser.

But I wonder just who God worked through to pay my rent? she pondered, as she found the bathroom cleaning supplies and sprayed the shower. *I've only told James and Jessica that I was struggling. Was it them? It couldn't have been James... surely if he cared that much, he would have at least called me this week. But if it was Jessica and Peter why would they pay my rent anonymously? If I were to do something like that for a friend I would make them a big card and tell them what I've done. Or send them a dozen roses and tell them to talk to the landlord. Or...hmmm,* she pondered, as a new idea occurred to her, *perhaps James talked to Laurie, and Laurie sent the money?*

Scrubbing the sink and polishing the taps in the bathroom, Sandra imagined James telling Laurie about her circumstances, and Laurie's terrible remorse that he hadn't even asked his sister if she needed any help. "Oh, if only she had told me!" she could hear Laurie saying, running his plump hands through his curly gray hair. It was easy enough to imagine him writing a cheque on the spot, completing his signature with a grand flourish. "Here, James," she could hear him saying, "Please take this to her landlord and let me know if she needs anything else!"

Cleaning the toilet, Sandra saw herself running up to her brother and throwing her arms around his plump, sturdy frame in total gratitude for his great generosity. His kind blue eyes beamed down at her as he expressed his deepest sympathies... "Any time you need help, just say so. Don't wait for me to find out from somebody else."

No, she said to herself, standing up and jabbing the toilet brush back into place. *I must stop thinking that Laurie is the perfect brother. What if...Peter and Jessica paid my rent, or... somebody else? How would I feel about them? And what would I do to thank them?* Hanging a clean towel in place of the other, and picking up the mop, Sandra considered this carefully. *My friends have been so good to me,* she thought, dipping the mop into the bucket of warm water. *Jess comes over every Thursday night to help me study the Bible. She's helped me find promises that are real - promises that surpass anything I've ever dreamed up before.*

She's helped me find work with their landscaping company...work that I enjoy...and she's invited me to her wedding...

Carrying a pail of warm water to the kitchen, Sandra began mopping the tiles. On the kitchen table was the Heart Smart cookbook and Sandra noticed a yellow sticky-note on the cover. She took a break from mopping to read what it said:

> *Sandra,*
>
> *Just in case you're looking for ideas,*
> *the Grilled Chicken Salad looks fantastic!*

Sandra smiled. Another note from James was very welcome indeed. *He has been kind too,* she thought. *He may not have called all week but he drove me home when I was crying and probably had to work late because of it. He gave me his box of delicious Chinese food. He says so many lovely things about my cooking... He's always paid me faithfully on the day... I wish he hadn't talked me into coming to that luncheon to meet my brother, but... even so,* Sandra considered, as she squeezed out the mop, *he was only trying to help. Yes, he was trying to help me. He truly was. He knew how much I wanted to see my brother. He was worried my brother was going to let me down again. He tried...he actually cared... cared enough to suggest that I come along with him...*

Suddenly Sandra stopped mopping and stood up with a horrified look. *That luncheon was James' idea,* she told herself, *and he probably hoped it would have made me happy...but instead, I was upset – very upset. I hardly ate the meal that he'd paid for. I blamed him for talking me into something that...only failed because... because of my own foolish high expectations...It was my fault, not his!*

With a rush, Sandra realized that James might have been very hurt by her negative response. *In a way, I blamed him for it,* she recalled with a foreboding sense of gloom. *Maybe that's why he didn't call me all week. Maybe he's been waiting for me to apologize! After all, he tried to apologize to me. Maybe that's why his message is so short... Oh drat it! What a fool I am! Will he forgive me? Have I lost another friend?*

Discouragement filled her heart. When it came to guys, this was the usual pattern. Friendships never lasted very long. Sooner or later mistakes were made and the downward spiral began. *It's not worth it,* she told herself. *I should just avoid friendships with guys. It always leads to pain...to rejection...*

However, Sandra had learned too much in the last couple months to just leave it at that. *But what if James is hurt,* she thought, *after he tried to be so kind? What if it was James who talked to Laurie about the rent? I've got to say I'm sorry, regardless of what he now thinks about me.*

From that moment on, Sandra gave the condominium the best cleaning ever and planned out how she could best say sorry. *I'll make him that chicken salad and the yummiest dessert ever*, she decided, *and surprise him with it in the courtyard. By nine o'clock it will be almost dark ...so it can be a candlelight dinner. I'll buy some candles at the store...and I will apologize!*

Then she reconsidered. *Hmmm...Will all that seem a little too romantic? He didn't call me all week. Our friendship may be over.*

But I'm still his housecleaner. And if we don't have candles how will we see what we're eating?

Sandra finally decided to make everything as nice as possible and hope for the best.

It was nearly seven that evening when all her preparations were done. A small note was left for James, which read,

James,

Dinner will be served at 9:00 in the courtyard. Please meet me there. I'd like to talk to you.

    Sandra

Apologies

Chapter Twenty-Five

It had been a hot day and the evening was still quite warm. Sandra took a shower, straightened her hair and chose a light, breezy sundress to wear. She picked up a blue necklace which had once belonged to her mother and hooked the clasp around her neck. She liked the way the swirled, glass beads sparkled brightly against her white cotton dress. Putting her glasses back on, Sandra carried the dinner in a small cooler down to the courtyard. The metal-work table was quite small but Sandra set it as nicely as she could. All around the garden, roses had come into bloom. Right next to the table were the prettiest, apricot roses she'd ever seen. *A couple of those would be just the perfect thing to add a little elegance,* she thought with a smile. *But no, I don't want to make James feel uncomfortable. This is not a romantic dinner – it's an apologetic one.*

Running back upstairs to get her Bible, more determined than ever to keep reading, Sandra took it out to the courtyard and settled down to wait.

Jessica had recommended that Sandra should read the book of Ruth and continue through the books of Samuel, Kings and Chronicles. Half an hour later, Sandra looked at her watch. She had been absorbed by the story of Ruth, a young widow who had followed her Jewish mother-in-law back to the land of Israel. It was a beautiful story of loyalty, devotion and service. In the end, God had provided so wonderfully for both women and Sandra could fully empathize with their thankful hearts.

At twenty after nine, James had still not come. Pale orange and yellow clouds dotted the evening sky and danced in the rippling water. *I'm glad I didn't prepare something hot,* she thought wryly. With the grilled chicken salad and the dessert in the cooler she had no concerns that anything would spoil. Instead another thought troubled her. *Maybe James isn't going to come,* she worried, beginning to play with her necklace. *Maybe he was so appalled by my lack of gratitude that he isn't interested in having dinner with me. Or...maybe he was invited out somewhere else.*

I'll wait till nine thirty, she thought sadly. *If he's not here by then, I'll pack it all up and put the dinner in his fridge.* Her stomach growled loudly. *Oh, I'm so hungry!*

Smoothing out the page of her Bible under the slowly fading light, Sandra began the story of Samuel. Running her fingers along the smooth, glass beads of her necklace, she read about Hannah's earnest, silent prayer in the temple and how Eli, the priest, mistakenly thought she was drunk. She hardly noticed her stomach growl the second time.

"Hey, sorry I'm so late!"

Sandra looked up to see a tall, slim man standing in front of her. Having changed out of his suit into navy shorts and a striped polo shirt, he looked ready to attend a courtyard dinner, except that... his kind brown eyes – the kindest eyes in the world - were full of uncertainty.

With just as much uncertainty in her own, Sandra waved awkwardly towards the chair opposite from her. "Please, have a seat," she encouraged.

James slid in. "I'm glad you're not still mad at me," he remarked.

"Was I mad?" she asked in surprise.

With a flustered look, he explained, "After I talked you into meeting your brother..."

"Oh, James, I'm sorry!" she said sincerely, thankful she could make the apology right away. "I wasn't mad at you. I was mad that my beautiful bubble had burst. I spent *eighteen years* dreaming about meeting my brother! You were just kind enough to be there while I was venting and to ...take me home, and to give me that box of food. It was so thoughtful of you to even invite me to that luncheon. I'm very sorry I reacted ungratefully."

"Oh...really?" James said with astonishment. "I spent the whole week thinking you were never going to talk to me again. You...you never called...I thought..."

Sandra's hand flew up to her mouth as she tried to suppress a laugh. *James was hoping I'd call him?* "Sorry," she apologized earnestly again. "I was... hoping you might call me."

They both shared a laugh and heaved a sigh of relief.

This was the right thing to do, Sandra assured herself, no longer concerned that things might look too romantic. *James was worried how I felt about him! This apology needed to be made.*

With a smile, she pulled the plates of salad out of the cooler.

Looking hungrily at the meal she set before him, James said, "The *chicken salad!* I'm glad you saw that note. It looks even better than it did in the recipe book! Perfect thing for a hot night."

"Thank you," she said, blushing a little with his enthusiasm. "I hope you like it."

The plates were on the table and the knives and forks in place. For a moment they both hesitated. James went to pick up his fork and then put it back down. Sandra was waiting too.

Hoping that James was thinking the same as she was, Sandra asked shyly, "Would you mind giving thanks for the food?"

They had never done this before but James smiled. "Sure. I can do that."

Bowing his head, he prayed, "Heavenly Father. Hallowed be Your Name. Thank you so much for this good food you've abundantly provided. Thank you for the friendship Sandra and I enjoy. All good blessings are from you. Please be with Sandra and help her through this tough time. Please lead both of us to your truth. Amen."

When he had finished, Sandra looked up at James with surprise. A warm feeling was filling her heart. Their friendship was something James had thanked God for! And he'd asked that God would lead both of them to His truth! Had something changed?

"Is that what you want?" she asked timidly.

"What do you mean?" James replied, digging eagerly into the salad.

"Do you want us both to find truth?"

Looking at her steadily, James nodded. His mouth was too full to answer.

Something is different, she thought. "You mean we can talk about it...to each other?" she questioned timidly.

Laughing at her wide-eyed expression, James nodded. "I'd like to."

With a look of grateful perplexity, she pierced a lettuce leaf with her fork.

"You're wondering what's changed?" James prodded.

"Something sure has!"

"It's as simple as this," he admitted solemnly. "I finally took the time to read some of the lengthy manuscripts Peter has emailed me over the last couple of years, and believe me *they are lengthy*, and I've come to realize he might not be as crazy as I first thought."

"You've never read them *till now?*" Sandra was astonished.

James shrugged, slightly embarrassed. "I thought he had...well, *left the faith*," he explained. "I was worried I'd get confused...just like everyone else in my family. But last week I didn't turn on the TV once," he added cheerfully; "I just read and checked things out – looking up all the passages Peter gave me."

With a happy sigh, Sandra looked at James admiringly. "So, I can ask you questions now? Can I tell you what I'm learning?"

"You can talk to me about it all you want," he assured her. "I want to talk *to you* about it. I want to sort it out and make sure that I understand what the Bible says. I'm through with relying on other people to tell me what I believe. It's going to have to make sense to me from beginning to end. It's going to have to be clear and simple from the Bible alone."

"James, I'm so proud of you!" she said earnestly, just barely suppressing an urge to jump up and give him a big hug. *"Truth fears no questions,"* echoed through her mind. *James is no longer afraid!*

Shifting in his chair, James' long legs bumped against hers. Sandra didn't move out of his way. An indigo sky stretched around the little courtyard scene. Sandra lit the candles. Automatically, one by one, the carriage lights surrounding the gardens flickered and came to life.

Suddenly, the backdoor of the Manor opened and footsteps sounded on the stone pathway. "Hey, that looks cosy," a voice rang out. "Anyone else invited?"

"Hi, Brett," Sandra said, recognizing his voice and looking up in a friendly, guarded way.

"Any word on your car?" he asked.

"It's finally going in for service tomorrow," she replied with a light laugh.

"Well, I can see you don't need a driver," he chuckled, walking past. "Enjoy your dinner."

James looked inquisitive. "What was that all about?" he asked.

She told him the story of her car.

"Your car has been sitting there for *five weeks* and you never said a word about it?" he chided gently. "Sandra, I would have helped you out. Same goes for financial difficulties and *the 'brown rice diet'!* I can't believe you were making me all those wonderful meals and then going home to nothing! How can anyone know you're in trouble if you don't tell them?"

Sandra's pretty blue eyes sparkled merrily as she enjoyed another forkful of salad. The flickering candlelight highlighted the angular shape of James' face and the deep concern in his eyes. *James is so wonderfully different from any other guy I've known,* she mused. *I can tell that he cares about me as a person, and that he's honest, sincere, and kind. It's all there in his eyes. I love his eyes and his smile!* Then an astonishing thought came to her. *Could he have…is it possible…that James paid my rent?*

"It's okay," she said softly. "Today when I went to pay my overdue rent, I discovered that someone - some incredibly generous, thoughtful person had already paid it for me. I could hardly believe the receptionist."

"Seriously?!" James said with a look of genuine astonishment. "That's a fair bit of money!"

"It is," she agreed, watching James' reactions very carefully. "And all day long, I've been trying to figure out who it was."

James was silent. Having finished his plate of food he sat back against his chair. "I'm sure that was the best chicken salad I've ever had," he raved. "Thanks so much for making it." Then he chuckled. "You know, I have to watch how much I brag about your cooking to my mom. I don't want to make her jealous."

If he's pretending to act as though he knows nothing about my rent, he's doing a superb job! Sandra thought. "Your compliments make it all worthwhile," she responded warmly. "Are you ready for dessert?"

"Mmmm, what is it?" he inquired.

Taking it out from the bottom of the cooler, Sandra slowly uncovered the dessert. "This is also from *your* cookbook," she assured him, "but you're not going to believe it. It's strawberry *cheesecake!*"

"No way!"

Sandra had to explain that it was made with yogurt and cottage-cheese, before James was fully convinced it was really low in fat. And he loved it!

When they had eaten their fill and all the plates had been stacked on the tray, James looked up pleadingly. "Hey, I know it's already past ten," he said, "but I've been sitting all day and I'm dying for a walk. Care to join me?"

"I'd love to!" Sandra replied eagerly.

Leaving the dishes stacked on the tray and the leftover food in the cooler, Sandra and James set off towards the boardwalk.

"Did you have a class with Jessica last week?" he asked quietly.

Looking over in surprise Sandra nodded.

"What did you learn?"

A warm feeling spread over Sandra from head to toe. James meant what he'd prayed! He was inviting her to share what she'd learned. *I really care about this man,* she thought.

Without her Bible, Sandra couldn't remember all the passages they'd looked at but she explained the best she could about the resurrection and immortality; she even told him what Jessica had said about paradise and the thief on the cross. Some aspects of the subject James seemed to know more about than she did; others he prodded and probed until he could see how it all fit together.

Walking slowly as they were, it took longer than usual to reach the boardwalk that led to the wharf. The moon was rising slowly on the horizon. Almost full, it brightened the deep blue sky and streamed radiantly across the bay. A few little boats were coming in, putt-putting noisily across the water, aglow with light.

The moored vessels rolled and heaved with the incoming waves, groaning as they rose up and slapping heavily back down against the water.

"Hey, there's the north star," James said, pointing up to the sky.

"Where?" Sandra wanted to know. "How do you find it?"

Stepping in behind Sandra, James pointed over her shoulder. "First you find the Big Dipper," he explained. "See it there?"

Sandra nodded.

"Then you draw a line through the two stars on the outer edge of the cup, towards the Little Dipper, which is always close by..."

"Okay," Sandra said uncertainly. "So, you draw a line through the outer edge..." Pointing upwards, she tried to draw the line.

James took her outstretched hand and drew with her. "That's right," he said softly. "Follow through those two stars and see the Little Dipper there? Join it up with the handle," he said, helping her to make the line. "The brightest star at the end of the Little Dipper's handle is the North Star. If you can find that star you can always find North."

"Wow – that's cool. Thank you!" Sandra said, hoping she would always remember and wondering if there were any other stars she could ask James about. However, she couldn't think of the names of any other stars. Too many tiny, magical lights seemed to be dancing all around her, especially down one arm! There was no doubt about it; James was becoming a special friend.

Letting go of her hand, James strolled over to the railing and leaned on it. Looking out over the harbour towards the rising moon, he asked quietly, "Are you still thinking of heading back to Ontario?"

Sandra had to think for a moment why James would even ask that question. She certainly wasn't making any plans to go away. Then she remembered their last conversation in the car when everything had seemed to be caving in and her future had seemed so glum.

She joined him along the railing. "A lot has happened since we last talked," she said, smiling softly. "I have an interview at a private school on Thursday for a job that starts in September. Jessica's parents have said I can board with them when my lease with the Manor is over. And," she paused meaningfully, "now that my rent's been paid for this month and Peter is giving me so much landscaping work, I think I can manage fine."

"All that happened this past week?" James asked with astonishment, looking at her. "And you never called to tell me?" he added teasingly.

She nodded with a smile; then they both looked out over the water.

A moment later she asked quietly, "James, do you know who covered it?"

"Covered what?"

"My rent."

James was watching the waves intently. "Did your friend leave a name with the payment?" he asked.

"No," she answered, "and the receptionist doesn't know anything. The money order came through the mail."

"Then I guess your friend, *or friends,* perhaps, wish to remain anonymous. Maybe they don't want you to feel obligated."

From the way James had initially reacted at dinner, Sandra had been unsure. But now that James had suggested there might be more than one person involved, she was sure he knew something about it.

"They don't want me to feel obligated," she considered. *Yes, I can see that. If I knew who it was I would certainly feel*

obligated to repay it somehow - no doubt about it. Fifteen hundred dollars is a lot of money!

"Well, whoever they are," she replied with deep appreciation, "I would like them to know how thankful I am! I didn't know I had friends who cared so much."

For a moment there was no response from James. A few crickets chirped. A gull squawked. Waves splashed up against the wooden wharf.

"You do have friends who care, Sandra," James said at last, earnestly. "They care very deeply. Don't worry about that."

The moon was now above their heads. Sandra sighed peacefully. The gentle intensity in James' voice was most reassuring. She stole a glance in his direction and he met her eyes with a smile.

"I guess we should head back," he said with sudden resignation. "Unfortunately it's getting late and I have to go to work tomorrow."

They walked back quietly to the end of the boardwalk.

"So, you'll be meeting up again with your brother this weekend," James prompted. "How are you feeling about that?"

Sandra looked up with a smile. She was glad James had thought to ask. "I'm okay about it all now," she said. "You were right. I did have really high expectations and meeting Laurie brought them *all down to size* - a little too quickly perhaps, but it had to happen sometime. However," she said hesitantly, "I actually called this morning and cancelled my plans with them for this weekend."

"Why?" James asked in surprise.

"Because I want to go to the wedding," she explained gently. "Peter and Jessica mean a lot to me. There will be other times I can visit my brother, but this is the only chance I'll ever get to go to their wedding."

James sighed deeply. In the silence of the evening, their footsteps shuffled noisily against the wooden planks. "I've been feeling really bad about it too," he confessed. "Did Peter ever find a fifth groomsman?"

"No, he still hasn't," she said, trying not to sound too hopeful. Was James about to change his mind?

"Well, there are only four days left before the wedding," James reflected. "I don't want to mess up their plans at this late date, but I wish I'd said I would come."

"Really?" she clarified. This was almost too good to be true!

"I've been wrong about Peter," James admitted with a sigh. "After reading all his emails, I can see now that he's only been trying to help me. I've treated him...well, rather poorly this last year. I wish I could make it up to him somehow."

"I know they would *love* to have you come, James!"

"Are you sure?"

"James, if you came to their wedding they would know that you care."

Pausing uncertainly, James reached for his Blackberry; then he hesitated again.

"Is it too late for me to give him a call?"

Sandra was thrilled. "Definitely not!" she exclaimed, turning to face him. "Peter will be so happy!"

With a sad, thoughtful smile, James slowly pulled his Blackberry out of his pocket. He looked at Sandra, took a deep breath and tapped in Peter's number.

Standing next to James, Sandra could faintly hear the phone ring, and then a sleepy "Hello."

"Hey, Pete," James said awkwardly. "I'm...I'm sorry to call you so late. I'm sorry to wake you up...Thanks...but look, I've just been talking to Sandra...Yeah, things are much better now...Yeah, I know it's late, but we didn't eat dinner till nine-thirty...*I know.* I'm not sure how much longer I can put up with these hours! It's great to have a job, but it's important to have a life. Anyway, umm...I know this is kind of last-minute-ish and all, but... would I still be able to come to your wedding? Do you still have a spot for me?"

There was a burst of elation and James tipped back the phone from his ear so Sandra could hear Peter's voice. "Seriously?! James, I would be overjoyed to have you come!"

Sandra eyes shone merrily.

"Thanks, Pete," James smiled. "I'm sorry I've messed things up so badly..."

"Not a problem. Actually...I'm still short one groomsman...Could I...well... talk you into standing up for me?"

James swallowed hard. "Ah, that's not fair to you, Pete," he said. "How can you fit me in at this late notice?"

"If you have a black suit, you're set," Peter answered. "The guys are all just wearing their best black suit."

"Sure, I can do that easy enough."

"But what about the convention?" Peter inquired.

"I'll have to sort that one out tomorrow," James smiled. "There might be someone who can fill in for me. And if not, well, I just might be looking for a new job anyway," he laughed.

After the brothers had said goodnight to each other, James put away his Blackberry. He looked over at Sandra with a sheepish grin. "Any chance you could take my suit to the drycleaners this week?"

She laughed. "With pleasure!"

Sandra went to bed that night with a thankful heart. She was so happy! She was going to the wedding. James was going to the wedding! Peter and Jessica were going to be so happy!

"God you've been very good to me," she whispered. "You answered my cry for help and provided in many more ways than I asked. Thank you for James! Thank you for what you have done in his life and for the friendship he's extended to me. I'm so happy we can now talk about everything together. Please help us to find your truth and be sure about it.

"And Heavenly Father," she added, "I want to be at that special wedding *you've* invited me to. I know that what you've promised for the future is beyond all that we could ask. Please help me to trust you even when things don't seem to be working out. Help me to remember that you have only promised true happiness when Jesus returns! And that is where I want to be – in your Kingdom, with your Son, *forever.* In Jesus' Name. Amen."

Help With the Car and a New Idea
Chapter Twenty-Six

Even though James had told Sandra he would help her with anything, she couldn't bear to ask him to drive her old car to the auto shop for her. *He has to leave home at six in the morning as it is,* she reasoned, *and he gets home so late! I'll try to get it there myself.* However, the little Escort had no interest in responding to even an initial start. Turning the key produced only a faint clicking sound. Sandra got out of her car with a sigh. *Oh, well, I guess I'll call a tow truck.*

A happy whistle sounded behind her and turning around in the darkened, underground garage, she saw Brett Lawson coming around the corner. In a crisp, white, short-sleeve shirt, wearing the same brilliant blue sunglasses that he always did, Brett was looking as handsome as ever. *Okay,* she cautioned herself. *Careful with the eyes. No more flirting with Mr. Blue!*

Brett chuckled when he saw Sandra standing beside her car. He pushed his sunglasses up and looked at her appraisingly. "So," he surmised, "is that car taking you someplace today, or has it let you down again?"

Sandra sighed. "Well, I have an appointment at Gord's Auto Shop this morning, but I'm just heading back inside to call a tow truck. It won't even start."

"Hmm," Brett murmured, looking down at his watch. "I'm on my way to see a client, but he won't be upset if I'm a little late. Your battery's probably dead. Let me give it a boost."

Sandra tried her best to relay her appreciation as Brett told her to put the car in neutral. He pushed it out of the tight parking space as she steered. Bringing his own car over to face hers he soon had the Ford Escort roaring and screeching to life. "I really don't know how far this is going to get you," he admitted loudly.

245

"At some point that belt is going to snap. We may be calling the tow truck yet."

Brett told Sandra that he would follow her to Gord's, and they both set off across town. The car died once; Brett got it going again, but the last twenty meters they had to push it in to the shop.

"We did it!" Brett cheered as the old white car rolled to a gentle stop in front of the garage. "Tell that man of yours he owes me a game of golf."

Sandra laughed. "I'm not sure he plays golf," she said, "but here," she offered, reaching into her purse for fifty dollars. *It's so nice to have money again!* she thought. *I can actually be generous!*

When she passed the money towards Brett, he only smiled and shook his head.

"No, I was just joking," he assured her. "I love a challenge, especially when it comes to cars and...well, *pretty women in distress!*" There was just a little too much admiration shining through his sapphire-blue eyes, but then he added, "Just ask Natalie!"

With a slight blush, Sandra quickly dropped her eyes to the ground. *Don't return that look,* she thought, *I want to be his friend and nothing more!* However, she wished there was some way she could thank him. He had helped her out in a number of ways. She told him about the job interview she had the next day. "Tutoring Matt led to this interview," she added. "Thanks for helping with the car and a job!"

"I'm sure you'll get it," Brett nodded. "See you around."

Suddenly, Sandra remembered the pamphlets she'd picked up at the Kingdom Feast. She still had a few in her purse. "Hey, Brett," she called, pulling one out as he began walking back to his car. "Please take this."

Brett turned around and came back. He took the pamphlet she held out to him, curiously.

"I don't know if this information will be new to you or something you've known all along," she said, "but I picked it up at the Kingdom Feast. I've found it fascinating! It's worth a read."

With a nod of thanks, Brett skimmed through it briefly.

"By the way, if you don't mind me asking," he said, "what is the fellow's name that you were dining with the other night? He looks vaguely familiar."

"James Bryant."

"Bryant," Brett mused thoughtfully, as though he'd half-expected to hear that very name. "Wow - I haven't seen him for ages! He used to go to the same church that I do, and his brother was our pastor!"

"Seriously!" Sandra laughed. "So you know him then?"

Brett looked at her with an odd expression. "Andrew - James' brother, was the pastor I really liked! I was so disappointed to find out that he had left. Is he still in this area?"

"Yes," Sandra smiled. "I see him on Sundays. He lives near Peggy's Cove."

"That's good news!" Brett said, reaching into his shirt pocket. He held out a business card to Sandra. "Could you please give Pastor Bryant this card and tell him to give me a call when he has a chance? I'd like to ask him some questions. He was always a good man to talk to."

"Sure," Sandra smiled. "Thanks again for helping me with the car."

Brett departed to his Mustang and Sandra turned to go into Gord's Auto shop. She inserted the little card into her purse. *How interesting,* she thought. *I must remember to give this to Andrew - Pastor Bryant indeed!"*

It was a very happy Sandra who drove out to the Star Academy Private School the next day. There were no more squealing noises, just an odd rattle or two. *Finally,* she thought, *I have a reliable car again. I don't care if it's not flashy or new. I just need it to work!*

She dropped James' suit off at the dry cleaners in the Plaza nearby and walked up to the bright red doors of Star Academy with a box of activity kits in her arms. The little school was a navy-blue clapboard building with a large, wooden, dinosaur skeleton out front. All along the big, rectangular windows were life-sized, poster-painted pictures of the children.

The interview went smoothly and proved successful. After the Lawson's glowing recommendation it could hardly have failed. Marnie was very impressed by the box of activity kits that Sandra had put together and the enthusiasm she exhibited towards teaching. Sandra was offered the job on the spot. She toured the whole school with Marnie, looking at all the special science equipment the school had collected and the great variety of books. It looked like such a fun place to be. *I can hardly wait to tell James about this when I get home,* she thought.

However, James was at work when Sandra tried calling him at six. She tried again at eight but only reached the answering machine. Finally, at nine-thirty James called back.

"Guess what?" she cried out. "I got the job!"

"Good for you, Sandra," he praised. "But I'm not really surprised. I know you deserve it!"

"Thanks, James."

James wanted to know all about the school and the interview, so Sandra relayed her day's experience. Then she remembered the pressing matter James was facing.

"So, did you get someone to take your place at the convention?" she asked hesitantly.

"It's been a rather awkward day," James admitted. "I'm not in anyone's good books right now. My manager even went so far as to tell me that Drayton's is cutting back with the recession and all, and there will be layoffs in two week's time."

"Hmmm, that's somewhat threatening..."

"It is," James agreed. "But I took this job when I came back from travelling around the world because I felt good, the pay was excellent and it sounded exciting. I didn't have much else in my life at the time..."

That's changed? Sandra wondered hopefully.

"Anyhow, I had no idea I would be working this many hours! So, if they give me the axe and a severance package, I'll enjoy a few weeks holiday and try to find something more reasonable."

"You don't sound too worried."

"I'm not really. I have a few connections that will help me out. One day, I'd like to work for a little, private accounting firm somewhere out in the country."

"Your own perhaps?"

"It might have to be...but, hey, I had an idea!" James said hesitantly, changing the subject abruptly, "and it might be another *dumb* idea but tell me what you think."

"You haven't had *any* dumb ideas that I know about," Sandra assured him. "I just maybe didn't appreciate how good they were at the time."

James chuckled. "Well," he began, "ironically, one of the important people I need to talk to at this convention is your brother. So..." He paused for a long moment. "So, I was just thinking that since you were supposed to visit with them this weekend, why don't *we* invite them to *your place* for dinner Sunday night? The conference will be over by then."

Sandra wasn't sure. "To *my place?*" she questioned. "Not a restaurant?"

"I was thinking you could make the meal," he explained, "the kind of meal you make for me, and blow him away with your culinary arts!"

Laughing appreciatively, Sandra thought about the many times she had imagined visiting her brother in his magnificent mansion and being served the grandest entrees created by some famous chef. Now James was suggesting they invite her brother to visit them in a rented condominium and that she do the cooking! But before she dismissed the idea carelessly, she stopped. *James is making this suggestion because he cares,* she reminded herself, *and because he wants to help. Maybe, just maybe, it might actually work out...*

"You think he would enjoy it...?"

"Sandra," James implored, "he's just a man. Sure he lives a pretty fine life, but I doubt he eats out every night. Michelle probably serves him frozen dinners every now and again. Anyway," he added, "your cooking would rival the best restaurant in town. I'll get the food, if you'll work your magic."

It's worth a try, Sandra thought. "Okay," she said. "I'll call them tonight."

After planning a tentative menu with James, which she hoped Laurie would love, she nervously called her brother. To her great surprise, not only did her brother actually answer the phone but as soon as she mentioned that James wanted to discuss business, Laurie readily agreed to come.

Wow! Sandra thought to herself as she hung up the phone. *There was absolutely no hesitation... And oddly enough... it wouldn't have mattered so much anymore, if there was.*

The Wedding
Chapter Twenty-Seven

Sandra felt a shiver of excitement as she arrived at the Bryant's home, on a very special Saturday afternoon in July. So many cars were lined up all along the winding driveway that she had to park on the road. Stepping out of the now *almost* reliable Escort in a new pink dress, Sandra walked eagerly down the shady driveway, lined with tall, dense evergreens. As always, when she rounded the last corner, the glossy blue expanse of the ocean came instantly into view. More than ever before, the scene took her breath away; it was all so beautiful! A white, wedding tent fluttered daintily in the moist, salty breeze, stretching out over a collection of fancy, little tables, impeccably set for dinner. On a flat, uniform stretch of the lawn, nearly all the rows of white, plastic chairs were filled with finely dressed guests. Rainbow-coloured flower gardens surrounded the scene, running in gentle curves towards the white, Victorian gazebo.

Scanning that very gazebo, which had the most attractive gardens of all, Sandra looked for James. He had stayed overnight at his family's house and she imagined he would be with them now. As happy as she was that James had decided to be in the wedding, Sandra felt a little overwhelmed by all the people that she didn't know. *It would have been nice to have had his company today,* she thought, still looking for James, *but I'm glad he's there for Peter.*

Up near the front, a tall, lean figure in a black suit waved discreetly and Sandra recognized her friend. James was standing with his brothers near the gazebo, where the vows were to be given. She waved back with a smile.

Thomas and Allan stood with James and were easy to recognize as well. However, the fellow with the rugged features and curly, auburn pony tail was someone new. *That must be Peter's friend from Australia,* she decided. *I think his name is Jono.* She looked around for an empty seat.

Music was playing from large speakers set up on the lawn – beautiful piano music that she'd never heard before. Derrick stepped towards her, dressed in a black suit just like the others. The suit was an astonishing contrast to his usual tattered appearance. His wild curly hair had been trimmed short and he'd even shaved closely that morning. "Where would you like to sit?" he asked pleasantly. "I'm ushering people in."

Oh, so that's what they do at weddings, Sandra realized. *I'm glad he reached me before I seated myself!*

"You actually look like a proper gentleman this morning," she teased.

With a quiet laugh, Derrick took her arm. "Boss' orders!" he said.

"Are there any places beside someone that I know?"

"Probably not," he replied, "but I'll try to find someone you'll get on with."

A few rows up, Derrick stopped. "See that lady with the white hat?" he whispered. "She's in the third row." When Sandra nodded, he said, "That's Kara Lovell, Thomas' mother. There's a seat beside her. I'm sure you'll enjoy her company."

Sandra allowed Derrick to lead her to the third row and then she slid in beside Kara. The older woman turned and smiled amiably. She introduced herself and Sandra did the same.

"So how are *you* connected to Peter and Jessica?" Kara inquired in a friendly fashion.

With Derrick's assurance that she would like this lady, Sandra felt she could talk freely. She told her about the first talk she'd heard on Israel and world events, the classes she had been having with Jess and her friendship with James. This time she didn't identify herself as James' housecleaner, just simply *a good friend*.

As the melodious music played on and the guests continued to arrive, Kara told Sandra of her connections. With growing fascination, Sandra listened as Kara explained how she'd first met Peter as the romantic interest of her teenage daughter and how Verity's untimely death had sent Peter into a tailspin. Remembering many of the details from her talks with Peter and Jessica, Sandra was interested in Kara's perspective.

"Seeing this relationship with Jessica blossom, has had a healing effect on me," Kara admitted. "Of course there's a certain amount of sadness, as I know Peter would have been a wonderful husband to Verity," she smiled regretfully. "And I would have *loved* to have been his mother-in-law. But his pain has always made mine worse, and now I can just see he is *so very happy* again. Jessica will look after him well. Verity desperately wanted Peter to be loved and cared for."

"He and Jess are very happy together," Sandra agreed. She couldn't imagine Peter with anyone else. Looking up to the front where Peter stood with his groomsmen, Sandra met the eyes, the sincere, kind eyes, of the tall man beside Andrew and smiled. She felt as though she would never stop smiling. The tall, wonderful man gazed steadily back and Kara noticed.

"Is there someone special in your life?" she inquired, her eyes twinkling.

Sandra nodded with a slight blush, "Someone…who is becoming more and more special every day!"

The conversation might have continued for hours, but a new piece of music began. It was a processional piece and everyone began turning to look behind. Jessica was coming across the lawn, walking slowly, following her bridesmaids and holding on to her father's arm. Radiant in the afternoon sun, Jessica's simple white dress flowed around her. Purple hydrangeas filled the bouquet she held in her arms, matching the colour of her bridesmaids. Behind the fine veil trimmed with white ribbon, Jessica's hair was pulled back into a loose knot. Stray curls hung softly down to her shoulders.

She looks so beautiful! Sandra sighed happily. As Jess approached closer, however, Sandra noticed that tears were streaming down her face and she was dabbing them away with a tissue. They could only be tears of joy. Her eyes were locked with Peter's and her smile didn't waver.

It was a lovely ceremony and Sandra took it all in, fresh with wonder. So many allusions were made to the greater marriage to come between Christ and his bride. Sandra had never realized how elevated and symbolic a wedding could be. Reading from Ephesians chapter five, Mr. Henderson, the older man giving the service, described Peter and Jessica's new roles in ways that related to Jesus and the believers. Just as Jesus had given his life to save those who would come to him, so Peter was to give himself for Jessica.[133] Just as the believers were to submit to Jesus as their head and leader, so Jessica was to submit herself to Peter.[134] It was another whole new way of thinking, and Sandra was impressed with the beauty of following such lofty ideals.

Everyone was friendly as Sandra mingled around after the service. Pictures were being taken of the wedding party and James seemed to be in most of them. She looked over to see the photographer arranging Andrew's five children in front of the rest of the family. Walking towards the refreshment table, she overheard a couple of Peter's friends from Australia.

"Whoa! Is he ever a different bloke now!" a young, handsomely-dressed woman was saying to another man. "All this

---

[133] Ephesians 5:25-28
[134] Ephesians 5:22-24

stuff about the Bible *and Jesus* – Jessica's done one heck of a number on him!"

"What does Jono think of it all?" the other man chuckled, with the same strong Australian accent.

"He thinks it's a joke!" she laughed. "But he says he always thought Peter was rather strange. He never cursed or swore and he wouldn't rip anyone off, not even the aggros[135]!"

"I hear his business isn't going so well back home."

"We're lost without him!" the woman laughed. "Sure he trained his mates to cut lawns and water gardens and Jono's quite handy with the pruner, but no one has Peter's vision. I do the accounting and I can tell you, we used to make a good profit but we've lost a third of our customers and we're slipping into the red."

"And that's just from losing Peter?"

"The drought hasn't helped any. With the Murray drying up and all the water restrictions, there's not the same demand for elaborate gardens."

The conversation carried on, but Sandra decided to take a tray of drinks to the wedding party. They were out in the hot sun and hadn't had a refreshment break. *And besides,* it was an opportunity to have a little visit with everyone. She loaded up a tray and walked out to the gardens as the twins came running in the opposite direction. *Their pictures must be over,* Sandra thought to herself, watching them race towards the punch bowl.

James was posing with the rest of his siblings and their partners in front of the large pines. Peter and Jessica were in the middle, smiling happily. Peter's arms were wrapped around his new wife, looking so pretty in her white, organza dress. Mrs. Bryant was on Jessica's side and Mr. Bryant on the other. Andrew

---

[135] "a person who is upset and aggravated"

and Lisa were together, next to Mr. Bryant and...James stood alone by his mom.

"That's good," the photographer called out. "Grandparents next."

"Ah, just what we need!" James exclaimed, as Sandra drew close. Taking the cups from the tray, he handed out the drinks to everyone. They all expressed their appreciation to Sandra. James took the last one for himself. "Thanks, Beautiful," he said, with a grin.

The comment wasn't made privately and Sandra wasn't the only one who looked up in surprise.

He smiled at her. "I like the dress. You look great!"

All eyes turned on Sandra and she met Jessica's astonished gaze. She could feel her face turn as pink as her dress.

"Hey," James said to Peter. "Mind if we do another picture with Sandra in it?"

Everyone agreed readily, although in a baffled and bemused fashion. James drew Sandra in beside him.

I'm being included in an official family photo? she thought wonderingly, trying to remember to smile and hide her amazement.

"Is there something you should be telling us, man?" Andrew called out, trying to keep his smile intact.

The photographer snapped a few shots and then called for 'grandparents only'.

"The picture just needed a little balancing," James grinned as they relaxed the pose and moved out of the way. "I was the only guy there without a pretty girl beside him."

Andrew raised his eyebrows and looked from his brother to Sandra and back. Everyone in the family was looking over but James wasn't giving anything away.

Stepping off to the side with Sandra, James watched Peter and Jess take a picture with the only grandparent there - Beth's mom.

"Hey, I hope I didn't embarrass you just now," James whispered. "That was a little impulsive. I'm sorry. Call it the 'pink dress phenomenon'"

"I don't mind," Sandra smiled, "as long as I get a copy of that picture."

"Most certainly!" he grinned.

They watched the photographer take a few close-ups of Peter and Jessica alone and then James said quietly, "I'm glad I'm here, Sandra. I'm thankful you've helped me to remember how important my family is to me...but I feel bad you're hanging out by yourself. The people you know best are all in the wedding party."

"I'm okay," she said, grateful for his concern. "You're where you need to be. But," she added hesitantly, "it would be nice to have your company."

Reaching over, James squeezed her hand quickly and smiled. "After we clean up tonight," he said, "I'll have time to show you around this place. In fact," he said, "why don't you stay over? You can have the guest room. I'm happy with the couch downstairs."

Sandra considered the offer. She didn't have any extra clothes but it was a welcome idea, especially if it meant time to talk things over. *I can always zip over to the Manor in the morning,* she thought, *and get changed for the Sunday service.*

"Okay," she said. "I'd love to!"

"Great!"

James was being called for the next picture, so Sandra collected the glasses onto the tray and took them back to the marquee. Her head was in a whirl and her heart was beating quickly.

Sandra wandered around for the next hour, chatting to various people she met and helping herself to the lovely spread of fruit and goodies in the tent. It wasn't until the roast beef dinner was over that she had another chance to visit with James. He strolled over to the table where she sat chatting with some of Jessica's friends from the community and pulled up an empty chair to sit down.

Sandra looked up with surprise.

"Formalities are over," he shrugged. "It's time for the speeches."

Sandra glanced towards the head table to see that Purity had moved to sit beside her husband Thomas, and Jono had left to sit with his girlfriend. Peter caught Sandra's eye, winked and gave her a 'thumbs up'.

There was so much noise and happy chatter in the marquee that James had slipped over to Sandra's table without a whole lot of notice. But a minute later, when the Master of Ceremonies stood up to announce that it was time for the speeches to begin, James' nieces suddenly noticed where their uncle was sitting.

As Thomas, the best man, walked up to the microphone, Sandra could see excited whispers being traded back and forth between the girls. The eldest even took out her camera and focused it towards Sandra and James.

"The paparazzi have discovered us," James remarked wryly.

"Mmm," she agreed, feeling colour creep into her face again. "Most eligible bachelor sitting beside unknown housecleaner!"

James laughed quietly and squeezed her arm. "Naw," he said, looking down at her warmly. "Despairing bachelor falls for beautiful, top-chef, Five-Star-Academy teacher!"

Sandra liked James' news headline much better than her own and laughed appreciatively. *James really does care,* she marvelled.

Thomas' speech was funny, sad and serious. He talked about his friendship with Peter in their teen years, relayed a few humorous stories and talked about the changes they had both made. He finished off recalling that he'd asked Peter, two years earlier what he was looking for in a girl and that Peter had replied, "Someone gorgeous and fun, I guess."

There was a ripple of laughter around the room and leaning back in his chair, with his arm around Jessica, Peter grinned.

"He's added a lot to the list, since then," Thomas smiled. "Yes, *he has* found someone gorgeous and fun but when I asked Peter, last night, what was important to him, he had far different priorities. Since he's met Jessica he's come to value honesty, kindness, loyalty, godliness and someone who wants to pull him forward not drag him back." Picking up his notes, Thomas looked over towards the new bride and groom. "I can't express how happy I am for both of you!" he said.

Peter stood up, pulled a laughing Jess to her feet and gave her a kiss.

With his best wishes and a toast to the new couple, Thomas walked over to embrace them both before he sat down.

In the lull between speeches, one of the twins found his way over to James. Sandra wasn't sure which one it was; they looked so much alike.

"Can I sit with you?" he pleaded.

James laughed. There weren't any spare seats nearby. Without waiting for a reply, the boy settled on James' lap. "How do you make those stunt planes again?" he asked his uncle, producing a wrinkled name card from his pocket.

"This is going to be pretty small, Jake," James smiled, taking the rectangular card from his hand.

"That's okay," Jake assured him. "I like 'em small."

As Uncle James folded and shaped the small plane, Jake looked over at Sandra. "My dad says you're a teacher. Are you going to come to my school?"

Sandra smiled and began to tell him about the new school she planned to be at. While she was describing the large dinosaur that stood outside the front door, Zach slipped over with a chair in tow, and placed it beside her. The two boys wanted to hear all about the little private school with its scientific equipment and special arts program.

James had just finished the stunt plane, when Mr. Bryant stood up to welcome Jessica into their family. "Just wait, guys," James said, stopping them from running off. "You'll have to test fly your *mosquito* plane later. Grandpa is giving his speech."

Mr. Bryant told everyone how happy they were that Peter had found such a lovely young lady. He talked about the gradual changes he had noticed in Peter for good, and then Mr. Bryant thanked the Symons for all that they had done for his family and especially his son.

Jessica's father gave the next speech, which was surprisingly emotional, expressing how close they had all become to Peter over the years. Craig thanked Mr. and Mrs. Bryant for raising such a kind-hearted and responsible young man and thanked God for bringing Peter into their family.

Jake and Zach were getting rather restless. As soon as Craig sat down, James told the boys they could run outside the marquee and try out their plane. "Just keep it quiet guys," he cautioned.

Peter and Jessica were the last to take the stand and thank the audience for coming. They ran through an extensive list appreciatively, as Sandra realized with astonishment how many people had been involved in cooking food, designing the invitation, sewing dresses, accommodating out of province guests, and so much more. Then Peter thanked Jessica's parents for taking him in as one of their own and entrusting him with their beloved daughter. "I've always wanted to call you mom and dad," he laughed, "and today it's official – that's who you'll be to me from now on!"

Turning to his wife he took her hand and said, "I thank God everyday for you, Jess. You've made me whole and brought laughter and happiness back into my life. I didn't know twelve years ago that the cutest, little girl with the big, blue eyes would one day stand tall beside me." Peter smiled sadly, recalling the painful memory. "When my heart was breaking at the funeral and I thought it would never be repaired," he told the audience, and everyone knew exactly which funeral he meant, "this little girl came over and slipped her hand into mine. She only promised to be my little sister, back then," Peter laughed, with a catch in his voice as he and Jess smiled adoringly at each other, "but here you are, Jessica, and here I am, and we're together – man and wife! All I can do is praise God for His grace and mercy."

Sweeping Jessica up in his arms, Peter gave her the biggest kiss of the evening, to the delight of the audience, who clapped and whistled in appreciation.

"Jess did that?" Sandra whispered in surprise to James, once the tent was quiet again. She had never heard this part of the story. "That's so sweet!"

James nodded. "She was just a pip-squeak then," he whispered back.

Turning serious again, Peter thanked each of his groomsmen for the important part they had played in his life. Thomas had been his conscience, his support, and a friend whom he credited with bringing him back to God.

Jono had been a good mate when times were tough and his right-hand man while their new business was being developed. "Those were the days," Peter recalled, "when I simply needed to 'chill out' and let time heal the wounds. Thanks for giving me the space to do so," he smiled.

Andrew had been a brother he had always highly respected and always would in the future. Allan had been like a younger brother while Peter had stayed at the Symons and a very good friend.

And then, Peter spoke about his fifth groomsman.

"We all have someone in our life that we grow up with," he began, "someone who we play with and fight with and learn to love as we develop and grow. That person for me has always been my brother James from as early as I can remember. He might remember life without me, and perhaps he even enjoyed more attention before I came along but I can't remember life without him. Even though James left for Nova Scotia when I was just fifteen, we always kept in touch – quite regularly, in fact, considering my *track record* - and we always knew we were there for each other."

There was a pause in Peter's speech and Sandra could tell he was trying to compose himself.

"For the most part, James was always a good listener," Peter relayed, his voice unsteady, "very kind and very generous and he's taught me many things."

Sandra looked up at James with pride, but his eyes were transfixed on his brother's and his face unreadable.

"Today wouldn't have been right without him," Peter continued emotionally, looking directly at his brother. "I'm not sure how you wrangled yourself out of that convention, but I just want to thank you…" Peter choked up and struggled to say the last words, "for…for being here."

Peter paused, with his hand over his eyes. Holding onto his arm, Jessica looked up at her new husband tenderly and passed him a tissue.

Sandra whispered. "I think he needs you."

James looked down at her uncertainly and Sandra nodded encouragement. "He needs a hug," she said quietly.

Getting up from his chair, James strode awkwardly up to the front. Jessica stepped back smiling, as Peter embraced his brother warmly. They stood there for a minute or more, while James patted Peter's back and Peter clung to him tightly. Sandra looked over at James' mom and dad. They were struggling with emotion themselves and his mother was wiping her eyes with a handkerchief.

When James returned to his seat looking rather moved by the experience, Sandra looked up with admiration. "I'm proud of you," she said. "I know that wasn't easy."

"It's been a long time," James admitted quietly, "and Pete and I still have a long way to go. But thanks…thanks for your help."

When the speeches were over, Andrew's youngest daughter pranced over with her camera in hand. "You should see all the pictures Sadie took of you!" she told James and Sandra. "They're beautiful!"

Sandra smiled and reached over to draw the little girl close. "And what is your name, cutie?" she asked.

"I'm Esther," the child replied, fumbling with the buttons on her camera. She held it up so that James and Sandra could see. "There are *twenty-five* pictures of you!"

James laughed and Sandra giggled and they bent their heads close together to look at the screen. Esther displayed them with great pride one by one.

Most of the pictures were almost identical but one was extra special. James was looking down at Sandra with a look of loving amusement. Sandra was looking up at him gratefully.

"I'd love a copy of that one," Sandra said to Esther. "Please, pretty-please!"

"Me too," said James. He took a five-dollar bill out of his pocket. "Do you think you could get us both one? You can keep the change."

Esther looked delighted to be asked and readily pocketed the money. "Really? I can keep the change?"

James nodded with a smile.

"I'll get them for you ...as soon as Mom takes me to the Atlantic Superstore! I think I took that picture." She looked at it more carefully and then screwed up her cute little face. "Oh, no, maybe Sadie did..."

As abruptly as she'd come, Esther dashed back to tell her sister. Sandra could see a conference quickly take place over who had taken the winning picture.

James brought Sandra over to talk with his parents. He let them know that he was giving up the guest room that night, so that she could stay over. They were both happy for Sandra to do so. Mrs. Bryant commented on how much James raved about Sandra's cooking and Mr. Bryant said he'd be more than happy to try a little of that cooking himself. "It's not that I would question my son's culinary discernment," Mr. Bryant grinned, his eyes twinkling brightly, "it's quite the contrary. I'm looking forward to a chance to validate the high ratings!"

Sandra laughed. *I like him,* she thought. *He's kind and funny, like James.*

"Tell you what, Dad," James smiled, with a wink in Sandra's direction. "I'd like to bring Sandra over and show her around the lodge some weekend. If you'd like to invite us for dinner, I'm sure you could talk Sandra into making dessert."

"I'd be more than happy to," Sandra agreed.

"We'd love to have you come for dinner," Mrs. Bryant smiled. She suddenly remembered something. "Oh Sandra," she said, fumbling in her purse, "Peter gave me a CD to give you today. He didn't think he would remember at the wedding, but he said he promised to give it to you."

Producing the small case from her large black purse, Mrs. Bryant handed it to her.

"Oh, thank you," Sandra said with enthusiasm. She slipped the CD of music into her handbag.

After Peter and Jessica had cut the cake they handed out all the pieces, saying goodbye to everyone along the way. When Jessica handed Sandra a piece of the cake, she leaned close and whispered in her ear. "Having you included in that family photo was a *most pleasant* surprise!"

The two friends looked at each other with laughing eyes and embraced.

When Peter and Jess had given out all the cake, they stood together on the stone path and announced they had a parting song to sing. Thomas gave them the portable microphone and a karaoke machine provided the accompaniment. With the ocean waves crashing in behind them and a colourful sky in front, they joined hands and sang the most beautiful wedding song Sandra had ever heard.

Peter began the song with a verse that thanked God for the wonderful wife he'd been provided. Then Jess sang the second verse as the bride to her husband, choking up with emotion a couple of times. They sang the third part together.

> "As we 'wait Messiah's reign,
> When we, by God's grace will form that glorious train,
> Of faithful ones, joined to His Son.
> We must strive to be righteous as His chosen ones.
> A faithful bride we pray He'll find,
> A multitude of faithful servants undefiled.
> In garments white, stars shining bright,
> And in immortal glory shine with everlasting light:
> In one mind, as man and wife."[136]

---

[136] "In One Mind – the song of Boaz and Ruth," by Dan Osbourne. Used by permission.

It tied in so much with what had been said during the ceremony and left everyone with tears in their eyes, *even James!*

Amid a shower of grass seed and flower petals, which had been Allan's bright idea, Peter and Jess left in the car they had borrowed from his parents. A succession of firecrackers, which had been Jono's brilliant idea, went off behind them. Everyone waved goodbye until they were out of sight. Then it was time to clean up.

In the Moonlight
Chapter Twenty-Eight

A full moon was shining bright when the cleanup was complete, and there were a vast number of stars in the sky. When all the others started heading indoors, James and Sandra ventured down the weed-free stone pathway with the well-trimmed edge. "I'd like to take you for a walk along the shore someday," he told her, "when it's not so dark and we're not all dressed up. But for now I want to show you my favourite spot!"

The stone pathway led to the beach and in the bright moonlight Sandra followed James eagerly. For a moment or two they stood watching the waves roll in noisily and draw back foaming. "Is this your favourite spot?" Sandra asked. "It's a lovely little beach."

"It's one of them," James smiled. "But I want you to see a place up on the cliff."

Together they made their way along a winding, narrow footpath close to the edge of the low cliff. Rising only ten meters or so above the waves, the sandy bank sloped gradually down into the ocean. The footpath led to a large, flat rock with an unobstructed view across the water. On one side Sandra could see the harbour inlet with all the shining lights of Stirling illuminating the sky. To the other side, a single lighthouse beckoned brightly in the distance.

Taking off his suit jacket and placing it carefully on a tree branch behind him, James sat down on the large flat rock. "It's a clean spot," he encouraged Sandra, dusting it off with his hand, just to be sure. "Your dress will be fine."

"Peter said some nice things about you," Sandra beamed, joining James on the rock. "I love your family!"

James looked over. "I really don't feel I deserved Peter's kind words. I've shut him out so many times in the last year. He has good reason to hate me."

Sandra thought back on the conversations she'd had with Peter and Jess. "But he doesn't...not at all!" she exclaimed. "Peter understands completely."

"He told you that?"

"Yes."

Nodding slowly, James contemplated the matter.

Thinking back on all she'd learned from her friend, Sandra added, "Jess would say that *we* don't deserve the love Jesus has shown us. She says God wants us to show the same love to others."

"She's taught you a lot, hasn't she?"

"She has."

Picking up a little stone that lay beside him, James tossed it over the cliff. "Sandra," he said, rather nervously, "I made a few assumptions today and I'm sorry that I put you on the spot with that family photo. I hope I didn't put you in a place you didn't want to be."

"No, you didn't," she assured him, as her heart started to race. "I might be blushing bright red in that photo...but I didn't mind...at all."

"I'm glad to hear that," he smiled. "I felt there was something between us, but I should have talked it over with you first."

Sandra wasn't sure what to say. "That's all right," she smiled. "Everything has just sort of fallen into place."

"You're okay with it?"

"I am now," she smiled.

"You weren't before?"

"James," she sighed, "I've had a few misgivings...or *misunderstandings,* I should say. But I've come to see that you're a very sincere person; that you do love your brothers; that you do care about truth and want to find it with me and ...well, it has taken time to figure all that out."

With a wry grin, he nodded. "I can appreciate your struggles," he admitted. "I've been working through a tough time with my family. I still regret the night I got mad at you and scared your kitty!"

Sandra laughed.

"But..." James added solemnly, looking out once more towards the ocean, "there's something else...a couple more things you need to think through carefully..."

Sandra looked up with apprehension. "What's that?"

"I'm not a hundred percent healthy," he confessed reluctantly. "I still get these strange heart palpitations...I could have another heart attack tomorrow and be an invalid the rest of my life...or...*worse!*" He paused; then added quietly, "I don't want to ruin your future."

For a few moments Sandra was dumbfounded. James' health issues had been there from the start, but she had never considered the implications. It didn't bother her so much that James might become an invalid needing constant attention – such a thought seemed almost romantic. But did she really want to become emotionally involved with someone who might be taken from her suddenly? Losing someone she loved dearly would be very difficult! Looking out across the ocean towards the twinkling lights of Stirling, Sandra considered such a possibility carefully. *I finally find someone I love, who loves me, and he's ill!* she thought with dismay. *He may be taken away from me at any time. It's not fair! Why isn't life fair?!*

But, what if I was the one who was ill? she pondered. *What would I hope James would say to me?* Her perspective shifted.

"I could discover I have cancer next week," she murmured, "or be hit by a bus. Neither of us knows what tomorrow will bring."

James shook his head. "Sandra," he pleaded quietly. "Is it fair for me to ask you to become involved in my life? Are you going to want to look after a sick man – if it comes to that?"

"You're my friend, James," she said earnestly. "I'd be there to look after you whether I was invited to or not. I mean that!"

Looking back towards the bay, Sandra's eyes were drawn to the shining path of the moon reflecting brilliantly in the water. Suddenly, she realized that all she had been learning about God's promises and the hope for the future made life fair – even if everything went wrong! God would continue to take care of her…regardless of whatever might happen to James, or her brother, or anyone else that she loved. God's plans went on forever! It wasn't all about the 'here and now.' There was something greater, and bigger, and surer than any of the foolish fantasies that often evaporated as quickly as she dreamed them into existence.

She looked up with steady, earnest eyes. "James," she said, "if you come to share the hope I've found, then we won't have to be afraid of anything. We'll see each other again and it will be *forever!*'"

James turned away abruptly.

Puzzled, Sandra waited a moment before gently asking, "Did I say something wrong?"

Tossing another stone into the ocean, James remained quite serious. "No," he replied with a shake of his head. "You didn't say anything wrong. It's just that while I *am* committed to searching for truth, I'm not sure where that's going to lead. Right now all I know is that I made a big mistake simply trusting others to tell me what God's truth is. I don't want to believe something now, just because my brothers do, or because I feel I'm committed in...in other ways. I'm going to check out a number of churches and ask *lots* of questions. I have to sort this out personally," he said almost defensively, as if she might choose to argue the matter. "I have to prove it to myself...*from the Bible*. Until then, we both need freedom to choose logically. If we have to diverge we don't want to break...each other's hearts."

It was a fervent outpouring. Such edgy intensity was part of the man she was coming to care for so deeply. Sandra smiled. As much as she agreed that their friendship was dependant on choosing the same path, she didn't feel overly worried that they might diverge. After all, they were both determined to find their answers in the Bible. Rightly or wrongly, she felt confident that with an open mind, James' search would lead to the same conclusions she had made.

"That's integrity, James. I'm glad you feel that way... I do too."

It was a lot to think over and Sandra wasn't exactly sure what response James was looking for. Beside her lay a smooth, white stone - the perfect size for throwing. She picked it up and handed it to him with a smile.

James grinned and tossed it over the cliff.

"Okay," he said, in a calmer fashion, "so I guess what I'm trying to say is that I love you, Sandra, and I think that's something you need to know. But I don't want to get overly involved in a relationship until we have both determined where Truth lies. Are you okay with that?"

"Yes," she agreed reluctantly, while the words, "I love you," danced around her mind. "Yes, that's sounds wise. You need the freedom to choose and so do I."

"So then...do we search things out together, or on our own?"

Sandra thought it over for a moment and then said, "I've enjoyed the discussions we've had, even when we disagree. I'd like to do it *together*. I think we can help each other."

He smiled. It was a very happy smile. "That would be nice. I'm glad you feel that way." Reaching over, he covered her hand with his. "Thank you," he said quietly. "Thanks for all your understanding. You've already been a big help to me."

They sat quietly for a moment or two. The warmth of James' hand was quietly reassuring and one hundred percent real. Instinctively, he reached for another rock with his free hand. Sandra passed him two more from her side.

James laughed, but he didn't throw. Instead, he looked at her with a grin. "Do you know what I thought that first day you showed up to clean my house?"

"What did you think?"

"I thought that housecleaning ad was the best twenty-five dollars I've *ever* spent!"

Sandra laughed. "You seemed so uneasy that day," she recalled.

"Yeah, and I guess so!" he chuckled. "I would have been quite comfortable showing a little old lady around my messy apartment, but not someone as…well – someone as beautiful as you!"

James has Some Questions
Chapter Twenty-Nine

A few clouds were moving across the sky and threatening to block out the moon. "Let's get back while we can still see," James said, rising to his feet and gently pulling Sandra to hers. She brushed her dress off while James retrieved his jacket.

Following the winding footpath, they came again to the long, weed-less stone pathway. Looking up from the beach, Sandra was surprised to see the purple log house sitting so quietly. It was such a contrast to the beehive of activity it had been all day. A soft glow emanated from one dorm window above. Bright light shone through the large, main-floor windowpanes, but everything else lay in shadow.

"Looks like everyone has gone to bed," James remarked with surprise. He checked his watch. "It's only ten-thirty."

"They've all had a tiring day," Sandra mused.

"A tiring week!" James added.

However, Andrew was still up, sitting by the glowing, decorative lampshade in the living room, typing away on his laptop. He looked up with a smile when they came in. "And I suppose you just needed someone to help you find your way in the dark?" he teased his brother.

James and Sandra looked over at each other with amusement.

"Sandra is *very* helpful in many ways!" James exclaimed with a wink in Andrew's direction. Then he looked back at Sandra, "Can you stay up for a bit?"

She nodded. She wasn't tired at all, not after the conversation they'd just shared!

"What did you think of your place, this morning?" Andrew inquired as James walked into the living room. "Pete's crew sure made a difference!"

"I was blown away!" James agreed. "We'll have to hire them every summer."

Looking back, James motioned for Sandra to join him on the leather couch. However, Sandra was still standing in the hallway with a look of confusion. *"Your place",* she repeated to herself. *Why is Andrew speaking as though James owns this house?* She looked from one brother to the other.

"Isn't this *your* place?" she asked Andrew.

Andrew laughed. "I guess it looks that way," he replied. "But no, James owns this place with my parents. Thankfully for Lisa and me, James has been letting us stay here."

With astonishment, Sandra looked over at James.

He shrugged. "I was travelling around the world for most of the year," he explained. "It didn't make sense for the place to sit empty."

"Yes, but without your generosity," Andrew replied, "I would have been pumping gas, or…"

James cleared his throat. "Come join us," he encouraged Sandra.

Walking over to sit next to James, Sandra's thoughts whirled. *James could be living in this lovely place by the ocean with his mom's good cooking every day, rather than paying exorbitant rent at the Manor! And it sounds like James doesn't even charge them anything! No wonder they are so thankful for his generosity. And he just brushes it off as if it were nothing!* Any last lingering doubt about James' affection for his family faded completely away. Admiration took its place.

"So, anyway, I know I caught you off guard today, with the family photo and all," James was saying to his brother.

"All of us off guard…" Andrew clarified with a chuckle.

"Even ourselves," James grinned, looking over at Sandra.

Still processing all the new information Andrew had given her, Sandra could only smile in response.

In a more serious fashion, James explained, "The truth is that Sandra and I have become very good friends but we are both trying to sort out our religious convictions. Sandra has spent a lot of time with Peter and Jessica, and has become quite convinced that you all have it right. I'm willing to consider anything from the Bible at the moment but I'm still not sure…"

Nodding with a pleased expression, Andrew inquired, "What's puzzling you, James?"

With a sigh, James hesitated as though he was trying to figure out where to begin. Sandra looked up with interest. *Thanks for asking, Andrew,* she thought. *I'd like to know the answer to this.*

"I have lots of questions," James confessed. "I've come to understand that there will be a kingdom on this earth and that Jesus Christ is coming back here, soon. But I've always believed that we have an immortal soul. That when we die, our soul goes to heaven *or worse* – to hell. The resurrection, to me, has been the time when the body and soul are reunited…but from what I can determine, you don't believe that anymore."

"No, I don't," Andrew agreed. "Not since I've really searched it out from the Bible."

"So, what's changed your mind?" James asked.

Andrew reflected for a moment or two and then said, "Well, it's probably best to start in Genesis. There we have God's formula for a soul."

James looked blank. "Formula?"

Andrew laid his laptop on the floor beside him and took down a couple of worn King James Bibles from the bookcase. He handed one to James and kept the other.

"Where in Genesis do you think we would first come across the word 'soul'?" he asked.

With a shrug, James shook his head. "When the first two people were created, maybe?"

"That's right," Andrew nodded, sitting back down. Turning up the reference in his own Bible, he said, "When God created Adam, he created *a soul,* as it says in Genesis chapter two, verse seven."

Sandra leaned over to look at the passage as James read it out loud, "And the LORD God formed man of the dust of the ground, and breathed into his nostrils the breath of life; and man became a living soul."

"Do you see the formula?" Andrew smiled.

"That's a strange way of putting it," James remarked.

"Perhaps," Andrew nodded, "but look at it carefully. God formed a man from the dust – that's the first component, and then He breathed into him 'the breath of life' – the second component, and man *became* a living soul."

James studied the passage with a furrowed brow. He still didn't see where Andrew was going with this line of reasoning. Andrew sensed his confusion.

"It's an equation," Andrew explained. "*Dust* plus *the breath of life* equals *a living soul*. Take away the breath of life and man returns to dust. He ceases to exist, as is described in Ecclesiastes chapter twelve, verse seven. Death is the reversal of what happened when God created Adam."

Pondering the words in Genesis two, verse seven, Sandra observed, "It does say man *became* a living soul, not that he was *given* a soul."

"Good point, Sandra," Andrew nodded. "Adam was given 'breath', or as Solomon describes it - 'spirit'. Turning up Ecclesiastes twelve, a chapter which speaks about the aging process leading to death, Andrew read verse seven, "'Then shall the dust return to the earth as it was: and the spirit shall return unto God who gave it.' God's spirit is the power that sustains life all over this planet," Andrew explained. "God's spirit returns to Him when we die."[137]

"So is God's *breath of life* the 'soul' that people talk about?" asked James.

"It's the same *breath of life* that was given to all the animals," Andrew told him.

"Are you serious?" James questioned.

"Yes." Andrew nodded. "If you were to do a study of the word 'soul' you will find the same word used for all living creatures – man and animal."

James read Genesis two, verse seven out loud again – more to himself than to anyone else. "I don't even remember seeing the word 'soul' in this passage before," he mumbled.

"What translation do you use?" Andrew asked.

"The New Living Translation."

"It gets a little confusing with all the different translations today," Andrew nodded. "You won't always find the English word *'soul'* in other translations of Genesis two," he agreed. "The New International Version and the New King James Version both use *'living being'* in verse seven, instead. But the original Hebrew word is *'nephesh'* – the same word that is used extensively throughout the Old Testament for 'soul'."

"Do you know Hebrew?" Sandra asked in surprise.

"No. I don't know Hebrew," Andrew admitted, "but I'll show you how we can discover what the Hebrew words are." Bringing his laptop over to the coffee table to face them, Andrew took a seat beside James. "It's a simple task with modern technology! There are plenty of Bible programs that are linked to Strong's Exhaustive concordance. Strong's is a complete listing of

---

[137] See also Psalm 104:29-30; Job 34:12-15

all the words in the King James Version, with numerical links to each original Hebrew word for the Old Testament, or Greek word for the New. It's like a dictionary."

Seeing a quizzical look on Sandra's face, Andrew went on to explain, "In the translation process, decisions have to be made about which English word best suits the word from the original language and gives the proper sense. For the most part, translators have done an amazing job, but there are times when their own preconceptions have influenced the choices they made." Clicking on a Power Bible icon that stood out on his screen, Andrew continued, "Sometimes it's very handy to be able to check the original wording."

With the Power Bible program open, Andrew transported Genesis chapter one onto the screen. He chose an interlinear setting and tapped the mouse-pad to check the meaning of the word 'soul'. A box came up with a Strong's Concordance number, definition and a listing of the variety of ways 'nephesh' had been translated into English.

> 05315. nephesh, neh'-fesh
> Search for 05315 in KJV
> from 5314; properly, a breathing creature, i.e. animal of (abstractly) vitality; used very widely in a literal, accommodated or figurative sense (bodily or mental):--any, appetite, beast, body, breath, creature, X dead(-ly), desire, X (dis-)contented, X fish, ghost, + greedy, he, heart(-y), (hath, X jeopardy of) life (X in jeopardy), lust, man, me, mind, mortally, one, own, person, pleasure, (her-, him-, my-, thy-)self, them (your)-selves, + slay, soul, + tablet, they, thing, (X she) will, X would have it.

"Now, see where it says 'Search for 05315 in KJV'?" Andrew pointed out.

James and Sandra nodded.

"A search like this can be very informative," Andrew smiled. "When I search for 05315, I will get a list of all the places where the Hebrew word 'nephesh' occurs. In this way I can see how the Hebrew author used the word 'nephesh' and get an accurate, scriptural definition."

Andrew clicked on the 'search for 05315' and up came an enormous list that he had to truncate in order to view easily.

> Ge 1:20 ¶ And God <'elohiym> said <'amar>, Let the waters <mayim> bring forth abundantly <sharats> the moving creature <sherets> that hath **<nephesh>** life <chay>, and fowl <`owph> that may fly <`uwph> above <`al> the earth <'erets> in the open <paniym> firmament <raqiya`> of heaven <shamayim>. {moving: or, creeping} {creature: Heb. soul} {fowl...: Heb. let fowl fly} {open...: Heb. face of the firmament of heaven}
> Ge 1:21 And God <'elohiym> created <bara'> great <gadowl> whales <tanniyn>, and every living <chay> creature **<nephesh>** that moveth <ramas>, which the waters <mayim> brought forth abundantly <sharats>, after their kind <miyn>, and every winged <kanaph> fowl <`owph> after his kind <miyn>: and God <'elohiym> saw <ra'ah> that it was good <towb>.
> Ge 1:24 ¶ And God <'elohiym> said <'amar>, Let the earth <'erets> bring forth <yatsa'> the living <chay> creature **<nephesh>** after his kind <miyn>, cattle <b@hemah>, and creeping thing <remes>, and beast <chay> of the earth <'erets> after his kind <miyn>: and it was so.
> Ge 1:30 And to every beast <chay> of the earth <'erets>, and to every fowl <`owph> of the air <shamayim>, and to every thing that creepeth <ramas> upon the earth <'erets>, wherein there is life <chay> **<nephesh>**, I have given every green <yereq> herb <`eseb> for meat <'oklah>: and it was so. **{life: Heb. a living soul}**
> Ge 2:7 And the LORD <Y@hovah> God <'elohiym> formed <yatsar> man <'adam> of the dust <`aphar> of <min> the ground <'adamah>, and breathed <naphach> into his nostrils <'aph> the breath <n@shamah> of life <chay>; and man <'adam> became a living <chay> soul **<nephesh>**. {of the dust...: Heb. dust of the ground}

"Wow!" Sandra observed. "In just the first chapter of Genesis, the word 'nephesh' is used quite often."

"What else is a 'nephesh'?" Andrew prodded. "What else is a *living soul?*"

"The fish!" Sandra replied with amazement.

"And beasts," James added thoughtfully.

"So living, breathing animals are 'souls', just like people are souls," Andrew stated.

"Wow!" James replied. "Animals have souls?"

"Animals *are* souls," Andrew corrected with a smile. "They were created with the same formula as man. Dust plus God's breath equals a soul – a living creature!"

"Right," James nodded, accepting his brother's clarification.

Scrolling quickly through the long list of passages, Andrew pointed to a few other telling usages of the word in the Bible. In Joshua chapter eleven, it said, "And they smote all the souls *(nephesh)* that were therein with the edge of the sword, utterly destroying them: there was not any left to breathe..." Ezekiel eighteen, verse four said, "...the soul *(nephesh)* that sinneth, it shall die."

"Well, if a soul can be killed or die," Sandra observed, "then it certainly isn't immortal."

"So where did the concept of the immortal soul come from?" James asked, perplexed. "It's one of the most widespread Christian beliefs of today. Almost everyone would hold that belief – even people who are not Christian!"

Andrew typed the words 'immortal soul' into his search engine. Zero results came up. "See, it's certainly not a Biblical term," he replied. "In fact, if we enter the word 'immortal' we will only get *one* result." He demonstrated this on his laptop. The only verse to come up was First Timothy one, verse seventeen, which said, "Now unto the King eternal, *immortal*, invisible, the only wise God, be honour and glory for ever and ever. Amen."

"Try 'immortality'," James suggested.

Andrew put in the word. Five results came up.[138]

Skimming through them, Sandra noticed that immortality is something we are to seek for, [139]and at the resurrection our mortal body must 'put on immortality'. [140]It was all exactly as Jess had described it to her. However, she was puzzled by what she read in First Timothy six, verse sixteen, which said, "Who only hath immortality, dwelling in the light which no man can approach unto; who no man hath seen, nor can see…"

"Is this saying that only God has immortality?" she asked. "I thought the angels were immortal and isn't Jesus immortal too?"

"What I believe it's saying," Andrew explained, "is that God is the *only source* of immortality. He has always been immortal and is the only being that can give immortality to others."

James was nodding. "So you're saying that there's nothing immortal inside us?"

"That's right." Andrew nodded. "The message from the Bible is that eternal life is a gift – given at the resurrection to those God deems faithful to Him.[141] In Romans chapter six, verse twenty-three, it says that '… the wages of sin is death; but the *gift* of God is eternal life through Jesus Christ our Lord.'"

"Where does it say we are given eternal life at the resurrection?" James asked.

Andrew took them to First Corinthians chapter fifteen, verses fifty to fifty-four. He suggested that James read it out loud.

James read, "'Now this I say, brethren, that flesh and blood cannot inherit the kingdom of God; neither doth corruption inherit incorruption. Behold, I shew you a mystery; We shall not all sleep, but we shall all be changed, In a moment, in the

---

[138] Romans 2:7; 1 Corinthians 15:53, 54; 1 Timothy 6:16; 2 Timothy 1:10
[139] Romans 2:7
[140] 1 Corinthians 15:53,54
[141] 1 Corinthians 15:50-54

twinkling of an eye, at the last trump; for the trumpet shall sound, and the dead shall be raised incorruptible, and we shall be changed. For this corruptible *must put on* incorruption, and this mortal *must put on* immortality. So when this corruptible shall have *put on* incorruption, and this mortal shall have *put on* immortality, then shall be brought to pass the saying that is written, Death is swallowed up in victory.'"

"Now if the 'immortal soul' theory was correct," Andrew deduced, "and we all possessed immortality within our corruptible bodies, then it would make sense to say that our immortality *must put off mortality – the soul must depart from the corruptible body*. Instead, this passage states that our mortal body is going *to put on immortality!* Corruption must be transformed by incorruption."[142]

A look of confusion came over James' face again. He was thinking deeply. "But God is a loving God," he argued. "It's all very fine for those of us who have heard the gospel message to look forward to a resurrection when we'll be made immortal, but what about those who have never heard what God has offered? What about all the people in places like China, or other communist countries, where the Bible is a forbidden book? How could a just and loving God not give those people another chance in a better world?"

Sandra looked over at Andrew with interest. James had raised a very good question and she was glad he was asking Andrew and not her!

Andrew sat back in his chair. "That *is* a good question you've raised, James. I think the reason we struggle with the answer to that is because we live in a humanistic world, where we have become indoctrinated to think *it's all about us*. Many people think that God is primarily there to pander to our needs and give us

---

[142] See also 2 Corinthians 5:4; Romans 8:11; Philippians 3:21; 1 John 3:2

everything we want. The truth is that God has asked *us...to serve Him.*"

"Yes, I used to think it was all about me!" Sandra agreed.

"And God *will* be there to care for those who put their trust in Him," Andrew assured her. "He's promised He will. [143] But, even the life we have now is a gift of God's mercy; it's not something we could ever say we deserve! God has told us that His purpose in creating this world is to fill it 'with the knowledge of the glory of the LORD, as the waters cover the sea.'[144] His purpose isn't just to sustain human life, but to have a world that brings glory to Him through people who are willing to become like Him. The *glory of the Lord* is His attributes of justice, kindness, mercy, and so on,[145] which God is able to develop in us through His Word."[146]

"But not everyone has access to a Bible," James argued.

"True," Andrew replied. "And obviously God knows all things and will be completely fair and just.[147] His mercy is great. It's His prerogative to raise from the dead whomsoever He will. But those who have access to a Bible have the responsibility to search out the conditions God has clearly revealed in His Word. We will be judged on the conditions God has revealed.[148]

"You see," Andrew continued enthusiastically, "God has created an intricate and marvellous world, which He says is a witness to His existence. In Romans chapter one, God says that His Creation alone is enough to witness to His existence and compel people to seek out His plan of salvation.[149] None of us can demand anything from God. Life itself is a marvelous gift. Eternal life is

---

[143] Psalm 37:25; 55:22; Matthew 6:25-26;
[144] Numbers 14:21; Isaiah 11:9; Habakkuk 2:14
[145] Exodus 33:18- 34:8
[146] Galatians 5:22-24; John 6:63
[147] Genesis 18:24-25; Romans 3
[148] John 12:48-50
[149] Romans 1:18- 32; Psalm 19:1; Acts 14:15-17;

God's prerogative to grant,[150] and throughout the Bible ignorance has never been presented as an acceptable excuse."[151]

James didn't reply. Looking up at him, Sandra could see that he was pondering the matter.

"Let me show you a passage in Psalm forty-nine," Andrew suggested.

Turning up the passage, James held the Bible for Sandra to see. At Andrew's request, she read, "'For he seeth that wise men die, likewise the fool and the brutish person perish, and leave their wealth to others. Their inward thought is, that their houses shall continue for ever, and their dwelling places to all generations; they call their lands after their own names. Nevertheless man being in honour abideth not: *he is like the beasts that perish*...Like sheep they are laid in the grave; death shall feed on them; and the upright shall have dominion over them in the morning; and their beauty shall consume in the grave from their dwelling. But God will redeem my soul from the power of the grave: for he shall receive me. Be not thou afraid when one is made rich, when the glory of his house is increased; for when he dieth he shall carry nothing away: his glory shall not descend after him. Though while he lived he blessed his soul: and men will praise thee, when thou doest well to thyself. He shall go to the generation of his fathers; they shall never see light. Man that is in honour, *and understandeth not*, is like the beasts that perish.'"

The words were sobering to Sandra and she could tell that James was taken aback himself. *What if I had never come to know about the promises God has offered?* she pondered. *I would have died like an animal, to never see life again!*

"I suppose," she remarked out loud, "that if this life is the only chance any of us have to get it right, then we need to do all

---

[150] Romans 3:8; 5:12,17,21; 2 Corinthians 5:10; Revelation 20:12
[151] Leviticus 4:13-14; 5:15-18; Numbers 15:22-25

we can *now*, both for ourselves and to help others who haven't yet heard the message!"

As she spoke the words, Sandra thought of how desperately Peter had wanted to share the message with James. Now, she could appreciate his urgency!

Nodding, Andrew agreed with her. "God has done all He can to provide the invitation and give us the guide book to bring us to Him, but He's also given us free choice. We don't have to take part in His plan of salvation – He isn't forcing us. But if we want something more than the short existence we have in this life, then the offer is there – 'the wages of sin is death, but the gift of God is eternal life through Jesus Christ our Lord.'"[152]

For a moment or two the room was quiet as Sandra and James mulled this over. Then Andrew spoke again. "You know, James," he said, "the problem with the belief that everyone possesses an immortal soul, is that it spawns other false teachings. If everyone has something that lives on after death then you need some place for all those immortal souls to go."

"Like heaven and hell?" Sandra suggested.

"Yes," Andrew agreed. Looking at his brother, he said, "James, you spoke up about a just and loving God. Do you think a God of love would condemn a person to *eternal* torment for a *finite* life of sin?"

James shrugged.

"I certainly don't believe that He would," Andrew said. "Death is simply the cessation of life – and it's what God says we all deserve because we sin – 'the wages of sin is death'.[153] Eternal life is a *gift*, given to us by the grace of God, so that we can bring glory to Him!"

The discussion went on for much longer as Andrew took the word 'hell' and used his Bible program to examine the word in

---

[152] Romans 6:23
[153] Romans 6:23

the same way he had for 'soul'. James was most surprised by the discoveries they made. [154]When Sandra's eyes began to get heavy, she looked over at James' watch. It was one o'clock in the morning!

"I think I'm going to head off to bed now," she told the two brothers. "This has been most interesting but I'm not sure I can concentrate any longer."

James smiled warmly. "Thanks for staying up with us," he said. Pointing to the wooden staircase that led to the loft above, he told her, "Your room is the first one on the right, at the top of those stairs. I hope you sleep well."

As Sandra made her way up the stairs and entered the dimly lit room she could only barely hear the soft voices below. The clouds had cleared away and moonlight streamed through the dormer window. Walking over to a padded window seat, she had an unobstructed view of the restless ocean below. Through the open window she could hear the waves breaking heavily against the rocky shore; it was such a peaceful sound! *This is your place, James,* she marvelled. *You and your parents own this cozy log home! You've allowed your brother and his family to stay here, while you rent at the Manor. You're special, James - so very, very special!*

Slipping out of her new pink dress, Sandra hung it carefully on a white wicker chair. Reaching over, she switched off a tiny reading light and turned back the old-fashioned, flowered quilt that lay neatly on the bed. Wearily she climbed in, hearing a muffled laugh from below. *It's all making so much sense to me,* she thought. *I hope it does for James. I love him so much...I love his family...God please help us both to find your truth!*

---

[154] Psalm 16:8-10; 139:8;Genesis 42:38; 44:31; Ecclesiastes 9:10; Isaiah 38:1-3, 10-18; Jonah 2:2; Acts 2:31; Revelation 20:13

Lay Down Your Life
Chapter Thirty

The next morning Sandra rose early and rushed back to the Manor to shower and change. Even so, she arrived at the little white meeting hall, ten minutes early.

To her great surprise, James pulled into the parking lot, just after she did! He had still been asleep on the couch when she had left the lodge that morning.

"You came," she remarked with astonishment, as he got out of his car. "What a lovely surprise!"

Striding over with a cheerful expression, he lifted her chin tenderly with his forefinger. "I thought I'd check things out here," he replied casually. "It's all part of the process."

"Is your family expecting you?"

He nodded. "I told them at breakfast."

Even though she was tired, Sandra smiled brightly as she walked into the hall with James. He was coming with her...they were going together to a place that she wanted to be!

"Hey, how many cups of coffee did you have this morning?" Andrew chided his brother, as James walked in. Andrew looked very bleary-eyed himself.

"Mom says you had more," James replied with a smile.

Sandra looked at them curiously. "How late did you two stay up?"

"It was past four!" James grinned. "I was wired. If Andrew hadn't fallen asleep on top of his Bible we might still be talking!"

"What did I miss out on?"

"Lots," James replied. "I'll share it with you sometime."

"Tuesday night over dinner?"

"Tuesday night sounds good. I only have to work till six. That's if... I still have a job," he added with a chuckle.

287

As others filtered into the hall and greeted one another cheerfully, Sandra sat down beside James. They were right behind Andrew and his happy clan. Suddenly, Sandra remembered the business card she had in her purse. She found it easily enough and tapped Andrew on the shoulder.

"I was asked to give you this," she said, when Andrew turned around. "Do you remember Brett Lawson?" she asked. "He wants 'Pastor Bryant' to give him a call."

Andrew smiled to hear his former title. He took the card thoughtfully. "Brett Lawson," he mused. "The name sounds vaguely familiar, but…"

Lisa, Andrew's wife, turned to Sandra. "Is he fairly tall, with blond, wavy hair?"

Sandra nodded.

"You'll remember him," she encouraged her husband. "He was in your Sunday school class for years…"

"Okay, *now* I remember," Andrew smiled. "I think he was more interested in the girls than the class…but he was a good kid. I'll call him," he assured Sandra.

'More interested in the girls than the class,' Sandra smiled to herself. *Maybe not much has changed.*

Beth began playing music on the piano and everyone finished up their conversations and settled back quietly to focus on the reason they had all come together. They were there that morning to remember their Lord Jesus Christ and the sacrifice he had made for the world.[155]

Thomas gave the exhortation that morning and it was on Jesus' willing sacrifice. He talked a lot about the crucifixion and the wonderful plan God had from the beginning of the world [156]to forgive our sins in Christ. He talked about the pain Jesus would

---

[155] John 3:14-17; Luke 22:14-20
[156] Revelation 13:8; Genesis 3:14-15; 22:2-18 cp. Galatians 3:8-9; Isaiah 53; Acts 15:18

have endured, the rejection and the humiliation. And then, Thomas directed everyone's attention to the practical implications. "'By this we know love,'" he quoted, "'because He laid down His life for us. And we also ought to lay down our lives for the brethren.'[157]

"Jesus died for our sins so that we could be forgiven," Thomas reminded his audience, "and Jesus died to show us the way. He said, 'If anyone desires to come after Me, let him deny himself, and take up his cross, and follow Me. For whoever desires to save his life will lose it, but whoever loses his life for My sake will find it.'"[158]

Throughout Thomas' exhortation Sandra had been reminded of the many powerful, perspective-altering verses she had come across in the last couple of months. "Whatever you want men to do to you, do also to them."[159] "And be kind to one another, tender-hearted, forgiving one another, just as God in Christ forgave you."[160] It was the perfect exhortation for what lay ahead later that evening with Laurie and Michelle. After all the lonely years, Sandra's brother was coming for dinner!

Once the congregation had taken the time to remember the Lord Jesus Christ in the bread and wine, a special collection was passed around to help with a school for orphan children in India. Sandra was only too happy to put in a twenty! James looked at her thoughtfully for a moment and then contributed something as well.

A final hymn and prayer were sung and then there was an announcement that caught almost everyone by surprise. Craig Symons stood up and said that he had a letter to read.

"To all our dear friends," Craig began reading from the letter. "As you know we have been attending your meetings

---

[157] 1 John 3:16
[158] Matthew 16:24-26
[159] Matthew 7:12
[160] Ephesians 4:32

regularly and have had many personal classes with you to discuss the Bible. We have found the Bible speaks clearly and consistently from beginning to end of God's plan for His glory to be manifest in this earth. We're so thankful that God has called us to repent of our former ways and be heirs of salvation in Christ and citizens of the coming Kingdom. Please make the necessary arrangements for the four of us to be baptised. Sincerely..."

James had been listening politely as the letter was read, but now he looked down at Sandra with a smile.

"Jim and Mary Bryant," Craig read, "and Andrew and Lisa..."

"Your family?!" she whispered in astonishment.

"They told me about it this weekend," he whispered back.

There was quite a stir about such wonderful news and James and Sandra were caught up in the excitement.

"I've never seen a baptism before," she told James, as they left the hall to head to their separate cars. "Where will it happen?"

"I think they've decided on the small lake in behind the chapel," James replied. "My mom and Lisa are somewhat squeamish about it, but Dad and Andrew think it's the obvious choice."

"If there wasn't a lake," Sandra asked, "what would they do?"

"Find water, somehow," he smiled. "I guess they would look for a river, rent a pool, fill a bathtub - whatever works."

Sandra mulled it over as she drove to the Manor, following James.

As they walked into the Manor together, James stopped hesitantly and took Sandra's hand. "I hope you don't mind if I work on my bank presentation this afternoon," he said. "I know it's unfair to ask you to put on a dinner and then be too busy to help," he added apologetically, "but...I really do have some more work to do and ..." Pausing uncomfortably, James shook his head. "Well, you see, the full truth is, I don't like to visit women alone in their apartments for any extended length of time."

"You don't?" Sandra clarified in surprise. "Why not?"

"I just don't think it's right," James smiled firmly. "It's a set up for temptation."

Sandra looked up uncertainly. In university, she and her friends had been in and out of one another's dorms freely. "Really?" she said. "I would never have thought of it like that."

James shrugged. "I was raised rather conservatively," he explained, "but the older I get, the more I appreciate the wisdom behind it all. I'll come over in half-an-hour," he promised, "so save me a few things to do. And just call if you want me to pick anything else up at the store."

Looking up, Sandra smiled. *This man has integrity,* she thought. *How did I ever get so lucky ... or was God guiding me? I feel like I can trust James completely...and that's unusual for me.*

The dinner was planned for seven and it was only two o'clock in the afternoon. "I have all the time I need to get the dinner ready," she assured him. "Don't worry about it."

"Thanks for understanding," James said, as they reached his floor. "I'll bring up the groceries."

After the groceries were put away in the fridge and James had left, Sandra looked around the kitchen and living area. Some cleaning needed to be done. *A little music would help,* she thought. Remembering Peter's CD, she took it out of her purse. As she opened the case to take out the disk, a small note fell out. She picked it up and read,

Sandra,

When you listen to my favourite song on this CD, I want you to know that we thank God for the way He's worked through you with

my brother. You're an answer to our prayers! James and I had a long talk, the best talk we've had in years! I know James has a lot of searching to do and it may take a long time, but at least he's opened the door. He's willing to look at what we've been trying to show him.

Thanks, and may God be with you and your brother!

Your friends,
Peter and Jessica

I never thought I might be an answer to someone's prayers! Sandra thought with astonishment. *How interesting.*

Putting the CD on, she gave her apartment a quick tidy as she listened to the music. It brought to mind plenty of beautiful memories of warm, sunny days in gorgeous gardens with great friends to talk to and inspiring thoughts to consider. *God, I've been so blessed by you,* she thought, *in ways I would never have thought to choose for myself.*

It was going to be a couple of busy weeks ahead while Peter and Jessica were on their honeymoon. Derrick was taking charge of the gardening crew. Sandra and Allan were booked to work every day, except weekends. Finally she would work a full five-day week again!

As she vacuumed the living room floor, Sandra still wasn't completely convinced that this second meeting with her brother would go any better than the first, but for James' sake she was determined to give it her best effort. When the vacuum had been put away, she opened the fridge door and took out the food that she needed to prepare for the meal. As she chopped up the garlic for the steak marinade and washed mushrooms to pan fry, she thought long and hard about meeting Laurie again. Only this time it wasn't a fanciful daydream, it was a thoughtful consideration of the facts. *I always envisioned Laurie looking after me,* she thought with a smile, *and here I am preparing to look after him. How ironic! But maybe,* she considered, *this is the better way. After all, Laurie hasn't really ever had a family either. He grew up without a dad and saw little of his mom, just like me. He probably doesn't know how to treat a sister any more than I know how to treat a brother. And,* she mused, *since I've been learning about God's love and Jesus laying down his life for us while we were sinners...I guess I'm the one who needs to show this kind of love.*

Scrubbing the potatoes, Sandra thought about all she had learned. Even the exhortation that morning and the little note she'd just received from Peter and Jess had been reminders of a new way of thinking. *Perhaps,* she considered, *it's not about what God can do for us. It's about what God can do through us.* With that in mind, she thought through the kind of sister she wanted to be, regardless of how Laurie might respond. *I'm going to show God's love to him,* she decided, *whether or not he cares about me. I want to make him and Michelle feel welcome here. And I do actually have something to share with them that is far more valuable than anything they own. I doubt we'll discuss it tonight, but maybe someday we can. God has freely given me this invitation and I can freely pass it on to others! How wonderful!*

With such an objective in mind, Sandra did her best to make everything as special as it could be. The raspberry cheesecake – made with yogurt and cottage cheese, was picture-perfect, the tablecloth carefully pressed and the dishes set out neatly. She ran over to the grocery store for a bouquet of zinnias and lime-green napkins. In the middle of the table, she arranged the giant, brightly coloured flowers in a tall, blue vase, surrounding them with a flourish of swirled, green napkins in every glass.

A soft song began quietly as Sandra stepped back to observe her work. It was "Peter's Prayer", as she had come to call it. She listened to the melody with new meaning, carefully pulling one wilted flower from the vase.

"Lord, I pray that you will be with Laurie," Sandra whispered. "Even if things don't go as I want them to, even if he doesn't care about me, I'm going to do the best that I can and leave him in your hands. He belongs to you. Please help me to always remember that."

There was a knock on the door. Sandra ran to open it and was pleased to see James.

"Wow, Sandra! This is even better than I expected," he exclaimed, looking at the table.

Sandra smiled up at him, always thankful for his praise.

"So what can I do to help? Do you want me to barbeque the steaks?"

Not having any idea whether or not James was an incompetent cook - as he so often proclaimed, Sandra hesitated. The steak was the most important part of the meal. However, she could see in James' eyes that he really wanted to help. *James' feelings mean more to me than my brother's,* she thought.

"I'd love you to help," she replied sincerely, taking the veggies out of the fridge to make a salad. She looked over at the clock and calculated a plan. "They'll only take five minutes a side…and Laurie should be here around seven…so why don't we wait till we've welcomed them in, and then they won't get overdone?"

James was happy to comply but there was still half an hour to wait. Sandra handed him a knife. "You could help me chop the salad," she smiled warmly.

For the next half an hour they chopped up the veggies, as the mushrooms sizzled, the potatoes baked and the steaks marinated close by. Tiger came over and purred contentedly around their legs.

"Do you think he's forgiven me?" James asked with a twinkle in his eyes. Without another word, he uncovered one marinating steak and sliced off a tiny piece of meat. "Here kitty, kitty," he called, holding out the tidbit.

"James!" Sandra laughed, taking out cans of frozen pina colada. "You're giving him *steak?*"

Tiger devoured the morsel. From then on he selectively purred around James' legs, reaching up now and then on his haunches to see if any more tidbits were coming.

"I think I won him over," James smiled, "the same way you won me."

"What do you mean?!" Sandra questioned, adding ice to the blender.

He chuckled. "When you made me that raspberry pie and insisted I keep it, I thought, 'Now, this is the kind of compassion I've been looking for!'"

Sandra smiled thoughtfully. *Was it compassion?* she asked herself. *Or was I serving myself in a roundabout way? It doesn't matter,* she decided. *Compassion is now the spirit I choose to have.*

Looking up at James with admiration, she replied quietly, "I was looking for compassion too. And I know I've found it... in you."

James was suddenly at a loss for words, but that was okay because just then the intercom buzzed. Laurie and Michelle had arrived. Sandra felt her stomach do a flip-flop inside. She looked up at James nervously and he looked down at her with a smile. "Are you ready?" he asked.

"I hope so," she said.

295

Pressing the buzzer, James let them in to the ground floor Lobby. Then they waited for the knock on the door.

Seeing Sandra's anxiety, James squeezed her arm. "You'll be fine," he said encouragingly. "Any guy would be proud to have a sister like you!"

With a grateful heart Sandra followed James to the door. Mentally she rehearsed all her thoughts from before. *I'll be the sister he needs to have,* she reminded herself.

"Welcome, come on in," James said, opening the door.

Laurie and Michelle stepped forward a little awkwardly, dressed in fairly normal, everyday attire, looking like normal, everyday people.

James shook their hands and Sandra who had planned to give hugs, chickened-out and followed suit. "I'm so glad you've come," she said, beaming brightly.

Laurie was quiet but Michelle bubbled over. "At last we meet, Sandra!" she smiled. "And you're as pretty as Laurie told me you were! Thank you for inviting us."

James took Laurie outside on the deck to barbeque the steaks. "Five minutes a side?" he clarified, looking over at Sandra.

She nodded, still reeling from Michelle's unexpected compliment. *Did Laurie really tell her I was pretty?*

"Would either of you like a drink?" she inquired timidly, looking at Michelle.

Michelle quickly chose from the selection on the counter. "Pina colada would be great for both of us, thanks!" she said. "It's our favourite."

Passing her a drink to take to Laurie on the deck, Sandra smiled appreciatively at Michelle. She wasn't a blond like Sandra had always imagined. Instead, Michelle had short, highly-stylized brown hair. Wearing white-heeled sandals, she was quite petite with small, elegant facial features and hazel eyes. Well-placed makeup made her attractive. A heavy gold necklace and diamond studs were the only conspicuous evidence of superfluous wealth.

The dinner went well. The steaks were perfectly grilled. *James may know more about cooking than he's ever let on!* Sandra decided. She did her best to be a gracious hostess and James made a great effort to keep the conversation going.

"How long have you been in Stirling?" James asked her brother, picking up a forkful of sautéed mushrooms and a slice of tender steak.

"I came out here in my teens," Laurie told him. "Great steaks, by the way!" he said with a nod in James' direction. "A good friend of mine moved here with his family and invited me to come along. I've never gone back."

"Same here," James nodded. "Only, my brother and I came to Nova Scotia to work for my uncle. I was just out of high school."

Laurie and James compared notes and discovered they had both moved out within a year of each other.

"What about you, Michelle?" James asked.

"I grew up in the Maritimes," she replied. "I'm one of the lucky ones!"

James continued asking interesting questions involving everyone at the table. But suddenly it became a little more personal.

"So, Laurie," James asked, passing around the salad for the second time, "what do you remember about Sandra, when you were growing up? Was she always as sweet as she is today?"

Laurie chuckled, glancing briefly at Sandra and then back over to James. "I can't say that I was the greatest brother," he admitted. "I think we were too far apart in age. Sandra was always begging to tag along but I was seven years older. It just wasn't cool. I thought I was finally going to have the chance to make it up to her this weekend," he said, looking furtively in Sandra's direction again, "but that's just how things go for me. *Michelle and I* rarely even see each other..."

Resentment rose in Sandra's heart but she dismissed it evenly. *His plans and his status have always been more important to him than people,* she thought. *Maybe that's how it always will be, but it doesn't matter anymore. Laurie isn't all I have. God has shown me His love and brought me to James and so many others.*

As Sandra enjoyed the dinner, she watched Laurie talk amiably to James. *I wish I could have such an easy conversation with my brother,* she thought, and then she caught herself. *No,* she decided, *I'm not going to get upset about this. I'm just going to show Laurie the love I wish he would show me.*

With such constant self-talk and determination Sandra didn't allow anything to get her down. She served the dessert graciously, enjoying James' compliments and overlooking the fact that Laurie never once praised her for anything.

"Hey, Beautiful," James said to her, looking over affectionately, "do you think I could have another *tiny* slice of that cheesecake? It's just too good to resist."

Blushing just a little, Sandra served James another slice. The term of endearment James used was flattering and the public acknowledgement that she was more than just his housekeeper meant a great deal. Laurie looked over with interest but he didn't seem surprised.

"Did you hear that your sister landed a new job this week?" James asked Laurie, as he took a forkful of the cake.

"No, I didn't," Laurie replied, "but that second helping looks good. Another slice for me too, please," he asked, holding his plate out to Sandra. "Same size as James'."

Sandra cut another slice as James relayed the news. "Yes, Sandra's going to be working for the Star Academy Private School. You know the one just near the Atlantic Superstore?"

"With the big dinosaur in front?" Michelle clarified.

"That's the one," Sandra and James both replied simultaneously.

"I've heard some really good things about that school," Michelle said. "Good for you, Sandra!"

Laurie nodded his approval but didn't meet his sister's eyes. "So, I guess you'll be better off financially, then," he queried. "That must be a relief."

"It's a great relief!" Sandra replied with a smile, thinking, *I just don't understand why he hardly even looks at me!* Then she began to absorb what Laurie had said. *He knows I've had financial struggles,* she mused. She looked up quickly at James but his eyes were firmly fixed on his unfinished cake. *Hmm, James must have talked to him,* she reasoned. *Maybe Laurie is one of my 'friends'!*

Later on when James and Laurie were having their business discussion huddled over laptops in the living room, Michelle helped Sandra clean up in the kitchen. "You did a fabulous job, tonight," she praised, drying off the salad bowl. "I'm not a cook; we have to eat out a lot."

"I'm glad you enjoyed it," Sandra said evenly, looking over at Michelle. *She's a nice person,* she thought. *I could get along with her easily, but how does she ever put up with my brother?*

As if reading her thoughts, Michelle put a hand on Sandra's shoulder. "I'm sorry about Laurie," she said compassionately, speaking quietly so no one else would hear. "I know he comes across as uncaring…sometimes." Michelle sighed. "He's not really like that, deep down. You see, Laurie's very good at what he does because it consumes him; he lives and breathes every decision he makes. But he can be completely oblivious to everything else that's going on right in front of him." In a sensitive tone of voice, she added, "I think, Sandra, that for some reason with you, he has this burden of guilt. He feels he's always let you down and I think that makes it difficult for him to just relax and enjoy your company. He's been very anxious about meeting you."

Sandra stopped scrubbing the barbeque fork and stared at Michelle. "Is that it?" she clarified. "It's not that he just doesn't like me?"

"No, it's definitely not that," Michelle assured her, laying down the plate she was drying and picking up another. "I know he thinks you're a great person…He just…doesn't always know how to show it."

Maybe I've been too intense with Laurie, just as Peter was with James, Sandra considered. *Maybe I need to back off a bit…and leave it in God's hands…*

"So, if you're right," Sandra surmised as she resumed scrubbing, "then what can I do to make things better?"

"What you did tonight was really good," Michelle nodded. "Just let him know you accept him as he is and you're happy to enjoy the time he has to give you."

James and Laurie talked for at least a couple of hours, while Sandra and Michelle visited in the kitchen. They had both lived completely different lives and had very different goals and aspirations but when it was time for everyone to go, Sandra felt they had paved the way for their relationship to grow. And while she didn't feel much closer to her brother than she had before, Sandra felt she could now at least understand him. A raw, bleeding wound had begun to heal.

"Goodbye, Michelle," she said warmly, giving her a hug. "It's been lovely getting to know you."

Sandra looked over at Laurie. He stood aloof with his hand on the doorknob. *Should I give him a hug, or not?* she wondered. *Is that too much pressure?*

No, it isn't, she decided. *He's my brother and he needs to know he's completely accepted.*

"Goodbye, Laurie," she smiled, stepping towards him with outstretched arms. "We'd love to have you over again sometime."

Laurie responded to her hug stiffly at first, but then he patted her back. "You're a wonderful hostess, Sandra," he said. "We will gladly come again."

Sandra and James walked out to the hallway to watch until Laurie and Michelle had reached the elevator. They waved goodbye and when they were gone, Sandra turned to James.

"I'm so glad you thought to invite them," she said thankfully. "You were right; they are *just people* and I think we made them feel welcome."

James smiled down warmly. "You did very well, Sandra," he said. "I know it wasn't easy."

"Thanks for your support. I could never have pulled it off without you!"

He nodded. "You're welcome. It was no trouble at all."

Sandra had expressed her thanks but she didn't feel she had truly expressed her gratitude. "James," she said earnestly, "It's more than that. It was a *fabulous* idea! I am so very thankful for a friend like you!"

Had Sandra not felt bound by the agreement to keep their relationship from becoming too involved, she would have thrown her arms around his neck and said, "I love you!" But it was okay. She could see in James' eyes that he understood. Reaching out his hand, he squeezed hers tight.

Warm, Cleansing Water

Chapter Thirty-One

A week and a half had elapsed since four members of James' family had requested baptism. After deciding to wait until Peter and Jessica could be back to witness the event, the special evening had finally arrived.

What a busy time we've had! Sandra reflected, as she waited in the courtyard for James to take her to the baptism. She had worked with Derrick and Allan from eight till six every weekday to maintain all the gardens and lawns. Not only had she been busy gardening, but true to his word, James was asking lots of questions from pastors near and far and he had taken Sandra everywhere that he went. Early on in the previous week, they'd visited the pastor of the church that James used to attend. It had been an interesting experience and Sandra had welcomed the opportunity to hear another side. She had been most surprised, however, when the pastor had 'spiritualized' so many passages that seemed clearly literal.

James had printed off Peter's manuscripts and given them to Sandra to read. They were lengthy, but very helpful and had given them both plenty to discuss. On the weekend, she and James had attended a Bible Convention that some friends from his work had invited him to up in the Cape Breton area. The scenery had taken her breath away! The Highlands were just that – rugged and very high above the sea, covered in thick, green grass with unusual wildflowers and so many birds! Everyone at the convention was friendly and welcoming - especially James' friends from work. The talks had been Bible-based and very helpful in practical ways. However, when she and James had asked questions of a doctrinal nature, neither had been satisfied by the answers they had received. Many people simply wanted to reason things out from their own logic and opinions; only a few knew where to find a Bible passage to support what they believed. However, one of the few Bible passages that had been given in support was still disconcerting. Sandra hoped James had talked to Andrew about it. If not, they were supposed to meet with Andrew and Lisa on Friday night, just as they had the week before.

When there had been no meetings to run off to, Sandra and James had spent time together in the Manor lobby. *It's just the perfect place,* Sandra thought to herself with a smile, as she watched a small fishing boat chug noisily out of the harbour. Swarms of seagulls were hovering above, hoping for some remains of the catch. *Hardly anyone else ever uses the lobby. It's quiet and comfortable, with great lighting and we've had so many good talks about everything - our past lives, our futures and all that we're learning!* She laughed at herself. *Three months ago, I wouldn't have dreamed that sitting in a lobby discussing the Bible would be something I'd look forward to so much!*

She checked her watch, hoping James would appear soon.

At last a tall, familiar – *wonderfully* familiar figure emerged from the doorway and Sandra's face lit up.

"Hey, Beautiful," he called out. "Hope you haven't been waiting long?"

With a careless shrug, she inquired lovingly, "Did you get something to eat?"

James smiled down at her. "Don't worry. I had a big lunch. I'll be fine till afterwards."

"I made you a sandwich."

James laughed appreciatively. "I'm one lucky guy! You were gardening all day; you had enough to do."

Nevertheless, he was more than happy to receive the chicken and tomato sandwich.

As they were driving out to the meeting hall, and James was munching on the first half of his sandwich, Sandra asked about the Bible verse she found hard to understand. "Did you talk to Andrew today about that passage in John?"

"I did," James smiled, turning onto the highway. "I called him up on my lunch break."

Sandra opened up her Bible and turned to John chapter fourteen.

"You want me to tell you the answer right now?" he chuckled, picking up the second half of his sandwich.

"Is there one?"

"Read it out to me again," James requested.

Sandra read, "In My Father's house are many mansions; if it were not so, I would have told you. I go to prepare a place for you. And if I go and prepare a place for you, I will come again and receive you to Myself; that where I am, there you may be also."

"Well," James began, pausing in between bites of his sandwich, "apparently the word for 'mansions' simply means 'an abode' or 'an abiding place'. Jesus is saying that the Father has many abiding places for us - in other words - there's enough room for everyone. While Jesus is in heaven now, he's arranging all the future plans for his Kingdom."

Glancing quickly over at the Bible on Sandra's lap, James asked, "When does he say he will receive us to himself so that we can enjoy those 'places'?"

Sandra looked at the verse carefully. "...I will *come again* and receive you to myself..." She looked up at James with a smile. "Of course!" she said, wondering why she hadn't seen this before. "It's quite clear. He's talking about when he returns to the earth to give us places in his Kingdom!"

"And since he's going to stay on the earth, when he returns," James continued, slowing down to exit the highway, "then we'll all be together here – here on earth."

"It really is simple, isn't it?" Sandra smiled.

James nodded, as he finished off his sandwich. "It's all beginning to make a lot of sense to me. I'm not sure why I didn't see it before."

Pulling up to the hall, Sandra noticed that many cars filled the parking lot and lined the road. They drove past a bright red Mustang that was just like Brett's. Had Andrew contacted him?

Parking on the side of the road, James and Sandra wandered over to the small, white meeting hall. The service was almost ready to begin. Stepping inside, Sandra realized there was only standing room at the back. *Where are all these people from?* she wondered. At least half the audience was unfamiliar.

Looking around, she could see Peter and Jessica up in the front row, next to the rest of the Bryant family. Brett and his girlfriend were only a few rows behind.

"Sorry I was late," James whispered close to her ear. "I guess we missed out on seats."

"That's okay," she whispered back with a smile, "at least we're here together."

The service began with a friendly welcome to everyone and an opening hymn, prayer and a Bible reading from Romans chapter six. Then Craig Symons was called upon to give the talk.

He's had a lot to do lately, Sandra considered, *but this must be a very special day for him. I know how close he is to Peter's family.*

"It's wonderful to see so many faces, this evening," Craig began. "You've chosen to witness a very special occasion; one that would be completely overlooked in this world but is the most important moment in the life of a believer. Tonight, four members of the Bryant family are making the decision to choose life – *eternal life*; to turn their back on sin and its *wages of eternal death*, and to find grace to become heirs of the promises that God will very soon bestow."

With emotion, Craig described how fond he had become of the Bryants. "So much so," he said with a wink in Jessica's direction, "that I convinced my daughter to marry one!"

There were a few light laughs from the crowd, including Sandra; most knew that Jessica hadn't needed any convincing.

Craig went over some of the passages that were now becoming so well known to Sandra – the 'forever' promises. He talked about the promises to the Old Testament faithful, that Abraham and his descendants would inherit the land *forever,* and David's son would sit on the throne *forever,* and that this all primarily revolved around the Lord Jesus Christ. He turned to Galatians and showed that God has invited everyone to share in these promises by doing what the Bryants were choosing to do that night - understanding the Gospel message and being 'baptized into Christ'.

"Forever," now had a new meaning to Sandra, as she stood beside James. *It's God who promises 'forever',* she thought. *And only God truly means life that never ends!*

Reading the words of Jesus to Nicodemus in John chapter three, Craig demonstrated that Jesus had said, "unless one is born of water and the Spirit, he cannot enter the kingdom of God."

"Today," he said, looking towards the Bryants from where he stood on the stage, "you are choosing to be 'born of water'. The 'Spirit' has already begun its work to bring you to this birth, as you've allowed God's Word to mould your lives and change your thoughts to His."[161]

When Craig turned to Romans chapter six and read the first eight verses, Sandra began to fully understand what baptism was all about.

Craig told the audience that just as 'circumcision' in the Old Testament had been a sign of a covenant made with God,

---

[161] John 6:63; Romans 8:5-14

baptism is the New Testament covenant with God. Baptism is a symbolic identification with Christ's sacrifice. Going down into the water, the believer symbolically demonstrates they are choosing to put to death their sinful desires – just as Jesus crucified the flesh with all its affections and lusts, both in his life and on the cross.[162]

"...our old man was crucified with Him," Craig read from Romans six, "that the body of sin might be done away with, that we should no longer be slaves of sin."

"As you see them enter the water this evening," Craig told the audience, "realize that they are choosing to give up their allegiance to the kingdom of sin.[163] Tonight they will be set free – set free from themselves - from their old master – sin - who only pays wages of death.

"As the water passes over them," Craig continued. "God has promised to see this covenant they are making in identifying themselves with His Son, Jesus Christ. He promises to wash away all their sins! Those sins will be gone, forgotten – as though they had never been.[164]

"And then," Craig smiled. "When you see them come up out of the water, remember that Jesus rose again to newness of life. [165]From this day on, they have chosen to give their lives to be servants of God - to be citizens of the coming Kingdom, to live for God's will, His purpose and His desires."

With an encouraging smile, Craig looked once more at the Bryants. He quoted directly from Romans chapter six, "Likewise you also, reckon yourselves to be dead indeed to sin, but alive to God in Christ Jesus our Lord. Therefore do not let sin reign in your mortal body, that you should obey it in its lusts. And do not present

---

[162] Galatians 5:24; Romans 6:6; 13:14; Hebrews 2:14-18; 5:7-9; 4:14-16
[163] Romans 6
[164] Colossians 2:12-14; Acts 2:37-38; 1 Peter 3:21; Psalm 103:11-13
[165] 1 Thessalonians 5:10; Galatians 2:20

your members as instruments of unrighteousness to sin, but present yourselves to God as being alive from the dead, and your members as instruments of righteousness to God."

"Will you fail?" he asked them rhetorically. "Yes, sadly, at times we all forget we are no longer part of the kingdom of sin, and we do things we regret. Always remember that because of your identification with Christ tonight – 'If we confess our sins, He is faithful and just to forgive us our sins and to cleanse us from all unrighteousness.'"[166]

After Craig was finished speaking, the Bryants were given time to head out and prepare for baptism. When they were ready everyone else filtered outside to walk to the edge of the lake. Having stood near the door for the whole talk, Sandra and James were now in front of the crowd. Sandra could see Jessica by the edge of the water with some of Peter's family. Andrew was the first to be baptised. Since Peter was going to baptise him, they were both already wading in. Seeing Sandra and James, Jessica came towards them.

"We were saving you seats, at first," she whispered, "but there were so many guests from the church where Andrew was once the pastor, we eventually gave them up. But come," she encouraged, "come, stand here with us."

The whole family was together by the lake, as a glowing red sun sank slowly in the sky. James reached over and took Sandra's hand.

There were still many people coming across the lawn. With a smile, Lisa asked her husband quietly, "What's it like in there? Is it cold?"

Andrew was shivering just a little, but he laughed. "It's warm as a bath, sweetheart. You'll be fine."

---

[166] 1 John 1:9

"I hope it stays warm for a few months more," James remarked softly.

Andrew heard him and looked up. "You and your evasive comments," he smiled, shaking his head. "I'm going to hold onto that one."

Sandra was pleasantly surprised by James' remark and looked up as well. He didn't return her look but he did squeeze her hand.

At last the whole group was gathered around the shoreline. The sky was turning quite pink and little crickets were chirping noisily.

When Craig moved close to the edge, a hush fell over the crowd. He said, "Let us pray," and everyone bowed their heads. After giving an appropriate prayer for the occasion, Craig asked Andrew directly, "Andrew Bryant, do you believe the things concerning the Kingdom of God and the Name of our Lord Jesus Christ?"[167]

Andrew gave his firm assent and Craig said, "With this confession of your faith, and before these witnesses, it is with great joy that I command you to be baptised into the saving Name of the Lord Jesus Christ for the remission of your sins."[168]

Peter completely immersed his brother into the water and then brought him back up. Andrew's face was radiant as he sputtered and wiped the water from his face.

"I've been set free!" he rejoiced. Then embracing Peter heartily, he chuckled, "And now we're brothers *in Christ!*"

Andrew and Peter both stayed in the water and Andrew baptised his wife in the same way. Then Andrew baptised his mom and Peter baptised his dad. Each time the same questions were asked and the same responses given. Sandra watched carefully,

---

[167] Acts 8:12
[168] Acts 2:38

remembering Craig's words about the death and resurrection of Christ and the forgiveness of sins.

Jessica had plenty of towels to hand out to everyone who came up out of the water, dripping wet. She threw her arms around each one of them, even though their wetness was soaking through her cotton sweater and skirt. It was a very happy time.

"You're drenched," Peter laughed, the last one to hug his wife, "and you didn't bring any clothes to change into."

"I don't mind," she smiled. "It's warm, cleansing water. It's brought our family into Christ and I'm delighted to wear it!"

Warm, cleansing water. All our sins forgiven! Sandra considered, as the crowd moved away towards the hall and she and James stayed watching his family hug and congratulate one another. The prospect of forgiveness was wonderful. Looking at the pond, she saw the pink water still spreading out from the center in slow, wide ripples rolling right towards her.

What a difference from that frigid, black water in May, she thought with a shudder; *water that was all too ready to welcome a death, but completely inept to give birth to life!*

Unknown to James, or to any of the others, Sandra looked up to the evening sky where the first star had just appeared and breathed a silent prayer of thanks. Regardless of her brother's lack of care, or whether or not James would ever commit his life to God… and to her, no longer did she have a sad, lonely existence with candyfloss dreams and broken promises. She had been invited to a royal wedding; a *forever* wedding, planned for thousands of years and promised by the most faithful of all, [169]and she, Sandra Marie Carrington, fully intended to accept.

"God," she spoke inwardly, "Thank You so much for inviting me! I want to accept with all my heart. I do want to come to the banquet!"

---

[169] Hebrews 6:12-19

Unknown to Sandra, the tall man standing close beside her, clasping her hand firmly in his, was praying as well. "Heavenly Father, please forgive me for the way that I've treated my brother," he begged. "And thank you for giving me time to learn about the promises you've made to the world and the response you've asked us to make. Thank you so much for bringing Sandra into my life!" And then he pleaded silently, "Lord Jesus, remember us *when you come into your Kingdom.*"

Acknowledgements

    I would like to thank many people who took the time to read this developing manuscript and give me so much helpful advice.

    Thanks to Greg and Miriam Pullman – who suggested this story in the first place and encouraged me throughout its progress. Thanks to my husband and children - my cheering-squad and first-draft editors! I would also like to thank my mom, my in-laws, my sisters, especially Julie who always gives me the Nova Scotia details. Thank you to my sisters-in-Christ - Ruth Knowles, Nancy–Lee Braux, Carolyn Runge, Carol Link and Hadassah, all of whom added many helpful comments, suggestions and great editing advice. Much thanks also to Dan and Linda Wilton for their 'kingdom feast' ideas and to Ben Link and Pam H. for their thoughtful insights. I greatly appreciate the many helpful editing suggestions given to me by Christadelphian Scripture Study Service and Michael Owen as well. Thanks also to Jason Grant (Fifth and Missing) for designing such a beautiful book cover and Jessica Crandlemire for the photo!

    I would also like to thank God for the time, valuable experiences and the helpful support that always came just when it was needed the most.

    Feel free to contact me at: **annatikvah@yahoo.ca**
"An Invitation to Forever" may be ordered at:
http://www.createspace.com/3961150

Agape in Action

The proceeds from the sales of this book will be donated to Agape in Action. Agape in Action is a Christadelphian based relief and development organization dedicated to working with children, adults and communities to overcome the challenges of extreme poverty. The Scriptures guide all their activities and their motivation comes from the love shown to us by the Father and the compassionate example of His Son.

Agape in Action is currently working in Kenya, Uganda, Mozambique, India and Sri Lanka. Although the needs are enormous, Agape in Action aims to effect change one person at a time. We are committed to nurturing both the physical and spiritual needs of children and families living with the effects of extreme poverty, and we are committed to their care for the long term.

www.agapeinaction.com
info@agapeinaction.com

Other books in the Series:

In Search of Life begins the story, when Verity Lovell meets Peter Bryant in high school. A strong friendship develops as they attend a Bible reading seminar and put their beliefs to the test with the Bible in hand. But will the answers they find support them through tragic, heart-breaking pain?

Who Are You Looking For? delves into the life of Peter Bryant returning home, after ten years overseas, lacking faith and harbouring a deep grudge against God. When his mom hands him a popular Christian novel on "Antichrist" Peter is alarmed by the future scenarios portrayed by the authors. With the help of his good friend Thomas, Peter takes a second look at the evidence, and discovers 25 clues from the Bible which guide him towards a very different conclusion than the one his family has embraced. Tensions rise and family ties are strained as Peter attempts to share his findings, deal with his pain and open his heart to love and forgiveness once more.
The first two books may be ordered through www.csss.org.au

Coming Soon, Lord Willing:

A novel about the Last Days involving the teenage twins, Zach and Jake, in the final few months before the return of the Lord Jesus Christ to the earth. Will apathy, discouragement and the temptations of this world, fatally eclipse their view of the coming Messiah? How will they feel when the angel comes to call them away? What will it be like to meet the Lord Jesus Christ face to face? Probing deep into the future, this novel challenges all of us to be ready and waiting for our Lord.

Appendix

How do we know we can believe the Bible?

It claims to be the "Word of God":
2 Timothy 3:15-17
"And that from childhood you have known the Holy Scriptures, which are able to make you wise for salvation through faith which is in Christ Jesus. All Scripture is given by inspiration of God, and is profitable for doctrine, for reproof, for correction, for instruction in righteousness, that the man of God may be complete, thoroughly equipped for every good work.
2 Peter 1:20-21
"Knowing this first, that no prophecy of Scripture is of any private interpretation, for prophecy never came by the will of man, but holy men of God spoke as they were moved by the Holy Spirit.
Helpful resources: Bible Basics by Duncan Heaster, Study 2.2 (4th ed. Published by Gospel News Publishers, 2001.http://www.bbie.org
God's Living Word: How the Bible Came to Us by D. Banyard, published by The Christadelphian,1993.

What evidence proves the Bible was Divinely Inspired?

- **Advanced Health Laws**

Advanced health laws given to the Nation of Israel – an understanding of health and hygiene in the first five books of the Bible, thousands of years ahead of its time.
(ie. Leviticus 11:4-8;10-12; Deuteronomy 23:12-13)
Helpful resource: The Bible and Medicine by John Hellawell, published by Christadelphian ALS, c.1998; Modern Medicine and the Bible by Alan Fowler, Ortho Books, 2000; None of These Diseases by S.I. McMillen and D.E. Stern, revised ed. Baker Book House, 2000)

- **Archaeology**

Archaeological finds shed light on Bible history and demonstrate Bible accuracy.
Helpful resource: The Stones Cry Out by Randall Price, published by Harvest House, 1997.

- **Consistent Detail**

Consistent Detail from the beginning to the end, even though the Bible was written by many different authors over a period of 1600 years.
Helpful resource: Undesigned Scriptural Coincidences by J.J. Blunt, 19th ed. 1983, The Christadelphian: Birmingham. On apparent contradictions: Encyclopedia of Bible Difficulties by Gleason L. Archer, published by Zondervan, 1982. Hard Sayings of the Bible by W.C. Kaiser Jr, P.H. Davids, F.F. Bruce and M.T. Brauch, published by InterVarsity Press, 1996.

- **Fulfilled Prophecy Concerning the Nations**

Daniel chapter 2 is another prophecy which outlines the four major world empires: Babylon, Persia, Greece and Rome, that would dominate the Middle East. It is a completely accurate vision given at a time when only the first of the empires existed.
Helpful Resources: Wonders of Prophecy by John Urquhart, revised ed. 1939, Pickering and Inglis: London. Bible Prophecy by Fred Pearce, published by The Christadelphian.

- **Fulfilled Prophecy Concerning Israel**

Here are a few of the fulfilled prophecies concerning Israel:
Israel would be a nation – predicted in 2000 BC by God to Abraham.
Genesis 15
Israel's disobedience to God's Laws, scattering, preservation and revival was predicted by God to Moses in 1500 BC.
Deuteronomy 28
Fulfilled: taken captive to Babylon in 605 BC, returned to land in 538 BC
Fulfilled: scattered - AD 70, returned to land - 20th century, nation reborn -1948.
Israel is a continuing witness to God's existence
Isaiah 43:1-2;10-12 given in 700 BC
Though scattered throughout the world, Israel would be preserved – given by God to Jeremiah in 600 BC
Jeremiah 30:3,10-11; 31:10
Fulfilled: The Jews have survived the Spanish Inquisition, the Russian pogroms, the Nazi holocaust and many other attempts to destroy them as a people. Throughout their history, God has preserved a remnant of his people.
Israel would, in the 'latter days' (just before Christ's return) come back to their land and become a nation again. This prophecy was given by God to Ezekiel in 590 BC. and is in the process of being fulfilled.

Ezekiel 36-37
There are many more prophecies concerning Israel in the 'latter days':
Psalm 83; Isaiah 19:23-25; Ezekiel 38-39; Zechariah 3:8-9; ch.8 & 12-14; Joel 3:1-17; Luke 21:20-24; Micah 4:9-13 etc.
Helpful Resources: Israel: Land and People of Destiny by John Collyer, Christadelphian Office, 1988. Great News for the World by Alan Hayward, Christadelphians Worldwide, 1976. Israel- Ruler with God by Paul Billington, The Bible Magazine, 1985.

Does it matter what we believe?

The Bible is clear that we must hold fast to the teaching of Jesus and the Apostles:
Galatians 1:6-9
I marvel that you are turning away so soon from Him who called you in the grace of Christ, to a different gospel, which is not another; but there are some who trouble you and want to pervert the gospel of Christ. But even if we, or an angel from heaven, preach any other gospel to you than what we have preached to you, let him be accursed...
Matthew 15:8-9
These people draw near to Me with their mouth, and honor Me with their lips, but their heart is far from Me. And in vain they worship Me, teaching as doctrines the commandments of men.'"

God predicted many would fall away from truth:
2 Timothy 4:3-4
For the time will come when they will not endure sound doctrine, but according to their own desires, because they have itching ears, they will heap up for themselves teachers; and they will turn their ears away from the truth, and be turned aside to fables.
2 Thessalonians 2:9-12
The coming of the lawless one is according to the working of Satan, with all power, signs, and lying wonders, and with all unrighteous deception among those who perish, because they did not receive the love of the truth, that they might be saved. And for this reason God will send them strong delusion, that they should believe the lie, that they all may be condemned who did not believe the truth but had pleasure in unrighteousness.
Helpful Resources: One Bible, Many Churches. Does it Matter? Dennis Gillett, The Christadelphian. Bible Basics by Duncan Heaster, Gospel News Publishers, 2001. http://www.bbie.org (biblebasicsonline.com)
All the material above in this appendix has been used by permission of Rob Hyndman from his book The Way of Life, Bethel Publications, 2002.

What is the Gospel message that Jesus and the Apostles preached?

Teachings about the Kingdom of God and the Name of Jesus Christ:
Matthew 4:23
And Jesus went about all Galilee, teaching in their synagogues, preaching the gospel of the kingdom...
Acts 8:12
But when they believed Philip as he preached the things concerning the kingdom of God and the name of Jesus Christ, both men and women were baptized.
Acts 28:30-31
Then Paul dwelt two whole years in his own rented house, and received all who came to him, preaching the kingdom of God and teaching the things which concern the Lord Jesus Christ with all confidence, no one forbidding him.

What does the Bible teach about The Kingdom of God?

God has a plan to fill this earth with His glory:
Isaiah 45:18
For thus says the LORD, Who created the heavens, Who is God, Who formed the earth and made it, Who has established it, Who did not create it in vain, Who formed it to be inhabited: "I am the LORD, and there is no other.
Habbakuk 2:14
For the earth will be filled with the knowledge of the glory of the LORD, as the waters cover the sea.

With this plan in mind, God made promises to the Old Testament faithful:

- After the first act of disobedience and the resulting curse upon creation, God promised a 'seed' who would bring deliverance.

Genesis 3:14-15
So the LORD God said to the serpent: "Because you have done this, you are cursed more than all cattle, and more than every beast of the field; on your belly you shall go, and you shall eat dust all the days of your life. And I will put enmity between you and the woman, and between your seed and her seed; he shall bruise your head, and you shall bruise his heel."
(See also Rom. 5:12-21; Isaiah 7:14; Hebrews 2:14; Galatians 4:4; 1 Cor. 15:54-55)

- **Abraham (the 'friend of God') was promised that he & his descendants would inherit THE LAND of Canaan forever :**

Genesis 13:14-17
And the LORD said to Abram, after Lot had separated from him: "Lift your eyes now and look from the place where you are-northward, southward, eastward, and westward; for all the land which you see I give to you and your descendants forever. And I will make your descendants as the dust of the earth; so that if a man could number the dust of the earth, then your descendants also could be numbered. Arise, walk in the land through its length and its width, for I give it to you."
(See also Genesis 12:1-3 [great nation, blessing/cursing/a blessing to all nations]; 15:5-8,13-21;17:4-8,15-16 [kings, son of Sarah, Canaan forever];22:16-18 [many descendants, all nations blessed in Abraham's seed])

- **This land was MAPPED OUT by God:**

Genesis 15:18-21
On the same day the LORD made a covenant with Abram, saying: "To your descendants I have given this land, from the river of Egypt to the great river, the River Euphrates...

- **Abraham never received this inheritance in his lifetime:**

Acts 7:1-5
The God of glory appeared to our father Abraham when he was in Mesopotamia,... and said to him, 'Get out of your country and from your relatives, and come to a land that I will show you.' ...He moved him to this land in which you now dwell. And God gave him no inheritance in it, not even enough to set his foot on. But even when Abraham had no child, He promised to give it to him for a possession, and to his descendants after him.

- **Abraham understood that this promise was for the FUTURE:**

Hebrews 11:8-16
By faith Abraham obeyed when he was called to go out to the place which he would receive as an inheritance...By faith he dwelt in the land of promise as in a foreign country, dwelling in tents with Isaac and Jacob, the heirs with him of the same promise; for he waited for the city which has foundations, whose builder and maker is God. These all died in faith, not having received the promises, but having seen them afar off were assured of them, embraced them and confessed that they were strangers and pilgrims on the earth. For those who say such things declare plainly that they seek a homeland...they desire a better, that is, an heavenly country. Therefore God is not ashamed to be called their God, for He has prepared a city for them.

- **These promises were the foundation of the GOSPEL message, involving Jesus Christ and those in him:**

Galatians 3:7-8,16,27-29
Therefore know that only those who are of faith are sons of Abraham. And the Scripture, foreseeing that God would justify the Gentiles by faith, preached the gospel to Abraham beforehand, saying, "In you all the nations shall be blessed..." Now to

Abraham and his Seed were the promises made. He does not say, "And to seeds," as of many, but as of one, "And to your Seed," who is Christ... For as many of you as were baptized into Christ have put on Christ...And if you are Christ's, then you are Abraham's seed, and heirs according to the promise.

- **God also made promises to King David, involving his THRONE and A KING that would come from his line:**

2 Samuel 7:12-16
When your days are fulfilled and you rest with your fathers, I will set up your seed after you, who will come from your body, and I will establish his kingdom. He shall build a house for My name, and I will establish the throne of his kingdom forever. I will be his Father, and he shall be My son...And your house and your kingdom shall be established forever before you. Your throne shall be established forever."'"

- **JESUS CHRIST is the fulfillment of this promise to David:**

Luke 1:31-33
"And behold, you will conceive in your womb and bring forth a Son, and shall call His name JESUS. He will be great, and will be called the Son of the Highest; and the Lord God will give Him the throne of His father David. And He will reign over the house of Jacob forever, and of His kingdom there will be no end."
(See also Psa. 89:20-37; Isa. 53:4-11; Heb. 2:9-18)

Acts 2:29-31
"Men and brethren, let me speak freely to you of the patriarch David, that he is both dead and buried, and his tomb is with us to this day. Therefore, being a prophet, and knowing that God had sworn with an oath to him that of the fruit of his body, according to the flesh, He would raise up the Christ to sit on his throne, he, foreseeing this, spoke concerning the resurrection of the Christ, that His soul was not left in Hades, nor did His flesh see corruption.
(See also Isaiah 9:6-7; Philippians 2:9-11)

When will this Kingdom come?

- **After Israel is established in the 'promised land' as a nation:**

Ezekiel 37:21-22
Then say to them, 'Thus says the Lord GOD: "Surely I will take the children of Israel from among the nations, wherever they have gone, and will gather them from every side and bring them into their own land; and I will make them one nation in the land, on the mountains of Israel; and one king shall be king over them all; they shall no longer be two nations, nor shall they ever be divided into two kingdoms again.

Joel 3:1-2,16-17
...When I bring back the captives of Judah and Jerusalem, I will also gather all nations,...And I will enter into judgment with them there on account of My people, My heritage Israel, whom they have scattered among the nations; They have also divided up My land. So you shall know that I am the LORD your God, dwelling in Zion My holy mountain. Then Jerusalem shall be holy,...

- **After the resurrection of the dead**

Daniel 12:1-3
...there shall be a time of trouble, such as never was since there was a nation, even to that time. And at that time your people shall be delivered, everyone who is found written in the book. And many of those who sleep in the dust of the earth shall awake, some to everlasting life, some to shame and everlasting contempt.

1 Thessalonians 4:13-17
For this we say to you by the word of the Lord, that we who are alive and remain until the coming of the Lord will by no means precede those who are asleep. For the Lord Himself will descend from heaven with a shout,...And the dead in Christ will rise first.

2 Timothy 4:1
I charge you therefore before God and the Lord Jesus Christ, who will judge the living and the dead at His appearing and His kingdom: (see also 2 Thessalonians 2:7-10)

- **After a Russian-led invasion sweeps through the Middle East and into Israel and brings Divine intervention:**

Zechariah 14:1-9
For I will gather all the nations to battle against Jerusalem;...Half of the city shall go into captivity,... Then the LORD will go forth and fight against those nations... And in that day His feet will stand on the Mount of Olives, which faces Jerusalem on the east. And the Mount of Olives shall be split in two... Thus the LORD my God will come, and all the saints with You...And in that day it shall be that living waters shall flow from Jerusalem... And the LORD shall be King over all the earth. In that day it shall be-"The LORD is one," and His name one.

Ezekiel 38:3-23
Thus says the Lord GOD: "Behold, I am against you, O Gog, the prince of Rosh, Meshech, and Tubal. I will turn you around, put hooks into your jaws, and lead you out, with all your army...Persia, Ethiopia, and Libya are with them, all of them with shield and helmet; Gomer and all its troops; the house of Togarmah from the far north and all its troops-many people are with you...In the latter years you will come into the land of those brought back from the sword and gathered from many people on the mountains of Israel, which had long been desolate; they were brought out of the nations, and now all of them dwell safely...And it will come to pass at the same time, when Gog comes against the land of Israel," says the Lord GOD, "that My fury will show in My face...Surely in that day there shall be a great earthquake in the land of Israel...I will call for a sword against Gog throughout all My mountains...And I will bring him to judgment with pestilence and bloodshed...Then they shall know that I am the LORD."
(see also Joel 3, Zechariah 12 & Ezekiel 39)

- **After Jesus and the Saints take the Kingdom**

Daniel 7:13-14; 27
I was watching in the night visions, And behold, one like the Son of Man, coming with the clouds of heaven! He came to the Ancient of Days, and they brought Him near before Him. Then to Him was given dominion and glory and a kingdom, that all peoples, nations, and languages should serve Him. His dominion is an everlasting dominion, which shall not pass away, and His kingdom the one which shall not be destroyed...

Then the kingdom and dominion, and the greatness of the kingdoms under the whole heaven, shall be given to the people, the saints of the Most High.'
Revelation 11:15
Then the seventh angel sounded: and there were loud voices in heaven, saying, "The kingdoms of this world have become the kingdoms of our Lord and of His Christ, and He shall reign forever and ever!"

(see also Daniel 2:44; Psalm 2; 2 Thessalonians 1:7-10; Revelation 2:26-27)

How do we know that Russia is "the prince of Rosh"?

"Gog (a name which means 'all that is powerful, gigantic, and proud'-Companion Bible) is to be 'of the land of Magog' as well as prince-or ruler-of Rosh, Meshech and Tubal (c/p R.V.). It is fascinating to follow the clues provided by both Scripture and history in order that we may trace these ancient names and places.

'The land of Magog' is geographic information and must be considered with the further statement that Gog's 'place' is in 'the north parts' (v. 15)-or more correctly, 'the uttermost parts of the north' (R.V.) The Hebrew text is crucial to our consideration and speaks of the remotest extremities of the north. In fact the word 'north' actually carries the idea of 'hidden, unknown.' The land of the Magog, to which this prophecy refers, obviously lay beyond the civilised world of Ezekiel's time...

In the third century BC, the Hebrew Scriptures were translated into Greek. This translation has survived and is known as the Septuagint Version or LXX. These early translators understood the Hebrew word Rosh (meaning head or chief) as a proper name, and rendered it by the Greek word Pws.

Now the Encyclopaedia Britannica, in discussing the origin of the term Russia, says, 'It is certainly derived, through Rossiya, from the Slavonic Rus or Ros (Byzantine Pws or Pwsoi).'

Edward Gibbon likewise, in his Decline and Fall of the Roman Empire says of the same 'Russians' that 'Among the Greeks, this national appellation has a singular form, Pws.'"

(Paul Billington. 'Russia's conquest of Europe'. The Bible Magazine, Vol. 21, Issue No. 4, October 2008, Pg. 22-24.)

Who will be the Administrators of this Kingdom?

The faithful believers - the saints:
Daniel 7:18,27
'But the saints of the Most High shall receive the kingdom, and possess the kingdom forever, even forever and ever.' Then the kingdom and dominion, and the greatness of

the kingdoms under the whole heaven, shall be given to the people, the saints of the Most High. His kingdom is an everlasting kingdom, and all dominions shall serve and obey Him.'
Revelation 5:9-10
And they sang a new song, saying: "You are worthy...For You were slain, And have redeemed us to God by Your blood out of every tribe and tongue and people and nation, And have made us kings and priests to our God; and we shall reign on the earth."
(See also Matt.5:5; Lk.19:11-19;22:28-30; 1 Cor. 6:2-3; Rev. 20:6)

What will be unique about the Administrators?

Immortality!
Psalm 37:9,29
For evildoers shall be cut off; But those who wait on the LORD, they shall inherit the earth. The righteous shall inherit the land, and dwell in it forever.
Matthew 5:5
Blessed are the meek, for they shall inherit the earth.
Luke 20:35-36
But those who are counted worthy to attain that age, and the resurrection from the dead, neither marry nor are given in marriage; nor can they die anymore, for they are equal to the angels and are sons of God, being sons of the resurrection.
1 Corinthians 15:49-53
And as we have borne the image of the man of dust, we shall also bear the image of the heavenly Man...flesh and blood cannot inherit the kingdom of God; nor does corruption inherit incorruption...For the trumpet will sound, and the dead will be raised incorruptible, and we shall be changed. For this corruptible must put on incorruption, and this mortal must put on immortality.
(See also Job 19:25-27; Dan. 12:2; Rom. 2:7-8; John 5:28-29)

How will the Jews feel about Jesus?

Of the one-third that will be saved by Christ, they will finally recognize their Messiah and repent.
Zechariah 12:8-10
"In that day the LORD will defend the inhabitants of Jerusalem; ...It shall be in that day that I will seek to destroy all the nations that come against Jerusalem. And I will pour on the house of David and on the inhabitants of Jerusalem the Spirit of grace and supplication; then they will look on Me whom they pierced. Yes, they will mourn for Him as one mourns for his only son, and grieve for Him as one grieves for a firstborn.

Romans 11:25-27
For I do not desire, brethren, that you should be ignorant of this mystery, lest you

should be wise in your own opinion, that blindness in part has happened to Israel until the fullness of the Gentiles has come in. And so all Israel will be saved, as it is written: "The Deliverer will come out of Zion, and He will turn away ungodliness from Jacob; for this is My covenant with them, when I take away their sins."
(See also Ezekiel 36:25-28; ch.39; Zechariah 13:8-9)

Will the Jewish people have a special role?

Yes. They will continue to live in the land of Israel and many will serve in the Temple.
Ezekiel 44:9-14
And the Levites who went far from Me, when Israel went astray, who strayed away from Me after their idols, they shall bear their iniquity. Yet they shall be ministers in My sanctuary, as gatekeepers of the house and ministers of the house; they shall slay the burnt offering and the sacrifice for the people, and they shall stand before them to minister to them. And they shall not come near Me to minister to Me as priest, nor come near any of My holy things, nor into the Most Holy Place; ...Nevertheless I will make them keep charge of the temple, for all its work, and for all that has to be done in it. *(see also Ezekiel 36 to 39)*

What about the Arabs around Israel?

Those who submit to Christ will enjoy the blessings of the land.
Isaiah 19:18-25
In that day five cities in the land of Egypt will speak the language of Canaan and swear by the LORD of hosts; ...for they will cry to the LORD because of the oppressors, and He will send them a Savior and a Mighty One, and He will deliver them...In that day there will be a highway from Egypt to Assyria, and the Assyrian will come into Egypt and the Egyptian into Assyria, and the Egyptians will serve with the Assyrians...In that day Israel will be one of three with Egypt and Assyria-a blessing in the midst of the land, whom the LORD of hosts shall bless, saying, "Blessed is Egypt My people, and Assyria the work of My hands, and Israel My inheritance."
Zechariah 9:5-7
Ashkelon shall see it and fear; Gaza also shall be very sorrowful;...A mixed race shall settle in Ashdod, and I will cut off the pride of the Philistines. I will take away the blood from his mouth, and the abominations from between his teeth. But he who remains, even he shall be for our God, and shall be like a leader in Judah, and Ekron like a Jebusite.
(See also Psalm 83)

Who will be the SUBJECTS of this Kingdom?

Those who survive Armageddon.
Zechariah 14:16
And it shall come to pass that everyone who is left of all the nations which came against Jerusalem shall go up from year to year to worship the King, the LORD of hosts, and to keep the Feast of Tabernacles.
Revelation 11:15
Then the seventh angel sounded: and there were loud voices in heaven, saying, "The kingdoms of this world have become the kingdoms of our Lord and of His Christ, and He shall reign forever and ever!"
Micah 4:1-4
Now it shall come to pass in the latter days that the mountain of the LORD'S house shall be established on the top of the mountains,...Many nations shall come and say, "Come, and let us go up to the mountain of the LORD, to the house of the God of Jacob; He will teach us His ways, and we shall walk in His paths." For out of Zion the law shall go forth, and the word of the LORD from Jerusalem. He shall judge between many peoples, and rebuke strong nations afar off; They shall beat their swords into plowshares, and their spears into pruning hooks; nation shall not lift up sword against nation, neither shall they learn war any more.

To what extent will this Kingdom have DOMINION?

The whole earth!
Psalm 72
Give the king Your judgments, O God, and Your righteousness to the king's Son. He will judge Your people with righteousness...He will save the children of the needy, and will break in pieces the oppressor. They shall fear You as long as the sun and moon endure, Throughout all generations... In His days the righteous shall flourish, and abundance of peace, until the moon is no more. He shall have dominion also from sea to sea, and from the River to the ends of the earth...The kings of Tarshish and of the isles will bring presents; the kings of Sheba and Seba will offer gifts. Yes, all kings shall fall down before Him; all nations shall serve Him. His name shall endure forever; His name shall continue as long as the sun. and men shall be blessed in Him; all nations shall call Him blessed.
Psalm 2
..."Yet I have set My King on My holy hill of Zion. ""I will declare the decree: The LORD has said to Me, 'You are My Son, Today I have begotten You. Ask of Me, and I will give You the nations for Your inheritance, and the ends of the earth for Your possession.
Daniel 2:44
And in the days of these kings the God of heaven will set up a kingdom which shall never be destroyed; and the kingdom shall not be left to other people; it shall break in

pieces and consume all these kingdoms, and it shall stand forever.
Revelation 17:13-14
The ten horns which you saw are ten kings who have received no kingdom as yet, but they receive authority for one hour as kings with the beast. These are of one mind, and they will give their power and authority to the beast. These will make war with the Lamb, and the Lamb will overcome them, for He is Lord of lords and King of kings; and those who are with Him are called, chosen, and faithful.

Where will the CAPITAL CITY be?

Jerusalem
Matthew 5:34-35
But I say to you, do not swear at all: neither by heaven, for it is God's throne; nor by the earth, for it is His footstool; nor by Jerusalem, for it is the city of the great King.
Psalm 48:1-3
Great is the LORD, and greatly to be praised in the city of our God, In His holy mountain, beautiful in elevation, the joy of the whole earth, is Mount Zion on the sides of the north, The city of the great King. God is in her palaces; He is known as her refuge.
(See also Isaiah 62:1-7;Jeremiah 3:17)

Where will the nations go to WORSHIP?

To God's Holy Temple in Jerusalem
Isaiah 2:2-4
Now it shall come to pass in the latter days that the mountain of the LORD'S house shall be established on the top of the mountains...and all nations shall flow to it. Many people shall come and say, "Come, and let us go up to the mountain of the LORD...he will teach us His ways, and we shall walk in His paths." For out of Zion shall go forth the law, and the word of the LORD from Jerusalem.
Ezekiel 48:10,21,35
To these-to the priests-the holy district shall belong: on the north twenty-five thousand cubits in length, on the west ten thousand in width,...The sanctuary of the LORD shall be in the center...All the way around shall be eighteen thousand cubits; and the name of the city from that day shall be: THE LORD IS THERE."
(The master plans for the temple are in Ezekiel 40-48)
Zechariah 6:12-13
Then speak to him, saying, 'Thus says the LORD of hosts, saying: "Behold, the Man whose name is the BRANCH! From His place He shall branch out, and He shall build the temple of the LORD;...He shall bear the glory, and shall sit and rule on His throne; so He shall be a priest on His throne, and the counsel of peace shall be between them both.
(See also Jeremiah 23:5-8; 2 Samuel 7:12-13)

What will LIFE be like in the Kingdom?

Perfect!
Isaiah 65:17-25
For behold, I create new heavens and a new earth; and the former shall not be remembered or come to mind...I will rejoice in Jerusalem, and joy in My people; the voice of weeping shall no longer be heard in her, nor the voice of crying. No more shall an infant from there live but a few days, nor an old man who has not fulfilled his days;...They shall build houses and inhabit them; they shall plant vineyards and eat their fruit...They shall not labor in vain, nor bring forth children for trouble; for they shall be the descendants of the blessed of the LORD, and their offspring with them. It shall come to pass that before they call, I will answer; and while they are still speaking, I will hear. The wolf and the lamb shall feed together, the lion shall eat straw like the ox, and dust shall be the serpent's food. They shall not hurt nor destroy in all My holy mountain,"

Revelation 22:1-5
And he showed me a pure river of water of life, clear as crystal, proceeding from the throne of God and of the Lamb. In the middle of its street, and on either side of the river, was the tree of life, which bore twelve fruits, each tree yielding its fruit every month. The leaves of the tree were for the healing of the nations. And there shall be no more curse, but the throne of God and of the Lamb shall be in it, and His servants shall serve Him. They shall see His face, and His name shall be on their foreheads. There shall be no night there: They need no lamp nor light of the sun, for the Lord God gives them light. And they shall reign forever and ever.
(See also Psalm 72; Isaiah 2:2-4;11; 25:6-9; 35:5-10; 51; 60:12,18,21; 65:17-25; Jer.33:14-16; Micah 4:1-8; 1 Corinthians 15:24-28; Rev.7:13-17)

What will happen after 1000 YEARS of this Kingdom?

There will be a rebellion amongst the mortal population, a final judgment and resurrection, after which Jesus will give the Kingdom over to God, who will then be "all in all".

Revelation 20:2-6
He laid hold of the dragon, that serpent of old, who is the Devil and Satan, and bound him for a thousand years;...so that he should deceive the nations no more till the thousand years were finished. But after these things he must be released for a little while. And I saw thrones, and they sat on them, and judgment was committed to them... And they lived and reigned with Christ for a thousand years. But the rest of the dead did not live again until the thousand years were finished. This is the first resurrection. Blessed and holy is he who has part in the first resurrection. Over such the second death has no power, but they shall be priests of God and of Christ, and shall reign with Him a thousand years.

1 Corinthians 15:20-28
But now Christ is risen from the dead, and has become the firstfruits of those who have fallen asleep...For as in Adam all die, even so in Christ all shall be made alive... Then comes the end, when He delivers the kingdom to God the Father, when He puts an end to all rule and all authority and power. For He must reign till He has put all enemies under His feet. The last enemy that will be destroyed is death.
For "He has put all things under His feet." But when He says "all things are put under Him," it is evident that He who put all things under Him is excepted. Now when all things are made subject to Him, then the Son Himself will also be subject to Him who put all things under Him, that God may be all in all.

Revelation 21:1-4
Now I saw a new heaven and a new earth,...And I heard a loud voice from heaven saying, "Behold, the tabernacle of God is with men, and He will dwell with them, and they shall be His people. God Himself will be with them and be their God. And God will wipe away every tear from their eyes; there shall be no more death, nor sorrow, nor crying. There shall be no more pain, for the former things have passed away."

How can we have a part in this Kingdom?

Believe, repent, obey Christ's commands, be baptized into him and preach the true Gospel Message.
Mark 16:15-16
And He said to them, "Go into all the world and preach the gospel to every creature. He who believes and is baptized will be saved; but he who does not believe will be condemned.

John 14:15,21-24
If you love Me, keep My commandments. He who has My commandments and keeps them, it is he who loves Me.

John 3:5
Jesus answered, "Most assuredly, I say to you, unless one is born of water and the Spirit, he cannot enter the kingdom of God.

Galatians 3:27-29
For you are all sons of God through faith in Christ Jesus. For as many of you as were baptized into Christ have put on Christ... And if you are Christ's, then you are Abraham's seed, and heirs according to the promise.
(See also Matthew 28:19,20; John 3:5; John 6:63; Acts 2:38; 8:12,13, 36-39; 16:15,33; Romans 6; 1 Peter 3:21)

What does the Bible say about Heaven?

It is the dwelling place of God
John 3:13
"No one has ascended to heaven but He who came down from heaven, that is, the Son

of Man who is in heaven.
Psalm 115:16-17
The heaven, even the heavens, are the LORD'S; but the earth He has given to the children of men. The dead do not praise the LORD, nor any who go down into silence.
Matthew 5:5
Blessed are the meek, For they shall inherit the earth. (See also Psalms 37:9-11,22)
Acts 2:29,34
Men and brethren, let me speak freely to you of the patriarch David, that he is both dead and buried, and his tomb is with us to this day...For David did not ascend into the heavens...

Do all human beings possess immortality?

No, immortality is a gift from God.
Ezekiel 18:4,20
Behold, all souls are mine; as the soul of the father, so also the soul of the son is mine: the soul that sinneth, it shall die.
Romans 6:23
For the wages of sin is death; but the gift of God is eternal life through Jesus Christ our Lord.
Romans 2:6-7
Who will render to every man according to his deeds: to them who by patient continuance in well doing seek for glory and honour and immortality, eternal life:
Ecclesiastes 9:5-6,10
For the living know that they shall die: but the dead know not any thing... Also their love, and their hatred, and their envy, is now perished;...Whatsoever thy hand findeth to do, do it with thy might; for there is no work, nor device, nor knowledge, nor wisdom, in the grave, whither thou goest.
Psalm 146:3-4
Put not your trust in princes, nor in the son of man, in whom there is no help. His breath goeth forth, he returneth to his earth; in that very day his thoughts perish.
Psalm 115:17
The dead praise not the LORD, neither any that go down into silence.
(see also Josh. 11:11; Psa. 22:29; Matt. 10:28; 1 Cor.15:50-55; Rev. 16:3)

When Will We Receive Immortality?

At Christ's return when he judges the living and the dead.
Matthew 16:27
For the Son of man shall come in the glory of his Father with his angels; and then He shall reward every man according to his works. Verily, verily, I say unto you, The hour is coming, and now is, when the dead shall hear the voice of the Son of God: and they that hear shall live.

John 5:26-29
For as the Father hath life in himself; so hath he given to the Son to have life in himself; and hath given him authority to execute judgment also, because he is the Son of man. Marvel not at this: for the hour is coming, in the which all that are in the graves shall hear his voice, and shall come forth; they that have done good, unto the resurrection of life; and they that have done evil, unto the resurrection of damnation.
John 6:39-40,44
And this is the Father's will which hath sent me, that of all which he hath given me I should lose nothing, but should raise it up again at the last day. And this is the will of him that sent me, that every one which seeth the Son, and believeth on him, may have everlasting life: and I will raise him up at the last day. No man can come to me, except the Father which hath sent me draw him: and I will raise him up at the last day.
2 Corinthians 5:10
For we must all appear before the judgment seat of Christ; that every one may receive the things *done* in *his* body, according to that he hath done, whether *it be* good or bad.
2 Thessalonians 1:7 -10
And to you who are troubled rest with us, when the Lord Jesus shall be revealed from heaven with his mighty angels, in flaming fire taking vengeance on them that know not God, and that obey not the gospel of our Lord Jesus Christ: who shall be punished with everlasting destruction from the presence of the Lord, and from the glory of his power...
2Ti mothy 4:1,8
I charge *thee* therefore before God, and the Lord Jesus Christ, who shall judge the quick and the dead at his appearing and his kingdom; ...Henceforth there is laid up for me a crown of righteousness, which the Lord, the righteous judge, shall give me at that day: and not to me only, but unto all them also that love his appearing.
1Corinthians 15:49 -55
And as we have borne the image of the earthy, we shall also bear the image of the Heavenly... flesh and blood cannot inherit the kingdom of God; neither doth corruption inherit incorruption. Behold, I shew you a mystery; We shall not all sleep, but we shall all be changed, In a moment, in the twinkling of an eye, at the last trump: for the trumpet shall sound, and the dead shall be raised incorruptible, and we shall be changed. For this corruptible must put on incorruption, and this mortal *must* put on immortality. So when this corruptible shall have put on incorruption, and this mortal shall have put on immortality, then shall be brought to pass the saying that is written, Death is swallowed up in victory...
Acts 24:15: Daniel 12 :2-3; Matthew 25:1-12,31-36; 7:21-23; 13:47-50; Rev. 20:6

Will Everyone Rise From the Dead?

No. Those who are without the knowledge of the Gospel will remain in the grave.
Psalm 49:19
He shall go to the generation of his fathers; they shall never see light. Man *that is* in honour, and understandeth not, is like the beasts *that* perish.

Ephesians 2:1,12
And you *hath he quickened*, who were dead in trespasses and sins; That at that time ye were without Christ, being aliens from the commonwealth of Israel, and strangers from the covenants of promise, having no hope, and without God in the world:
Ephesians 4:18
Having the understanding darkened, being alienated from the life of God through the ignorance that is in them, because of the blindness of their heart:

Does God want us in His Kingdom?

Yes. He hopes we will all choose to come!
Ezekiel 18:23
Do I have any pleasure at all that the wicked should die?" says the Lord GOD, "and not that he should turn from his ways and live?
Luke 12:32
Do not fear, little flock, for it is your Father's good pleasure to give you the kingdom.
1 Timothy 2:3-4
For this is good and acceptable in the sight of God our Savior, who desires all men to be saved and to come to the knowledge of the truth.
2Peter 3:9
The Lord is not slack concerning his promise, as some men count slackness; but is longsuffering to us-ward, not willing that any should perish, but that all should come to repentance.
Revelation 22:17
And the Spirit and the bride say, "Come!" And let him who hears say, "Come!" And let him who thirsts come...

Printed in Great Britain
by Amazon.co.uk, Ltd.,
Marston Gate.